**"I've wanted to do this since that damned slow dance
the other night."**

Keira looked at Finn, startled, but he saw no alarm in her
gaze.

"Someone might come in," she whispered. She stroked
her fingers down his cheek, letting her thumb play across
his mouth. He assumed she wasn't overly concerned by
the possibility of being interrupted.

He took a moment to listen to the sounds in the gallery.
He couldn't hear anything but the music and the faint
sound of their breaths. He pressed a kiss to the pad of her
thumb. "We're the only two in here right now," he murmured back.

She looped her arms around his neck, her hands
cradling his skull. Her eyes were as blue as he'd ever seen
them. "Well, then," she said with a delectable lilt in her
sultry voice, "let's not waste any time."

He bent his head and set his mouth on hers...

ACCLAIM FOR THE WARRIORS OF THE RIFT SERIES

SECRET OF THE WOLF

"Garner returns to her paranormal world, where supernatural beings are in constant conflict with each other and humans often become collateral damage. Filled with hefty doses of action, suspense, and romance, Garner's latest is an intriguing read."
—*RT Book Reviews*

"With mystery, romance, and plenty of paranormal, this series will appeal to a variety of genre lovers."
—*Parkersburg News and Sentinel* (WV)

"Fast-paced...Tori is a terrific individual torn between the two most important people in her life...Readers will appreciate the fascinating Garner mythos."
—GenreGoRoundReviews.blogspot.com

"This was a quick read with a good mystery, a memorable heroine, and a hero that will charm you."
—ParanormalHaven.com

KISS OF THE VAMPIRE

"An inventive spin on supernatural mythos draws readers into this fast-paced paranormal series launch...Garner shows promise with great characters, constant action, and steamy sex."

"Intriguing...Garner provides both a cool premise and interesting characters. One to watch!"

"A deliciously dark and scorchingly sexy treat for fans of paranormal romances."

"Various characters in the story have complex, yet compelling, backgrounds...As for the ending—*awesome*!...I closed the cover of this book while wishing that the second title was available for me to dive immediately into."

"A refreshing look at the origin of vampires, werewolves, and other myths. Fast-paced, the romantic and police procedural subplots deftly balance a strong story line...never slows down as Cynthia Garner provides a fascinating take on the supernatural."

"I cannot wait for this series to continue...Garner seamlessly combines paranormal romance and romantic suspense that has you on the edge of your seat."

Also by Cynthia Garner

Kiss of the Vampire
Into the Rift
Secret of the Wolf

Heart of the Demon

Cynthia Garner

FOREVER

NEW YORK   BOSTON

Forever
Hachette Book Group
237 Park Avenue
New York, NY 10017
www.HachetteBookGroup.com

Forever is an imprint of Grand Central Publishing.
The Forever name and logo are trademarks of Hachette Book Group, Inc.

The Hachette Speakers Bureau provides a wide range of authors for speaking events. To find out more, go to www.hachettespeakersbureau.com or call (866) 376-6591.

The publisher is not responsible for websites (or their content) that are not owned by the publisher.

Printed in the United States of America

OPM

First Edition: February 2013

10 9 8 7 6 5 4 3 2 1

To my wonderful critique group, who always come through for me.

Heart of the Demon

Prologue

Zombies got a bad rap these days. At least that's what the drunk one kept telling Finn Evnissyen as he sat at the bar nursing his beer.

"I mean, come on. Do I look like I'm rotting?" The guy held out one arm and turned it so Finn could see the underside. The action also sent a waft of ammonia covered up by too much cologne.

That hint of ammonia told Finn this guy had become a zombie within hours of death instead of days. Yeah, if he'd been dead longer he wouldn't be so pretty and he'd be much more odoriferous.

The zombie flexed his arm again. "Nope," he muttered, answering his own question. "Skin's as clear as a baby's bottom."

Finn didn't give a rat's ass about the zombie's skin or baby bottoms. "Uh-huh," Finn grunted as he swiveled around on his stool to look out over the crowd. It was just after three in the afternoon on a hot, humid Sunday, and the bar already had a healthy clientele made up of various preternaturals and humans. Finn brought his glass to his lips and sipped while he checked out the other drinkers.

A couple of blue-collar type humans sat at a back

booth with pretzels and beers, their eyes glued to the large
TV screen hanging on one wall. It looked like a pre-
season game of the Arizona Cardinals playing the Pitts-
burgh Steelers at the home stadium. Damn. He should've
bought tickets, since it was so close. It'd be better than
sitting here watching it on TV with a zombie yammering
in his ear.

There was a lone drinker at the end of the bar that
caught Finn's eye. Finn leaned around zombie guy for a
better look. The loner hunched over his drink, obviously
not wanting Finn to get a good look at him. Finn understood the need to be alone with a drink, but he was
curious to know what kind of pret was sharing the bar
with him. Doing his job as well as he did meant he'd
made a few enemies. Hell, more than a few. So using extra precaution was necessary to make sure the guy trying
to hide behind his drink wasn't a demon with a grudge.

Finn took a few sniffs of air and grimaced at the sickly
sweet smell emanating from the man next to him, a man
who was still going on about zombies getting negative
press.

"Really, man." The zombie lifted his drink. "Just because we happen to like brains...and intestines—"

"Mack!" Finn held up his hand to signal the bartender.
Enough was enough. He slammed his glass onto the bar
and scowled. He'd come here for a drink or three, not
to strike up conversation with some random smelly dude.
Since this guy wouldn't shut up, it was time to go. He
slapped a few bills down on the bar and pushed off his
stool.

"You gotta go?" The whiny zombie looked like he was
about to cry. "We were only gettin' started."

"Yeah, well, somebody's disturbing my quiet." Finn shot the guy a look and headed toward the front of the bar, taking a route that brought him behind the lone drinker. He didn't recognize the dude, and sensed no aggression coming from him. Just another guy trying to drown his sorrows.

As Finn pushed open the door, he slipped his sunglasses over his eyes. The sultry air of a late August afternoon in Scottsdale, Arizona, slapped him in the face. God, it was so hot it felt like he'd stepped into an oven.

"Highway to Hell" began playing on his phone. He dragged it out of his pocket and answered with a terse, "What's up, Dad?"

"I need to see you. *Now*." As always, Lucifer Demonicus got right to the point. "My office."

"I'm a little busy." He wasn't, but dear old dad didn't need to know that.

"My office. Ten minutes."

Finn realized his father had disconnected the call. "Damn it." He shoved his phone back into his pocket. He could blow off his dad, but if he did he had no doubt that the old devil would find him, or send some of his goons. "Damn it," he muttered again, and threw a leg over the seat of his motorcycle, wincing when heat from leather warmed by the sun seeped through his jeans.

One day he'd be free from his father's power. He was tired of Lucifer dictating his every move. As soon as he could find something to use as leverage, he'd be out from beneath the king of demons' tyranny. Until then, though... With a scowl he started the motorcycle and pulled away from the curb. The sooner he got this over with, the better.

He headed his bike down Scottsdale Road. The fronds
on the tall palm trees lining the street swayed in the
breeze. The sun beat down on him and reflected off the
pavement in shimmering waves. His shirt began to stick
to his perspiring skin. Luckily the wind he stirred up by
riding his bike cooled him off a little.

Finn made a turn onto the road that would take him
to the office building where the leader of demons in this
region conducted his many businesses, legitimate and
otherwise. Lucifer was crafty enough not to get caught
by the authorities. Finn had a lot to do with that as his
father's enforcer. When a demon stepped too far out of
line—and Lucifer was actually pretty lenient—Finn was
the one sent to dispense justice. Which wasn't always
quick, or painless.

Or neat for that matter.

But he got the job done because somehow in all the
mess that was the preternatural community, being the son
of the devil evidently meant he'd been born into inden-
tured servitude. Not that most prets knew of his blood
relationship to Lucifer. There were rumors, but very few
knew anything concrete, which was the way Finn liked it.
The less people knew about him the better. A man's private life should be just that. Private.

He stopped at a traffic light and glanced at the car that
pulled to a halt in the next lane. Flirty smiles on their
faces, two of the most beautiful women he'd ever seen
looked at him with invitation in their eyes. Despite their
beauty, he didn't get even a single twitch of interest from
his body. He blew out a sigh and looked at the light.
When a demon could look at two succubi and feel nothing, something was wrong. Really, really wrong.

What, exactly, he didn't know. It could be a bad case of the blues, he supposed, though he didn't feel particularly depressed. Maybe he was tired. He had been working a heavy schedule lately. The upcoming rift had everyone, prets and humans alike, on edge. And demons seemed to be cornering the market on orneriness.

The light switched to green and he took off, nearly burning a swath of rubber in his hurry to get away from nontemptation. When Finn reached his father's office building he drove up onto the sidewalk and brought his bike to a stop by the front door. He heeled down the kickstand and swung his leg over the seat. As he went through the automatic doors he tipped his head at the security guys at the front desk. "Fellas," he greeted. The air-conditioning was a welcome relief from the stifling midday heat.

"You should move that before Lucifer sees it." The guard gestured toward the motorcycle.

Finn merely grinned. Part of him recognized he was acting like a rebellious teenager, but he didn't care. If Lucifer had a problem with him, he could tell him to get lost. Finn would happily do so. Hell, he'd been trying to encourage his father to release him from his duties for years with no luck.

He took the elevator to the top floor, getting off at the penthouse suite. He crossed the inlaid-wood foyer, his boots thumping over the expensive flooring, and went straight into his father's no less than opulent office. "The master calleth?" he asked and flung himself down in one of the leather chairs across from Lucifer's desk.

"I did." Lucifer looked away from the bank of security monitors on the wall and leaned back in his chair. "Don't think that parking your motorcycle in front of the building is enough to cause me to release you from your...obligations."

"Obligations? Is that what my job is called?" Finn crossed his legs, resting one ankle on top of the opposite knee. He drummed his fingers on the arm of the chair. "How is it that by virtue of being your son I'm automatically at your beck and call forever?" He held his father's dark gaze. "Seriously, I've been doing this for over a thousand years. You have other sons you can foist this job on. Go make one of *them* miserable for a while."

"Miserable. Really?" Lucifer frowned, the action barely causing wrinkles to form. That was one of the quirky things about being a preternatural. Lucifer had been on Earth for over seven thousand years, yet he looked like he was in his early forties. Certainly not old enough to have an adult son as old as Finn appeared to be. Not that Finn looked old. He wasn't a vain guy, but he knew he looked good, roughly thirty-five years old.

"Yeah, killing demons gets old after about, oh, five hundred years, give or take."

"Is that so?" From the tone of Lucifer's voice, it was clear he didn't give a damn. "Well, I have another job for you."

Finn scowled. As usual, his father ignored Finn's objections and plowed ahead with his own agenda. "And if I say no?"

Lucifer's mouth twisted. "Let us tell you about it first before you turn it down, all right?" He pressed a button on his desk and Finn heard the elevator start up.

"Who's us?" Finn twisted around as the elevator doors pinged open. He frowned at the vampire who stepped into the foyer.

"Tobias, come in," Lucifer said, getting to his feet. The two men shook hands and the vampire took the chair next to Finn.

"What's this all about?" Finn asked as Lucifer sat back down.

A former liaison to the Council of Preternaturals, Tobias Caine had just been appointed to the council as their newest member. The council, made up of thirteen members of the various pret clans, governed the preternatural community. Every preternatural—vampire, shapeshifter, and fey—had representation. Only demons, by choice, did not participate in council governance. They had a strong abhorrence of anyone telling them what they could and could not do, especially when nondemons were the ones setting the rules.

Tobias shifted in his seat to look at Finn. "We're looking at statistics taken over the years to determine the breakdown of preternaturals who come through the rift opened by the Moore-Creasy-Devon comet," Caine said. "It's apparent that of all the pret clans, demons have the smallest representation."

"So?" Finn frowned. "There have always been fewer of us than other prets. We can hold our own."

"For how long?" Lucifer leaned his elbows on the desk. "Every seventy-three years, when the comet opens the rift between dimensions, there are fewer demons that come through than any other preternatural. Century after century this occurs. In a few hundred years we could very well be an endangered species."

"Then demons should have more babies." Finn wasn't sure what the fuss was all about. People became preternaturals by traveling through the rift and taking over bodies of human hosts. But all of them could procreate the good, old-fashioned way as well. "That's how I got here, after all."

"Demon women would have to be perpetually pregnant to make any headway at all," Caine said dryly.

"And the problem with that is..." Finn grinned at the annoyed looks on the other men's faces. "I'm kidding."

"Despite your ill-timed humor, this is a serious problem." His father shot him a scowl. "The only way preternaturals keep the community somewhat at peace is because there is a balance between all groups. As soon as one group becomes more powerful than the others, there will be a fight for control."

"I've never been much of a big picture kind of guy," Finn said. "You might need to explain why you're acting like this is my problem."

"Because it's *my* problem. Therefore, it's yours, too."

Finn blew out a sigh. Since this wasn't something that involved another demon directly, Finn's skills as an enforcer weren't being called upon. Which meant he could refuse the assignment. "Sorry," he said, not meaning a bit of it. He pushed to his feet. "Whatever it is you're asking me to do, I'll pass." He wanted to get away from doing his father's bidding, not do more of it.

"You can't refuse to help, Finn." Lucifer crossed his arms and glowered at his son.

"Are you asking me to hunt down a demon who's been attacking humans or other prets?"

"Not exactly."

"Then I believe I can refuse." He cocked a brow. "And I do."

"I realize you've never looked out for anyone but yourself, and you do a hell of a job at it. Can't you look past your own needs just this once?" Caine asked.

"You're such a sweet talker," Finn muttered. "You're really making me want to help." Finn thought a moment. "I have one question: What's in it for me?"

Caine's scowl mirrored Lucifer's. He muttered a curse. "Cut the crap, Finn. You're not as much of a loner as you make out. Listen to your conscience." He pressed his lips together. "And if that doesn't work, I'll give you half a mill to do it."

"To do what, exactly?" It had to be something good for Caine to toss around that kind of money.

The vampire shared a glance with Lucifer, then said, "We want you to infiltrate a rogue group that's planning something big at the next Influx."

The next Influx of preternaturals to come through the rift was due in four months. That didn't give him a lot of time to go undercover.

"We figure your reputation will speak for itself," Caine added. "It should open doors quicker than someone else could get it done."

"The thing is . . ." Finn sat back down. He stretched his legs out in front of him and clasped his hands across his stomach. "I don't need the money. I've got plenty."

"Two million." This from Lucifer.

That cut him deep. Since when had Finn ever done anything he'd been asked to because of a paycheck? He might be a lot of things, but mercenary wasn't one of them. He clenched his jaw and shook his head. "I don't need the money," he repeated.

"Three million."

Finn folded his arms over his chest and thought about the offer. He'd been truthful when he said he didn't need the money because he had more than he could spend in a couple hundred years. But there was something he'd been wanting, something that had been out of his reach for a long time. What he wanted was to be his own man for once. Do what he wanted when he wanted instead of having to ask permission from his boss, who also happened to be his father and the leader of the demon enclave in the region.

All his life Finn had felt more like one of Lucifer's subjects and less like a son. From the day of his birth his father had designed the course of his life, and Finn in his early years had gladly followed that map. Yet century after century his efforts to garner his father's approval had awarded him nothing. With his mother's death Finn had lost the only person who'd ever truly loved him. His father certainly didn't. At least he never showed it. Finn had never felt like he measured up to Lucifer's expectations, and about five hundred years ago he'd given up trying. He did his job well because that was the kind of guy he was—you do the job you're hired to do regardless of the pay or any issues you had with the boss. And now he didn't care if good ol' Dad was proud of him or not.

At least, that's what he told himself. And perhaps if he kept telling himself that, eventually he'd believe it.

For the chance to be his own boss he just might give in. He'd been tossing around the idea of running a private security firm, one that would cater to the rich and powerful—both preternatural and human—and this might be his chance.

"There's more to you asking for my help than my rep," he said, looking from his dad to Caine.

Lucifer cleared his throat, drawing Finn's gaze. "The chameleon abilities you got from your mother will prove useful."

Finn raised his eyebrows. "You told him?" he asked, amazed that his father would tell an outsider a closely guarded secret that not even the demons knew.

"I trust him."

"So I take it he also knows—"

"That you're my son? Yes." Lucifer leaned back in his chair and rocked it back and forth.

It wasn't common knowledge that Finn was Lucifer's child, and it was safer that way. Each of them had made enemies, and if a relationship closer than that of boss and employee were to become known, well, it wouldn't be a good thing. For Lucifer to not only have clued in an outsider on the existence of chameleons but his and Lucifer's kinship, he must trust the vampire implicitly.

Finn studied Caine. He didn't know him, not really. He'd had some dealings with Caine in the past, and the vampire struck him as intense. Dedicated and single-minded in his pursuit of justice. And someone capable of taking secrets to his grave.

"As I understand it," the vampire said, "you can take on the abilities of any preternatural. Does that mean you can enhance your hearing or sense of smell to the level of a werewolf's if you wanted to?"

Finn nodded. "There's a little more to it than that, though. For a short period of time I can actually become that preternatural."

"Meaning…"

"If I mimic a werewolf, I can shift into a wolf. Or if I want to imitate a vampire..." He paused and got to his feet. "Here, let me show you."

It had been a while since Finn had impersonated a vamp. He studied Caine, took a deep breath to get his scent, then closed his eyes to concentrate on summoning his chameleon demon abilities. There was a burst of heat deep inside him, then his body temperature plummeted. His jaw began to ache and his canine teeth lengthened into fangs. When he opened his eyes, it was to see Caine staring at him in shock.

The vampire stood and walked over to him. "What the hell?" He stopped and drew in a deep breath. "Damn. You even smell like a vampire." He glanced at Lucifer. "I can see how this could prove useful."

Lucifer gave a sly smile. "Indeed."

Finn let go of the pretense and became his normal self again. He dropped back down into his chair and exhaled. Since he was only part chameleon, he was unable to hold on to a deception as easily as a full-blooded chameleon could. Even that little bit had taxed his energy. Not that he'd ever admit out loud that he was tired.

"Come on, Finn." Caine shoved his hands in his pockets. "We need you."

Finn thought about it a moment longer then, looking at his father, said, "I'll tell you what. You free me from my enforcer duties, and I'll do this."

"Done."

Finn's brow furrowed. "I mean forever, not just while I'm on this particular assignment."

"Agreed."

Finn couldn't hide his shock. He hadn't expected it to

be that easy. It hadn't been when he'd asked before. He knew this was some serious shit for his father to so readily agree to his demand. "Fine." Finn looked at Caine. "Tell me what you want me to do."

Caine nodded. "One thing first." He leaned forward, his gray eyes darkly intent. "No one, and I mean no one outside of this room, other than my wife, knows what we're asking you to do. Make sure you keep it that way."

Chapter One

Three months later

Finn walked into the Devil's Domain nightclub and paused to let his eyes adjust to the dimness. The warmth inside the club, produced by a furnace and the heat of the assembled crowd, contrasted with the coolness of the November evening.

Not that heat bothered him. He was a demon after all; he could handle a little heat. Once he accomplished his task tonight, he'd see what kind of hookup he could make and then he'd generate another type of heat altogether. *If* he could. He scowled a little, remembering those succubi he'd seen a few months ago. He'd had similar reactions since, but hoped that very soon his disinterest would be a fleeting thing.

First, he needed to make some progress on that little matter his father and Tobias Caine had asked him to take care of. Things had been slow moving thus far. Infiltrating the rogue group of preternaturals would be the key to his freedom.

He'd been working on it for the last few months, using his current contacts and making new ones. Going to the leader of the group head-on would be too obvious, so Finn had been coming at them sideways. He was so close, he could feel it. All he needed was one person to buy that he was a true believer and he'd be in. He planned to make some headway to that end tonight, especially since he was running out of time. The next rift was set to occur in only four weeks.

Moving a few more feet into the club, he looked out over the assembled crowd. Prets of every type as well as several humans filled the place almost to capacity. A handful of vampires congregated in the booths near the door that led to the area where they could dine in private if they wanted. Some vamps, though, were exhibitionists and got off as much on audience reaction as they did the actual ingestion of blood, which explained why a few of them were leaning over donors in booths that lined the back wall, fangs in arms or necks.

Shapeshifters—werewolves, various werecats, and even a werebear or two—gathered near the bar. A couple of succubi led entranced humans by the hand toward the restrooms where, no doubt, they'd suck off some of the men's energy while, well, sucking them off. And they'd probably lift their victims' wallets while they were at it, but the men wouldn't care about that, not for a while, anyway.

The club smelled like it usually did, a combination of booze, sweat, and the underlying dark, silky feel of carnal, preternatural hunger. Between the music and voices of people trying to talk over it, the noise level was at a low roar. Finn tapped into his chameleon abilities and took on the hearing of a shapeshifter. He listened to several conversations, none of which were all that interesting. Certainly none pertained to the rogue group he was still trying to get close to. He eased up and shifted his attention to the dance floor. Several demons he knew, most of whom he had no desire to engage in conversation. One guy, an incubus, caught his attention, though. Not because of what he was doing, which was dancing badly, but because of *whom* he was dancing with.

Finn would recognize that long hair anywhere. It flowed down her back to the top of her shapely buttocks in a fiery cascade. Keira O'Brien.

His body tightened. On some level he recognized the reaction and registered the relief he felt in knowing he hadn't completely lost his interest in the opposite sex. But on another level he wondered if Keira had ruined him for other women.

He reflected on their first meeting. They'd met here, at the Devil's Domain, right at the bar. Finn had just come off a job. He'd been tired, in need of a shave, a haircut, and a small supply of give-a-damn. A husky, shamrock jeweled voice ordering a scotch had caught his attention and set his nerve endings on fire. When he'd seen the owner of that voice, a slender, curvy woman in a barely there black dress, he'd been a goner.

The attraction had been mutual and instantaneous. She'd been as irreverent toward him then as she was now. Unafraid of his strength, she saw right through him to the man he was inside, the man he could become if he wanted it badly enough.

Keira had been new to the city, still trying to find her way. They danced for a while, shared another drink, and agreed to see each other again. Over the following months they had enjoyed a flirtation that had deepened each time they were together, finally culminating in a night filled with overheated bodies straining together against silky sheets.

The evening had started out as their dates usually did—dinner and dancing at the Devil's Domain. That night, though, they'd both been more than ready to take things to the next level. Slow kisses and a little heavy petting in a dark booth at the club barely held their lust in check until he could get her to his bed.

Her dress had stayed on her for all of two seconds, only as long as it took him to get her from the front door to his bedroom. He'd laid her down on the crimson and plum comforter and she'd given him a slow, sultry smile that told him she knew exactly what she was doing to him, lying there in nothing but her smooth skin and a pair of red high heels.

"You're a naughty little thing, aren't you?" He stared down at her, his eyes burning as desire flamed white hot in his gut. He let his gaze drift over her slender body, taking in her hard-tipped breasts, narrow waist, and flaring hips. Soft auburn curls guarded a treasure trove he fully intended on plundering. "Do you often go without panties?"

"Only when I think they might slow things down," she murmured. A slim finger traced along his lower lip. When he sucked it into his mouth, her breath caught and her eyes flared with passion. With a low moan that fired his blood, she pushed him onto his back. Holding his eyes with hers, she began to unbutton his shirt, her fingers brushing against his skin, sending shivers of reaction racing to his cock. By the time she'd pushed the material to the sides of his torso, he was grinding his jaws to keep from hauling her beneath him.

When her fingers went to the button on his pants, he knew he'd never keep control if she wrapped them around the part of him that most wanted her attention. With an oath he surged off the bed and finished undressing.

When he came back down, she curled her legs around his hips and surged against him. He'd been surprised by the strength in her body, though he knew he shouldn't have been. When he moved one hand to stroke through the soft folds of her sex, the slick heat he'd found had made the breath catch in his throat.

"Ordinarily I'd insist on a short getting to know you period," she husked, trailing her hands across his chest. Her brogue was more pronounced than usual, and he realized she slipped back into the familiar and perhaps comforting cadence of speech when her emotions were heightened. "But you've been teasin' and tormentin' me somethin' fierce these last weeks, boyo." Her thumbs raked across his nipples, making him jerk in response. That slow, sexy smile curved her lips again. "Let's get down to business, then, shall we?"

What had followed had been the hottest sex of his life.

They'd fit together like they'd been custom made for one another. Afterward, though, things had gotten awkward between them. Instead of curling up in his arms for a postcoital snooze, Keira had muttered something about not wanting to get into a serious relationship, and he'd mumbled something along the same lines.

By unspoken agreement they'd put distance between them. The truth of the matter was, while their lovemaking had been fulfilling on a level he'd never before experienced, he wasn't about to trade one type of servitude for another. Doing this "job" for his father was the means to an end. He wanted to be free, not tied down.

Since Keira had also denied any desire for a serious relationship, he figured she'd be a safe bet for what he needed tonight. No-strings-attached sex. Even if she was the only woman who'd enticed him in a long while, he didn't have time for anything else, not in the short period he had to complete his mission.

He wended his way through the couples on the dance floor until he reached her. Her dark blue dress glimmered in the light. As she danced, he could see the bare skin of her back each time her hair moved. Or when the incubus slid his hand down to cup her ass.

Finn clenched his jaw. With two rigid fingers he tapped her companion's shoulder. Hard. "I'm cutting in." His voice came out in a low, predatory growl that irritated him. It wasn't like he and Keira were exclusive, after all. She could dance with whoever the hell she wanted to. She could also have sex with whoever she wanted to.

That didn't mean he had to like it.

With the mood he was in, Finn wouldn't have minded a decent, down and dirty fight, but unfortunately her dance partner wasn't an idiot. "Sure thing." The incubus gave a smile to Keira, handed her over to Finn, and turned away without another word.

Finn watched him walk away and then looked down at the woman standing in front of him. Her dress was almost as low cut in the front as it was in the back, showing off the delectable slopes of her breasts and the pale, smooth skin of her upper abdomen. The fresh, sweet-grass smell of heather he always associated with her wafted to his nostrils. He drew in a breath, holding her scent in his lungs a moment before exhaling. "It's nice to see you, Keira. You look beautiful as always."

"Thank you." Her gaze tracked the incubus for a moment before she looked at Finn again. Her lips curled upward, her reaction one of indulgent amusement rather than outrage at his high-handedness. "You're looking fine yourself. How've you been?" she asked, her tones as lilting as if she'd just arrived off a plane from Ireland the day before. "I haven't seen much of you lately."

"I've been busy. Work," he explained. He didn't want to talk about what he'd been doing the last few months. He *couldn't* talk about it. She knew enough about him to know he was no stranger to keeping secrets. In his line of work it was necessary. Couldn't have his target running off because they'd heard Finn the Enforcer was after them. Or have the rogue group close its doors because they found out a nonbeliever was trying to infiltrate them. "What've you been up to?"

Suddenly serious blue eyes stared into his. "Oh, a little of this, a little of that."

Keira was no stranger to secrets, either. She was one of the most private people he'd ever met, and that was saying something. Every preternatural alive' had learned to exist by hiding their true nature. But Keira took keeping her privacy to a whole new level.

She freed her hand from his. "I've been around, boyo. You're the one who's been scarce." Her fingers drifted across his shoulder to stroke through the hair at the nape of his neck. Heat spread from her fingertips down his torso and wrapped around the base of his cock. When her softly rounded belly brushed against the slight rise beneath his fly, she gave a slow, wicked smile. "You're glad to see me then."

"Yeah, I am."

The song ended and the DJ started another slow ballad. Finn rested his hands on Keira's hips. "Dance with me," he murmured in a voice gone low and raspy with desire. When she nodded, he pulled her even closer. This was his kind of dancing. Nothing too fancy, just the shuffling of feet and the brushing of bodies against each other.

She twined her arms around his neck, fingers still sifting through his hair. The motion sent darts of sensation throughout his body. She shifted nearer, the tips of her breasts brushing his chest. Her high heels put her at cheek level with his jaw, and she rested her face against his.

Her skin was like satin against his stubble-covered jaw. He drew in a breath, enjoying the light floral scent of her hair. She was the essence of femininity—soft, seemingly delicate—yet every once in a while she'd get a look in her eye that made him think of Boadicea, the fiery Briton queen. He had no doubt Keira would be fierce in a fight.

He knew from experience she could be fierce in bed.

The feel of her in his arms made him ache to slide her beneath him on the closest horizontal surface. Or up against a wall. Finn slid his hands to the small of her back and linked his fingers, pulling her closer. He focused on the woman in his arms, the warmth of her body against his, the softness of her skin beneath his palms. He drew in a breath, trapping the fresh scent of her shampoo in his nostrils before he exhaled.

Her fingers continued combing through his hair. With each stroke his muscles tightened. Going horizontal was looking better and better. To regain some control, Finn drew back a smidgin and glanced around the club for potential contacts. He had to focus on something else or he'd end up dragging her out of the club like some Neanderthal. Any other time that wouldn't have bothered him, but tonight he had other things he had to accomplish. He couldn't forget his mission, though this sensual woman surely made him want to. Even as his eyes searched the crowd, his mind replayed images of Keira stretched out beneath him in bed, her slender body naked to his gaze, his touch. He drew in a shuddering breath and fought to rein in his rampaging libido.

The song ended, and Keira stepped back from him. He took one of her slender hands in his. *Want to get a drink?* he meant to say, but what came out was, "Come home with me."

She tipped her head to the side, one delicate eyebrow climbing.

"For drinks," he hurried to add. He could tell by her expression that she was thinking what he was. The temptation for more was there. And, like him, she looked like she was about to give in.

Her lips parted, her gaze bright with agreement. Then her eyes flicked to something over his shoulder and she said, "Rain check? There's someone I need to talk to." Genuine regret colored her sultry voice.

Finn gave a nod. "Sure, no problem."

She stroked her hand down his cheek and let her fingertips linger on his lips. Then she went up on her toes, moving her fingers aside to press her mouth against his. He parted his lips, allowing her inside, tangling his tongue with hers. God, she tasted good. Better than good.

She tasted of sweet honey but with a tartness that was un-expected yet welcome.

"I'll see you later," she whispered against his mouth. Another lingering kiss, then she brushed her hand across his shoulder as she walked past him.

Finn turned and watched her head toward the back of the club. Because of the crowd he couldn't see who her target was, and soon the crush of bodies forced him to move off the dance floor.

He couldn't take his gaze off the auburn-haired woman who was pure temptation. Still watching Keira, his mood soured. Scowling, he realized his interest in being at the club had waned, but as much as he wanted to get the hell out of there, he had work to do.

Keira glanced over her shoulder to see Finn staring at her. He'd shoved his hands into the pockets of his jeans, the broad shoulders beneath the soft T-shirt and leather jacket slightly hunched. Blue eyes gleamed with a faint demon-yellow glow. His expression, one he seemed to wear a lot around her, contained a mixture of desire, determination, and befuddlement.

She was just as confused as he seemed to be, because he purely baffled her. And as much as she told herself she didn't want to solve this particular puzzle she knew deep down she was lying to herself. The demon was compli-cated, and she loved every complicated piece of his puzzle.

Maybe once she was done with this...project, she could put more effort into the mystery that was Finn Evnissyen. All she knew about him was that he was hand-some, sexy, a great lover, and as badass as they came. While she would trust him to watch her back in a dangerous situation, he wasn't the type of guy a woman should give her heart to.

Definitely not the sort a girl brought home to meet her parents.

Luckily for Keira, her parents—both the set in the other dimension and the ones of her human host—were long dead and buried. All of them—shapeshifter, fey, or vampire—were mortal in the other dimension. They lived and died the same way humans did. It was the combination of their otherworldly essence with human souls that created their immortality here on Earth. Although she didn't have to worry about gaining approval, that didn't mean she was going to entertain any ideas about having some sort of long-term relationship with Finn. He was strictly a love 'em and leave 'em kind of guy. She'd heard about him around town.

Yet she couldn't deny that he was a mighty temptation, as well as enigmatic. Even with her abilities she had trouble figuring him out. She was fey, and like all of her kind she had the ability to use glamour. The older the fey, the stronger the ability. With her specifically, she was an empath. She could read the emotions of others, even influence those emotions. She could make people feel what she wanted them to, believe what she thought they should. And if she pushed hard enough, she could alter their perception of their surroundings to the point that she became invisible.

Her glamour was something she rarely used anymore. In the other dimension before she'd become Keira O'Brien she'd used all her skills as a grifter to swindle a handsome living off unsuspecting marks. Since she'd come to Earth, though, she'd tried to do better, *be* better.

The personality of her human host had a lot to do with that. The human Keira of the O'Brien clan had been an honest, honorable woman. So, to pay homage to that, the new Keira had determined to live her life the way her human host would have.

While she could have used her gift to influence Finn, she hadn't. And she wouldn't. Ever. Not for something as important as love.

But to get the information needed for her task from a vampire? In her experience, any tactic employed in war was fair. She'd use her ability faster than a bartender could pour green beer on St. Paddy's Day. She turned toward the back of the club and hurried after the vampire she'd spotted. "Javier!" she called.

With one hand on the knob of the door that separated the public area of the club from the rooms where vamps went to dine in private, a short, swarthy-skinned man stopped and looked at her. She'd met Javier Alvaro initially at a formal meet-and-greet at council headquarters that all newcomers to Scottsdale had to go through. While she wouldn't call him a friend, they were at least on friendly terms. Of sorts.

"I need to talk to you," she said upon reaching him.

"Keira." He gave her a once-over, which set her teeth on edge, but she plastered a pleasant expression on her face and projected a sense of sexual interest she was far from feeling. When his dark gaze came back to her face, he said, "If you want to talk, *bonita*, you'll have to donate, because I'm going in there"—he tapped two fingers against the door—"to feed." Crimson hunger rimmed his cocoa-colored irises. "I have a powerful thirst for blood. And maybe something more."

She wasn't thrilled with the idea of letting this smarmy vamp fang her, and she had no intention of letting him "something more" or anything else with her either. However, she was no stranger to making hard choices to get what she needed. She'd use her glamour on him. It would take some doing to fool a vampire, but she'd been around a long time and had the strength necessary. And if it didn't work for some reason, she'd do what she needed to do to get the information she was after.

She widened her smile and swept her arm toward the door. "After you."

His nostrils flared as did the red in his eyes. He opened the door and murmured, "No, please. After you."

She went through the door, aware of Finn's burning gaze on her. He'd want to know why she'd chased Javier down and, more importantly, why she'd gone into the back rooms with him. The fact that she was going off with a vampire would automatically anger him because of the animosity between vamps and demons. But it wasn't like she and Finn were exclusive. She never pressed him for details about his comings and goings, because she knew it'd be a waste of breath. By the same token, what she did was none of his business.

Keira pushed back the tinge of sadness that crept over her at the thought. Finn didn't seem like the kind of demon who craved hearth and home. She sensed a restlessness about him, a desire to shake off the trappings of his current life so he could live the way he wanted to. Perhaps so he could be who he wanted to be, not who the pret world painted him as. And she had a feeling a woman didn't fit into those plans in any permanent fashion. He was far too self-centered for that.

She walked into the small room that Javier indicated and seated herself on a little leather sofa, crossing her legs and stretching her left arm along its back. A strong scent of cinnamon colored the air, no doubt to help cover up the smell of blood. No matter how hard or how often they cleaned these rooms, blood had a way of lingering.

Javier sat beside her and leaned forward. The scent of peppermint wafted from his breath. He licked his bottom lip, no doubt thinking it made him look sexy. She forced herself to keep a sultry smile on her face as he ran his fingers lightly up and down her arm.

"So, *bonita*, a little bite to eat first, yes?" He curled his fingers around her wrist and lifted her arm from the back of the couch.

She trilled out a laugh, made sure she was projecting a general feeling of satisfied indulgence, and whispered, "How about you answer a question for me, and then you can have a big bite?" She leaned closer and trailed her right hand from his knee up to his inner thigh, almost but not quite hitting his sweet spot.

"Deal." His voice came out guttural, barely sounding like that of a man. It matched the predatory gleam in eyes that had gone completely crimson.

"I don't know if you know it or not," she said, making sure to keep the soft Irish lilt in her voice, "but I moved here from back east to do more than get away from cold winters."

"Oh?"

"Aye." She stroked her fingers back down to his knee and lingered there, letting him feel the warmth of her palm through the fabric of his trousers. "We preternaturals have always had to be so careful. Before our public outing, we had to hide what we were so we didn't provoke humans into hunting us."

His lips twisted. "Yes, we have historical accounts to back us up on that one. The witch trials of the fifteenth, sixteenth, and seventeenth centuries, and werewolf trials in the sixteen hundreds." His lips curled back to show his fangs. "And of course they've been frightened of vampires from time immemorial."

"Exactly!" Keira agreed. "And now it's all 'Don't do this or you might make the humans around you aware of what you are. Don't do that or you'll expose us all.'" She sighed and started a halting trail back up his thigh. "You'd think that since we've become common knowledge things would have changed, but they've only gotten worse."

"Yes, they have." Javier rested one hand on her left shoulder. The other lay on the thigh opposite the one she currently teased. "What's your point?"

"My point is . . . I'm tired of it." She held his gaze with her own. "We're stronger than humans. *Better* than humans. We should be living loud and proud, not denying who we are." She halted high up on his thigh, still not touching where she knew he wanted her hand the most. "I'm tired of us being in the minority and not allowed a say in how this town, this *country*, is run."

"I'm still not connecting the dots, *bonita*." His fingers tightened on her shoulder. "And neither my time nor my patience, nor my willingness to continue to go hungry, is limitless."

"I've heard you can put me in touch with like-minded folk here in town. I want to contribute to the cause." She watched his face carefully and tried not to look like she was watching carefully. "I'd like to help."

"I think maybe you got some bad information." Javier moved his hand from her shoulder to curl it around the back of her neck. His skin was cool against hers, and she could feel the strength in his grasp. With a flick of his wrist he could snap her neck, and that'd be it for her. She didn't know of any preternatural who could survive with their body being cut off from their brain.

Javier's hand on her nape made her nervous. But she couldn't let him see it. The last thing she should do now is show any sort of weakness to a predator like him. Without losing her smile, she said, "Well, I hope my information isn't bad, because I'll be very disappointed." She let her fingers drift a little higher.

He studied her a moment. Carnal hunger sparkled in his eyes. "And if I could make sure you're not disappointed?"

"I'd be very...grateful." Keira pushed extra breath into her voice so it came out throaty. She also pointed feelings of good will and sincerity his way.

Those red-tinted eyes stayed fixed on her. She reached out with her empathic sense but couldn't discern his true feelings. Damn, he was a hard one to read. Most vampires were. She could only suppose it was because they were reanimated corpses. Thankfully, they weren't that hard to influence.

"If I hear something," he said, "I'll let you know." The dip between his brows and the downturn of his mouth told her in spite of her gentle pushing he was skeptical of her sincerity. Then his lips twisted up. "Now, it's time to pay up, *bonita*." He moved his hand from the nape of her neck to her left wrist, lifted her arm off the back of the sofa and started to bring her wrist to his mouth. His lips parted, pulling back from his fangs.

Keira focused on her breathing, reached deep within her and drew even more upon her fey power. With a soft sigh she projected a feeling of contentment and growing satiation to Javier. His mouth never made contact with her skin, but his eyes drooped and his face took on the expression of a vampire who was enjoying every swallow.

After a few minutes, she slowly pulled her arm away. He smiled, a vacant one of overindulgence, and slumped back, his body limp and replete. She left the room, closing the door softly behind her. She blew out a breath and leaned against the door for a few moments.

Drawing as deeply as she did on her power always drained her. She fisted her hands to conceal her trembling. It wouldn't do for someone to remark upon how exhausted or weak she'd seemed when she left the back room. It might be expected if she'd actually donated, but since there wasn't a bite mark on her, it wouldn't do at all.

Secure in the knowledge that she'd left Javier with the feeling he'd had the best meal of his life, Keira pushed away from the door and headed toward the front of the club. As she entered the main area, the heat and babble slapped her in the face. By Dagda's beard, she was tired. The life energy flowing from the gathered crowd and the noise they made was usually something she enjoyed. But not now. It only made her want to get out of there.

She focused on putting one foot in front of the other even as a satisfied smile curled her lips. She'd done it. She'd finally been able to get someone who was willing to put her in touch with the rogue group of preternaturals.

She needed to report in, but she wanted to refuel and

rest first. Which meant getting outside and at least putting her bare feet against the ground so she could take in energy from the Earth. Completely naked would be better, but she wasn't an exhibitionist so feet or hands would have to suffice.

Keira reached the front door and paused to glance back into the club. As if drawn by a magnetic force, her gaze lit upon Finn. He was seated at a high-topped table, leaning close to a blond-haired woman. When the woman threw back her head and laughed at something he'd said, Keira saw the small lotus blossom tattoo behind her left ear. Her mouth firmed. Of course Finn would have hooked up with a succubus. He'd been cruising for a sexual partner, and who better to see to his needs than a sex demon?

He wore what she'd come to think of as his flirty look—the smile just a bit too practiced, the interested expression in his eyes a little too forced. Most women in here wouldn't look closely enough to be able to see it, but Keira had been around a long time. She'd seen men at their primitive worst in the Celtic tribe she'd become part of during the early Bronze Age at the time of her rifting. And she'd seen them at their best when the age of chivalry had reached its height.

Regardless, it had been a long enough time for her to know the signs. Yet she couldn't seem to help herself from being jealous. A sudden wave of light-headedness assailed her, making her sway and reminding her she needed to recharge. She turned away from the temptation that was Finn and pushed open the door.

As soon as she got outside, she headed to the easement between the sidewalk and the street. Remembering what this strip of land was called back in Northeast Ohio where she'd lived for a time, she smiled. It seemed appropriate that outside the Devil's Domain she'd be standing on the devil strip.

Keira reached it and looked down. The security lighting from the club's parking lot made it as light as day even out by the street. The devil strip was gravel, not soft grass like in Ohio, but at least it wasn't concrete or asphalt like the parking lot. It also had several clumps of prickly pear cacti growing in it. Any time she could be on a patch of ground where other living things were also nourished, it provided a stronger surge of nature's vitality.

She slipped off her shoes and scraped the gravel aside with the edge of one foot then stepped onto the cool packed dirt. Immediately renewing energy from the Earth and everything it nourished flowed into her, like warm tendrils snaking around her muscles, curling through her veins. Her fatigue lessened enough so that she felt she'd be able to make it home without passing out.

She put on her shoes and walked to her car. She'd get back to her house and lie down on the patch of grass she had in the backyard, a small circular area she maintained so she could have a place to literally commune with nature. Sheltered beneath a mesquite tree, it was a tiny oasis in the dry desert landscape. And she definitely would use it tonight. This little bit she'd done was only a Band-Aid solution for what she really needed, but she didn't have time for more. In a little over two hours she had to meet her contact on the Council of Preternaturals and fill him in on her progress.

Chapter Two

Keira sighed and shifted against the grass. The night air was cool against her bare skin, and with the six-foot-tall privacy wall that surrounded her backyard, she was assured none of her neighbors would catch the late show she was currently putting on.

She'd been home less than fifteen minutes, and other than the few seconds it had taken her to shed her clothing, she'd been out here, lying on her stomach, skin to ground on the small patch of grass she maintained with meticulous grooming and much care in this desert clime. She'd kept the lights off. Closing her eyes, she breathed deeply, letting the scent of grass permeate her. The Earth generously gave of its vitality, filling her with strength and peace.

With another soft sigh she turned onto her back and stared up into the night sky. The moon, slicing a slender crescent in the star field, peeked at her through the branches of the mesquite tree that grew at the outer edge of this small patch of grass. During the day the tree gave the grass and the small patio behind her house additional shade. At night it was a welcome friend, standing as a silent sentinel.

After several more minutes Keira had the healing energy she needed. Getting to her feet, she shrugged into her robe then sauntered to the house. She glanced at the old carriage clock on the fireplace mantel. Good, she had time for a shower, which she took in five minutes. After towel drying her hair, she pulled it back into a ponytail then looped it up into a haphazard chignon at the nape of her neck. She'd thought several times about cutting it, but every time a feeling of dread had stolen over her. She sensed that having long hair was something that had been very important to her human host, so she'd left it long. But damn if it wasn't a pain in the arse to care for.

She debated wearing jeans and a simple T-shirt, but decided that, as good as she felt now, she wanted looser clothing. Instead, she donned a thin strapped sundress in bold turquoise and slid her feet into bright orange sandals. She slipped her gold cuff watch over her wrist and gathered up her purse, making sure her cell phone and other essentials were in it, and headed back out again.

She guided her car south on 101 then went east on State Route 60. After she went through the small town of Apache Junction she started north on Apache Trail. In the blackness of the desert, her headlights were the only illumination until she reached a tiny mom-and-pop diner just before the boundary of the Lost Dutchman State Park. She pulled into a parking space and shut off the engine.

From the outside, the diner looked like it was caught in a time warp with its sleek metal design and neon signage. When she entered the restaurant a bell above the door jangled, making her smile. It was such a cheery sound. She paused and looked around, deciding that the place was as fifties on the inside as it was on the outside. The floor was black and white square tiles, and there were red stools at the counter. The rest of the modest restaurant contained booths with red seat cushions. She liked it.

"Sit anywhere you want to, hon," a middle-aged woman in a worn blue-and-white-striped uniform told her from behind the counter.

"I'm meeting someone." She spotted her companion in a booth at the very back of the diner. "There he is," she said with a soft smile at the waitress. She walked back and slid onto the bench opposite Caladh MacLoch, a senior member of the Council of Preternaturals.

"You're late," he muttered. He folded the newspaper he'd been reading and set it to one side. His white shirt was crisply pressed, as if he'd just picked it up from the cleaners. Lifting a spray bottle, he spritzed his face with water. Caladh was a selkie—a seal shapeshifter— and hated being in the desert. His term on the regional council wouldn't be up for several more years, so he'd learned to adapt as best he could. He'd told her more than once that someday he hoped to finally make it to San Diego, where he was sure he'd live a long and fulfilled life.

"Sorry. You couldn't have picked something closer to home?" She pushed the silverware lying on a paper napkin to one side and leaned her elbows on the table, which was set for two and already had a small bowl of creamer containers sitting in the middle. "You already ordered?" she asked Caladh.

He gave a nod. "My stomach has been reminding me for a few hours now that we went long in today's council session. I missed dinner."

The waitress approached, and Keira leaned back and

gave her another smile. The woman returned it. "You know what you want, hon?"

"I'll take a coffee, black." Keira leaned over to read Caladh's menu upside down. There wasn't a huge selection to choose from, mostly burgers, breakfast dishes, and dessert. Looking back at the waitress, she asked, "How's the peach pie?"

"Best pie this side of the Superstitions," came the reply.

"Coffee and a slice of peach pie, then."

"Ice cream with that?"

"Oh, of course."

The woman smiled. "You got it."

Keira waited until the waitress was gone before she asked, "Why on Earth did you pick way out here to meet? I like it, but it's like a pimple on God's arse. It's to hell and back again to get out here."

"I think you exaggerate." Caladh's grin showed off his small, bright white teeth. "I believe the drive is worth it. The landscape around here is quite beautiful."

"I didn't mean..." She heaved a sigh. "It is beautiful. I only meant it's not a very convenient place to get to."

"That would be the point." He glanced around. "It is quiet, and everyone in here is human."

"Except us."

"Except us," he agreed. "Regardless, the humans should have no interest in our conversation, should any of them chance to overhear it."

The waitress returned, and he stopped speaking.

Keira had to hide a smile. Even though he thought no one would have any interest in their discussion, he still wasn't willing to talk in front of them. Not that she disagreed. They had to be careful.

The waitress set a plate with a burger and fries in front of Caladh and then flipped over two coffee cups on the table. As she poured the coffee, she said, "I'll be right back with your pie."

"Thanks," Keira murmured. She and Caladh remained silent until the waitress deposited a big piece of peach decadence topped by a large scoop of vanilla ice cream in front of Keira and walked away. Keira speared a peach and put it into her mouth, her eyes briefly drifting closed as the sweet fruity goodness hit her taste buds. Then looking at Caladh, she said, "I think I'm about to be invited into the group."

His dark eyes lit up. "Most excellent! I knew my favorite grifter would get the job done."

"Favorite *former* grifter," she reminded him. He might not appreciate her effort, but she'd been living a quiet, law-abiding life for decades. Just one slip in all that time and he'd taken advantage of it.

"Not all that much former." He broke open a small container of creamer and poured it into his coffee.

She tightened her lips. By Dagda's balls, how many times would he be throwing that in her face? As long as it suited his purposes, she acknowledged to herself. Seventy-five years ago she'd found herself on hard times. Partly out of desperation she'd taken up with a charming confidence man. They'd made good money, enough to get them through several lifetimes, but he'd been a con artist through and through and had wanted to do one last job. She'd been so much in love with him, she'd agreed. But it had gone arse over elbows and the mark—the man they'd chosen to swindle—had died. Not by their hands, but certainly because of their actions

He'd returned to his business earlier than expected, and rather than simply calling the police, he'd given chase. Keira and her partner had barely made it across a busy street unscathed. Their mark hadn't been so lucky. He'd been hit by a car that had tossed him through the air, landing on the pavement where he'd been run over by another vehicle.

To this day she carried the guilt of that like a gaping wound deep in her soul. Caladh had learned about it and now the crafty old seal used that knowledge to his advantage, pressing her into service free of charge.

Not that she disagreed something needed to be done about this rogue group. Caladh had drawn her aside after the last council meet-and-greet of new arrivals to Scottsdale, and told her that he'd become aware of the group's usage of a small device that opened a mini rift between the dimensions. That was distressing enough. Even more alarming, though, was the fact that by using the small gadget the group had been communicating with prets in the other dimension, and he didn't know why. That was the reason he'd wanted her to infiltrate the rogue group— to find out who the members were and discover their plans. And, if possible, put a stop to those plans by any means necessary.

In all the jobs she'd pulled, both here and in the other dimension, she'd never killed anyone. When she'd first gotten to Earth, the tribe she was part of had had several skirmishes with other tribes. She'd killed in self-defense or to protect her village. She wasn't naive enough to think she shouldn't be prepared to kill now. She only hoped it didn't come to that.

"So," Caladh said now, "give me the details."

She told him about the vampire at the club. "The only thing I can do now is wait for his call."

"That is fine work, Keira. Truly outstanding." He pointed at her with his fork, a French fry suspended from its tines. "Remember, though, I am authorizing this investigation on my own. The rest of the council remains unaware of this situation, and until I know whom I can trust I wish to keep it that way."

"I understand." She scooped up a bite of pie. If she got caught, Caladh wouldn't step in. He couldn't help her and still maintain the secrecy that was needed.

He leaned forward and said, "No one else is to know you're doing this, or that you're doing it for me. You're to tell no one," he repeated.

"All right." Jesus, Joseph, and Mary, did he think she was daft? She'd been around a hell of a lot longer than he had. He'd only been on Earth two hundred and twenty years. She'd been here over three thousand, starting out her new life with a small Celtic clan from the green hills of present-day County Galway.

As a matter of fact, now that she thought on it, Caladh had come through the rift the same time as Tobias Caine, the newest vampire member of the council. She wondered if they'd known each other before.

"No one is to learn about this," Caladh stressed, his dark gaze fixed on her. "And you are to update me in as much detail as possible."

"I've got it." She scowled and shoved the last piece of pie into her mouth. "I'm not stupid," she said after she swallowed.

"No, you're not. You're very clever. Possibly one of the most shrewd and cunning people I have ever met." His liquid black eyes glittered. "Sometimes, though, a person can be too slick for her own good."

She let her fork clatter onto her plate. "What is that supposed to mean?"

He swiped his napkin across his lips and leaned back in his seat. One wide hand crumpled the napkin and dropped it onto the table. "Do not think for a moment that you can use this information to manipulate me."

"What information? And manipulate you for what purpose?" Keira shook her head. She wasn't sure where he was headed with this, but she knew she didn't like it one bit. Her aggravation showed in her next words. "Just what the feck are ya on about, Mr. MacLoch?"

He pulled out his wallet and dropped a ten-dollar bill on the table. As he slid out of the booth, he picked up his water bottle and murmured, "Do not think you can blackmail me into anything by threatening to go to the rest of the council with what you know."

She frowned. "I don't—"

"That's what grifters do," he said. "They use situations to their own advantage." He leaned so close she could smell coffee on his warm breath. "I know you're trying to mend your ways, and I do appreciate the effort it takes for a person to change. I also know how easy it is to slide back into old habits."

As he walked away she drew in a deep breath and held it a moment, then blew it out slowly from between pursed lips. Caladh was the damned reason she was "sliding" back into old habits, the old bugger. He always presented himself with an air of affability, but she'd seen the ruthless side of him that had gotten him where he was on the council. She was under no illusions that she was working with a friend on this. He was her handler, pure and simple.

If he thought he had to threaten her to keep her on task, he was wrong. Her conscience dictated her actions. She didn't need any additional pressure from him.

"Want me to top off your coffee?"

Keira glanced up at the waitress and nodded, watching her pour the hot brew into the cup.

"We're not busy, hon, so no need to rush." The waitress put the bill facedown on the table. For the first time Keira noticed the lines of exhaustion tugging at the woman's eyes. "And let me know if you want anything else."

Keira took a sip of coffee and watched the woman go back to the front counter. The waitress put her hand on an older customer's shoulder, saying something that made him laugh. She seemed like a kind woman, taking time to cheer up a customer even while tired. For a moment Keira felt wistful that she couldn't be more like her. Oh, she could be as nice as the next person, but it was usually an act. No, more like a persona she slipped on. Random kindness to strangers wasn't her first inclination. Her true nature was to look out for herself. As Caladh said, to twist situations to her own advantage.

She had to work at being kind. And she did, but no mistaking, it was *work*. But she knew she didn't ever want to go back to being the person she was before. This was her second chance, hell, it was more like her fourth or fifth chance, and she refused to squander it. By helping Caladh, and therefore the council at large, she would hopefully be scoring some points on the goodness scale.

With a sigh she reached for the newspaper Caladh

had left behind. The first article that caught her eye was a doozy: LEGISLATIVE COMMITTEE APPROVES MICROCHIP BILL.

"For the love of..." She read on. "HB 3762, the preternatural tracking bill sponsored by Senator Glenn Martin, has been approved by legislative committee. If passed by both the House and Senate, this bill would include provisions for the forced insertion of microchips into every preternatural in the state of Arizona. The bill further assures that humans will not be part of the mandate."

Her lips tightened. *Yeah, right. Just give them time.* Soon enough they'd set their sights on their own kind and make it seem like it was for the greater good. If the state government allowed forced microchipping of prets, that slope was slippery, indeed.

She grabbed Caladh's ten and the bill from the table and walked to the front. The waitress rang her up. Keira handed her a twenty with a "Keep the change." The poor woman had probably been on her feet all day; she deserved something for her efforts.

"Thanks, hon."

Keira pushed open the door, smiling again at the jingling bell, and walked to her car. She pressed the remote to unlock the doors and, as she got behind the wheel, her cell phone rang. She dug in her purse and pulled it out. She pressed the phone icon and brought the cell to her ear. "Hello?"

"It's Javier." The vampire's voice was as silky as ever. Keira's empathy didn't work over a phone line, but he didn't sound upset, so she could only assume he didn't know she'd used glamour on him. "You'll be invited to the next meeting, which is in a week. One hour before the meeting you'll get a text message with the location. It'll also have a special code that ensures your entrance."

"Great. That's wonderful." She threw as much gratitude into her voice as she could without overdoing it. "I appreciate it, Javier."

"Just make sure you show up, *bonita*. It won't end well for you if you don't."

From the dark tone in his voice, she knew he wasn't joking. She had no doubt that anyone who expressed an interest in this rogue group and then didn't follow through on their membership wound up dead. "Oh, no worries, I'll be there." She started to say more but didn't get a response from him. Pulling the phone away from her ear, she saw that the call had ended. "What is it with people not saying good-bye?" she muttered and dropped the phone back into her purse.

She started up her car and fastened the seatbelt. On the drive home, she went back over her conversation with Caladh. She understood his paranoia about getting other people involved. It would only take one person who was sympathetic to the rogues' cause to muck up the works. And muck her up as well.

Her thoughts drifted to Finn. Was he part of the group? And what if he was? How would she handle that? She couldn't tell him why she was in the group—they'd have to carry on with their relationship, such as it was, with her pretending she was genuine to the cause.

If he were part of the group, on one hand she wouldn't be surprised. He was such a nonconformist. On the other hand, it would shock her to find him with the rogues because he really didn't seem to give a rat's ass about anyone but himself. She didn't think he'd care about what happened with the rift or with other preternaturals. Not unless it would directly affect him.

She pressed her lips together. That was the biggest reason she shouldn't get involved with him. He was too much like the person she used to be and she was doing her best to make amends for past wrongs. He didn't give a flying feck about whatever sins he'd committed or those he was about to commit.

He defined what being a demon was all about. Be damned, be unrepentant, and be on your own.

Finn pulled his motorcycle into the garage and killed the engine. Getting off the bike, he pressed the garage door switch and waited until the door was fully down before he went inside the house. Without turning on any lights, he headed straight back to his bedroom. As inviting as his king-size bed was, he needed to get himself cleaned up before he could collapse between the sheets. It was after three a.m. and he was exhausted. He'd never had such a hard time getting women to cooperate. He'd spent a small fortune buying drinks and had gotten nowhere.

He shed his clothes, leaving them in a pile on the bedroom floor, and padded naked into the bathroom. He turned on the shower and jumped in. The lighted overhead water jet and four side shower heads wet him down in seconds. Goose bumps popped out on his skin until the water warmed up. A few minutes later he haphazardly toweled off and then crawled into bed naked. His body immediately relaxed against the memory foam mattress, but his restless mind wouldn't let him sleep.

His questioning at the club tonight had been subtle. He'd bought drink after drink, showered women with flattery and cajoled them with charm, but none he'd encountered was involved with the rogue pret group. He was sure of it. He could tell when people lied—there was a twitch of a muscle here, a slight flicker of an eye there—and none of the lovely ladies had so much as fluttered an eyelash except when they were flirting with him.

There was only one person who came to mind that could hide when she was lying. Keira. He knew her background, that she'd been a con artist with her husband in the other dimension. Her husband had died before he could be sent through the rift, so Keira had been sent alone. In the past she'd relied on her grifting skills from time to time, but for the last several hundred years she'd pretty much walked the straight and narrow as far as he knew.

He admired her for that. She had been strong enough, determined enough, to change who she was. He hadn't, and she deserved better than him. He should keep his distance.

Now if only his body, and his heart, would pay attention, he'd be all right while he lived out his life alone.

Chapter Three

The next evening, Finn rolled his bike to a stop in a parking spot near the front door of the Pixie Dust Lounge. He cut the engine and sat for a moment. The parking lot was well lit. The large sign on top of the building was neon, the pink outline of a woman with back arched and breasts outthrust was the main component. A glitter of cascading sparkles created the illusion of fairy dust streaming down from one of the figure's outstretched hands.

He wasn't a stranger to these kinds of joints; he actually spent quite a bit of time in one or another. In reality he ended up in places like this not because he wanted to be there but because he'd tracked down a demon that needed to be reminded of the rules.

There weren't many guidelines for demon behavior, but Lucifer demanded absolute adherence to the few that were in place. When a demon broke one, Finn tracked him down. Usually at a strip club, because most demons—like any other male—had a thing for naked girls.

Tonight, though, he was here on his own. To talk, not watch pole dancers, though he was just as red-blooded as the next guy. He foresaw lots more talking in his future even though he was used to banging heads together to get what he wanted. He *preferred* banging heads together to get what he wanted. This whole business of trying to persuade people through verbal communication was making him psycho. He realized head bangings wouldn't get him the desired results, so he was adapting.

See? Anyone who said he couldn't learn and grow was just shooting shit.

He heaved a sigh and got off the bike. Pocketing the key, he swiped his palms down his jean-clad thighs and headed toward the front door. As he reached out for the knob, the door swung open. Finn jumped back to avoid getting hit, and scowled when a Surtur demon named Phoebus walked out of the building.

Surturs were called fire giants by humans, but among their own kind they referred to themselves by the name of the planet they came from. They could put their hands on someone and, if they wanted to, literally kill them with a touch by heating up the victim's body temperature. They could cause anything from a raging fever to spontaneous combustion. Even with the advances of modern medicine, Finn had never known of anyone who'd been touched by a Surtur and survived.

As Phoebus stood before him, arms crossed over his chest, Finn made sure to keep some distance between them. He didn't think the other demon would start anything, but he couldn't be sure. While he wouldn't call Phoebus his nemesis, they sure as hell weren't friends, each holding an active dislike for the other. He curbed his natural inclination to reach out and pop the guy on his big schnoz. Instead, he tipped his chin in greeting. "Phoebus," he muttered and started to walk around the other man.

"That's it? No trading of insults? No veiled threats?"

Finn turned to look at Phoebus. The Surtur's irises were almost completely yellow, which they hadn't been until he'd gotten a look at Finn. Now his emotions were riled and it showed in his eyes. Finn figured his own eyes were probably showing a spark of his demon as well, but he didn't have the time or the inclination to tap dance with the bastard. "Nope," he said and turned back toward the club.

A hand fell onto his shoulder.

Finn stiffened. So far Phoebus was only touching him, but at any minute he could decide to let loose with a kind of heat not even Finn could take.

"Just one damn minute," Phoebus said. "Since when do you let an opportunity go by to remind me of my place in the grand scheme of Lucifer's domain?" His voice rasped with suspicion and animosity.

"You sound disappointed." Finn glanced at the hand on his shoulder and then raised his gaze to Phoebus's face. He lifted a brow and waited.

With a great show of compliance, Phoebus lifted his hand and shoved it into his front pocket. "Well?" he prompted.

"I'm letting you slide because I have better things to do with my time." Finn headed toward the club again.

"So the rumors are true, then?"

Finn heaved a sigh and stopped. "What rumors?" he asked in a tired voice without turning.

"From what I understand, you've been telling anyone who'll listen that you're fed up with how restricted we are by Lucifer. By the council." He paused and then, his voice thick with barely contained glee, said, "I also hear you and Lucifer are on the outs. That true?"

"Even if it was," he grated, turning to shoot a glower the other demon's way, "you'd be the last person I'd confirm it to." The thought that Phoebus could be a viable connection to the rogue group flashed through Finn's mind, and he dismissed it. There was no way in hell he could pretend to be chummy with Phoebus and have anyone believe it. Especially Phoebus. No, he'd just have to carry on as usual with the Surtur, which generally meant being snarly and trading insults. That was fine by him.

A smile tilted one corner of Phoebus's mouth and a sly look entered his eyes. "Would you at least tell me if you're his son?"

"No." Finn folded his arms over his chest.

"No, you're not his son? Or no, you won't tell me?" Phoebus's expression darkened with guile. "Come on, give me a little somethin' here."

"I wouldn't give you my last mouthful of spit if you were on fire." Finn dropped his arms to his sides and turned back toward the club. As he pulled open the door, he threw over his shoulder, "Think what you want to."

He went into the building without waiting to hear what Phoebus's comeback might be.

He headed straight to one of the tables near the pole area and settled into a seat. Two women halfheartedly danced around poles at opposite ends of the raised platform. He didn't blame them for their lack of zeal; other than him, there were only three other guys in the place.

Little white bulbs lined the edge of the stage, only half of them working. Overhead colored lights blinked, spotlighting the dancers in blue, then red, then yellow. It didn't help. He guessed the lights were an effort to make them more appealing, but to Finn it only made them look tired. Besides, he wasn't there to watch the gyrations of exotic dancers.

Within seconds a pink-haired, eyebrow- and nose-ring-sporting pixie came over to him. She wore skintight black pants and a red halter top that barely covered her breasts. Finn had been here before; he knew her outfit was the standard uniform for the waitstaff. Aroused customers tended to drink more, though it took skill to keep them sober enough so they stayed aroused and kept spending money.

And Sinead, the pixie standing in front of him, possessed mad skills. She also had ties to the rogue group, or so he'd been told, so she was on the top of his list of people to talk to. She flicked pink-streaked blond bangs out of her eyes and gave him a lusty stare. "What's your pleasure, Finn?" she asked in a sultry, husky voice.

He had to keep up his bad-boy rep, so he slung an arm around her waist and pulled her near, not close enough to scare her, but enough to be friendly. "I'll take a beer, sweetheart. And some company, if you've got the time."

"I have the time." She glanced around the nearly empty club with a grimace. "And I'm due a break, anyway. I'll be right back."

He watched her saunter away, her hips swaying with a promise he wouldn't take her up on. Though it would be a different story if she had long, red hair...he pushed that thought away. He was here to get Sinead to open up to him about the rogue group, not finagle a free lap dance. For him to succeed, she had to think he would follow through on the temptation she presented with lots of cash. Actually, either way he'd probably have to give her money, but if it got him closer to his goal, he'd consider any outlay of cash a wise investment in his future.

He watched the pole dancers with as much enthusiasm as that which they performed. The music coming over the sound system sounded like something from a low-budget seventies porn film. The women's apathetic performance was as painful to hear as it was to watch.

After a few minutes Sinead was back, a bottle of beer in one hand and a glass of wine in the other. She gave him the beer and sat down in the chair next to him. After taking a sip of wine, she placed the glass on the table and crossed one slender leg over the other. She idly swung her leg, the tip of her red stiletto coming close to his calf with each upswing. "So, you're not here on business, I take it?" she asked. She gestured toward the three other patrons. "You barely even looked at them. I'm guessing you're not on somebody's trail."

"I'm taking a break from work," he murmured. He watched her slim fingers slide up and down the stem of the wineglass. Knowing he needed to feign interest in what other long thing she could move her fingers over, he let a hint of lust show in his expression. He rolled his shoulders and met her eyes. "Today's all about fun."

"Good for you. You know what they say about all work and no play." She smiled and kept toying with the glass.

"Mmm. And I think you know I'm not a dull boy."

She snickered. "Not by a long shot."

He stretched an arm along the back of her chair. "What keeps you here, Sinead?" He met her bright blue gaze. "You could do so much better."

"Are you asking 'What's a nice girl like you doing in a place like this?'" She lifted delicately arched brows. From the look on her face he guessed she was mildly amused at his tactics.

"I guess so." He gave a one-shouldered shrug. He wasn't here to piss her off. He was here to butter her up and get information. It always helped when he could tell the truth when he flattered someone. He said, "You're smart enough to do more. You have a degree. Why are you still here?"

Surprise lightened her eyes. "Well, thank you. Most guys don't look past my assets." Sitting up straighter, she preened a little, showing off those assets while pink pleasure spread over her cheeks. She looked around the club and a tinge of sadness stole some of the pleasure away. "Arnie's worked so hard on this place, and I've been with him from the start. This job is the reason I was able to put myself through school and earn my B.A. It wouldn't be right for me to abandon him now."

Knowing the owner as he did, Finn was surprised the joint had stayed open as long as it had. The Oneiroi clan of demons was better known for causing night terrors, not for being astute businessmen. And in his heyday, Arnie Mitress had been one of the best nightmare-invoking guys around. "I admire your loyalty," he said. And he did. "But you might not have a choice if it comes down to either being loyal or eating."

"Sure I do. Arnie looks out for me." Sinead shifted her position so that her shoulder bumped against Finn's hand.

When she didn't move, he knew he'd been given the go-ahead. He slid his fingers over her soft skin and cupped her shoulder, feeling the frailty of her bones beneath his palm. "He's doing a helluva job," he muttered, a frown pulling between his brows. He genuinely liked Sinead, even if he was using her to get information. "When *is* the last time you ate?"

A smile curved her lips and brightened her eyes. "You're sweet. I'm fine, Finn. Really." She bent her arm and laced her fingers with his. "What made you decide to take a break today? Is it your boss?" Her features scrunched in commiseration. "I heard you two had a falling out."

"You did, eh?" He stroked his thumb along hers. When had his business become everyone else's?

She nodded. "Phoebus was just in here and—" Her eyes widened and her mouth formed a small *O*. "You probably ran into him on your way in."

The animosity between him and Phoebus wasn't a secret. "We saw each other, yeah." At her look of concern, he added, "He walked away uninjured, don't worry."

Sinead grimaced. "I wasn't worried about Phoebus," she said. As Finn started to feel good about her concern for him, she stated, "He can take care of himself."

He raised his brows. "You thought *he* might have hurt *me*, is that it?"

"Don't get your shorts in a twist," she muttered. She flicked her finger at the back of his hand before twining their fingers together again. "I know you can take care of yourself, too. It's just that Phoebus fights dirty." She shook her head. "You men and your egos. Really, it's ridiculous the things you get upset over."

"You think?" He let his voice come out in a low growl and wiggled his brows.

She giggled. "I do. And sometimes it's cute." She

leaned closer, nestling in the crook of his arm. "So, your break?" she asked, redirecting the conversation back to her earlier question. "Why aren't you working today? And does Lucifer know?"

Finn gave a little growl. "I guess he knows. Seems like everyone else does." He smiled at her giggle. "I've been doing this for a long, long time. A break is overdue." He lifted his gaze to the ceiling and blew out a sigh. "I get so fed up with it all, you know?"

"What do you mean?"

"Policing behavior we shouldn't have to police. Being a minority within a minority. Kowtowing to humans, making sure we don't do things to spook them." Finn looked at her. "It's especially galling for me."

"Why you?"

"Because I'm a demon. We don't answer to anyone. Well, other than Lucifer." He scrubbed his hand across his jaw. Answering to his father was bad enough. He couldn't imagine also being brought to heel by the council. "But we *don't* answer to the Council of Preternaturals, and I'd prefer to keep it that way."

"Do you think Lucifer would ever allow it? I mean, there have been councils for millennia, and demons have never been represented. They've never *wanted* to be represented. Why would that change now?" Sinead took a sip of wine, staring at Finn over the rim of the glass.

He glanced around the club. Both of the pole dancers had left the stage and no one had taken their places yet, though the cheesy porn music still played over the speakers. The other three patrons remained where they'd been when Finn had come in, so they weren't close enough to overhear what he was about to say. However, just in case one of the others in the club was a shapeshifter with preternatural hearing, he lowered his voice and said, "Because I've heard this next rift might be different."

"Different how?" She leaned toward him, her expression a mixture of curiosity and suspicion.

He couldn't tell if she wondered how much he knew, or if she was legitimately curious. "It's going to be open longer than usual, and more prets are going to come through."

Her eyes widened. "The rift will be open longer... how could that happen? And how would more prets come through from the other dimension?"

"I have no idea. I'm only telling you what I've been hearing. And I want in."

She blinked. "In on what?"

He withdrew his arm from around her shoulder and scooted his chair around so that he faced her. He hunched his shoulders, leaning his elbows on his knees, and stared into her face. "I've heard there's a group that has a device that can keep the rift open. Hell, someone told me the machine could maybe even open a rift on its own. We wouldn't have to wait another seventy-three years for more of us to get here; to take over more human bodies." Keeping his voice low, he said, "I want in on that group."

Sinead sat quietly, looking at him, and didn't respond.

He couldn't tell what was going on behind those eyes. "It's no secret that demons are in the minority among preternaturals," he went on. "We have fewer numbers than any other group. And compared to humans," he shook his head for effect, "I'm tired of the status quo. I want to shake things up."

She continued to stare at him for several moments before she took a breath and leaned back in her chair. "I might know someone. I'll give him a call."

Finn focused on keeping his heart rate steady. He couldn't show the savage satisfaction he felt. "Who?" If he could get a name, he'd be that much closer to his goal. And independence.

She waggled a finger and laughed. "Nuh-uh. It doesn't work that way, Mr. Impatient. I'll make a call, and if he's interested in letting you in, you can expect a text message." She stood. "Don't go anywhere. I'll be right back."

As she walked away, he muttered, "Don't worry, sweetheart. I'm not gonna budge."

Sinead returned with a pad and pen, which she put on the table in front of him. "Give me your cell phone number, and I'll pass it on."

He wrote down his number and handed the pad to her. "Thanks, Sinead. I appreciate this."

She gave him a look of warning. "I'm not making any promises here. Maybe you'll get a text, and maybe you won't. If you do receive one, you'd better follow the instructions."

Finn got to his feet and dug out his wallet. To make it worth her time, he handed her a couple of twenties along with the pen. "And if I don't?"

She took the money and pen, clicking the end to retract the tip. "If you don't want to die, you'll do exactly what they tell you to." With that warning she walked off with much less sway in her hips than she had earlier. He guessed she was through trying to entice him.

He settled his tab at the bar and left the club. Several minutes later, after making a few hard turns to discourage anyone who might be tailing him, he pulled his bike to the curb a couple of blocks over from his father's house. He followed a man-made wash running like an alley behind a row of homes until he could climb over the tall privacy wall that separated Lucifer's property from his neighbors, and knocked on the back door.

He was getting ready to knock again when the door swung open. His dad's longtime girlfriend Betty stood there, neither hostile nor welcoming. Her short black curls glinted with blue from the overhead light, and her round dark eyes framed with sooty long lashes were still youthful and reminiscent of a famous cartoon that had been created based on her back in the early thirties. "Hello, Finn," she said. She peered over his shoulder, a slight frown finally bringing some sort of life to her face. "Why are you sneaking around in our backyard?"

"I'm not." He bit back a sigh of impatience. "I was just making sure I wasn't being followed. Can I come in? I need to talk to my father."

"Sure." She stepped back to allow him entrance, then closed the door behind him. "Luc's in the living room. Go on in."

As Finn went into the living room, his father looked up from his computer tablet. "You have news?" Lucifer asked.

Finn shot him a look. For once he'd like to be treated like a blood relative, hell, like a son, instead of an employee. To get a *Hi, son, how are you?* instead of being asked for a status report. But this was the king of demons after all. "I do."

Lucifer smiled and set the tablet on the side table. "Let's hear it."

Finn glanced toward the kitchen. "Uh, I thought Calne

didn't want anyone but the three of us and his wife to know—"

"I don't keep things from Betty." Lucifer's face hardened with displeasure. "Besides, the day I let a vampire tell me what to do is the day you put me six feet under."

Apparently his father trusted Tobias Caine, respected him even, but wasn't willing to let go of the natural hatred that existed between vampires and demons. As far as Finn could tell, it stemmed from before any of them had come through the rift, and no one could or would tell him exactly where it all had started. "Fine," he said. "It's your call." At his father's nod, Finn filled him in, a feeling of satisfaction growing within him at the expression of pride on his father's face. "I was about ready to walk up to Caine's nemesis and introduce myself," Finn finished. "But it finally looks like our original plan is going to work after all."

"This calls for a celebration." Lucifer turned his head toward the kitchen. "Sweetheart, is there any cheesecake left?"

"You want to celebrate with cheesecake?" And here Finn thought he knew his dad, but the old devil pulled something new out of his bag of tricks.

Lucifer glanced his way. "It's good cheesecake."

"Uh-huh."

"*Very* good cheesecake."

Betty walked out of the kitchen and stopped under the arched entrance to the living room. "What kind do you want?"

"You have more than one kind?" Finn saw the sugar gluttony in his father's eyes. "Of course you do."

"I like cheesecake," Lucifer said with an arch glance

his way. "I'll have a piece of both," he said in a softer tone to his girlfriend.

"And both would be?" Finn looked at Betty.

"Caramel apple and white chocolate raspberry."

"You made them?"

Betty trilled a laugh. "Oh, hell no. I can't cook worth a damn."

Finn opted for the caramel apple.

Betty served them and took a seat next to Lucifer on the sofa. She curled her legs to one side and leaned against his shoulder, one hand curled around his inner elbow.

It struck Finn, not for the first time, how this woman, a succubus, could be so attentive and attached to his father yet spare barely a thought for her own daughter, Nix, Caine's new wife. And now that Nix was part vampire, the mother-daughter relationship was even more strained.

He supposed it was none of his business, though he was still curious. Certainly Nix didn't want him poking his nose into her relationship with her mother. And he couldn't care less how Betty treated him. As long as his father was happy with her, that was all that mattered.

As Finn dug into his piece of cake, Lucifer said, "I hear you and the new fey woman are on friendly terms with each other."

"Which fey woman would that be?" Finn scraped the last bits of cheesecake from his plate and set it on the table next to his chair.

"Keira Something-or-Other."

"O'Brien." Finn crossed his legs, resting one ankle against the opposite knee. He didn't like the dismissive way his father said her name, but he kept that hidden.

Now wasn't the time to get his father riled up. After he was released from duty, well, that was a different story. "Her name is Keira O'Brien."

Lucifer gave a nod and took another bite of cheese-cake. He pointed his fork at Finn and said, "Don't let your dick get in the way of the job."

"Have I ever?"

His father stared at him a moment and then shook his head.

"I won't now, either." Finn stood and looked at Betty. "Thanks for the cheesecake." To his dad he said, "I'll keep you posted." He said his good-byes and made his way back to his bike, his emotions churning. First his father seemed proud of the job he was doing, then he felt the need to tell him how to do it.

Finn couldn't wait for this final assignment to be over.

Chapter Four

Over the next week Finn kept working his contacts. By Saturday afternoon he needed something to take his mind off things, since his entire focus was on the text message that he still hadn't received. *Damn it!* What more could he do to convince the right people that he was a rogue? Go out and kill someone?

At three o'clock he pulled his bike into a spot behind one of the local art galleries. It was a favorite of his, a place where he could lose himself in beauty. Whenever he was stuck on a case or after he'd had to render ultimate judgment on a demon, immersing himself in art put some lightness back into his soul. Regardless of what others might think of him, he wasn't a stone-cold killer. Every life he'd ever taken weighed heavily on him.

He swung his leg over the bike, stood and stretched. He adjusted the legs of his jeans, then went into the gallery. When he pushed open the door, the chime above it sounded. As he walked into the main room, he glanced around. As far as he could tell, he was the only patron there.

Light classical music played softly in the background,

and a faint aroma of cinnamon and nutmeg scented the air. The staging of the various pieces of art was welcoming, and a few small sofas scattered around the large main room invited people to sit and enjoy their surroundings.

Within a few seconds the gallery owner, no doubt having heard the chime, walked out of the office. "Finn! I was hoping you'd stop by this week." The older man came forward and shook Finn's hand. "I missed you the other night."

"Rudi" Finn clapped the man on the shoulder. "I wanted to come to the opening but got tied up with work." Actually, he'd been so wrapped up in trying to get into the rogue group that the exhibition gala had completely slipped his mind. "You know how much I love putting on my tux."

"Ah, well." Rüdiger Zimmer rolled his eyes a bit. Finn had complained more than once at having to don his monkey suit for opening galas, so the gallery owner was well aware of his aversion to tuxedos. "At least you're here now." His round face wrinkled with his broad smile. Bright blue eyes sparkled from beneath graying eyebrows. "I think you'll enjoy the guest artist exhibit in the Cactus Room."

"Oh?" Finn glanced toward the smaller side room to his left.

Rudi nodded. "The artist does mostly western-inspired landscapes. You'll like the colors and composition."

"I'll go take a look, then." Finn patted Rudi's shoulder and headed toward the exhibit. He entered the room and was immediately bombarded with a sense of wild beauty and riotous color. A light citrus scent freshened the air, and Finn realized it came from small bowls of dried lemons Rudi had stashed on various tables and nooks in the room.

He was standing in front of a watercolor of a Monument Valley sunset when he heard the click of high heels behind him. He glanced over his shoulder to see Keira walk into the room.

She wore shiny dark blue, slim-legged pants and a sleeveless button-down blouse the color of lilacs. Pointy-toed turquoise spike heels and her gold cuff watch completed the outfit. Her long hair was pulled back in a haphazard knot on one side of her neck. As she caught sight of him, her eyes widened. "Finn? What're you doing here?" She stopped in front of him and looked up into his face. "This is the last place I would've expected to run into you."

He tried to ignore how good she smelled, because it made him want to bury his face in her neck and breathe deeply. "Really? Why?"

She gave a shrug. "You don't seem like the art appreciation type to me."

Finn figured that most people would be surprised to find out he was a man who enjoyed art. When he looked at paintings or sculptures, he not only recognized the talent behind them, but also found a calmness of spirit from the study of them. Somehow it stung to realize that Keira, in not discerning his connection to art, was the same as everyone else, even though he realized there was no reason she should know this about him. It wasn't like he'd shared that much of himself with her. "What are you doing here?" he asked without responding to her observation.

Her slender shoulders lifted in a dainty shrug. She

seemed a little self-conscious, and her next words told him why. "This is my work. I just stopped in to see if anything more had sold."

He couldn't hide his surprise. "You did these?" He glanced around the room, taking in the bright colors in the paintings, the subject matter of all of them connected to some aspect of nature. He decided it fit her, both the subject matter and the fact that she'd chosen to paint vibrant landscapes. It would figure that an earth fey would stick to a subject she was familiar with. "They're really good."

"Thanks." She paused a moment, searching his eyes. She grimaced at whatever she saw there. "I'm sorry. I guess I was wrong about you." She moved around him and looked at the painting he'd been studying. "So, what do you think of this one?"

Finn turned and stared at the watercolor again. "It's evocative. Powerful yet peaceful."

"Peaceful?"

He nodded. "The subject matter is so majestic, it makes you feel small, you know? And if you're small, your troubles are no big deal, either." He caught the wondering look she gave him and lifted one shoulder in a shrug. She acted like he'd said something profound. The heat of embarrassment crept up his neck. "You asked," he said with a pinch of defensiveness in his tone.

"I did, and I'm amazed." She stared at her work again. "I don't know why, but I never pictured you having such an appreciation for art." She shot him a sidelong glance. "And here I thought you were just another pretty face."

"Ha." He shook his head. "What you really mean is you thought me a mindless killer following my master's orders, right?" He caught the flicker of regret that crossed her face. For once he was able to read her reactions, and he wondered why. Was she letting him, or was she feeling particularly vulnerable around him? "I am more than my job." He couldn't keep the growl from his throat. He was, wasn't he?

Keira's slender hand rested on his upper arm. "I know and I'm sorry. Again." She shifted her position so that she faced him and slid her hand down until she clasped his. The smoothness of her skin made his callused palm seem even rougher. With a slight squeeze of his fingers, she said, "Not sure why I'm surprised that there's more to you than meets the eye. I know you're a complicated man."

"Complicated? Me?" Finn gave her the best innocent expression he could manage. "Nah. I'm the simplest of creatures."

From the look she shot him, she wasn't buying it. She let go of his hand, and he immediately missed the feel of her soft flesh against his. She walked a few feet over to another painting and crossed her arms. He shoved his hands into his pockets and sauntered after her.

"What about this one?" she asked. "How does it make you feel?"

He took a few moments to study the painting, another watercolor sunset, this one with Camelback Mountain as the subject. The sky was painted with vibrant purples, pinks, and reds. It gave him the same overall sense of peace. "Same as the other."

"Hmm." She stared at it a moment or two longer. "I remember when I painted this. I wasn't feeling particularly peaceful."

He looked closer at the painting. "It doesn't show," he

said. "You don't have wide, sweeping brushstrokes I'd expect of someone in a temper, or uneven tones in the paint itself."

Keira's expression showed a growing respect for his art acumen. She moved on to the next canvas.

"How long have you been painting?" Finn asked.

"Off and on, for about fifty years." She glanced at him. "It's only been in the last ten years or so that I decided to do something with my artwork other than stack it up in a storage facility."

He raised his eyebrows. "You had stuff like this sitting in storage? Seriously?" He looked at the closest painting and gave a little whistle. "I should have known you sooner."

She grinned. "You point to any painting here, and it's yours."

Finn took a look at the price tag on the painting to his right and shook his head. He wouldn't let her give him something that she could get thousands of dollars for. "Thanks for the offer, but I'm happy to support a friend." When Keira started to object, he waved one hand. "Let me buy the one I like, okay?"

A slow bloom of pink flushed her cheeks. She looked pleased to hear he considered her a friend. Why wouldn't he? They got along well and enjoyed each other's company before and after they'd had sex. Why would things suddenly be different now? Her eyes met his. "I'd rather give it to you—"

"Nope. And that's final." He stared around the display. "It must be nerve-racking, though, to put your art out there like this. You know, open yourself for Joe Public to criticize."

"I suppose so but I don't mind. Especially when I see how much pleasure my work gives to others."

"If that's the case, why not paint them for friends instead of selling them?" Finn turned so he could look at her straight on.

She shifted her feet, her gaze on the painting on the wall in front of her, though he had a feeling she wasn't actually seeing it. "I don't really have that many friends. Any, really. I've been on my own a long time."

He slid one hand along her jaw until he cupped her face in his palm. "Well, you have me now."

Her lips parted and she raised her eyes to his. "I do, don't I?" A slight smile crinkled the corners of her eyes. "And you know you can count on me, too, right?"

"I do."

Her smile widened. She gave his hand a quick squeeze and moved on to the next display of her work.

Feeling the need to appreciate beauty of a different kind, Finn watched Keira, enjoying the way the lighting, strategized to enhance the art, played off her dark red hair. As she scrutinized the painting she chewed on her lower lip. The longer she did it, the more he wanted to be the one to nibble on that plump lip. And he wouldn't contain himself any longer.

With a low growl, he took her arm and guided her to an alcove a few feet away. The atmosphere and contents of the art gallery might be calming to him, but this woman fired him up like no other. "I've wanted to do this since that damned slow dance at the club the other night."

She looked at him, startled, but he saw no alarm in her eyes. Then humor replaced the surprise. He wasn't discomfited by it because she always seemed to find something about him that struck her funny bone. Which was all right by Finn. He could laugh at himself, too.

"Someone might come in," she whispered. She stroked her fingers down his cheek, letting her thumb play across his mouth. He assumed she wasn't overly concerned by the possibility of being interrupted.

He took a moment to listen to the sounds in the gallery. He couldn't hear anything but the music and the faint sound of their breaths. He pressed a kiss to the pad of her thumb. "Other than Rudi, we're the only two in here right now," he murmured back. "And he's not going to bother us."

She looped her arms around his neck, her hands cradling his skull. Her eyes were as blue as he'd ever seen them. "Well, then," she said with a delectable lilt in her sultry voice, "let's not waste any time."

He bent his head and set his mouth on hers. The feel of her lips beneath his was as arousing as the first time he'd kissed her. Giving a low groan, he closed his eyes and pressed her deeper into the alcove, enticing her to part for the sweep of his tongue into her mouth. God, she tasted good. Fresh and sweet with a hint of tartness.

Finn left her lips to explore her jaw, the slope of her neck, the hollow of her throat. Keira shifted, slowly rocking her hips against his, the slide of her body making him hard all over. His muscles tensed, his hands tightened around her waist, pulling her closer. He went back to her lips, determined to make a meal of the honeyed depths of her mouth.

When she sighed, he drank down her breath like it was the finest of wines. She tightened her fingers in his hair, Keira's mouth becoming more demanding.

After a few minutes he drew back and rested his forehead against hers. She was breathing as harshly as he was, and once he had enough breath to talk he said, "You're addictive, you know that?"

"No more than you are." She lifted her head. Looking into his eyes, she said, "Why am I so drawn to you?"

To Finn she sounded like she was trying to work through a particularly knotty problem. "Because I'm so good-looking? And charming. And smart. And—"

"And so obviously modest, too." She grinned, making the smallest of dimples flash near the left corner of her mouth.

"You didn't let me finish." He leaned down and brushed his lips against hers. "And a fantastic lover."

Keira's expression went serious. "That you are." She reached up and pushed her fingers through his hair, the tips sliding against his scalp in a caress that made him tilt his head into her touch. "I'm not sure you're good for me."

He *knew* he wasn't. He was the son of a ruthless demon, and he'd done things he wasn't proud of. Things that had needed to be done, but still, his past wasn't something to be gloated over. He wished he could have met her a thousand years ago. A time when he hadn't been as hardened or as cynical. "If either of us was looking for a long-term relationship, I'd agree with you. But we're not, are we?"

She shook her head. Sadness flicked through her eyes before she chased it away with a smile. "You're a bad boy through and through, and pure temptation." She slid her arms around his waist. "Yet you've always treated me with nothing but respect and gentleness, in spite of that tough image you project." Her smile grew wider. "It's a good thing I like bad boys."

As he started to bend toward her again, her phone buzzed. She jumped in surprise and brushed against a small ironwork wall hanging. With a cry she jerked to one side, her hand coming up to cover her upper arm. Tears swam in her eyes and she bit her lip.

"What happened?" Finn took her arm in a gentle grip and moved her hand. A patch of skin the size of a man's wallet was reddened with small blisters. Damned if it didn't look like a burn. He looked at the wall hanging and backed carefully out of the alcove, drawing her with him. "What the hell?"

"It's iron," she said. She took a deep breath and held it a moment, clearly trying to work through the pain. "I should have paid more attention. Fey are allergic to iron. I'll be all right in a minute or so."

He felt like an unobservant idiot. He knew how deadly iron could be to the fey. Why hadn't he checked before he'd maneuvered her into the alcove? As usual, he'd had only himself in mind. He held her arm lightly. Even as he looked at it, the red faded and most of the blisters healed. He bent and placed his lips lightly against her skin. Her indrawn breath brought his head up. "I'm sorry. Did I hurt you?"

Her soft throat moved with her swallow. "No," she whispered.

He started to move back to her mouth but his phone beeped, signaling he'd received a text message.

Keira let Finn take a few steps back so he could check his phone. Her arm throbbed with lingering pain that quickly faded. She needed the space, too. She felt overheated, and not just from his kisses, though he was a great kisser. When he'd placed his mouth on her arm, it had been with such tenderness that he'd stolen her breath. She'd seen many sides of this demon—determination, arousal, playfulness, aggravation. Never had she seen this level of gentleness from him.

It made her want to believe he could be more than his demon, that he could be more than what the thousands of years of working for Lucifer had programmed him to be. Was she being naïve? While she was doing her best to overcome her own baser nature, trying to be a better person and atone for her numerous past wrongs, Finn had never expressed a desire to be anything other than what he was.

While his attention was on his cell, she quickly checked hers and saw she had a text message. She hoped it was from Javier, because all this waiting around was making her crazy. With a couple of clicks she had the message on the screen. It *was* from Javier, letting her know that the next group meeting was in an hour. He'd supplied the address with a promise that in the next few minutes she'd get the special quick response code that would permit her admittance. She tucked her phone into her purse as Finn put his cell back into his pocket and looked at her.

Regret and what looked like anticipation warred in Finn's eyes. "I've gotta go," he said.

"Something for Lucifer?"

He gave a nod. "Yeah. It's always work with him." His smile was forced, which Keira understood. From what he'd told her, the only time his boss got in touch with him was when he wanted something, and that seemed to be all the time. But there was an underlying note to his tone that made her think he wasn't telling the whole truth. Since she didn't use her empathic abilities on friends, she resisted the urge to reach out with her senses to read his emotions. She'd have to trust that he wasn't lying to her.

Though she suspected he was. Or, at least, he wasn't telling her everything. She didn't have time to pursue it now though. She had a meeting to get to.

His gaze slid to her arm, and he lifted it gently, turning it toward the light. "You sure you're all right?" he asked, his thumb sweeping lightly across her now completely healed skin.

The lump in her throat precluded speech. She could only give a slight nod.

He gave a satisfied nod of his own and then planted a hard kiss on her mouth. It was over before she got to enjoy it. "I'll see you later?" he asked, his voice deep and husky. As soon as she shook her head in agreement he kissed her again, this time a little softer and a little slower, pulling her close to him again. She relaxed into him, letting his big body support most of her weight, and rested her hands on his lean waist. The stubble of a couple days' worth of beard scratched her face, making her want to feel that roughness in her most intimate places. Too bad there wasn't enough time.

His mouth lifted and he sighed. "Bye," he murmured. He stroked his fingers over her jaw, then turned and left the room.

Keira heard him say something to Rudi about coming back later and to set something aside for him, but she couldn't hear all of it over the pounding of her pulse in her ears. She did hear the chime over the front door sound, and slowly moved out of the alcove. She left the Cactus Room and walked onto the main floor. After drawing in a deep, cleansing breath, she yelled, "Bye, Rudi."

The gallery owner came out of his office. "I'm sorry I haven't moved anything for you today, Keira."

"Oh, don't worry. I'm sure we'll get another sale soon." She wasn't worried about her art selling. In the past she'd had no trouble. It would move, eventually. She said her good-byes and went out to her car. She started it up but sat there, pondering her next move. She would go to the meeting and mask her emotions in case there were any other empaths in the room. She didn't want them to pick up on her true feelings. She'd listen. And watch.

Centuries ago, over a millennium actually, she'd been friends with some of the Fianna, the strong, powerful men who'd guarded the High King of Ireland. She'd admired their courage and the stoutness of their morals even while she had to fight so hard to have even a thimbleful of the same. The code by which they'd lived had been one she'd tried to adopt: *Honesty in our hearts, strength in our limbs, and deeds to honor our vows*.

Her natural instinct was to manipulate people to her advantage, not be honest. And while as a fey she had strength of body, in the past she had rarely put her promises into action and followed through with them. Which meant that no matter how difficult it might get, no matter how much danger she might get herself into, she'd keep her promise to Caladh. She owed it to herself. And because of that, she was being dishonest and manipulative. Doing what she did best for the greater good. No one but the two of them could know she was infiltrating the rogue group of preternaturals who were trying to mess with the rift. She couldn't even tell Finn.

Speaking of Finn, what was she going to do about him? In spite of herself that one time they'd made love had meant more to her than she'd expected. She might even be halfway in love with him, which tempted her to take their relationship to a deeper emotional level. Except her logical side told her he wasn't ready for—or interested in—that type of commitment. Not now, maybe not ever.

She'd been alone for so long. She'd never been one to make friends easily, perhaps because in her former life in the other dimension her "friends" had been people she could call upon for a con job. They'd been the kind of friends who wouldn't have hesitated to turn around and sell her out. Then she'd come to Earth only to discover she was immortal. Any human friends she'd made had grown old and died while she stayed the same. And, of course, there had been the whole having to pick up and move every fifteen years or so to keep her immortality hidden.

The few preternatural friends she'd made had quickly moved on as well. Before the computer age it was even more difficult to keep in touch. After the Internet and cell phones came on the scene, it was easy. Just not done.

Right now she would focus on the job she was doing for Caladh. As long as she was successful, it should garner her recognition among the prominent movers and shakers within the pret community.

She wanted, needed, to not be alone any longer. Most days she was fine on her own, but sometimes the loneliness seemed to eat her alive. If she got attached to Finn and he dropped out of her life without staying in touch, it would be too much for her to bear.

Without using her empathic abilities on him, she could sense there was something about her that made him hold back. She didn't know if it was her background, or that she was fey, or if she'd said or done something. Finn liked her, she knew. Maybe he thought his job was too dangerous to get deeply involved with her.

Which was fine. She had to keep reminding herself of that. She had work to do as well, after all. And regardless she seemed to have a penchant for falling for the wrong kind of guy.

Keira fastened her seatbelt and pulled out of the gallery parking lot. She had just enough time to go home and soak up some Earth energy before heading over to the meeting.

It was taking place at the Devil's Domain, which she wasn't sure was a good omen or not. She'd find out in an hour.

Chapter Five

Finn pulled his motorcycle into the rear parking lot of the Devil's Domain and cut the engine. He sat there a moment, watching people heading toward the back door. The big, beefy guy at the door double-checked the codes the attendees showed him on their cell phone screens. After a quick pat down for hidden weapons, he buzzed them in.

Everyone going through the door had varying natural weapons. They didn't need guns or knives, though no doubt some carried them. Hell, he usually had a gun and short sword on him. Sometimes he preferred the easier and less messy way of dealing with a problem over being hands on. Tonight he figured security would be tight, so he had only his body as a weapon.

If it came down to it, that would be enough.

He hopped off the bike and got into line behind a couple of vampires. When his turn came, he pulled out his cell phone and brought up the message that held the bar code. The bouncer gave a brief nod. "Raise your arms to the sides," he instructed. After giving Finn the same impersonal frisking he'd given the others, he let him into the building.

There was a small landing and then stairs leading

down into a sublevel. Finn followed the vamps down, aware that there were more prets coming in behind him. It made the hair on the back of his neck stand on end. He hated having anyone behind him—he was more exposed to an attack if he couldn't see it coming.

Once he got to the bottom of the steps he moved to one side and let the rest go ahead of him. Then he started off after them, passing a few closed doors on each side. There were double doors at the end of the hall, and he followed the others through into a surprisingly large room. Rows of chairs set up theater style were separated into three sections with aisles between. With a quick glance he figured the room seated about a hundred fifty to two hundred, and it was mostly full already.

A small portable stage area was at the front of the room with a podium and microphone in the center. Plenty of recessed lighting gave the room a bright, airy appearance. Finn looked around and figured the room was roughly half the size of the club upstairs.

And he'd never known of its existence. Interesting.

He directed his attention to the inhabitants of the room. He didn't know what he'd expected, but he was surprised at the variety. Preternaturals of every shape and size represented their clans. There were werewolves hanging out in the front near the podium, and several vamps talked in groups at the back just a few feet from where Finn now stood. Elves, pixies, sprites, leprechauns, and even a few trolls interspersed with werelions, werebears, and wereleopards. There were even a few of the elusive and shy brownies in attendance.

There were lots of demons, which didn't surprise him in the least. Most of them he knew, including Phoebus,

"So," the other demon said as he walked up to Finn, "I must admit I'm surprised to see you here."

Finn gave a lopsided shrug. Shoving his hands into his pockets, he continued to stare out over the crowd. He didn't want to give Phoebus the time of day. He also didn't want to alienate someone he might need later on. However, just because Phoebus might come in handy later on didn't mean Finn had to start being nice to him.

"Does Lucifer know you're here?" Phoebus crossed his arms and tilted his head to one side, curiosity bright in his eyes.

"Nope." Finn wasn't lying. He hadn't told his dad he'd gotten the actual invitation, so Lucifer didn't know that Finn was attending a meeting or where the meeting was being held. Though if it turned out that the vampire who owned the building had given permission for this particular group to meet here, it in all likelihood meant that he was part of this mess. If he hadn't given permission, then he didn't have a good handle on what was going on within his own empire. Either scenario spelled trouble.

"I suppose I shouldn't be so surprised to see you here," Phoebus said, his voice so smarmy it made Finn want to punch him in the face. Which was his usual reaction any time he was around the guy. "You follow Lucifer's direction only as far as you have to." Phoebus gestured around the room. "This must seem like an answer to your prayers."

"Oh?" Finn glanced at him. "Why is that?"

"Are you kidding?" Phoebus rested his hands on his hips. "Do you really think Lucifer will be able to hold on to power when people loyal to *our* leader arrive?"

Finn shifted his position to face Phoebus but was still able to keep an eye on the room at large. He couldn't appear to have prior knowledge of the intricacies of the group and, really, he only knew the name of the vampire who led things. He didn't know what he looked like, nor did he know who any of the members were. But since he suspected that most new members didn't know as much as he did, as little as it was, to keep up the act he asked, "And exactly who *is* our leader?"

Phoebus folded his arms across his chest again and shook his head with a smile. "You'll find out in a few minutes."

If it was longer than that Phoebus might find that smug smile pounded off his face. It would be worth having to put up with this rogue nonsense for the chance to take care of unfinished business with the bastard.

Finn shot Phoebus a look and moved away, walking along the back wall toward the corner. He ignored the curious looks he got from some of those he passed by. As he neared a couple of vampires, one of them lifted his lip in a sneer and muttered, "Fucking demons. We should call a blood feud and exterminate 'em like the vermin they are."

Finn didn't need to use any preternatural abilities to hear the guy. He hadn't exactly tried to be quiet with his comments. He'd obviously wanted Finn to hear him. So the guy wanted to rumble? Finn was willing to oblige.

"You know," he said in a musing tone, giving both vamps a dismissive glance, "some might say the same thing of vampires. Not me, of course." He lifted one shoulder in a shrug. "I think carrion feeders have their own ignoble place in the circle of life." When the two bloodsuckers scowled, he added in a nonchalant tone, "You should own your space, boys. Be proud of what you are."

"Son of a..." The vamp who'd made the initial comment took a step forward. He was slender, but tall and wiry. And he was a vampire, which automatically made him strong. "I'll make you eat those words, demon."

"Really?" Finn was of the old school that said you never backed down from a fight, and if you didn't start it you'd damn well better finish it. He cocked an eyebrow and glanced at the vamp's shorter companion. "You and who? Him?" He chuckled and shook his head in disbelief.

Both vamps' eyes went blood red. They moved closer to Finn, fangs out and ready for action.

Finn set his feet shoulder length apart, more than willing to take them on. He held the gaze of the mouthy vamp. "Take your best shot. I'll wad you up and toss you aside like a piece of paper."

"Take your seats, everyone."

The voice came from the front of the room. Finn shot a glance toward the podium to see a slender, swarthy man standing behind it. Was that the guy? Caine had given Finn the name and a vague description, but not an actual photo.

The mouthy vamp glared at Finn. "This isn't over, demon, not by a long shot."

"I'd be disappointed if it were," Finn murmured silkily. It was just as well their altercation had been curtailed. The last thing he needed to do was let his desire to bash some heads together get him kicked out of the group before he'd even gotten a chance to sit through one full meeting. He waited until the two vampires settled into seats, then he went to the end of the last row and stood next to a troll taking up two seats.

The large man looked up at him but didn't move. Finn stood there, staring down at him, until finally the troll sighed and moved onto one seat. Finn gave him a brief lift of the chin in acknowledgment, then pulled the chair on the end of the row away from the troll to give them both some room. He sat down and looked at the man at the front who was now talking to Phoebus.

Both men stood to one side of the podium, speaking in obviously hushed voices. Finn scooted his chair a little farther away so that his back was to the wall, then he called upon his chameleon abilities and ramped up his hearing like that of a shapeshifter. *Damn.* There was too much ambient noise in the room for him to filter out a conversation taking place at the front of the room. And as tempted as he was to get up and move closer, he didn't want to call attention to himself. So he stayed put.

About a minute later he was glad he had.

Gorgeous in a light green V-necked dress that bared her shapely arms and ended midthigh, Keira stopped just inside the doorway and looked around the room. As usual she wore high heels, this pair a bright yellow.

Shock at seeing her there, in this place, with these people, held him immobile for a second. Then, not wanting her to see him, at least not until he figured out how to feel about her being there and what to say about *him* being there, Finn slowly stood and moved casually behind one of the support columns in the large room. She must have seen someone she knew, because she smiled and lifted a hand in greeting, then walked down the center aisle and did her pardon mes down the row until she reached an empty seat next to the vampire Finn had seen her chase after at Devil's Domain one night. The guy for whom she'd blown Finn off after they'd shared that sizzling dance.

He stared at her, confused as hell. For all her talk about wanting to be a better person... Damn it, he'd believed her. She'd seemed so sincere; she certainly seemed to be above someone who would join this band of misfits.

Better than him, hands down. Even if he was here under false pretenses, this could have been something he might have joined to see where it would take him. For shits and giggles, and to break up the incredible monotony of being an enforcer for Lucifer.

She glanced around again, and Finn shifted his position so she couldn't see him. If he leaned backward he could get a look at her profile, and staying where he was he still had a good line of sight to the podium, where it appeared the Grand Poobah was about to speak. Finn folded his arms over his chest and leaned his shoulder against the column, settling in for what he hoped would be a short and sweet speech.

Keira opened her mouth to say something to Javier beyond her original greeting. Glancing his way, she realized she could save her breath. He was too busy flirting with the elf sitting on his other side.

"I can't wait for Natchook to speak." The young woman sitting to Keira's right, some sort of catshifter from what Keira could tell, leaned over and spoke softly, keeping her gaze on the front of the room.

Keira frowned. "Natchook?" She was at a disadvantage—she had been from the beginning—in not knowing who any of the players were. If Caladh knew, he'd never told her.

"Our leader." The catshifter looked at Keira, her surprised expression changing to one of understanding. "Oh, you're new." She pointed to the men standing next to the podium. "His name on this planet is Stefan Liuz, which is how most people refer to him, but I prefer to call him by the name he was known by in our original dimension— Natchook ot Renz." She sighed and stared forward again. The sound was as girly as a teenaged Justin Bieber fan.

Keira followed her gaze, trying to figure out which man was the leader of this motley crew. The taller one had his back to her and she couldn't tell which pret clan he belonged to. The one facing the group had a Latin look to him—dark hair, darker skin. Wiry build. She leaned over to the catshifter. "Which one is he?"

"The one facing us." Another sigh. "He planned all of this before he even came here, did you know that? He tried to make things better for all of us in our home dimension, and when that failed he already had plan B in place." The other woman stuck out her hand. "I'm Tracy, by the way."

Keira introduced herself and shook Tracy's hand. "How did Natchook try to make things better?" she asked with a glance at the man under discussion.

"He assassinated the leader of the Talisians."

Shock robbed Keira of speech for a few seconds. She'd heard of this man. He was the vampire Tobias Caine had been tasked with finding and punishing for the murder of Kai Vardan, the leader of Talis.

What had Caladh gotten her into? Did he even know that Natchook or Liuz, or whatever his name was, was involved? This was about more than a pret trying to bring more prets through the rift.

Much, much more.

"He's going to speak!" Tracy gave an excited clap of her hands, then clasped them together and sat forward on the edge of her seat.

Keira looked up front and, indeed, Stefan Liuz had stepped behind the podium. When he spoke, she was surprised at the soothing quality to his tones and his succinct style of speaking. She'd expected more verbosity.

But the affected importance she'd also expected was there in spades as he talked about his vision for preternaturals' place in society. "Will we allow humans to move forward with their plans to force us to have microchips implanted so they can track us? I say no! We must fight for our rights. Fight to create our own destinies, not settle for the ones allowed us by humans. And the only way we can truly create our destiny is through supporting and actively creating chaos," he said, punching his fist for emphasis. "It is our duty to subvert the hold on the preternatural community that every council around the world currently exerts. With anarchy we can establish our hold over humans around the world. Their governments will fall into chaos. Only through chaos can we truly be free."

He paused while the group applauded. Keira clapped as well, not wanting others to think she wasn't wholeheartedly in support of this nonsense. But really, this was batshit craziness.

She had the sudden sensation she was being watched, and she glanced around to see who was looking at her. No one seemed to be overtly staring her way. She gave a slight shake of her head and faced forward again. She was on edge and chalked it up to her imagination. Keira was finally where she needed to be, and because that was neck deep in trouble she was being paranoid. Though if anyone in this room found out she wasn't legit, she'd be in deadly trouble.

Stefan went on to blah-blah some more. Frankly, she wasn't all that interested in his rhetoric, so she only listened with half an ear. She was more interested in the people in attendance. As nonchalantly as she could, she looked around the room and saw varying degrees of attention from those around her. A few had the same rapt expression of fanaticism that Tracy did, while others looked like they were holding on until the meeting was over so they could head upstairs to the club.

Finally Stefan said, "We all have our parts to play. Each one of you is integral to our success." He swept his arms open. "The future is ours!"

More applause broke out, then Stefan stepped away from the podium. Prets of all clans, Tracy included, rushed to the front to speak to him directly. He smiled and clasped shoulders and shook hands, all the while wearing the wide smile of a seasoned politician. Keira hung back and watched, thinking these people acted like they were in a cult. Or was it that they were locked in such desperation that it made them willing to follow a madman who gave promises of glory?

Javier stood next to her, one of the few that hadn't run up to receive the touch of the charismatic leader. "So, *bonita*. What'd you think?"

Here we go. "I think it's about time someone says what Stefan said tonight. I've been on this planet a long time, keeping my otherworldliness a secret for all but the last three years." She looked at Javier. "It's been a relief to finally be who I really am." She shook her head. "It's still hard being outnumbered by humans. We don't have the same rights, and we should."

A werewolf standing in the row in front of them turned around. "Damn straight." Before he could say anything more, his attention was drawn to the other side of the room. He muttered an "Excuse me" and headed away from them.

"I'm glad you feel that way." Javier smiled at her, flashing a bit of fang. He glanced to the front of the room, then looked back at her. "Stefan wants to meet you, but he doesn't have time tonight. As soon as he finishes with them," he indicated the group, looking like mindless drones, gathered around the leader, "he has another meeting." He gave her a second fangy smile. "I'll see you later, *bonita*."

Keira walked slowly down the row until she reached the column at the end. As she started to skirt around it, she heard a man say, "Stefan says the device will be ready in time."

"He always makes good on his promises," a woman responded, her tone rife with satisfaction.

Keira paused. She needed to learn more about this, but she had doubts that they'd continue their conversation with a brand-new member, one they didn't personally know. Taking a deep breath, she called on the Earth energy she had stored deep inside. Her skin began to tingle as if small electric currents ran beneath the surface. She waited until they ran in a steady stream before she stepped out from behind the column.

The two vampires continued on with their discussion

as if she weren't standing three feet away from them. As far as they could tell, she wasn't.

By extending her empathic abilities, not only could she influence people's emotions, which colored the way they perceived events that occurred, she was also able to influence their perception of the world around them. It was basic physics, though done through preternatural means, making light bounce off of her body to reflect her surroundings. She was, for lack of a better word, invisible. She rarely used this power because it utilized a lot of energy, which meant she couldn't hold the illusion very long. But if she could glean some pertinent information it would be well worth the weak knees and exhaustion she'd later feel.

Because the motion of her clothing would make it harder for light to be reflected and thereby increase the likelihood some vague outline of her could be seen, Keira put her back to the wall and held still, taking in slow, silent breaths. A werewolf walked past her and paused, his head lifting as he sniffed the air. His brow furrowed and he looked around then shrugged and went on his way.

That was the other flaw to this ability. She might be able to conceal herself from others' sight, but she couldn't mask her scent.

"He said he's waiting on a special gold filament that fits in the oscillation unit," the male vamp said. "That jeweler guy over on Scottsdale Road is supposed to have it for him in a few days."

"That's cutting it a little close, don't you think?" the female vamp asked. She kept her voice low. Keira watched as the woman glanced toward the front of the room where Stefan chatted with a few of his followers.

When she looked back at her companion, a small frown furrowed her brows. "Why would he wait this long to actually finish the machine?" Worry entered her tone, making it not quite as satisfied as it had been a few seconds before.

The other vamp scowled. "Because of those delays a few months ago when the smaller rift device and schematics were stolen, remember? That pushed production of the larger machine back several weeks. Otherwise it would've been done days ago, in plenty of time." He, too, looked toward the front.

Say something more about the jeweler, Keira silently urged.

"Let's go upstairs," he said and looked at his companion. "I could use someone to drink."

The woman agreed and the pair walked away.

Damn it. Keira let out a long breath and eased back behind the column again. She relaxed her hold on her Earth energy. When the tingling in her skin ceased she leaned against the column, taking in deep breaths, and waited for her legs to stop trembling. As soon as she felt she could walk without crumbling to the floor, she headed toward the exit. She returned Javier's wave and pushed open the door.

As she headed toward the stairs, she wished the two vampires had given more specific information about the jeweler, but at least she had a place to begin a covert investigation. After all, how many jewelers could there be on Scottsdale Road?

Finn circled the column, staying out of sight until Keira left the room. He'd glanced at her off and on through all

Liuz's bullshit, and to his surprise she'd seemed interested. Her expression had been nearly as rapt as all the other lemmings in the room.

He was disappointed, and a little angry. She was supposed to be doing better than him, moving away from her old life. So what in the hell was she doing with this crowd?

For his part, he thought everything Liuz had said was bullshit, and hated the idea that now that he was "in" he'd have to put up with all this crap until the next rift. Thankfully that was only three more weeks away, then his mission would be complete and he'd be his own master for the first time in two millennia. Failure was *not* an option.

After listening to Liuz tonight, and seeing how everyone in the room cradled his words like they were precious newborn babes, Finn didn't disagree with dear old dad that having the demon-to-other-pret ratio swing even wider would be a bad thing. If vampire numbers grew and demons did not, it wouldn't be long before Finn and his kind were eliminated.

This was as much about maintaining the status quo as anything else. It was also about self-preservation, pure and simple.

And if there was one thing he understood, it was self-preservation.

Chapter Six

Over the next few days Keira came to realize there were more jewelers on Scottsdale Road than she would have thought possible. Without having a specific name it was very improbable that she'd find the one who was going to provide Stefan with the gold filament. Not that she was ready to give up, not yet. She was merely ready to move on to plan B as soon as she thought it up.

She stared down at a row of sapphire rings without really seeing them. This was the tenth store she'd been in, and everything was starting to blur together. She looked up at the salesman and gave him a smile. "I'm sorry, I just don't see anything that catches my eye."

She knew that wasn't what he'd wanted to hear, but his polite expression never changed. "That's all the sapphires we have, I'm afraid."

And yet again she'd struck out. "Well, thank you," she said with another smile. She left the store and headed toward her car. Then her stomach growled, and she thought maybe she should stop and get something to eat before trekking on to the next shop.

Thankfully there was a small café near the jewelry store. It was brightly lit with mostly small tables for two, a few tables for four, and stools at the counter. Against the far wall were three booths that were all occupied at the moment. She took a seat at a table near the back, sighing with relief to be able to sit down. While she liked expensive jewelry as much as the next woman and enjoyed spending hour after hour looking at diamonds, rubies, and sapphires, she didn't like pretending to be interested in buying something while she watched and listened to what was going on around her. It was too much like scoping out a place in order to run a scam.

It didn't make her feel good about herself at all, even as she reminded herself she was doing it for a good reason. It still seemed too much like what she'd done in her old life.

That's not who you are anymore.

Though she was beginning to think perhaps she should embrace that part of herself instead of fighting it. If she continued to feel so conflicted about this job, this mission she was on, eventually someone would pick up on that. Maybe, for this short period of time, she should become who she'd been before.

For the greater good.

If she did, could she get back to where she was right now? She was very much afraid the old habits were too deeply ingrained, and they'd overtake her again. If she didn't do this, how successful would she be?

A young man dressed crisply in a long-sleeved white shirt, black tie, and black pants with a small green apron tied around his waist approached her table. He placed a small menu in front of her with a smile. "Can I get you something to drink?"

Keira returned the smile. "I'll take an iced tea, please."

"One iced tea coming up." He grinned. "I'll come back in a few minutes to take your order."

After he walked away, Keira pulled the menu closer. She was so hungry, every last thing on the menu looked delicious.

The waiter came back a few minutes later with her tea. "Are you ready to order?" he asked.

"I'll take the bacon cheeseburger with fries. Oh, and a side salad." She wasn't particularly fond of salads. It was only in the last fifty years or so that humans had started using them as something other than a garnish. But she'd ordered the salad so she wouldn't feel as guilty about the burger and fries. She still had more jewelry stores to hit this afternoon, and the heightened stress alone would work off most of the extra calories she was getting ready to ingest.

"How do you want your burger cooked?"

"Medium, please."

"That's mostly done with a thin strip of pink in the center?"

Keira nodded.

The server gathered up the menu. "I'll put your order in right away." After giving her another dimple-producing smile, he walked away.

She sat back and glanced around the small restaurant. There was a woman with a young child a few tables over, and a couple of older men sitting on stools at the counter toward the front. A smartly dressed woman and a man in a suit sat at one of the booths against the wall, and men in ties sat at the other booths. They all seemed to be business people on their lunch breaks.

By their scent, everyone here except her was human.

Maybe it was all of Stefan's rhetoric still rolling through her head, but all of a sudden she felt outnumbered and hemmed in. At least one more pret would be nice. She pulled her phone closer, debated a moment, and then sent off a quick text to Finn, asking him to join her if he could.

She looked around, read the menu again, looked around some more, and wished she'd thought to bring a book with her. Ten minutes later the server approached with her food. After ascertaining she didn't need anything else for the moment, he went over to another table.

Keira checked her phone; Finn still hadn't responded to her text. She thought about sending him another message but pushed her phone away. He was probably busy, and she wasn't going to beg. She heard the door open but didn't look to see who was coming or going.

Footsteps sounded behind her, then Finn plopped down in the chair beside Keira. His hair curled against the collar of his shirt. Long sleeves were rolled up to his elbows, showing off his hair-roughened forearms. His grin crinkled the corner of his gorgeous blue eyes. Bloody hell. He looked good enough to eat.

"Hey, there, stranger. I got your text." He leaned over and placed a soft kiss at the corner of her mouth, his breath warm and sweet against her skin. "Where've you been keeping yourself lately?"

She inhaled, holding the fresh scent of him in her lungs a moment. She couldn't tell him what she'd really been up to. With a nonchalant shrug, she said, "I've been around. I've been doing some shopping today."

"For what?" His eyes twinkled with good nature and curiosity.

"Oh, this and that. Jewelry mostly." She picked up her iced tea glass and took a sip, and grimaced when she realized she hadn't put any sweetener in it.

As she reached for the small container of sweetener packets, his sensual lips pursed. He clearly didn't care for her evasiveness, but he didn't push it. When the server approached and asked for his order, Finn said, "I'll have a burger, rare, and fries. With a cola. Thanks."

After the waiter left the table, Finn snagged one of her fries. When he reached for another one, Keira fisted her fork and made a move to stab his hand. "Hey!" he protested. His grin told her he knew she hadn't seriously been ready to hurt him. "Look, you're the one who invited me to lunch, remember? You're not going to make me wait until my order comes out, are you? I'm starving."

She pondered a moment to tease him. "Fine," she finally said. "But when you get your food, you have to share with me." She cut her burger in half.

He grabbed the portion closest to him and took a big bite, giving an appreciative groan that made Keira grin, though she almost mimicked him after tasting her hamburger for the first time. The bite of mustard was tamed by the creaminess of mayonnaise, and the crispy savory taste of the bacon complemented the slightly sweet beef of the burger.

"They put a little brown sugar in the meat," Finn said as if he'd read her mind. "You wouldn't think that combination would taste good, but it does."

The server returned and handed Finn his soda. He took a sip and snagged another of Keira's fries. After a minute or so, he wiped his hands on his napkin and took one of the hands Keira had wrapped around her glass. He gently toyed with her fingers before lacing them with his. "I've missed you," he said, his voice husky and deep.

She tightened her fingers around his. "Have you?" Her own voice came out in a throaty rasp.

He gave a nod. "Even if you are being cagey," he said, a slight smile playing around his mouth. "I understand women need to be mysterious. Especially one like you."

Her brows shot up. "One like me? What does that mean?"

"I don't mean anything bad by it." He brought her hand to his mouth and pressed a warm kiss to her knuckles. His cerulean eyes darkened with the beginnings of desire. "Means you're full of surprises, and I like surprises."

The server approached with Finn's order. Finn released her hand and sat back. After they both assured the server they didn't need anything else, he walked away.

Keeping to their deal, Finn halved his burger and then picked up his half and finished it off. When she realized how much she was enjoying watching him eat, she shook her head. She was acting like a besotted teenager. While she didn't begrudge herself a friendship with Finn—and maybe something a little more, like friends with benefits—she still hadn't changed her mind about getting emotionally involved with him. Even though she couldn't help but wonder what it would be like to give her heart to him. To have him love her back.

To have a family again.

If they wanted it badly enough, she knew they could make it work. She wasn't sure, though, that they could move beyond their pasts with all their hurts and disappointments to build a future together.

Right now, if she let him get too close, he'd be more likely to figure out she was up to something, and she wasn't ready for that. She didn't like lying to him, because friends didn't do that to each other.

She focused on her own food and made sure to keep their conversation light, because Finn was one sharp cookie. Not much got past him, and without knowing where he stood on things she didn't want to clue him in on what she was up to.

Finished with his meal, he wiped his mouth on the paper napkin and crumpled it, tossing it onto his plate. "Damn, that was good." He glanced around. "Coming here was a great idea."

"Thanks. I'm glad you could join me." She'd eaten all of her salad and had made it through all of her fries and had only a bite or two of burger left, but she was close to being stuffed. She had to stop now, or she'd have to be rolled out the door. She crisscrossed her silverware on her plate to signal the waiter she was done.

"You're not gonna finish that?" Finn asked.

She shook her head. "I'm full."

"Hmm." He shoved his plate out of the way and slid hers in front of him. He finished off the food and then leaned back, patting his stomach. "No sense in letting it go to waste."

"No, instead we'll let it go to your waist," she murmured.

He grinned. "Demon metabolism," he boasted with another pat on his flat belly. "Plus my job keeps me pretty active."

"I imagine so," she said. She'd never really liked thinking about exactly what his job as Lucifer's enforcer entailed. But since he'd brought it up… "Chasing down rogue demons and killing them must use up a lot of energy."

"I don't always kill them," he muttered, his eyes flashing with yellow sparks of annoyance. "Sometimes I do, if the situation warrants it. I've never killed anyone who didn't deserve to die."

She kept her voice low. "If killing is wrong in the first place, how do you justify taking someone's life?" She leaned her elbows on the table and held his gaze.

He heaved a sigh. "I'm not going to get into a debate about capital punishment with you, Keira," he rejoined, his own voice soft and deep. "I know some fey are tree huggers, some of you more literally than others, but you're also preternaturals, and you know you can't judge prets by the same rules you use for humans. We can't build prisons for the deadliest pret criminals. It's too dangerous to keep them alive. That's one thing the council's gotten right." He signaled the waiter. "Anyway, I don't kill demons who keep their aggression within the pret community. Well, unless they've implemented an unsanctioned blood feud against another clan. Usually, it's only those who harm humans who pay the penalty with their lives."

She knew what he was saying had basis in fact. In order to keep peace with humanity, prets had to pay a higher price for their transgressions. Otherwise people like Senator Martin and the judicial committee would get their way and the wholesale tagging of preternaturals, maybe even internment camps. And that was unacceptable. Most of them hadn't asked to be here, and many of them, her included, had done their best to live good, decent lives since they'd arrived on Earth. They tried to make the most of a bad situation.

"Fair enough," she said quietly. "I'm not judging."

His eyes narrowed. "Sounded to me like you were."

Maybe it hadn't been such a good idea to invite him to lunch. She was feeling raw, off her game, because she was right back in the old life she'd tried so hard to leave behind. Even if it was the right thing to do, she couldn't feel completely right about it. And it was making her a tad cranky.

Reaching out, she placed her hand on his forearm where it rested on the table. His muscles flexed beneath her fingers but he didn't otherwise move. "I'm not judging," she stressed. "I guess this is one area where we'll just have to agree to disagree."

"Do you really think that a demon who's gone rogue, one who has gotten a taste for human blood or flesh, can really be kept locked behind bars for the rest of his life?" Finn took a sip of his soda. "The stress of being in prison tends to shorten folks' lifespan by a few years, so for most humans a life sentence might, at best, be fifty or sixty years. For a pret," he shook his head, "you're talking hundreds, even thousands, of years."

"I realize that, but—"

"Do you remember how being imprisoned felt, Keira?" He flipped his hand over and wrapped it around her fingers. His skin was warm and rough. "When you were in the other dimension and were brought to the Detention Center for trial, do you remember what that was like?"

"Of course," she responded in a quiet voice. It was a memory that would never leave her. Even with over three thousand years between her and the event, it remained as sharp in her mind as ever. The shock, the fear, the guilt, it was all still part of her.

As was the shock, fear, and guilt at taking over an innocent's life here on Earth, a woman who'd been a wife and mother. A queen. Granted, she had been queen of one of numerous Bronze Age tribes that inhabited Ireland back then, but she'd been a queen nevertheless. And while the queen no longer had control of her own body, her personality—her *soul*—had become woven with Keira's to make her the woman she was today.

A woman who wanted to do better. To *be* better.

He shifted on his seat. "Imagine what being imprisoned for thousands of years would be like. Think of what that could do to someone's psyche."

She couldn't picture it. She thought someone locked away, no freedom of choice, would indeed have damage to their emotional well-being. It would make her insane, that was certain.

As the waiter came to the table, Finn let go of her hand. He lifted his hip and pulled out his wallet. After looking over the bill, he fished out two twenties. He handed them to the young man with a murmured "Keep the change."

"I didn't invite you to lunch so you'd pick up the tab," Keira said. She looked at the waiter and held out one hand. "May I see the bill, please? I'd like to pay my half."

"I've got it, Keira." Finn motioned the server to leave. The young man walked away and Finn said, "Let me be chivalrous for once, okay? I don't get that many opportunities."

She sat back in her chair and crossed her legs. "Fine.

Far be it from me to insist on my independence at the cost of your male ego." She smiled to soften her teasing. "Thank you."

His answering smile reflected in his eyes. "My pleasure." He leaned closer and cupped his palm around the nape of her neck. His thumb rubbed lightly against the base of her head. The warmth and weight of his hand against her skin made her feel feminine and cherished. "So," he said softly, snagging her gaze with his, "will I see you later?"

She'd promised Javier she'd meet him at the club this evening—he'd said he had a message for her from Stefan—but she couldn't tell Finn that. He hadn't been too pleased to see her go off with the vampire before. He certainly wouldn't understand it now, and she couldn't explain why she was doing it.

"I have plans tonight," she murmured and tried to keep from moaning at his touch. Despite her efforts she couldn't keep herself from tilting her head to give him better access to muscles that were tight from stress. But it was more than that. She loved his touch, the feel of his strong fingers kneading her flesh. Taking a deep breath, she straightened and looked him in the eyes. "Finn, what are we doing?"

He cocked a brow. "I'm giving you a little neck massage, and you seem to be enjoying it."

"I am, but that's not what I meant." She reluctantly pulled away. She couldn't think straight with his hands on her. "Where are things going with us?"

She half expected him to prevaricate, to say something like *Where do you want things to go?* Instead, he studied her, his eyes dark, intent, and interested. He leaned toward her and brought his hand to her face, cupping her jaw. Her heart quickened as she waited for his reply.

His phone buzzed. "Hang on a sec." He pulled his hand away and fished his phone from the pocket of his jeans. It vibrated again before he pressed a button and stared down at the screen. His face twisted into a scowl. "Damn it." Looking up at her, he said, "I'm sorry, I have to go." He held up his phone. "Duty calls." He pushed his chair back and stood. "But I guarantee we'll finish this conversation soon." He bent and cupped her face in one broad palm, and pressed his mouth to hers, a long, lingering melding of lips that stole her breath as they always did. He straightened, letting his hand linger against her jaw a moment before his mouth twisted with regret and he turned away.

Keira watched him walk out, wondering what the text was about to put such a dark look on his face. Of course, with secrets of her own, she couldn't begrudge him his. With a sigh she took her napkin off her lap and placed it on the table, then stood and headed toward the door. She had more jewelers to hang out with this afternoon.

Joy.

Chapter Seven

Finn swung his leg over his bike and sat on the leather seat, wincing as heat bit through his jeans. The text he'd received was from Lucifer, telling him to call. Apparently his father had gotten tired of him not answering his phone.

He pressed the three-digit speed dial and waited for Lucifer to answer. When he did, Finn said, "What's up?"

"We've just got report of a demon attack against a human near Fashion Square mall," Lucifer said, his voice taut. "I want you to check out the crime scene. Discreetly, of course."

"Of course." Finn frowned. Keira came out of the restaurant and lifted her hand in a wave before turning and walking away. Where was she going, anyway? She'd been evasive at lunch, though that was nothing new with her, especially lately. She seemed to love to tease him, which he didn't mind in the least. Someone who liked you well enough to tease you without malicious intent, well, there was promise of something more there. Something deeper.

Which he couldn't give her, he reminded himself. She already had more of a hold on him than anyone else ever had, and it made him jittery. He didn't like feeling jittery. If things went further between them, well, he had a lot of enemies. Someone could decide to use her to even a score.

With his gaze centered on her swaying ass, Finn asked his father, "Since when do we go check out anything at a crime scene? We don't report to the council, remember?"

"Yes, I remember." His father's aggravation came over the line with clarity. "But the closer the next rift gets, the more volatile things are between humans and prets. And since most humans are still ignorant of demons' true existence, I'd like to keep it that way. It's better for them. It's definitely better for us."

"Right." Finn watched Keira until she turned a corner and went out of sight. He'd figure her out one day. He focused his full attention back on the phone call. "It won't do for humans to start thinking that maybe their holy books are actually true."

Lucifer heaved a sigh. "Do you remember what happened when they became aware for the first time that vampires and werewolves were real? And living next door? Fathers set sons on fire. Sons staked fathers through the heart. Special orders of silver bullets went through the roof." He paused then said quietly, "What do you think will happen when they realize that demons who tempt them to wickedness, who thwart God's will at every turn, as they believe, are real?"

The reaction wouldn't be pretty. "And in order to downplay that, you stuck with the name Lucifer Demonicus?" Finn couldn't wait for his father to wiggle out of that one.

Another long-suffering sigh. "Up to this point people

have thought it was my shtick. A gimmick. Besides, how many dealings do I have with humans? Very few. A miniscule amount, really, and usually by accident."

He was right. Most of the companies Lucifer controlled that had anything to do with humans were set up very carefully to keep his name off the record. Ninety-nine percent of humans had no idea that Lucifer existed, let alone that he owned the company that built the mall they shopped at, or held major shares in the company that financed their home mortgage.

As long as those companies operated legitimately, and Lucifer was adamant that they did, his name was never brought up. He'd grown quite wealthy over the millennia directing things from behind the scenes, and Finn knew he aimed to keep it that way. Those who knew him regarded him with respect. Those who didn't know him, had heard of him and held him in awe. And fear.

Which was the way Lucifer preferred it.

"Where's the crime scene?" Finn asked. After his father gave the address, he ended the call. Finn slipped his phone into the back pocket of his jeans and started up his bike. The throaty roar of the bike's engine and the raw, powerful vibration beneath his body was the reason he had a bike and not a car. It somehow made him feel invincible and unrestricted.

After only a few minutes he pulled his motorcycle up to the curb in front of a vacant dirt lot on North Scottsdale Road as one of the human liaisons, Piper Peterson, got out of her car. She was in her usual attire, a dark gray pant suit with a no-nonsense button-down white blouse. Black boots with clunky heels completed the professional outfit. He didn't know her well, but every time he saw her he thought she needed to loosen up a bit. She ducked beneath the yellow tape that cordoned off the scene and began talking to a uniformed officer who stood just inside the perimeter.

Finn approached the area and saw the demon, shoulders slouched, sitting off to one side on the tailgate of a battered pickup truck. The truck had a bright orange sticker on the driver's-side window, signaling that it was an abandoned vehicle and was due to be towed. The human was in the back of an ambulance, blood on his face and hands, and a perpetual wince on his battered face.

As Finn started to stoop to go under the police tape, another uniformed officer stopped him. "This is a crime scene, sir," he said. "Only law enforcement personnel are allowed."

That drew Piper's attention. "Finn," she greeted him. She thumbed over her shoulder at the demon. "I just got here myself. Is he one of yours?"

"Yep." Finn stared at the police officer and then looked at Piper again. "I was asked to check things out."

"I'll vouch for him," she said to the uniform. "Let him in."

"Yes, ma'am." He lifted the tape without a word.

"Thanks," Finn murmured. He walked toward Piper, his boots kicking up dust as he went. "What's the story?"

She started heading toward the pickup truck where the demon waited. Finn fell into step beside her. "According to the first officer on scene," she said, "the man over there"—she gestured toward the ambulance—"was walking through this lot, minding his own business, and your demon attacked him without provocation."

"Uh-huh." Rarely did demons attack without provocation of any sort, but it wasn't impossible.

"The human has a broken nose and a few cracked ribs. Contusions and abrasions on his knuckles where he fought back. Nothing serious, though."

"Whether the attack was provoked or not, he should consider himself lucky his injuries weren't more severe," Finn muttered. Not many humans tangled with a demon and were able to walk away from the encounter.

"Yeah, well, you'd better keep that opinion to yourself. It won't go over well with the victim. And since you're here acting in the role of liaison, you should know that part of a liaison's job is to try to smooth things over. You know, rather than further enflame the situation." She shot him a sidelong glance.

"Funny." It was, actually. He'd had no idea Piper had such a dry sense of humor. "I'll do my best not to escalate things."

"Thanks. That'll make my job easier."

She turned and headed toward the ambulance. Finn kept going until he reached the pickup truck. "I'm Finn Evnissyen," he said.

The demon straightened from his slouch. His alarmed expression told Finn the guy knew who he was and, more important, what he did. "I didn't start it, I swear," the demon said. "That guy jumped me. I was only defendin' myself."

"Let's start with something simple," Finn said. "Like your name."

"Oh. Right. Sorry. I'm Sam Wiseman."

"All right, Sam. Tell me what happened."

As Sam began his story, Finn tapped into his

chameleon heritage and took on the abilities of a vampire. Not anything physical, but rather dipping into the way vampires could use their senses. This meant he could see little fluctuations of body temperature, blood flow and micro-expressions on the demon's face, and thus know when the guy was lying. Throughout Sam's explanation, from everything Finn was reading, the demon was telling the truth.

Finn dropped the chameleon routine and went back to his normal self. Sam glanced around, his brows drawn low over his eyes.

"What is it?" Finn asked.

"I thought…" The guy shook his head. "I could've sworn I got a whiff of vamp. Faint, and only for a few seconds, but it was there."

That was one of the hazards of drawing on his chameleon abilities. Whatever type of preternatural he drew from, the scent of that pret came along with it. Being only half-chameleon, Finn didn't have enough natural energy to hide the scent like a full-blood chameleon demon could. So any pret with a sensitive schnoz could smell him without much difficulty at all. Since few in the demon community knew about chameleons, and hardly any outside of demons knew about them, Finn had to play it cool. It was to his advantage to keep his abilities secret. "I didn't smell anything," he said with a dismissive shrug. Which wasn't untrue; he could never smell himself when he walked in another pret's skin, so to speak. He always had to assume the odor was there and try to deal with it the best way he could.

"Oh. Well, maybe it was a residual thing. A vamp could've passed this way a while ago."

"That's probably it," Finn said. It actually was a logical explanation. He'd heard plenty of shapeshifters talk about all the various scents they could pick up, some new, some hours old. "Look, you can go ahead and leave," he added. He pulled a small notepad out of his back pocket along with the stub of a pencil. "Write down your address. And let me give you some advice." He leaned forward and looked into Sam's eyes. Lowering his voice, he said, "Walk the ol' straight and narrow for the time being, or you and I will have another chat. And next time I won't be so friendly."

This was the first time he'd been asked to investigate a crime scene, and he hoped it'd be the last. If he didn't know better, he'd think his father was running scared, having him come down here to smooth things over. Since when did they care if the preternatural community or humans got upset?

Of course, there was the incentive of keeping the existence of demons on the down low. It was a sound strategy, he admitted, one that had allowed him certain latitudes over the centuries. If no one knew you existed, you could pull all sorts of crap and blame it on the other guy.

Sam jumped off the tailgate. He wrote his name and address on the pad and handed paper and pencil back to Finn while glancing at the ambulance. "Look, uh, Lucifer doesn't need to know about this, right? We can keep it between you and me?" He swung his gaze back to Finn.

Finn would say one thing for dear old dad. He still had the respect, and fear, of most in the demon community. "I hate to break it to you, buddy, but who do you think told me to come over here? I don't normally do liaison work, you know."

"Oh. Right." Sam met Finn's eyes. "Thanks. And don't take this the wrong way, but I hope we never meet again."

Finn grinned. "I agree." He sobered and put one hand on the guy's shoulder. "Seriously, don't fuck up again, Sam. We don't want humans to start getting itchy trigger fingers, you know what I mean? From now on, some human gets mouthy with you, you walk away. You get me?"

"Yeah, I got you." A muscle twitched in Sam's jaw and finally he started acting more like a demon. "It's hard, though. Letting some puny human spout a bunch of tripe and not do anything to make him regret it."

"For now, that's how it has to be." And for a split second Finn wondered why. Preternaturals were stronger than humans and in most cases more intelligent, more capable. After all, they'd come from technologically advanced people in the other dimension. Maybe keeping the rift open longer wasn't such a bad idea after all.

Finn pondered that for a moment, and as Sam walked away he decided that his father was right, about the rift at least. Maintaining the status quo with humanity was the best way to keep everyone in the preternatural community safe, including demons.

But as soon as he was done with this final mission for his father, he was done with being told what to do. He'd be the boss, and others could do the legwork.

"What's your guy's story?"

He turned to see Piper standing a few feet away. She had her own pad and pen in hand.

"The human attacked him, not the other way around. He defended himself enough to get the guy off him."

"Huh." She glanced back at the ambulance. "And yet

your guy walks away without a scratch, while the alleged attacker sits in the back of an ambulance with a broken nose and busted ribs."

"Hey, I can't help it if *your* guy can't hold his own in a brawl. He should be more careful who he picks fights with." He walked until he could see the human. "Sam told me the truth when he said the human started it."

"How do you know that?" she asked. Her head tilted to one side. "You carry a box with you?"

Finn had been around enough law enforcement officers to know when they referred to a "box," it was shorthand for a polygraph machine.

Since Piper knew he was a demon, he didn't mind giving up some information. "In a way." He shrugged. "I just know when someone's lying."

"That's a handy little trick to have."

"You can't tell me you've never seen it done. Vamps do it all the time. You've surely seen Knox do it," he said, referring to one of the quadrant's vampire liaisons. "Or even Tobias Caine," he added. "You know him, right?"

"Yeah, I know him. I worked with him, briefly, on a case several months ago. I haven't seen much of him lately, though, now that he's a council member." She put one hand on her hip, and it drew his attention to the gun holstered at her waist. He had a feeling she was as sharp with that gun as she was at doing her job.

"What do you need from me?" he asked.

She sighed. "Nothing, really." She directed a frown at the man in the back of the ambulance. "I tripped him up and he admitted he jumped the demon first. Not knowing, of course, that he was a demon."

"And does he know now?"

Piper shook her head. "I know how secretive you guys are."

"I'm gonna take off, then," he said. "If you want, I'll e-mail you a report of sorts."

"Yes, please. Be sure to include his contact info. Thanks." She headed back toward the ambulance, then paused and turned toward him. "You might pass along to Lucifer that perhaps now is the time for demon representation on the council. The next rift is only two weeks away. More prets will come through and people are going to flip out. It's only a matter of time before they are painfully aware that demons are as real as every other preternatural on the planet." Without waiting for his response, she walked away.

Finn sauntered to the edge of the crime scene and ducked under the yellow tape. At his bike he paused and reflected on what Piper had said. She wasn't wrong. People were going to find themselves with family members and friends who were human one minute and preternatural the next. And some of those prets would be demons.

Their secret would be out, in a big way.

By that time he'd be a free man, and none of this would be his problem anymore. He'd finally have the time and energy to devote to pursuing a real relationship with Keira without having to worry someone would come after her because of his job.

Chapter Eight

Keira went into the Devil's Domain and stopped at the bar to order a drink. "Glenlivet Eighteen, straight up," she told the vampire behind the bar. He handed her the whiskey and she made her way toward the back of the club. She tried to ignore the press of bodies, both preternatural and human, and the extreme noise level. The place was packed to capacity tonight, and everyone had to yell in order to be heard over the din.

Javier stood next to the door. His brown eyes lit on her as she neared. "I was wondering when you'd get here, *bonita*." He flipped his wrist to check his watch. "You're late."

"Traffic," she said by way of explanation. Trying to get anywhere quickly in the greater Phoenix metro area was an exercise in futility. "I'm here now." She placed her free hand on his arm and let part of her energy wash over him, creating a slight euphoric satisfaction in Javier. She could feel it bouncing back at her, so she knew it was working.

"Let's go inside," he said and opened the door to the private rooms where the vampires fed.

She followed him through the door and into a tiny room off to the left of the narrow corridor. The space was only large enough to hold a regular-size red sofa and a small table at the end opposite the door. Javier motioned for her to sit, and she did. As he sat down next to her, she took a sip from her glass, hoping the burn of whiskey down her throat would bolster her courage.

Javier took the glass from her and twisted to place it on the table behind him. Then, picking up her hand, he played with her fingers while he mused, "I've been hungry for you, *bonita*. So hungry." He raised his gaze to hers. His pupils had completely dilated, leaving them rimmed in the thinnest circle of brown, and the whites of his eyes had filled with red. "Will you allow me to nourish myself on your sweet vitality again?"

Oh, sweet Morrigan, she wanted to throw up. At least she knew the fake feeding she'd foisted onto him still held. This time, though, she didn't need to let him do anything to her. She was in the group. With a smile she pulled her hand away. "Not tonight, I'm afraid. You said you had a message for me?"

His mouth firmed but he answered readily enough. "Our next meeting is in two days. Stefan wants you to stay afterward."

Her mouth went dry. Had she somehow given herself away? "Why?"

"He didn't say." Javier seemed a bit put out by that fact, making Keira wonder if he didn't hold as much sway with the group leader as she'd been led to believe. He might be as much a foot soldier as she was hoping to be.

"Where's the meeting?"

"Here. At six p.m. In the basement, as before. You'll get another QR code sent to your phone." He put one hand on her shoulder and lightly squeezed. "This you don't want to be late for."

"I won't be." She stood. "Thank you, Javier. I appreciate you introducing me to the group."

He got to his feet and stared into her eyes. "You don't act so appreciative, *bonita*."

Damn it. She took his hand in hers and pushed with her empathy, creating a sense of well-being and that same sense of satisfaction she'd imparted before they'd come into the room. "I would show you in a more substantial way if I could. I just can't afford to be weakened right now. I'm sure you understand."

He withdrew his hands. "I do understand." He held her gaze a moment longer, somber and disappointed before a small twinkle appeared in his eyes. "That doesn't mean I have to like it, does it?"

She gave him an answering smile though what she really felt like doing was giving the little shite a swift kick in the arse. "No, it doesn't." She opened the door. "I'll see you around."

"Count on it," he murmured.

Half an hour later Keira stood barefoot on the small patch of grass in her backyard. As she absorbed energy from the Earth, she felt her body relaxing, her spirit calming. With a sigh she sank onto the grass and lay on her back, eyes closed against the early evening sun. When darkness arrived she might come back out here naked, but for now having the Earth against her heels, palms, and the back of her head would have to do.

In order to prepare for the upcoming rogue meeting, she decided she would take it easy over the next forty-eight hours. She needed all the energy she could muster, especially since she'd been commanded to stay afterward to meet with Stefan.

Her skin went cold again at that thought. Surely if he suspected she was a fraud he wouldn't bother to have her sit through a meeting. So what the hell could he want?

Two days later Keira took a seat in the last row and watched as other preternaturals entered the room. The last time she'd attended a meeting she'd ended up sitting in one of the middle rows, so she hadn't been able to see everyone. Now, from back here, she had a great view. And she was on the outer aisle, so if she needed to she had the ability to stand up and lean against the wall. She could always explain that she didn't like sitting for prolonged periods of time, which wasn't untrue.

She watched a variety of prets come into the room, and a few seconds later Finn strolled in.

Finn. At this meeting. He was dressed as he usually was, in a soft black T-shirt that showed off his muscular torso, black leather jacket, worn blue jeans that hugged his hard thighs, and heavy shit-kicker boots encasing his large feet.

Shock ran through her all the way to the tips of her neon green toenails. Yet she wondered why she was surprised to see him here. He had always seemed like such a *What's in it for me?* kind of guy, so she assumed he had some other agenda than the one the group followed. What, she couldn't say.

Disappointment followed on the heels of her shock. She believed Finn could be so much more than what he was if he'd only allow himself to try. If the rumors were true, and she suspected they were based on his attitude, then he was Lucifer's son. Much of Finn's behavior reminded her of a son bucking up against his father's authority. If theirs was a difficult father-son relationship, it would explain so much.

It could also explain what he was doing here. If Lucifer was against integration of demonkind into the other pret groups, which he'd certainly seemed to be, then this could be another way that Finn had to stick it to the man.

She watched as he made his way across the room. He started down the aisle on the opposite side of the room from her. She knew exactly when he saw her. He stopped cold and a funny expression crossed his face. She couldn't decide if it was astonishment, disappointment, or distress. Maybe it was all three for he certainly seemed gobsmacked to see her. He began to walk the rest of the way down the aisle, his intention to reach her clear in his manner, but Stefan Liuz stepped up to the podium and called the meeting to order. Finn paused, then took the nearest seat he could find, which put him several rows in front of Keira. For him to look at her he'd have to twist round, but she had a grand view of him. Or, at least, of the back of his head and powerfully built shoulders.

Stefan went through his tiresome, illogical rhetoric again. And at the end of his speech the room exploded into applause. Keira clapped along with everyone else and watched Finn for his reaction. He seemed just as enamored as the rest of the crowd, which really disappointed her. She'd thought if nothing else his innate intelligence would save him.

"Now, before I dismiss you all," Stefan said, beaming a look around the room like a doting father, "I'd like Keira O'Brien and Finn Evnissyen to stay afterward so we can talk."

Her stomach dropped. Most of the people in the room turned to stare at her. The curiosity in their eyes made her wonder if Stefan requesting audience members to stay behind was an unusual occurrence. Or maybe they were curious about her, since she was new to town. Whatever the reason, she'd find out soon enough what he wanted with her. And Finn.

Stefan met her eyes, his own expression unreadable, and she did her best to suppress her growing panic. With another glance at the room he said, "Thank you all for coming. Victory will be ours!"

There was more applause, which eventually petered out and stopped. Keira slowly made her way up front, her pace in no way reflecting the racing beat of her heart, and reached the rogue leader at the same time that Finn did. While Stefan finished a conversation he was having with another follower, she murmured, "Fancy meeting you here."

"Yeah, well, you're not the only one who's surprised." Finn stood close and gazed down into her eyes. His voice low, he said, "What the hell are you doing?"

She raised her brows. What did he expect her to say with Stefan—a vampire with very good hearing— standing right there? "I'm here for the same reason everyone else is," she said. "I'm tired of being treated like...no, worse than second-class citizens. It's time we do something about it."

"I'm so glad to hear you say that," Stefan chimed in before Finn responded. The leader murmured something to the man he'd been speaking with, and the man walked away, purpose in his strides. Stefan put an arm around Keira's shoulders and then did the same to Finn, though he had to reach up quite a way to do so. "Come with me," Stefan said.

He led them to one of the rooms that lined the corridor outside the large meeting room. He closed the door behind them and took a seat in an overstuffed armchair. That left a loveseat for Keira and Finn. She sat down and tried to stay as far away from Finn as possible, though the settee was so small she could feel the heat from his strong body next to hers.

"Now, let me say first of all how pleased I am to have the two of you on our side." Stefan leaned forward and clasped his hands between his knees. "You both bring such solid abilities to the team, we're fortunate to have you."

"Thank you," Keira murmured.

Finn stayed silent and watchful. Keira knew he was wondering the same thing she was: What the hell was Stefan up to?

Stefan gave a slight smile and went on. "I have an assignment for you that will put those skills to good use."

There it was. She exchanged a glance with Finn. Stefan was going to test them—both their skills and their loyalty, she had no doubt.

Stefan stood and pulled out a small clasp envelope from the inner pocket of his jacket. "Hold out your hand, Keira," he said and walked over to her. Opening the envelope, he poured several rough diamonds onto her palm. He smiled at her gasp. "Each of these is at least two carats. They're fake, of course."

Keira picked one up and looked at it more closely. It was a damned good fake, that was certain. She'd seen a lot of diamonds in her days, and at a glance this would fool even the most reputable jeweler.

"I want you to go to a local shop and swap out a couple of these for real ones." Stefan sat back down. "Specifically, Beynard Jewelers. They just received a shipment of raw diamonds. We need additional funds, and the money from those real diamonds will fill our coffers nicely." He stared at her, his gaze tracking over her face. "I've been told you're really good at grifting. I want to see how good you are."

"Of course." Keira was unable to fight back the tinge of sadness at the thought that people still wanted to use her because of her abilities to be a con artist, though she did think she was successful in hiding it. Stefan needed to think she was eager to prove herself to him. To the cause.

She couldn't deny the slight embarrassment that this was happening in front of Finn. While he was aware of her history, he'd never seen proof of it like he was now. She also couldn't deny the slight thrill of excitement at the thought of pulling a heist. The adrenaline rush was still there even after all this time.

"And if you're successful with this assignment, I can promise you that you'll be relied upon more and more."

If she was adept at swapping out the diamonds, she might get into the shadow cabinet of advisers and fixers for Stefan. She had to do this; time was running out. The next rift was only two weeks away. She had to get into that inner circle, become part of Stefan's closest confidants so she could find out where he was building his machine.

"For you, my friend," Stefan said, looking at Finn, "I have a job that is perfect for your rather unique skill set." He didn't say anything more.

Keira glanced at Finn and could tell he was going to

be stubborn enough to try to get Stefan to make the first move instead of doing what Stefan wanted him to do, which was solicit the information. She slowly moved her foot over and nudged his.

He glanced at her out of the corner of his eye. With a slight huff of air, he looked at Stefan. "What job is that?" he asked.

Stefan's face wore a hint of satisfaction that Finn had blinked first. With an air of magnanimity, the rogue leader said, "I want you to kill Tobias Caine."

The words hung there, bald and desperate. Vile.

Keira's jaw went slack with shock. She saw the muscles of Finn's back go taut. "You what?" He scooted forward to the edge of the sofa.

"You heard me. Now, if you also want to take out his wife, I'm all right with that, too." Stefan gave a careless shrug. "I don't have anything against her personally. But if she dies first, I'll at least have the satisfaction in knowing that Tobias suffered before he drew his last breath." He leaned back in his chair and crossed his legs. "I realize you have something of a relationship with the wife because her mother and your ... employer are lovers."

"That's right." Finn didn't offer up anything more than that. If Stefan knew that Finn was more than Lucifer's employee, Finn wasn't going to confirm it.

"And why do you want me to kill Tobias?" Finn's voice gave away nothing of what he felt.

"That's my business." He steepled his hands beneath his chin, tapping his fingers together. "Let's just say he's gotten in my way before and is likely to get in my way again, and I like to remove all obstacles I can anticipate."

"Fair enough." Finn folded his arms across his chest. "And you prefer that I also kill Nix?"

Keira couldn't believe how calm he was. How calm they both were. They were sitting here talking about murdering two people with less heat than they would if they'd been talking about a ball game.

"Like I said, I realize you and she have a relationship."

"Of sorts." Finn shrugged. "It's not like we're close. We really don't get along." He paused and lifted his hands. "I actually think she doesn't like me too much. Needless to say, we haven't had a lot to do with each other."

Stefan gave a nod and looked as if he'd heard something that confirmed what he already knew. "From what I understand, every time the two of you do come into contact, you give her a hard time."

"That might be true," Finn drawled.

"Yes, I had heard of an altercation between the two of you at Devil's Domain some months back. You and Caine got into it, too, as I recall." Stefan's slow smile glittered in his dark eyes. "Look, do whatever you want with Nix. Kill her or leave her be. But I want Tobias dead. Somehow I don't think that will be too much of a hardship for you."

"Nope."

Keira looked from one man to the other, feeling like she ought to interject something, evince some protest at their machinations. Yet, she couldn't find the words.

Stefan leaned forward. "Bring me proof."

Keira stared at Finn, aghast that he seemed more than willing to take out a council member. After all his protestations that he wasn't a cold-blooded killer...pain skittered through her chest. She really didn't know this man at all.

Finn's mind raced as he tried to come up with alternative solutions to the job Liuz had assigned to him. He couldn't, he *wouldn't*, kill Tobias Caine. Not to cement his role in the group, not to save his own life, which might be in jeopardy if he failed to carry out this job. This damned test. "What kind of proof do you want?" he asked.

"Bring me his head."

There was no way in hell *that* was going to happen. He shook his own head and folded his arms across his chest. "We're not living in the Middle Ages. I'm not carting anybody's head around town." He ran his tongue across his teeth, and inspiration struck. He'd always heard desperation was the predecessor to inspiration. Or some such thing. "I'll bring you his fangs." When Liuz looked about to argue, Finn said, "Take it or leave it. Or get someone else to do it." In which case he'd have to do what he could to stop the assassin.

It all depended on how badly this loony tune wanted Caine's head.

Liuz stared at him for a few moments, his gaze hard, face dark with displeasure. Finally he said, "Fine." He started to say more but stopped when his cell phone rang. He stood and walked away to stand in the corner of the room, his back to them, voice low.

Finn leaned over the arm of the sofa, trying to put a little distance between him and Keira so she wouldn't sense what he was doing. Then he called on his chameleon abilities and took on the hearing of a werewolf. Liuz seemed to be kowtowing quite a bit to the person on the other end of the line, even if Finn couldn't quite pick up exactly what he was saying.

Huh. Maybe Liuz wasn't the one in charge after all. Finn pushed his ability, trying to hear the voice of the other person, but he couldn't make out anything more than the cadence of speech. He couldn't even tell if it was male or female. When he heard Keira sniff a few times, he stopped what he was doing and allowed the chameleon to settle back inside.

She looked puzzled. While the fey didn't have olfactory senses as good as shapeshifters, vampires, and demons, they still could pick out scent better than humans.

Damn it, he hadn't been able to tell who Liuz was talking to.

The vamp finished his call and turned toward them. "Thank you both. I expect to hear results by midnight. Tonight."

Keira blinked, but Finn wasn't surprised. Liuz would want to ensure they didn't have time to cheat, so giving them a tight schedule would limit their opportunities to do anything underhanded. Well, other than the underhanded stuff they were *supposed* to do.

"Tonight?" Keira started shaking her head. "I can't possibly pull off a job with this kind of notice. I need to stake out the place, check on their security measures, figure out the personalities of the staff so I know which approach is best—"

"Tonight." Liuz sent her a hard stare, which he also turned on Finn.

Finn held up his hands in a surrender mode. He wasn't

the one who had a problem with the short notice they'd been given.

"Of course you wouldn't care," Keira muttered. "There's no finesse in running off and killing someone. However, I'm supposed to swap out diamonds at a moment's notice?"

"Are you saying you're not as good as I've been told?" Liuz asked. His voice had gone silky, dangerous like a spider waiting for unwary prey.

"No, of course not." Keira huffed a sigh. "I just . . hav ing only a couple of hours to do this is setting me up to fail."

"Or setting you up to succeed magnificently." Liuz once again wore his jovial expression, though his beady eyes held hardness. "Call me at this number," Liuz said and handed them both a business card. The only thing printed on it was a phone number. "Once you contact me, we'll arrange a meeting." He stared at both of them, his dark eyes steely. "Don't disappoint me."

"I'm sure we won't," Flnn said. He followed Keira out of the room.

They were both silent as they left the building, but once they were outside, she rounded on him. "What do you think you're doing?"

He frowned and put his hand up to shade his eyes. Since he was facing west, light from the setting sun was full on his face. He tried to ignore the way it seemed to set her hair on fire, reds and orange lights dancing along each strand. "What do you mean?"

"Joining this group! Why would you do that?" Her voice rose at the end.

This was not a conversation he wanted to have in the

parking lot of a trendy, popular club, well within earshot of anyone who cared to listen. "Where's your car?" he asked.

She sent him a scowl. "I want to talk to you about this, boyo, so don't be thinkin' you can just send the little woman on her way."

"I want to talk to you about it, too, but in private." He raised his eyebrows. "Now where's your car?"

"Over there," she muttered. After they'd gotten in, her behind the wheel, him in the passenger seat, she twisted to face him. "So?"

"Why are *you* part of this group?" he asked. He couldn't tell her the true reason he was taking part in the festivities, so if he could put her on the defensive maybe she'd stop haranguing him.

"Why do most prets join the group?" she responded. "There's something missing from their lives that this group can fill."

"That's why you joined?" He stretched his left arm out to rest his hand against the back of the driver's seat. "You have a void in your life?"

She stared at him. "What does it matter why I joined? Why do you care?"

He shook his head. "Look, I ran out of give-a-fucks about a lot of stuff a long time ago." He met her eyes. "But I do care about you." He softened his voice. "*What* are you doing here? I thought you wanted to be better than all of this." He made a circular gesture with his right hand.

Her blue eyes widened slightly. "I did. I do. But…" She trailed off and dropped her gaze to her hands. He watched slender fingers twist together. Finally she whispered, "It's so hard. And I'm tired."

Finn reached over and cupped her chin. "Get out now, Keira. While you still can."

For a moment he thought she might take his advice, but then she stiffened and pulled back. He let his hand drop onto his thigh. When her eyes lifted to meet his, they were hard with determination. "What about you? All I've been asked to do is a bit of stealing. You've been ordered to murder someone. And not just any someone. A member of the council."

"Like I said, I ran out of give-a-fucks." He lifted one shoulder in a careless shrug. "I think Liuz is onto something with this plan to keep the rift open longer to allow more prets to come through. Hopefully some of those prets will be demons, because we're outnumbered as it is."

"I wouldn't count on it if I were you."

"What do you mean?"

She grimaced. "He's said that it's his allies, and friends of friends, who have been greasing the palms of Detention Center employees in order to be 'rifted' without documentation. Do you really think his cronies, who are probably mostly from his home planet, are going to let a bunch of your people through? I reckon we'll end up with a lot more vampires."

"You're probably right." He wasn't overly concerned about the numbers, because Liuz's plans weren't going to come to fruition. Finn would see to it. In order for him to succeed, he had to kill Tobias Caine. And everyone, Keira included, needed to believe he was going to carry out his orders.

"Speaking of vampires," she said now, "don't kill Tobias and Nix. Please. You don't have to do this."

"Yes, I rather think I do." He cupped her chin again and leaned down for a quick kiss. "You have your assignment, and I have mine."

"You're not a cold-blooded killer no matter what you say. I know you're better than this."

He wasn't a cold-blooded killer, but Liuz didn't know that, nor did most people, even those who knew Finn. Except for this slender fey woman. Damn it. If she figured out what was going on with him, she'd blow his cover for sure, possibly without even meaning to. "I'm the kind of killer I need to be, Keira. Whatever it takes to get the job done."

Her eyes searched his. "Tobias is nearly family."

"Just because he's married to the daughter of the woman my…employer sleeps with doesn't make him family."

She jerked her chin out of his grasp. "Would you stop with all that? I know Lucifer is your father. There's no point in continuing to deny it."

"And how do you know that?"

"I just do. Your relationship is too dysfunctional for him to be anything other than your father." Even with a scowl she was the most beautiful woman he'd ever seen. "Don't do this."

He'd let her have her win on guessing his relationship with Lucifer. "If killing my almost brother-in-law is the price to pay for being accepted into this group, then I'm willing to pay it. Besides, killing a vamp won't be all that different than killing a demon." Before she could continue the argument, he leaned down and dropped another kiss on her mouth. "See you later."

He got out of the car and, as he walked toward his

motorcycle, resisted the urge to turn around for one last look. Keira seemed more concerned about him than she did about herself. It was telling. Exactly what she was trying to tell him, though, he hadn't quite wrapped his head around yet.

Chapter Nine

Keira watched Finn ride off on his motorcycle and muttered a few pithy words. She wasn't naive; she knew Finn had killed before. It was part of his job as one of Lucifer's enforcers. But she didn't want the murder of people who were essentially his family to be on his conscience. And it would weigh on him, no matter how badass he thought he was.

She wished she had a better handle on why he'd joined the group in the first place. He was not a team player by any stretch of the imagination. It didn't seem feasible to her that he'd joined because he wanted to help usher in a new age. He'd just as soon go his own way as to help create more preternaturals. At least, that's what she'd always thought.

Maybe she'd been wrong. And if she was wrong about him with respect to this, how wrong had she gotten everything else? The sense of fondness and friendship they'd formed, was that all an act? He used his charm and vitality to bait the trap, and then when it was sprung, would he lose interest?

She didn't know. And right now she had other things to

focus on. Namely, refreshing her skills so she could successfully complete her assignment.

Two hours later, after having practiced her sleight of hand in front of a mirror, she left the house and headed toward Beynard Jewelers. Along the way she noticed a black sedan a few cars behind her. It turned each time she did, and when she pulled into a gas station she watched as it veered down a nearby side street. She put a few dollars of gas into the tank and then pulled back out into traffic. As she drove past the side street she noticed the black car parked at the curb a few houses down. And from her rearview mirror she saw it ease back onto the main street.

She was being followed. Her first instinct was to lose them, and she sped up with that intention. But then the black car passed beneath a traffic light and she recognized the driver as someone she'd seen attending the meeting. So, Stefan had sent someone to keep an eye on her. He wanted to make sure she was really going to do the job. She didn't want to make him suspicious, and if she ditched her tail she probably would. She slowed down to the speed limit and made her way to the jewelers as sedately as possible.

Keira arrived at Beynard's twenty minutes before closing. As soon as she walked in she could tell the employees already had one eye on the clock. No doubt anxious to get their weekends started, which worked out perfectly for her. They'd be in a hurry and not paying as close attention as they should. Nevertheless, she projected her empathic energy, filling the store with a sense of happiness and peace, in order to keep everyone slightly less focused than they might otherwise have been.

When a well-dressed older man approached her, she

smiled. "I'm designing a ring and would like to see your raw diamonds, please."

"Of course, madam," he said. "Please, have a seat." He pulled out a padded chair at the main counter, and then walked behind the counter. "What size would you like to see?"

"I think two carats to start."

"Yes, madam." With his back to her and making sure he blocked her view of his hand, he punched in a few numbers to open a small wall safe.

While he was turned away, she unobtrusively pulled out two of the fake diamonds, being sure to keep her hands hidden from the overhead camera. She gave the stones a quick glance to view their relative size and shape. The salesman turned toward her and she smiled again and palmed the diamonds. He placed a tray covered in black velvet in front of her. On it were a dozen uncut stones worth, to her practiced eye, about sixty thousand dollars or so once they were cut and polished. And there were a few that closely matched the ones she held in her hand.

A man and woman came into the store, drawing the salesman's attention from her for a few seconds. And that was all she needed. She swapped out the diamonds, palming the real ones for the time being. When she stood up she'd be able to slide them into the tight cuff at the wrist of her long-sleeved blouse. She made a mental promise that when this job was over she'd get the real diamonds back to the owner if she could. She felt badly for what she'd done, but in this case the end justified the means.

When the salesman turned back toward her, Keira

asked him a few questions and then said, "You know, I don't see anything that suits my needs. Maybe I need larger stones." She flipped her wrist and checked her watch. "Unfortunately, I don't have time right now."

The man pulled the tray in closer and gave a quick perusal of the stones.

Keira held her breath.

He looked up with a smile. "Please come back any time," he said.

"Oh, I will. Thank you."

As soon as she was out the door she halted the flow of empathy, saying a silent apology to the workers inside the store who would now experience mild depression from no longer being surrounded by her peace-laden glamour.

Two minutes later she backed her car out of the parking lot and headed away from the store. She blew out a breath, part of her not quite believing she'd pulled it off. Another part felt pride that she still had what it took to get the job done.

After a couple of miles, she slowed and guided the car to the curb where she stopped and slid the gear lever into park. Drawing in a deep breath, she held it a moment before exhaling, and then dug around in her purse for a tissue. She retrieved the diamonds from the cuff of her blouse and dropped them into the tissue. She pulled out her phone and called Stefan. When he answered, she said simply, "It's done."

"Good! Good. I'm still at the Domain. Bring the diamonds to me now. Check in with Javier when you get here. He'll know where I am." He hung up before she could respond.

This was just great. If Javier was going to show her

the way that meant Stefan was back in the private rooms where the vampires went to feed. By Dagda's balls, he'd better not expect to feed off her. Not after all the energy she'd had to expend to keep everyone in the store feeling happy and calm. Plus, she had to draw the line somewhere. She pulled back into the flow of traffic and pointed her car toward Devil's Domain.

Once again she pushed her way through the crowd at the club, and stopped at the door to the private area. And, once again, Javier was waiting for her. "Come on, *bonita*," he said. "Stefan can't wait to see you."

As long as he didn't plan on trying to eat her, she couldn't wait to see him, either. She was glad she'd gotten her rest because she might have to drum up more glamour on him to make him think he'd fed on her. The sooner she saw him, the sooner she could get out of here. The sooner she left, the sooner she could take a shower and try to wash away some of the filth she was feeling. Even if it was all emotional dirt, a shower would help.

She found herself in the same room she'd been in with Javier, only this time Stefan was the one lounging back against the sofa. She pulled the packet of fake diamonds from her purse and handed them to him, then retrieved the bunched-up tissue from the pocket of her slacks. He sat forward, his gaze intent on her. "These are the real ones," she said as she handed the tissue to him.

He unfolded it and stared at the two raw diamonds in his palm. "Excellent," he breathed. He looked up at her, his smile crinkling the corners of his eyes. "Well done, Keira. Very well done." He leaned back and crossed his legs. "I'm sure we'll have other things you can assist us with, especially in the next several days." A hungry look flitted through his eyes, and she prepared herself to start deflecting his intent to feed. But just as he scooted to the edge of the sofa, his hand reaching toward her, two raps sounded on the door.

Stefan's lips tightened and he called out a terse, "Come."

The door opened and another vampire poked his head around the edge. "You're needed. Now."

A harsh sigh burst from Stefan. "Can't it wait?" His gaze drifted back to Keira, and she saw the crimson ringing his irises. His hunger was growing. If he stayed, she'd really have to pull out all the stops to fake him out.

"No." The vampire stooge winced at the sharp glare Stefan sent him. "You have a call, and he insists on talking to you now."

Stefan cleared his throat and stood. He took her hand in his and brought it to his lips. After pressing a light kiss to her knuckles, he murmured, "Later, my dear."

Keira scurried out of the club, but not before washing her hands...twice. She mulled over their conversation as she drove away from the club. What had he meant when he'd said she'd be able to help them with other things? There wasn't time to plan any elaborate scheme and pull it off before the next rift. So what else could he have planned for a grifter like her?

She glanced at the digital clock on the dash. Eight fifteen. She grabbed her phone and called Caladh. He picked up on the first ring. "I have news."

"Meet me at the contemporary art museum," he said.

Half an hour later, after doing her best to make sure she wasn't still being followed, she stood next to him in front of an abstract painting by a local artist and brought him up to date on what she knew of the rogue group. "For all his grandiosity," she said, "Stefan Liuz has plans that are well thought out. He may be crazy, but he's also very *smart*."

"I am not at all comfortable that they're raising the kind of capital they seem to be." The selkie councilor glanced at her and then put his gaze back on the painting. "Do what you can to foil his intentions. You're my best asset, so be careful. Don't do anything to jeopardize your position in the group."

"Or my life," she muttered.

"Yes, yes, of course." Caladh seemed irritated by her clarification. Was he becoming too focused on the goal to remember the asset he'd put in danger? "We cannot lose the foothold we now have." He glanced at her again. "You say Finn Evnissyen has joined the group?"

She gave a nod.

"I trust you'll not allow your personal feelings toward him to influence your decisions in any way."

She frowned.

"My dear, you haven't exactly made your flirtations secret. You and he have been seen together in public, dancing at Devil's Domain, having dinner. You're both, by all accounts, quite flirtatious with each other."

She couldn't deny that. Finn was fun to flirt with, and to *be* flirted with. "It won't be a problem," she promised.

"See that it's so." He paused and then exhaled on a soft sigh. "Keep me informed." He walked away, hands behind his back.

After a few minutes Keira left the gallery as well. It was time to slough off the unpleasantness of the evening. She had a long overdue shower to get to.

* * *

"Meet me at your mother's house, all right?" Finn gave a low growl at Nix's obstinacy. He'd been on the phone with her for five minutes, trying to get her to agree to see him. Sweet Jesus, but she was even more obstinate now that she was part vampire than she ever had been as half human. "I promise you I only want to talk," he said.

Finally she agreed and hung up. Quickly he dialed his father, letting him know he was on his way to Betty's.

"I'm leaving the office right now," Lucifer responded. "I'll be there in about fifteen minutes."

When he got to Betty's neighborhood, Finn parked his motorcycle a few blocks away and hoofed it to the house like he normally did. There was something about parking in front of his father's girlfriend's house that felt weird. He vaulted the back wall and knocked on the kitchen door.

Betty let him in. "Nix is in the living room," she said.

"Thanks." He went through to the main room.

Nix Caine was sitting on the sofa, leafing through a magazine, but looked up when he entered. She seemed a little thinner than she'd been the last time he'd seen her, but she looked fit. And content. He felt a brief flare of envy that he quickly quashed. If she wanted hearth and home and happily ever after, that was fine. For her. For him it was footloose and fancy free all the way.

"So what's this all about?" she asked. There were little yellow flecks in her eyes, which told him she was agitated and her demon half wanted to play.

He glanced back toward the kitchen. Raising his voice a bit, he asked, "Is there any more of that cheesecake?"

Betty poked her head around the corner. "You can wait

until Lucifer gets here," Betty answered. "No one's having any of his cheesecake without his permission."

For God's sake. The woman was more protective of a food item than she was of her own flesh and blood. No wonder Nix seemed brittle. If he had to deal with Betty like she did, he'd be on edge, too.

"Finn, you begged me to meet you," Nix muttered. "Tell me why."

"I didn't beg." He sent her a scowl. "And I'd rather wait until—"

"Tell. Me."

He heaved a sigh. "You know, I think I liked you better when there was a chance you'd go insane. You weren't as cranky then. You were sure a helluva lot more fun."

"Finn!"

There was no easy way to say this, so he'd just get it out. "I've been asked to kill Caine."

She shot to her feet. Eyes dilated and crimson rimmed what was left of her irises, now gone completely yellow. "The hell you say!"

"Slow down, little cousin," he drawled, holding out one hand, palm facing forward. "I didn't say I was going to."

Her eyes narrowed. "Don't call me that." Fang tips peeped out over her bottom lip as her vampire half made itself fully known. "Explain. *Now.*"

"You've gotten scrappy since you were turned," he said as he sat down in one of the plush armchairs that faced the sofa. Even knowing Nix could make a dash for his throat at any moment, he couldn't bypass the opportunity to play with her a bit.

Betty slipped into the room and settled on one end of the sofa, her gaze on her daughter. She held herself tensely, as if ready to spring into action at any time. She shot Finn a look that clearly conveyed her feelings at the moment. She thought he was being an idiot, baiting her daughter the way he was.

She was probably right.

"Ex. Plain." Nix crossed her arms and one booted foot began tapping on the carpet.

He figured if he drew this out any longer he'd end up with that boot up his ass, plus he didn't ordinarily turn his teasing into cruelty. "My test of loyalty to the rogue group is to kill your husband."

"Well, that ain't gonna happen." She plopped down on the sofa and curled her legs beneath her. Her relaxed pose in no way detracted from the fierceness still blazing from her eyes. "What did you tell them?"

"I said I'd do it. They know Caine and I had a run-in several months ago, and really, there's no love lost between us." When Nix shot to her feet again, he hurriedly assured her, "I'm not going to, of course. But I have an idea how we can do this, especially since I talked Liuz out of accepting Caine's head as proof the deed was done."

Nix went very still as only a vampire can do. "Son of a bitch."

"There's more," he cautioned.

"Oh, hell, there always is." She sighed and sat back down.

"The meetings that I've been to have taken place in the basement at Devil's Domain." He watched for her reaction to that bit of news. Nix knew the owner, Byron Maldonado, a vampire and an old friend and former employer to her husband.

"Byron is mixed up in this?" Nix jumped to her feet

once more and paced in front of the couch. "He and I will have to have a talk about that."

Finn tried to calm her down. "Be careful, Nix. We don't want to blow our cover. For now I think we need to sit on this."

"Now, Nix," her mother said, "just because you think you're some kind of big, badass vampire," her face crinkled in disgust for a quick moment, "you don't have the right to take the leader of the city's vampires to task."

"Watch me." Nix didn't show any reaction to the look on her mother's face that Finn was sure she'd seen. He knew she regretted not having a close relationship with her mother, and now that she was part vampire she probably never would.

The front door opened and closed, and Lucifer walked into the living room. When he saw Finn, he shook his head. "I didn't see your bike parked out front. I suppose you came over the back wall again?"

"He did." This from Betty, who got up and walked over to Lucifer. She placed a kiss on his cheek and wrapped her arms around his waist.

Finn saw the wince that Nix tried to hide. Damn her mother. Why couldn't she dole out some of the affection she reserved for his father to her own damned daughter some time? As a child starved for one little sign of approval from his own parent, he knew it wouldn't take much.

Lucifer kissed Betty's forehead and came with her into the room. They settled onto the sofa as he said, "Well, fill me in. How're things going?"

Finn brought him up to speed. By the time he got to the part about being asked to kill Caine, Lucifer's eyes blazed with yellow demon fire. "Son of a bitch,"

"Yeah, that's the consensus around here," Finn muttered. "Don't worry. Instead of taking him Caine's head, I told Liuz I'd bring him his fangs." He looked at Nix. "Caine is going to have to shed some blood, though."

Her eyes narrowed again.

"He's right," Lucifer said. "Liuz will be able to smell whether it's Tobias or not."

"Fine. But he's not shedding any more than he has to, so don't go getting any ideas." Nix shot Finn a warning glance. "How do you propose to pull this off?"

"We'll need a dead vamp brought to your house." He had something else to figure out, too. Like how to make sure Liuz or one of his shapeshifting buddies didn't smell the underlying odor of the original owner of whatever fangs he tried to pass off as Caine's. He finally settled on bleach. It would clean most of the other vamp's blood off and mask any remaining odor. Even a small amount of Caine's blood would provide enough of a scent to make a positive ID. "And we'll need bleach," he added.

"Bleach?" This from Betty.

Finn nodded. "I'll need to soak the wooden stake and the fangs in bleach before coating them in Caine's blood. The bleach should obfuscate the scent enough that Stefan won't be able to tell there's another vamp's scent underlying Caine's."

"Tobias has a friend at the council morgue," Nix said. "I think we can trust him to give us a dead vampire who's similar to Tobias in size. I'll let you know."

"It has to happen tonight."

"What!" Nix hopped to her feet again. "Are you kidding me?"

He shook his head. "It's a test. If I fail this, they'll

fail *me*." He stared at her. "Can you and Tobias get that corpse?"

"The alternative being that you make my husband a corpse?" She scowled.

"No." Finn put his hands on his knees and pushed to his feet. "I wouldn't."

"Sure you wouldn't," she muttered. "You don't like Tobias, why should killing him bother you?"

"Because Finn is not cold-blooded," Lucifer said. His voice was low, but steel threaded through the softness. "Don't mistake his adeptness at his job as anything other than what it is: dealing out justice."

Finn sent his father a look of gratitude. He'd been getting it from all sides lately, it seemed. It was nice to know his dad was in his corner on this one. "When you have things in place, send me a text that dinner's ready. I'll head on over."

Nix lifted her chin in acknowledgment. As Finn started toward the kitchen, her voice stopped him. "And Finn?"

He turned back toward her.

"Regardless of your protestations, I know you. If anything, anything at all, happens to my husband, you won't live long enough to celebrate it."

More often than not he gave Nix a hard time, but he'd always had a healthy respect for her skills. Skills that were now enhanced by virtue of her being half vampire. "I won't let anything happen to him," he said, hoping he could keep his promise.

He lifted a hand in farewell and left the house. When he climbed onto his bike, he caught movement from the corner of his eye from the house next to the one he was parked in front of. He paused, leaning over his bike as if he were checking something, and reached out with his senses. He couldn't hear anything beyond normal night sounds, and when he tapped into his chameleon abilities and took on the olfactory senses of a werewolf, he couldn't smell much of anything beyond the gasoline in his bike and the rubber and asphalt smell of the road. Except...

There was something vaguely feline in the air. Maybe Liuz had sent someone to tail him, to make sure he got the job done? All they would know at this point was that he'd gone to his father's house, and that Nix had been there. Which could be explained away as a family thing he couldn't get out of. For now, he wanted to see who was spying on him, and why.

He got off the bike and stood looking at it, giving whoever was hiding in the bushes time to relax. Then with a low grunt he turned and sprinted toward the house. He heard the bushes rustle as the other person tried to get away from him, but Finn was fast. Even faster when he took on the aspects of a catshifter himself.

Damn it. His shadow must have shifted, because the feline smell was stronger now. Finn chased him around several hedgerows before he was able to dive down and grab—

A cat. A damned ordinary orange tabby who hung in his grasp like a spitting furball of fury. Even with shapeshifters the laws of nature applied. A two-hundred-pound man could not downsize himself into a twenty-pound cat, no matter how hard he tried. Some mass could be lost or even expanded upon, but not *that* much. Cat-shifters were always big cats—lions, tigers, pumas, and the sort.

The tabby landed a lucky swipe of claws across Finn's inner forearm. He muttered an oath and dropped the cat, who growled and then hissed at him one last time and darted away.

Finn walked back to his bike and drove home, wincing as the scratches on his forearm tensed and pulled with the use of the hand gears. He'd never been fond of cats, and this solidified his dislike. Damned felines.

Once at home, he cleaned the scratch marks on his arm, though they were already healing. He wolfed down a couple of PB&Js, then geared up. He cleaned his seldom-used Glock and placed it in the holster. Clipping it to his belt, he moved on to his scabbard holding his short sword. It snuggled between his shoulder blades, the handle just where he could reach behind his neck to grab it. He tucked two wooden stakes into the inside pocket of his leather jacket. One final piece of equipment—a pair of pliers—and he was set. He sat down to wait.

Within an hour he received his text from Nix. Show-time.

Finn drove to Caine's house, fairly certain this time that he was being followed. His every turn was matched by a black sedan traveling a few cars behind.

The walkway to the house was well lit, making picking the lock on the front door like child's play. As he let himself into the darkened house he noticed all the curtains were drawn closed. He hesitated, letting his eyes adjust to the dimness. A dead vamp, a silent pale slab in front of the sofa like a morbid coffee table, lay on the living room floor. While Tobias and Nix stood without moving in a corner of the living room, Finn went about making it look like a struggle had taken place. He knocked over a lamp and shoved the sofa across the room. Then he slammed one of the wooden stakes through the vamp's heart.

He pulled the sharpened wood right back out again. "Do something with that," he said in a low voice, and held out the stake to Nix. Bits of tissue and congealed blood clung to the wood. She came forward and took the stake with two fingers and a thumb, wrinkling her nose slightly. "You're such a girl," Finn muttered, keeping his voice barely above a whisper. Even if anyone was lurking by the windows or door they wouldn't be able to hear him, preternatural hearing included.

"Shut up." Nix's voice was just as quiet as his had been.

"Both of you shut up," Caine whispered.

Finn couldn't hold back a grin. "Hang on," he said. "I'll have something else for you in a few seconds here."

He pulled the pliers from his jacket pocket and expediently removed the fangs from the dead vamp, ignoring the crunch and pop they made as they left the corpse's gums. He looked at Nix and held out his hand. "Take these, too." He pulled the other stake from his pocket. "Clean the fangs and this stake with bleach. Let them soak a few minutes. You can dispose of that one," he said, pointing at the used piece of wood.

"They'll be able to smell the bleach, right?" Her voice was as quiet as his.

"Sure they will." He glanced over at Caine and then looked at Nix again. "But they'll also be able to smell your husband's blood. I can explain away the bleach," he added with a shrug.

As Nix left to take care of the fangs and wooden

stakes, Finn settled himself on the floor by the corpse and looked at Caine, who hadn't moved a hair. "Did she tell you about where the meetings are being held?" Finn asked.

Caine gave an imperceptible nod. "She did." His voice was so low Finn had to strain to hear. Caine went on, "When this is all over, Byron Maldonado, Nix, and I will have a nice, long chat, don't worry."

"Do you think he's involved?" Finn leaned back on one elbow.

"I don't know." Caine sounded troubled by that. "I think if there was a big enough payout for him, he might."

"And that bothers you."

"It does." Caine took a step forward. Light from outside filtered around the curtains and streamed across his face. "If he's part of this rogue group, it means he's sold out every bit of integrity I ever thought he had."

Finn knew personal integrity meant a lot to Caine. "And what about Liuz?"

Caine's face went still and hard like marble. Except a marble statue's jaw didn't flex like Caine's was. His reddened eyes met Finn's. "I want to be there, at the end. I want him to die at my hands for what he did to Nix."

Just then Nix walked back into the room. Finn got to his feet and took the stake and teeth from her. "I need some of your blood," he told Caine.

The vampire lifted his wrist to his mouth and raked his fangs across the veins. Blood, rich and wet in the semidarkness, streamed down his arm. Without a word Finn handed him the stake, watching while Caine rolled it around, coating it in blood.

He took the stake and stared at it, watching a drop

of blood fall off the sharp tip. "Ah." He looked at Nix. "Could I trouble you for a towel?"

"Oh, for God's sake." She walked off, soundless even in her irritation, and returned less than a minute later with a hand towel and a washcloth. She handed him the towel. "For the stake," she said.

He slipped the terry cloth–wrapped wood into the inner pocket of his leather jacket while Caine repeated the process with the fangs. Nix gave him the washcloth, which he dropped the fangs into before folding it up and stuffing it into the back pocket of his jeans. With a slight smile, he said to Caine, "You want to flick some of that my way?"

"Good idea."

"Wait!" Nix said in a harsh whisper as Caine lifted his arm and flung it toward Finn a couple of times, flinging splatters of blood onto his clothing.

"Just so you know," she muttered, "I'm not cleaning this mess up."

Finn felt a hot splash across his cheek. "Okay, okay. I think we're good." He reached up and swiped at the blood on his face.

"You could've smeared him with blood," Nix said to her husband. "You didn't have to fling it all over the place." She huffed a sigh. "Men."

Finn reached inside his jacket and swiped his fingers against the towel that held the stake. He looked down at the corpse. "Uh, you guys'll take care of this one?"

Caine nodded. "We'll put him in my clothes and disfigure his face so no one can tell it's not me by looking at him. My friend at the morgue will make sure this vamp gets tagged as me."

"I'll wait a few minutes until after you've gone, then I'll call council dispatch to report my husband's murder." Nix stared at Finn. "If you know what's good for you, this is as close to actual death my husband will ever get." Even though Finn could tell she tried to add some lightness to the words, there was a protective edge to her tone. Anyone who wanted to get to Tobias would have to get by her first.

"Rest easy, little cousin," Finn murmured.

"Don't. Call. Me. That."

Caine sighed. "Get out of here, Finn. Keep us posted as much as you can."

"See ya." Finn made his way back to his bike and drove away, confident that Nix and Caine would take care of the corpse.

As he headed out of their neighborhood, he saw headlights in his side mirror, and knew for certain this time that he'd been followed. He realized he was enjoying himself, and looked forward to turning this stuff over to Stefan. It felt good to be underhanded. He could see why Keira had enjoyed being a grifter so much.

He pulled over to the curb and shut off his engine, giving a slight grin when the car behind him did the same. He punched in Liuz's number on his cell, and when the vampire answered, Finn said, "It's done. I have your trophies."

"Bring them to me." Liuz rattled off an address.

"I'll be there in about thirty minutes," Finn told him. He disconnected the call and started up his bike again. When he pulled away from the curb, his shadow did, too, and another grin tugged at his mouth. Now the fun was about to start.

He pulled up outside a modest house in the central part of town. As he started up the front walk, he waggled his fingers in a wave to the guy in the car rolling to a stop behind his motorcycle. Pressing the doorbell, Finn waited with his back resting against the side of the house. When the door swung open, he turned to see Stefan Liuz standing there.

"Come in," Liuz said. "You have what I sent you after?"

"I do." Finn followed him into the house and reached into his jeans' pocket for the teeth. As he handed over the crumpled washcloth, he looked around the living room where he now stood. If this was Liuz's house, and Finn didn't know for certain that it was, he clearly hadn't put a lot of effort in his living quarters. All of his furniture, from the worn green sofa to the battered end tables, appeared to be secondhand. Maybe even third.

He turned back to Liuz in time to see the smaller man lift the fangs out the washcloth. He let the cloth drop to the floor and brought the teeth to his face. Closing his eyes, he sniffed the teeth a few times. "Ah, Tobias. To finally have defanged you." His eyes flew open and he stared at Finn. "There's bleach on these."

"Is there?" Finn brought his hands to his face and smelled his fingers. "It must have transferred from my hands." He reached into his jacket and lifted out the towel-wrapped stake. He pulled the cloth away and showed Liuz the bloody wood. "I reuse this, and I don't like the smell of blood stinking up my house. So I soak it in bleach after each use. The smell lingers."

"Let me see that." Liuz held out his hand.

When Finn gave it to him, he brought it up to his nose and did the sniff test again. "This is Tobias's blood, too."

"Well, yeah. That's how I killed him." He hardened his gaze. "It's the best way to put down those damned bloodsuckers."

Liuz's mouth tightened. He was one of those damned bloodsuckers, too, and probably didn't like being called that. "And Nix?"

Finn lifted one shoulder. "She wasn't home."

"Well, that's all right. Like I said, I don't have anything against her." His eyes began to sparkle and his mouth curved into a wide smile. "My old nemesis is destroyed. Thank you." He looked down at the fangs. "I only wish you'd brought me his head." He closed his hand into a fist. As he walked Finn to the front door, he said, "Oh, and Finn?"

Finn paused at the open door and looked down at Liuz.

Crimson-rimmed eyes stared up at him. "Don't ever go against my wishes again. The next time I tell you to bring me someone's head, I expect it on a silver platter."

Chapter Ten

Three days later, Keira agonized over how she felt. She was falling in love with Finn and couldn't stop her developing feelings, especially since they had been spending more time together. The biggest reason she'd tried to slow things down after they'd had sex that one time was because everything had moved too fast. The sex had been mind blowing. So much so that she'd been afraid she wouldn't ask the hard questions about him, wouldn't look too closely at the type of man he really was.

And slowing things down had been the right thing to do. The desire was there, churning below the surface, but they'd actually shared things about themselves. She'd thought she understood what made him tick. She'd been so sure he'd turned a corner in his life. But it seemed like for every two steps she and Finn moved forward together, they got shoved three steps back. Now she found herself changing her mind about him again. Yes, she was attracted to him and believed he could be much more than what he was if he would let himself. But now, knowing he hadn't been bothered at all by being assigned a hit, that he seemed ready to kill in order to prove himself worthy of being part of Stefan's insanity, she wasn't as certain of

Finn's capability for goodness. For decency. To conduct himself with honor.

She also had serious doubts about her own judgment. How could she have been so taken by a man who could kill someone he knew as part of an assignment? Regardless that he'd killed before, this was Tobias Caine they were talking about. And from the word that had spread throughout the preternatural community over the last few days, Tobias was dead. Someone had staked him through the heart and removed his fangs. For trophies, some said.

She knew it was for proof. And she knew who'd done it.

She needed to talk to Finn about it. To get him to help her wrap her head around how he could do such a thing.

She set her cup of tea on the table in her small breakfast nook and grabbed her cell phone from where it rested on the counter. Without giving herself time to pause and reflect, she dialed him up. Finn answered on the first ring, his voice rough as if she'd woken him up. She'd been awake and showered since before dawn. The sun had risen hours ago. She hadn't even thought he might still be sleeping. But then he did a lot of his work later at night. She didn't want to think about what he'd been doing last night. "It's Keira," she said. "I'm sorry, did I wake you?"

"Yeah, but it's okay. What's wrong?"

She heard a slight rasping sound and pictured him rubbing his hand against his whiskered jaw. She pushed back the longing that action brought forward. She had to get things straight between them before anything intimate happened again.

"Nothing's wrong. I need to talk to you. About the group. Can you come over?" She held her breath.

"Sure." There was a slight pause, and a rustle of sheets. She closed her eyes against the image of his long, lean body stretched out on a bed, muscles taut with sexual tension, face hard and dark with passion. Had he been alone? Her eyes flew open and she pressed her lips together. It was none of her business. They'd never claimed exclusivity. For all their flirting and petting, they'd only had sex the one time.

"I'll be there in about forty-five minutes."

"Okay. See you then." Keira hung up and cupped her hands around her mug, letting the warmth of the liquid inside seep into her palms. She was still sitting there, sifting through her thoughts, through the argument she wanted to present him, when the doorbell rang. She stood and smoothed her hands down the sides of her jeans, and padded barefoot to the door.

Finn sauntered in as soon as the door opened. "I hear you were successful with your assignment the other night," he said with a smile playing about his lips. "I guess congratulations are in order. You're in. Part of the group. A bona fide rogue."

She crossed her arms and stared at him. So many emotions coursed through her, she had a hard time identifying how she was feeling. Mad, certainly. Frightened. Not of Finn, but of the situation she was in. Betrayed, definitely by Finn. Ignoring his snark, she drew in a deep breath and said, "I heard you completed your task as well. Though I can't offer up any congratulations."

His lips turned down in an exaggerated frown. "Why not?"

"You. Killed. Tobias." She stared at him, her eyes burning. This flippant attitude of his was going to get him in trouble someday, and that day might be today. Right now, as a matter of fact. "How could you revert to your old ways like that?"

"Revert to my old..." He folded his arms across his chest and met her glare with one of his own. "I never pretended to be anything but what I am, your feyness. I kill for a living; that's what I do as Lucifer's enforcer."

"But that's not what you want to do," she said, also ignoring his sarcasm. "You told me yourself that you want out. Yet what you did only dug you in deeper." She put one hand on her hip. "What did Lucifer have to say about all this?"

He gave that one shouldered shrug that usually seemed sexy but now just made her want to smack him into tomorrow. "You know how demons feel about vampires," he said. "The only good vamp is a dead vamp."

"You're telling me he was okay with it? And you don't think vampires will retaliate against demons?" What was wrong with him? He didn't seem worried at all that he might have started a blood feud. "Tobias wasn't any vamp. He was a well-liked and well-respected councilor."

"We don't concern ourselves overmuch about the council, either." He shoved his hands into the front pockets of his jeans. "Anyway, since when do you care about what happens between demons and vampires?"

"I care because of you, you great ignorant stump of a man." Her voice came out more shrilly than she would have liked. In exasperation she walked forward and poked her finger against his chest. His firm, muscular chest covered by the softest shirt she'd ever felt. She curled her fingers into her palm and dropped her hand to her side. "I just don't understand how you could do this. Tobias isn't the only victim here, you know. There's also Nix, and by extension her mother. And your father."

"Don't talk to *me* about victims," he said, his voice deep and hoarse. His eyes were as hard as she'd ever seen them. "You have victims, too. You may not have killed them physically, but many of them, maybe most of them, were broken financially and emotionally. Their families didn't feel any less victimized because their loved one was left alive." As his ire rose, yellow sparks floated in his irises. "I at least put people out of their misery."

"Oh, so you're saying Tobias was miserable, then? Is that what you're telling me?" Keira crossed her arms again and shot him a glare. "That's some crystal ball you must have, to be able to know when someone's so miserable they're pining for death." He opened his mouth to respond, but she forestalled him with a sharp slash of one hand through the air. "I'm not finished," she spat. "How dare you compare what I did to what you did? People recover financially; there's no coming back from the dead, boyo."

He took a step closer, looming over her. "There's not, I agree. But the ruin you've left in your wake, how can you defend that? Despite what you say, I'm sure there are plenty of people who were never the same after you finished with them. How many people committed suicide after you wiped them out financially?" He didn't wait for her shocked response before he said, "At the very least, they didn't trust people quite like they used to."

"And that's a good thing," she snarled. "Because people hurt you if you let them. They let you down, they use you—" She broke off as tears threatened.

She'd thought she had left that old life behind her, but

she'd taken to it again like a kid to candy. Maybe she hadn't been as adept at change as she'd thought.

She took a few breaths to regain some control, and said more quietly, "The first chance someone got, they used my past against me. The past I'd left behind, the one I'd wanted to forget. To escape. Yet here I am. Again." She raised her gaze to his. "And you. You wanted a different future than what your father has mapped out for you. Yet here you are; trapped in the present, doing what you've always done." Pain tore her insides to shreds. She gave an abrupt laugh, the sound as brittle as broken glass. "Aren't we the pair?"

"We're a pair of something, that's for sure."

They stood in silence a few minutes. Finally she sighed and raked a hand through her hair. "Look, I got you out of bed, the least I can do is feed you." She glanced at the digital display on the cable box. "It's almost lunchtime. Let me fix you a sandwich or something."

Finn stared at her a moment, then reached out and cupped her face. "I did what needed to be done, Keira. Someday I think you'll understand. And I'm not particularly hungry...for food that is." The yellow in his eyes intensified, obliterating the blue completely. He bent his head and pressed his mouth to hers in a kiss that wasn't nearly as gentle as his hands. "Open your mouth for me," he muttered, his voice harsh. Urgent. "I need to taste you." He angled his hips against hers.

She felt his need, and her lips parted on a gasp. He took her mouth with his again, hard, his tongue stroking inside to tease her. Tempt her.

Keira was tired of fighting her feelings for him. At this moment in time, right here, right now, it was just the two of them and their passion. That was all that existed. She'd deal with reality and regrets later.

Finn tilted Keira's head. God, she tasted better than anything he could remember. Sweet and spicy at the same time. He licked across her lips and dove back in.

Her tongue twisted around his, surging into his mouth when he retreated only to tempt him back to her when she withdrew. He forged forward. She suckled his tongue, drawing him deeper, making him groan as his cock hardened.

Her fresh heather scent made him crazy with need and her touch, soft and hungry and searching, made him ravenous. Leaving her mouth, he worked his way down her throat, stopping at the pulse pounding beneath her silken skin. He rested his lips there for a moment before touching the tip of his tongue to the spot.

He had to get her under him. Now. He pulled away. "Bedroom," was all he could manage through a throat gone tight with lust. There was something else there, too, something he didn't want to look too closely at. Something far more tender, but tenderness just got in the way.

"Yes." Keira's eyes held a gentle blue glow that threatened to enthrall him even without her using any fey glamour on him.

Finn swept her into his arms and carried her to her bedroom, where he set her on her feet next to the queen-size bed. He placed a kiss on the corner of her lips and eased off her clothing, his eyes narrowing at the sultry picture she made. Pink-tipped breasts billowed above a narrow waist and generous hips. He reached up and gently removed pins from her hair, letting it cascade over her shoulders and down her back in fiery waves. A rough groan left him. With economical movements he took off his clothes and then urged her onto the bed. He kissed her, his tongue sweeping between her lips to mate with hers.

Her hands came around him, fingers flexing into his back. She moved her legs and he slid between them, his cock stiff against her belly. He kissed his way down her throat, closing his eyes at the silkiness of her skin. Scattering kisses across her chest, he tongued each nipple to stiffness before kissing his way down her flat stomach.

His hands parted her thighs just a little wider, his fingers stroking a long caress in the folds between her legs. She jumped when he touched her, jerked against his hand, a sharp cry of pleasure escaping her.

He pushed a finger slowly inside her tight, hot sheath. At once her muscles clenched around him, velvet soft yet firm and moist. His own body throbbed and swelled in response.

Her hips pressed forward. Finn thrust another finger into her, stretching her, preparing her. More than anything, her pleasure mattered to him. Her velvet folds pulsed for him, wanting, *demanding*, and he fed that hunger, pushing deep, retreating, thrusting again so that her hips followed his lead.

"That's it," he breathed against her stomach. "Just like that. I want you ready for me."

"I am ready for you," she panted, her slender hands grasping his hair, trying to pull his face up to hers.

"No, you're not. Not yet." His mouth found the triangle of damp curls at the juncture of her thighs. Her breath hissed out as his tongue tasted her, his name a whispered plea. He lifted his head to look at her. "Open your legs wider. Let me have you."

To his surprise, she clamped her thighs together. Her grip on his hair tightened. "I don't want you playing nice, Finn. I want you inside me. Now."

Who was he to argue? He reared up and braced himself with his palms against the mattress on either side of her arms. "Condoms?"

"It's not like either of us can get STDs," she murmured. "And it's the wrong time of the month for me to get pregnant." She stroked one finger down the middle of his chest, circling around his navel.

His eyes widened as sensation jumped straight to his straining cock. He groaned when her hand curled around his erection.

"I want you inside me," she said. "Now. Naked. Skin on skin with nothing between us."

Her thumb swept over the tip of his cock, spreading the silky wetness over the fat head. With a gasp, he pulled her hand away and knelt between her legs to guide his throbbing shaft to the entrance of her body. She was unbelievably wet. Any worry he'd had that he would hurt her if she was unprepared went away.

He punched his hips forward, saw the ruddy tip of his cock slide past the slick folds of her sex and felt her, tight and hot, close around him. The sensation shook his control even further.

"Keira!" Her name burst from between his clenched teeth. He grabbed her firm ass and lifted her as he slid in another inch. "Tell me you're all right."

"I'm fine. I'd be better if you'd hurry it up," Keira

gasped, her eyes bright, her hands sliding around him to clutch at his back.

Finn laughed, a short, sharp burst of sound from a throat tight with need. With a hard flex of his hips, he buried his cock deeper. It had been like this the first time they'd come together. Their joining brought him pure ecstasy. It was all he could do to keep from ravaging her. Lowering his head, he flicked his tongue against the taut peaks of her breasts. The action tightened her body around him even more.

"I feel full, like you're part of me," she whispered. "But I want more, Finn. I want all of you." She slid her hands from his back down to grasp his buttocks.

"Me, too," he gritted his teeth and surged forward. Her sheath was slick, hot, velvet-soft, and so tight it was about to kill him. He buried himself deep, withdrew, thrust again with slow, easy strokes. He watched her face. When he saw passion glazing her eyes, heard her soft pants, carnal pride filled him with satisfaction. He loved seeing that look on her face, loved knowing he was the one putting it there.

Finn pumped his hips faster, gliding in and out of her, deeper with each stroke. God, she felt so good. So tight and hot and wet. He tilted her so he could thrust even deeper, wanting her to accept every last inch of him, as if by her body accepting his she could look past the facade he presented to the world and see *him*.

He buried himself to the hilt and moved his hand to her swollen clit. In seconds he felt the spasms of her climax beginning. "I've never felt like this." He needed her to know how he was feeling, what she meant to him. "Ever since I had you that first time, I've thought about only you."

Her dark blue gaze snagged his. Desire and something deeper flared in her eyes. "I need you, Finn." Her fingers dug into his buttocks as her hips rose to meet his. Soft gasps escaped her as his hips surged forward, his rhythm faster. Harder.

With her silky wetness wrapped around him, he was beyond any pretense of control. He moved his hand against her clit again, and Keira cried out. Her body bowed, heels digging into the mattress, fingers digging into his flesh. Finn felt the strength of her inner muscles gripping him in the intensity of her orgasm. He pumped into her frantically, the explosion ripping from his balls through the top of his head.

When he could make his mind work rationally again, he eased out of her, groaning as her inner muscles clung to his sated cock. He tucked her against his side and blew out a sigh. Finally he had her where he wanted her—in his arms, limp and sated.

"Can you stay?" Keira's voice, soft and sleepy, held hesitancy.

The only other time they'd had sex, she'd been reluctant to have him stay, mumbling something to the effect that snuggling allowed emotions to creep in and ruin a good thing. Finn was a little shocked, but happy, that now she wanted him to linger. He wanted Keira like he'd wanted no other in all his years, even with the doubt this rogue business had thrown into the mix. They couldn't go on ignoring it, and he knew they eventually needed to talk about it. But not now.

Now he was going to hold his woman. He rubbed his hand up and down her arm. "I'd like to stay," he murmured. When she rubbed her cheek against his chest and then placed a kiss on his shoulder, he let out a sigh of contentment.

After a few moments of silence, she said, "This is nice."

"Hmm." He pressed his mouth to her temple.

She tipped her head back to meet his gaze. Slender fingers stroked his side in an absentminded caress. "I used to think if we spent time like this, cuddling after sex, it would complicate things."

"And now?"

"Now I think cuddling after sex will definitely complicate things." Her smile was tinged with sadness. "But I can't help myself. I'm addicted to you, I guess."

"You're not alone in that." Finn stroked his fingers through her hair before wrapping several thick strands around his hand. It was like holding silken fire in his palm.

He hadn't been averse to their relationship growing more intense, no matter what he might have told himself. But he'd never really been certain how she felt about him. He wasn't willing to risk his emotions only to have her reject him. He'd gotten enough rejection from his father over the years to know he didn't want more of the same from a lover. Treading lightly was called for. "I care about you, Keira. You have to know that."

She rested her face against his chest. "Sometimes I think you do, but then I'm not sure." The warmth of her sigh drifted over his skin.

"Be sure." He tightened his arms around her a moment. He wanted to ask her what she was doing in the rogue group, wanted to come clean about his own role.

He especially wanted to confess to her that he wasn't capable of the cold-bloodedness she thought he was, but then he'd have to reveal that Caine was still alive. He'd also have to reveal the only reason he was part of the group was to stop Liuz at Caine and Lucifer's behest. But he couldn't take the chance. She had joined this group for a much different reason and he wouldn't have his mission, and his chance at freedom, be ruined. Rising up on one elbow, he smiled as she grumbled at being dislodged from her comfortable position. He stared down into her lovely face. "We're cut from the same cloth, you and I," he said. "We both have, or have had, occupations that have us walking a fine line between right and wrong. Some of your empathic abilities mirror abilities I've honed over the years." He wasn't going to tell her he was a chameleon demon without consulting Lucifer. It wasn't like he needed his father's permission, but being demon was like being a member of a secretive sect, so he wanted to make sure he wasn't divulging the wrong information. "I know that there are reasons we shouldn't be together. But for now, don't ask me to walk away from you, Keira."

She cocked an eyebrow and the smile that curved her lips bounced in her eyes. "Didn't I ask you to stay only a few minutes ago?"

Finn's lips twitched and he settled back against the pillows. "That you did." He sensed the good in her, the part that wanted to leave the old life behind. A goodness that he could use in his life. Her beauty—of face, body, and spirit—did for him what the paintings at the art gallery did. Gave him peace among the violence he was surrounded with every day. Above that, though, he was attracted to her for her sense of humor, her wry wit. Even her habit of poking fun at him held him enthralled. But for the sake of the mission, he had to remain silent.

"Look, why don't we—" He broke off as his cell

phone rang. He sent her an apologetic look and rolled out of bed to retrieve it from the back pocket of his jeans. A glance at the display showed him it was Nix. "Excuse me," he said to Keira and moved a few feet away. With his back to her he connected the call and brought the phone to his ear.

"We need to see you," the half demon, half vampire said in a no-nonsense voice. But he heard the underlying tension in her tones. "Now."

That tone of voice was one he couldn't argue with, but he did anyway. "Can't it wait?"

"It can't. Get here as soon as you can."

"I'll be right there." He ended the call and turned to face Keira, meeting her questioning gaze. She'd moved to the edge of the bed, as unconcerned with her nudity as he was with his. "I have to go. It's something to do with Lucifer." He quickly dressed then came to stand in front of her and rested his hands on her slender shoulders. Then he bent and pressed his mouth to hers, once. Twice. Three times before he tore himself away. "God above, you're addicting." He lightly rubbed his thumb over her lips. "I'll see you later."

As he made his way to his motorcycle, he cursed the interruption even while he felt grateful for it. He was never one who'd been comfortable talking about his feelings, and it was even worse now that things were so mixed up.

The next week and a half could not go by fast enough, though he knew the danger would escalate. And when this was all over, and he'd been shown to be a fraud where the rogues were concerned, what would that mean for him and Keira?

Chapter Eleven

Keira stood at the door, in jeans and a T-shirt, the tile floor cold against the soles of her bare feet, and watched Finn swing one long leg over his bike. She'd wanted to tell him she'd joined the rogue group at Caladh's request, that she was one of the good guys. By all the gods how she had wanted to confess. She wished she could explain that she was there to stop them, not help them, that in order to put an end to Stefan's idiocy she had to assist them in the short term. She wanted more than what they had, but she couldn't risk the mission, or her heart. She believed him when he said he cared for her. She could see that in the way he looked at her, the tenderness he displayed while they were together. But Finn only thought of himself and would never be able to give her what she needed emotionally. She had to be prepared to be the one to walk away when the relationship stalled, which she was almost certain it would do.

Even as she believed that deep down, where it counted, Finn was good in spite of the violence that surrounded him, she also believed he didn't want to change. And until he figured that out about himself, she couldn't trust that he wouldn't betray her if she told him the truth. So she'd kept quiet.

And it wasn't as if she was the only one with secrets. She watched him rev up his bike, the sound echoing throughout the neighborhood. When he waved at her, she summoned a smile and lifted her hand in farewell. Of everyone she knew Finn was the best at skullduggery. As he pulled away from the curb, the thought of following him to see what he was up to flitted across her mind. Before she could talk herself out of it, she turned back inside, locking the front door behind her, and grabbed her purse as she headed to the garage. Because she was barefoot she had to move the driver's seat forward before she could back out. Within a few seconds, she was heading down the road after him.

She did her best to keep a few cars between them so he wouldn't know he was being followed. She'd never really done this before, but she watched a lot of television. When he turned into a subdivision, she pulled over to the curb and waited a few seconds, her heart pounding like bongo drums in her throat, before she made the same turn.

It took a few minutes of driving around the neighborhood before she saw his motorcycle parked in front of a territorial-style house. The outside was adobe with an arched entryway leading to a large courtyard. The front door was red and had just swung open as Keira stopped across the street. She didn't recognize the woman who greeted Finn, but they didn't act like lovers. She was glad of that. The two of them might not have made any declarations of love, but they had made progress. She didn't like the idea that he might love or care for someone else.

Of course, he would never have sex with her while he was in love with another woman. He, at times, seemed more werewolf than demon, because he was as faithful a hound as any wolf she knew.

Knowing she wouldn't be able to hear what was going on inside, she made a mental note of the address and drove back to the main road. Caladh hadn't been returning her calls, and she not only wanted to talk to him about the misgivings she was beginning to have about this whole thing, but she also wanted to find out what was going on, why she suddenly seemed persona non grata with him. Maybe if she could corner him at council headquarters he'd agree to set a meeting with her, just to get her out of his hair.

Her agenda set, Keira drove to the main council building and parked in the rear. She stepped out onto the pavement in her bare feet and popped the trunk with her remote. She reached inside and pulled out a pair of yellow heels. Because she sometimes needed to take off her shoes to feel the earth beneath her feet, and she'd ended up losing more than one pair that way, she always kept a few extra in the trunk. Now she was glad she had.

After donning the shoes, she walked around to the front of the building. As she pushed open the door, she immediately had to step to one side as a black-clad security officer pushed past her. Other security guards milled around the entrance to the main chamber. Voices came from the big room, some shouting, and she thought she also heard weeping.

One of the officers, a big fey warrior named Conal, walked past her and locked the front door. On his way back he stopped and frowned down at her. "What are you doing here?" he asked.

"I wanted to see Councilor Caladh," she said. She

glanced around at the chaos. "What's going on here?"

"You've arrived just in time for us to go on lockdown," he said. "Lucky you."

She shot a look at the door and then stared at him. "I gathered we were on lockdown when you locked the door, boyo," she drawled, trying to hold on to her patience. "Why are we on lockdown?"

"Deoul has been murdered."

Shock ripped through her. The president of the council was dead? Murdered!

Conal motioned to one of the guards. "Stay with her," he instructed and walked into the main chamber.

"Wait!" Keira took two steps forward only to be stopped by the guard's big hand wrapped around her arm.

"Sorry, miss," he said. From his scent she surmised he was a feline shapeshifter—a lion, she thought, though of the African or American variety she couldn't say. She'd always had trouble sorting them out until, of course, they actually changed into their animal forms.

"Fine," she muttered, jerking her arm from his grasp. "Can I at least sit down?" She motioned to the row of chairs against the wall nearest the door.

"Of course."

Keira sat down. Who could have done this? At least she knew it hadn't been Finn, because he'd been with her all morning. Relief that he wasn't involved was short-lived as she began wondering who might have committed the crime. She tried to get a glimpse into the main chamber. She thought she saw a couple of liaisons inside the room, including two of the werewolf liaisons, Victoria Joseph and Bartholomew Asher. Then the guards at the door closed ranks, making anything more than their large brutish bodies impossible to see. They moved again, and Caladh walked out. Blood streaked the front of his white council robe and covered his hands.

She shot to her feet. "Caladh!" She started toward him, only to be stopped again by the burly guard. "Get out of my way, you damned beastie," she grated.

"It's all right, Jeff," Caladh said. To Keira he replied, "It's not my blood. It's Deoul's." He paused, his face pallid. "He's dead." He raised liquid brown eyes to hers. "Someone killed him. I went into the chamber to..." He shook his head. "He was lying on the floor, covered in blood. I tried to save him." He stared at his hands. "I tried."

She went over and took him by the arm. "Come over here and sit down," she said. She looked at Jeff. "Sorry about the damned beastie thing."

"No problem." His slight smile lightened the tension on his face for a moment. "But you need to stand back from him, miss."

"Oh, right." No sense in contributing to cross-contamination or whatever the hell it was called. She helped Caladh to a chair and then sat down herself, keeping an empty chair between her and the councilor. "Is there anything I can do for you?"

He shook his head then stiffened before turning toward her. His scowl brought some color to his pale face. "Later, when we can talk in private," he muttered so low she had trouble hearing him, "you can explain why you came here. For now"—he looked at the guard—"Jeff, make Miss O'Brien comfortable in the employee lounge, would you? She doesn't need to be mixed up in all of this."

"Yes, sir." Jeff motioned down the hallway. "This way, miss."

Keira stood and walked with him down the hall, casting one last glance over her shoulder to see Caladh sitting by himself, shoulders straight, eyes staring in front of him, while activity took place all around him. The calm in the eye of the storm.

Had Deoul's murder been at Stefan's instigation? It seemed too coincidental for it not to have been.

By Dagda's balls, would any of them make it out of this mess alive?

Finn accepted the bottle of chilled beer Caine handed him.

"Tori just called to let Nix know that Deoul was murdered at council headquarters." Caine walked toward an overstuffed armchair across from the sofa Finn was on.

"Murdered!" Finn leaned forward and rested his elbows on his knees. "By whom?"

Caine shrugged. "With all the prets that are in and out of there, it's impossible to know at the moment. But it certainly underscores the importance of what we're doing, and the need to keep it a secret, wouldn't you say?" He shook his head and sat down. "It can't be a coincidence that the council president was taken out three days after my 'murder.' "

Nix perched on the plump arm of his chair, and he reached behind her. From the way he moved, Finn assumed Caine was stroking his hand across her back. It was the penultimate picture of wedded bliss. Finn was actually happy for them.

"No, I imagine Liuz is behind this."

"And no one besides the three of us and Lucifer know what we're doing?" Caine stared at Finn, his gaze implacable. "Everyone *must* think you've joined the pret group as a viable, energetic member. One who will do what's necessary to further the group's cause." He let out a low sigh. "I don't even know who on the council I can trust. I think I can trust Caladh, but I'm not sure about anyone else, so at this point I haven't shared anything with anyone."

"I haven't told anyone, either."

"Not even your friend Keira?"

He stared at Caine and took a swig of beer. "What part of 'I haven't told anyone' did you not understand?"

"I'm just making sure," the vampire said. He leaned back against his chair, relaxed and at ease.

"Though my father did tell Betty."

"What?" Caine sat up, no longer so relaxed.

Nix also straightened. "Wait, what?" Her gaze narrowed on Finn. "So you're telling me that Lucifer really is your father, like all the rumors say?"

Finn merely raised a brow and took another sip of beer.

She looked at Caine. "Did you know?" she asked.

He glanced up at her. "Lucifer told me several months ago."

At the dark look Nix shot her husband, Finn figured Caine should've kept that last little bit to himself.

Eyes flashing with demon fire, Nix jumped to her feet. "Let me make sure I have this straight. Several months ago my mother's boyfriend told you that Finn was his son, and you didn't tell me? You know I've been wondering about that."

"It wasn't my story to tell, honey." Caine tugged her

down onto his lap. Finn noticed that she didn't put up much of a fight. "It was Finn's."

She turned her glare on Finn. "And why didn't you tell me?"

"Because I like to keep you guessing, little cousin. It keeps your mind sharp."

She let out an aggrieved sigh. "I don't know how many times I have to tell you. Don't call me that."

"The more you tell him not to, the more he'll do it," Caine murmured. "If he doesn't get a rise out of you, there's no more fun to be had, and he'll let it go."

"He's also right here, listening to you." Finn tipped the bottle to his lips and chugged several deep mouthfuls of beer. "Don't you pay him any attention, Nix. I like calling you 'little cousin.' And just think, if our parents ever get around to getting married, I can call you 'little sister.'"

"Aargh." Nix struggled off her husband's lap and glared at Finn, though he could see humor lurking in her eyes. "You are a pain in my ass, you know that?" She sidestepped Caine's attempt to haul her back down. "I'm going to make myself a grilled cheese sandwich and some tomato soup. You"—she pointed at Finn—"can go out to eat. And you," she said to her husband, her expression softening, "can come get a bite whenever you want to."

Finn watched her walk away. He was used to rubbing Nix the wrong way, and he ordinarily didn't care what she or anyone else thought about him. But he cared what Keira thought. She was light to his darkness, a breath of fresh air in the squalidness he found himself in day after day. He had to battle back unfamiliar guilt at deceiving her. What a mess he was in.

"There's something else you should know," Caine said.

"There usually is." Finn finished his beer and leaned forward to put it on the coffee table. Then he sat back and crossed his legs, resting his ankle on the opposite knee.

"Liuz is Tori Joseph's cousin."

Finn shifted against the sofa. "I'm sure I misheard you. What the hell did you say?"

"Stefan Liuz, known as Natchook ot Renz in the other dimension, was a cousin to Sirina lan Maro. After the rift, Sirina became Victoria Joseph."

"And you didn't think I should know that little fact when you asked me to infiltrate the group?" Finn pushed to his feet. "And you were worried about maintaining secrecy with me. I don't see how Tori will sit back and let her cousin be captured. She has to know he won't let himself be taken alive."

Caine shook his head. "No, he won't. But Tori's learned her lesson. She won't interfere in what has to be done."

"What do you mean?"

The vampire glanced toward the kitchen. "Natchook...Liuz is the one who caused Nix to be turned."

Finn had heard the story, or part of it at any rate. He'd known that Nix had been attacked and that Caine had turned her in order to save her life. He hadn't known that Stefan Liuz was the one who'd savaged her. "And Tori knows this?"

"She does now." Caine took a breath and blew it out. "Her brother went rogue a few months back and killed or turned half a dozen people or so. Including Dante MacMillan's sister."

Finn let out a low whistle. "I'd heard about all of that when it was happening, of course. Liuz was involved?"

Caine nodded. "Tori's brother was doing it as a way to prove his worth to Liuz." He sighed again. "Believe me, she knows better than to stand in the way. Liuz has been responsible for the loss of many lives in his quest for power, and there's only one penalty to pay."

Death.

Still, Finn sensed some hesitation on Caine's part. "You're not sure of her, are you?"

He met Finn's eyes. "She loves her cousin. On some level she has to be thinking of a way to get him out of this. I know I would be."

"Uh-huh." He stared at Caine. "Is there anything else I should know?"

Caine shrugged. "Not that I know of."

Before Finn could reply, his cell began to play "Highway to Hell." He tugged his phone from his back pocket and connected the call. "Dad," he greeted.

"I assume you've heard Deoul's been killed." Lucifer's voice was terse.

"Yeah, Caine told me."

"You're with him?"

Finn rubbed his brow. "I'm over at his house."

"Let him know that Caladh has been put in place as interim president until formal voting can be scheduled."

"That was quick," Finn muttered. "Both the action and you finding out about it."

Lucifer laughed. "You know I have people everywhere, son. Anyone who thinks I don't know what's going on would be mistaken."

And that made Finn wonder something else. "Which

begs the question: How long have you known about this rogue group?"

His father didn't respond right away. When he did, it was only to say, "I've known awhile. It doesn't matter how long, does it? I am doing something about it."

"Right."

"We'll touch base later," Lucifer said and ended the call.

Finn slipped his phone back into his pocket.

Nix came into the room, popping the last bite of grilled cheese into her mouth. "It got quiet in here. I couldn't hear anything from the kitchen," she said, admitting to listening in with a grin. She looked from Finn to her husband. "What's going on?"

"That's what I'm waiting to find out," Caine said.

Finn raised his brows. "Caladh's been named interim council president."

"Well." Caine looked at his wife and then met Finn's gaze again. "That changes things, doesn't it?"

"It certainly does." Finn blew out a breath. "Does this mean that we can trust Caladh more? Or less?"

"There's the sixty-thousand-dollar question." Caine put his arm around his wife's waist and pulled her close to his side. "I don't know. For now, let's keep things on the QT as we've been doing."

The dynamics, not only of the council but of the preternatural community on the whole, had changed. How, or if, it would impact the rogue group was anyone's guess.

Chapter Twelve

Later that evening Finn switched off the motorcycle and heeled the kickstand down. He sat on his bike a moment, studying the exterior of the "club" his father had sent him to. Seemed there was a demon named Julius Ferko who'd decided to bring some fire-and-brimstone-style terror to his human neighbors, and Lucifer wanted it stopped. There was only a little over a week to go until the next rift occurred and tensions among humans were running high.

Julius was one of the Sheddai, demons who could cause rising dread and paranoia in their victims and then feed off those emotions. Julius, though, topped it off with the fear that the devil was after them, which added exponentially to his victims' misery. He was suspected of being the cause of an attempted suicide at one house and an attempted murder at another. Finn would find out exactly what Julius had done and use his own judgment as to what needed to happen from here.

He heaved a sigh and got off his bike. Graffiti littered the outside east wall, and the sign above the door was missing some bulbs, so the name read OOBIE HAT H.

Why in the hell did these guys always have to hang out

at strip joints? Just once he'd like to have a conversation at a high-end steak place where he could get a good meal to go along with his trouble.

He went inside, wincing a little at the loudness of the music blaring from speakers mounted above the performance area, and headed straight to the bar. The bartender, a human, looked up. "What can I get you?" he asked.

"Information," Finn responded in a low voice. "And a beer. Whatever's on tap." He pulled his phone out of his pocket and retrieved a photo of Julius. As he showed it to the bartender he glanced around the establishment. The main room was roughly two thousand square feet, give or take. Three women performed pole dances, one at either end of the raised platform and one hot babe in the center stage that jutted out about six feet into the room and was very well lit.

The music at this joint was better than the last one he'd been at. It was upbeat and modern as opposed to cheesy and sad. The audience, if it could be called that, consisted entirely of men, a mixture of preternaturals and humans. Finn focused his attention back on the bartender. "I'm looking for this guy. You seen him lately?"

Curiosity filled the bartender's eyes. He absently wiped a glass and gave a nod. "He's here all the time. What'd he do?" He put the glass at the beer dispenser and pulled the tap.

"He here now?" Finn asked without answering the guy's question.

"He was just a few minutes ago." The man gazed out over the tables and Finn did the same. Men were seated generally by themselves, sometimes in pairs. One large group was particularly raucous, right in the middle of the room at the center stage. The bartender finally pointed to one man at the far side of the room. "That's him. The bald guy getting the lap dance from Treat." He wiped the outside of the glass with the rag and handed the foamy beer to Finn.

"Thanks." Finn slipped his phone into his pocket and accepted the beer. After paying for the drink, he strode toward the table the bartender had pointed out, stopping a few feet away to watch for several seconds. The lovely Treat—and Finn appreciated why she had that name— had Julius worked up for sure. She shimmied, shook, and rubbed her body all over him, leaving a smear of glitter on his chest and thighs, and everything in between. As Finn began to sense Julius's ardor beginning to peak, he drawled, "Well, hell. Julius! Fancy seeing you here."

Julius jerked with a startled "Hey!" and sent Treat tumbling off his lap.

Finn reached out to steady her and set her on her feet. Digging into the back pocket of his jeans, he tugged out his wallet and retrieved two twenties. "Go take a break, honey," he said, handing the bills to her. "You look like you can use it after this guy."

Her lips twitched but she was too much of a professional to actually laugh and agree with him. "Thanks," she murmured as she took the money from between his fingers.

Finn watched her sashay off. He flipped a chair around and straddled it, resting his forearms on the back. He took a sip of his beer and stared at a very nervous Sheddai. "Now, then. Julius. Why don't you tell me what you've been up to?"

"Nothing. I haven't been up to anything." He glanced

around the room. "I don't know what you heard that made you look me up, but I haven't done anything. Honest."

Finn took the opportunity to study him more in depth. It was time to push the guy even more off balance. "You know, Julius," he drawled, "it's a good thing you don't have to impress people with your looks in order to influence their emotions. With that shiny head and that paunch of yours, I bet the only way you get a woman to pay attention to you is if you pay her. Like sweet little Treat there." He let a slow smile curl up his lips. "Am I right?"

Julius sputtered, drawing himself straighter, his bearing one of affronted dignity. "I don't have to p..." He scowled. "I get plenty of action from women."

Finn gave an unconcerned shrug. "Well, that's neither here nor there, is it? I shouldn't have brought it up. What I'd really like to talk about is what's been going on in your neighborhood."

Julius went still except for a trickle of sweat that slid down his face in front of his left ear "I don't know." His gaze flitted around the room as if he were looking for an avenue of escape. Or rescue.

A quick glance told Finn that everyone else was either genuinely not concerned about what was going on in this corner, or they deliberately had looked away in order to not get involved. "Come on, Julius. You know what I'm talking about. Mrs. Peterson two doors down? Lovely little old lady, in her right mind and of sound health who, without warning, tried to hang herself from the second-story landing. Or what about Myra Davis right next door, who tried to hack off her husband's head while he slept?"

"I...I had nothing to do with that." Another drop of

sweat followed the first in a shiny trail down Julius's face.

"You're not nervous, are you, Julius?" Finn raised his brows. "It's actually quite cool in here."

Julius stood, knocking his chair over.

"Sit down," Finn said. "We haven't finished our conversation."

"It's finished as far as I'm concerned." The Sheddai demon took a couple of steps back, his hands fisted at his sides. "You... you can't just hunt me down and accuse me of... things. Whatever you think happened to my neighbors, you can't hang any of it on me."

"Funny you should put it that way." Finn put his palms on his thighs, ready to push to his feet if necessary. "Julius, don't make me tell you to sit down again. And do not make me chase you. You know I'll catch you, and the mild annoyance I'm feeling right now will be downright ugly when I do." He paused. "You won't like me when I'm angry."

Julius blanched, whether it was because he realized he was ill equipped to defy an enforcer, or because he had visions of Finn going all Hulk on his ass. Whichever it was, he righted his chair and sat back down.

"Good. Now, then, where were we?" Finn leaned his arms on the back of his seat again. He focused his gaze on Julius. Sweat broke out on the paunchy demon's forehead. Finn said, "Oh, that's right. We were talking about Mrs. Peterson and Mrs. Davis."

Julius stayed stubbornly silent for all of two seconds. "Oh, fine," he burst out, desperation raw in his strained voice. "I couldn't help myself. With the economy in the slump it is, there are so many people who are depressed and anxious. It's a veritable feast out there for those of us who feed on the misery of others." His expression turned placating. "I'll admit I was a little gluttonous. But I got really hungry, that's all." A pleading light entered his pale eyes. He made wide gestures with his hands. "I know we're not supposed to feed where we live. I won't do it again, I swear."

Finn pursed his lips. Julius had nearly caused the death of one human, but at this point the police had decided it had been a suicide attempt, and the family didn't seem to be fighting that conclusion. The Davises had been having marital trouble for some time now. Hell, the wife had admitted she'd often fantasized about Bobbittizing her husband. She'd obviously mistaken one head for the other, but she'd been docile enough when the police had taken her away. Maybe some time under psychiatric care would actually help her. And her husband could use the time apart to be grateful he still had his penis.

"You realize, don't you, that I'd be well within my rights to end you, right here. Right now," Finn held the other demon's gaze. "But I'm going to let you off with a warning, Julius. No more screwups like this. Or I'll be back, and I won't be so lenient next time."

Julius gave a nod. His brows furrowed. "Why do you care?" He leaned forward. In a whisper he confided, "I've seen you at the meetings. What do you care if humans get more upset than they already are? After the next Influx it won't matter. We'll be the ones in charge for a change. So again, why do you care?"

"I care because my employer cares," Finn responded in a hard voice. It wasn't the complete truth, not anymore. In dealing with the fanaticism that seemed to trail Liuz,

Finn suspected that humans would have a hell of a time if prets took over. Whatever was dished out to humans would be heaped upon demons, especially by vampires. The blood feuds of old would look like nursery school parties by comparison.

He had a moment of feeling a bit off his game as he realized he hadn't seen Julius at either of the meetings he'd attended. He knew why, too. He'd been too damned distracted keeping an eye on Keira.

Keira, who'd given him the best sex of his life the day before. Keira, who he had yet to call. To be honest, he needed some distance to try to sort out what he was feeling. To do his best to keep things in their proper perspective, and this last little bit of conversation with Julius was proof enough of that. Hell. So why hadn't he called? He'd told her to believe it when he said he cared. And he loved being with her. She made him want to be better, and when he was with her he could more clearly see the life he wanted. But he couldn't be sure she had the same depth of feelings for him.

He pushed all that back and responded to Julius. "I still have a job to do. An employer to keep happy. After the next rift... Well, we'll have to wait and see about that, won't we?" He stood and pushed his chair up to the table. "In the meantime, you'd better walk the straight and narrow, my friend. Or there's gonna be the devil to pay."

He stared at Julius a moment longer and then left the club. Getting back on his bike, he sat for a few seconds and rotated his tight shoulders. It hadn't been all that long ago that, emotionally, he'd been where Julius was. Did what he wanted, when he wanted, and didn't care about anyone but himself. He'd been spoiled. Childlike in his self-centeredness like many of the demons he'd handled. With Keira in the mix, though, he got how important his mission was.

So for now, he would keep sane by reminding himself that it would all be over in a little over a week. And if all went according to plan, he'd be a free man. Free from his servitude with Lucifer. And free to explore a life with Keira without having to worry about her safety.

Chapter Thirteen

Keira sat on the sofa and stared down at her smart phone. Two days. It had been two days since she and Finn had made love. Or, rather, had sex. There had been plenty of lust. Affection, even, but no love. Not on his part, anyway, even though he'd told her he cared about her. "Caring" was not the same thing as love. And that certainly was borne out by the fact that he hadn't contacted her at all since he'd walked out her door and went into a house with another woman.

Maybe she'd read the signs wrong. Maybe that other woman did mean something to him. Maybe the reason he hadn't called Keira was because he was too busy shagging that hussy.

At first she'd felt relief that he was apparently putting some distance between them. Distance was good and allowed her to get a better grip on her emotions, to try to stuff them back deep inside where they belonged. But then the second day without any contact from him rolled around, and relief turned to irritation and outrage. Just who the hell did he think he was to hop into bed with her and then go into silent mode?

Then irritation and outrage became hurt. Being intimate with someone wasn't something she did easily. For all her acting like she was into casual sex, she really wasn't. Not in the way most people meant it. She had to have an emotional connection to a man before she could bare her body to him. Because with the removal of clothing came a removal of pretense, like the removal of a mask so the lover could see the real person beneath.

She looked at the text message she'd typed moments before and still hadn't sent. *Miss you*, it read. *Please call me*. It certainly was more polite than the last one she'd typed where she called his parentage into question, but this one made her sound desperate. With a scowl she deleted the message. There was another rogue group meeting scheduled for tomorrow night. If she hadn't heard from him by then, she'd talk to him there. One way or another, she'd find out where they stood.

The next evening, Keira took her seat at the meeting and watched while other members entered the room. The next rift was only a week away, and excitement and tension filled the air. As Stefan stepped up to the podium to start the meeting, Finn walked in. He saw her and paused, a split second of indecision flitting over his face before he walked over and sat beside her. All the emotions she'd been battling for the last few days surfaced again—relief, irritation, outrage, hurt, and anger all rolled into one big, messy ball just waiting to slam him upside his hard head.

He must have picked up on some of what she was feeling, because he leaned over and murmured, "I'm sorry I didn't call. Demons have been particularly frisky lately, what with the next Influx due soon."

She shifted on her seat to look at him. For a moment

she debated having it out with him here because she didn't want to cause a scene, but her emotions were too raw to sit there and say nothing. "How long would it have taken for you to text me with a 'How are you?' message?" she said in a low voice. "Let me know you were thinking about me, that our being together meant something more to you than just a quick poke in the whiskers." She shook her head and faced forward again. "Typical male. Handing me a crock of shite like that. You're a real wanker, you are, Finn Evnissyen."

"Look, I said I'm sorry, and I am." He leaned closer. "I should have called you, or sent you a quick text. To be honest, I wasn't sure what to say." He shook his head and took her hand in his. "I've never felt this way about a woman before, Keira, and I'm a little off stride here."

She was shocked at the hesitancy in his voice and twisted in her seat to look at him. That same hesitancy was reflected in his eyes. She squeezed his fingers. "We both have a lot to learn about relationships, I guess."

She started to say more but Stefan called the meeting to order. She contented herself, for the time being, with giving Finn's hand another squeeze before releasing it and turning her attention to the front of the room.

As Stefan began speechifying, she couldn't keep from covertly glancing at Finn to gauge his reaction. He was focused on Stefan, seemingly rapt with attention. It crushed her to see how very much he bought into all this crap.

Finn had never had to put his acting ability to use as much as he did right now. God, this guy was a total nut job.

"With the death of Deoul Arias," Liuz said, "we see the

end of order and the beginning of chaos. First the council, then the local human government, then the Western states. We have members throughout the West who are dedicated to the path of anarchy." His eyes glittered with fanaticism, a slight tinge of crimson circling his irises.

"But the council already has another president in place," someone said. "Shouldn't we strike at every member?"

"And we will. Imagine, if you will, the fear that is rippling through them even now," Liuz responded. He lifted one hand, index finger pointing upward. "First we took out their newest member, Tobias Caine." His gaze held Finn's for a moment, and through all the crazy shining in his eyes there was a brief glint of approval. Liuz held up a second finger. "Now we've removed the president. Believe me when I say, they are more panicked than you will ever know." He went droning on, more of the same claptrap he'd been spouting from the beginning.

Finn knew in order to keep the trust he'd earned and move further into the inner circle, he would have to continue to act like he completely agreed with the narcissistic son of a bitch. He tried to ignore the fulminating glances Keira kept sending his way. It didn't help that the shiny bluish-green blouse she had on reflected in her eyes, making them look even more gorgeous than normal.

He knew he'd screwed up, big time. But there wasn't much he could do about it now. As a matter of fact, if anything had come out of these last few days it was the certainty that until this mission was complete, the less he saw of Keira the better.

She distracted him, as his father had figured she would. The other day, when he'd left her to go to Nix's house, he'd been so inwardly focused that he hadn't taken the ordinary precautions he would have to ensure he wasn't being followed. Even if he had been, it wouldn't have been all that unusual for his almost stepsister to have called him in her time of need. His presence at her house could easily have been explained.

Then something Liuz said caught his ear. "I and my comrades on the other side have been working on this plan for centuries. It wasn't until the last few years that technology on this planet has allowed a machine to be built that will keep the naturally occurring rift open longer than normal. What does this mean for us?" He paused and smiled, looking like a proud father announcing the birth of his first baby. "It means that more of our kind can come through the rift, perhaps double the normal numbers. Maybe even triple."

Finn frowned. Granted it had been a couple thousand years ago, but he himself had been born here on Earth. He hadn't traveled through the rift like Liuz. And like Keira and probably at least three-quarters of the people in this room. Unless there'd been a mighty increase in crime in the other dimension, he didn't see how those numbers were possible.

"My comrades have been gathering likeminded individuals and sending them through the Detention Center on the sly. There is no record of them being stripped from their bodies, and no record exists of which holding cells they've been placed in. The authorities on either side of the rift are completely in the dark, and will remain so until it is much too late."

Finn shared a glance with Keira. She looked alarmed, and he was sure the same feeling was plastered all over his face. And it shouldn't be, not if he really wanted to get deeper into the group. He schooled his face to impassivity and whispered, "Isn't this great?"

"Yeah," she murmured, her brows drawn in a slight frown. She didn't sound like she was thrilled. Far from it, in fact. Before he could comment on it, she looked forward again.

Finn did, too.

"This machine is waiting for one final part," Liuz said, "and then it will be operational. Don't worry, it's in a secure location that very few of us know about. Myself, of course, and three or four of my most trusted lieutenants." He wrapped his hands around the edge of the podium and leaned into the microphone. "My friends, our time has come. With this machine I will be able to keep the rift open indefinitely. Our compatriots from the other dimension will join us, and soon, very soon, we will outnumber the humans on this planet." He waited until the cheers died down and then said, "And then we shall rain chaos down on them, and take control. It will be glorious."

"Oh, my God," he heard Keira whisper just as applause broke out again.

He glanced at her but couldn't tell if she was appalled at Liuz's batshit craziness, as he was, or enamored by the vampire's alleged brilliance. Liuz adjourned the meeting and Keira hopped up right away. Without sparing a glance for Finn, she headed toward the end of the row.

He frowned. That was definitely a woman with a mission, and he had the sneaking suspicion she meant to go up to Liuz and offer her praises like a lot of other prets were doing at this moment. Finn stood and walked to the back of the room where he could keep an eye on things.

Damned female. He let out a breath. She was brighter than that, he knew. She was one of the most intelligent people he'd ever met. But for such a bright woman she was being too goddamned stupid right now.

Keira walked slowly toward the front, casting out with her empathy abilities to pick up on the emotions of those gathered in the room. Mostly she felt the highs left over from the galvanizing speech, but there was something, coming from two vampires just ahead, that seemed like secretive excitement. One of those *I know something you don't know* kind of things that she reckoned required further investigation. She stopped at a group of five other fey talking quietly on the opposite side of the vamps. Pretending to partake in that conversation, she focused her attention on the vampires. One of them mentioned a mine, but he didn't say the name or anything about the location.

Frustrated, she excused herself from the fey and turned toward the vampires. As she was about to outright ask them about the machine, she heard her name being called over the din of voices. She looked around and saw Stefan beckoning her.

As she walked over to him, she saw Finn heading that way, too. Hmm. What was this all about, then?

Stefan smiled at them. "Ah, you two. My shining stars." He took Keira's hand, cupping it between his palms. "I have another assignment for you. We are setting up bank accounts throughout the world, so that when our new brothers and sisters arrive, they can make their way to one of the banks, give a verbal password and be allowed access to funds. I've set up Scottsdale as the hub for orientation and to determine where in the country these new preternaturals can best be utilized."

"You're assuming these newbies will be able to speak English?" Finn's voice held a wealth of sarcasm and a darker tone that made her look at him. Flecks of demon yellow colored the bright blue of his irises, and his gaze was fixed on her hand in Stefan's before he raised his eyes. Was he jealous?

A thrill zinged through her at that thought. Of course, jealousy didn't necessarily equate to love, but it was a start.

Stefan shot him a sharp look. "No. I am not stupid, Finn, and don't make the mistake of thinking that I am." He looked back at Keira and his expression softened. She sensed that he was attracted to her and, even more, that he genuinely liked her. He gave a light squeeze to her fingers before releasing her hand. "We have people in place in these banks who can communicate with the newcomers in the standard language of the other dimension," he went on. "However, we need more money to fund these activities. Which is where you two come in."

"You want me to kill someone else?" Finn didn't sound eager about the idea. As a matter of fact, to her, he sounded resigned. Resentful even. The bits of yellow had grown his eyes, making it clear he was going demon.

"No." Stefan threw him another look. "Now that I see how good Keira is, I want you to have her back." He glanced at her and then stared at Finn. "Or was I misinformed when I was told the two of you have a relationship?"

"I wouldn't exactly call it a relationship," Keira hedged. She didn't want this insane vampire to know how much Finn had come to mean to her. She wouldn't give him that kind of leverage over her. "We're not a couple or anything."

"So, it's a friends with benefits sort of thing?" Stefan barked a laugh. "All the better. None of those messy emotions to get in the way."

He laid out the plan, and Keira bit back a sigh at learning she was to swap out yet more diamonds, though this time at another store.

And Finn was to be her lookout. Like it wouldn't be odd for a guy like him to be in a jewelry store. She said as much to Stefan.

Finn's "Hey! What d'ya mean, a guy like me?" was largely ignored.

Stefan said, "I see your point." He looked Finn over. "He's a big guy, good-looking enough, I suppose, but rather brutish. And that leather." He shook his head.

Keira looked Finn over, too, and privately disagreed. He'd look good in anything he wore, even though she'd only ever seen him in, and out of, jeans. She bet he looked downright tasty in a tuxedo.

Stefan snapped his fingers, dragging her attention back to him. A glint lit his eyes. "Go in as a newly engaged couple looking for diamonds to create your perfect engagement ring."

That wouldn't do at all. She couldn't go in and make googly eyes at Finn, pretending to be his fiancée. It would be too awkward and make her think all sorts of thoughts she shouldn't have, about Finn and a future. "I'm not sure that will work," she murmured. "I mean, we don't exactly look like we go together."

She ignored the disgruntled look Finn shot her way. She knew what Stefan saw when he looked at them. Finn was tall, broad, and aggressive, wearing his usual T-shirt, jeans, heavy boots, and leather coat. She was slender, gentle in demeanor, and wore a designer dress with shoes that cost as much as his coat had, if not more.

"Hmm. You may be right." Liuz stared at Keira. "You're a creative type, right? Let it slip that you're an artist designing your own ring. The store owner will eat that shit up." He pulled a familiar envelope out of the inner pocket of his suit coat and handed it to Keira. "At least three diamonds this time, please."

"Of course," she murmured.

"Go. Now."

"Now?" Keira stared at him. "I was able to do the other job with little notice, but with two of us it takes some planning. I need to know where the cameras are, what kind of security they have—"

"That's what he's there for," Stefan said, nodding toward Finn. "Let him act a little suspiciously, which should draw their focus away from you." He took her hand in his again and this time brought it to his mouth. He pressed his lips to her knuckles. "I have faith in you," he whispered. His pupils had dilated and she sensed a wave of pheromones directed her way. She should use this to her advantage, and if she wasn't so completely disgusted by him, she would.

"We should be on our way, then," Finn said, and gently wrapped his fingers around her upper arm. His action moved her hand away from Stefan's mouth.

The vampire straightened, his hard gaze going to Finn. "Yes, you should get moving," he said, though the look on his face promised retribution for Finn's continued lack of obeisance.

As they walked out of the room and down the hallway toward the stairs and the exit, Keira jerked her arm out of his grasp. "What is wrong with you?" she demanded.

Finn didn't respond until they were out in the parking lot. "What do you mean?"

"You know perfectly well what I mean." She stared at him, frowning. "Why are you being so adversarial with Stefan?"

"Oh, you're on a first-name basis with him, are you?" Finn shoved his hands in his pockets. His eyes glittered with demon gold and bad humor.

"I'm informal that way," she murmured. Then she laughed. "There's no need for you to be getting your knickers in a twist, boyo. You're the one for me. And anyway, stop changing the subject." She headed toward her car. "You keep trying to alienate him, and you're going to get your head handed to you."

"On a platter, no doubt." He sauntered after her.

She stopped beside her car and took a bracing breath. "I mean it, Finn. Stop provoking him."

"You worried about me?"

He said it with humor lightening his face, and she responded in all seriousness. "Yes, I am. He's dangerous. Look, let me go in first and get settled with a tray of diamonds. Then you can come in being your sly, shifty self and distract them."

He cleared his throat. "I'm not shifty."

She noticed he didn't deny being sly, and laughed at his dry glance. She sobered and said, "Well, just try to look as if you're about to nick something. That'll make you look right shifty enough." She used the remote to unlock her car. "Why don't you meet me at the jewelers?"

she suggested. "That way if something goes wrong, we have a chance of at least one of us getting away."

"All right," he answered easily enough. "I'll see you there." He grinned. "I'll practice looking shifty on my way over."

Keira shook her head at his playfulness. She got in her car and watched Finn walk back to his motorcycle a few rows over. He was multilayered, that was certain. And the most exasperating man she'd ever met. He was going to drive her to drink before this was all over. She only hoped they could salvage something from whatever they had between them once he found out she was a spy for the council. Or, at least, for the new council president.

Caladh as head of the council. That would change the dynamics of things around here, for the better, she hoped. Only time would tell.

She blew out a breath and started the car. It was time to pull another job. This time with Finn.

The thought filled her with a mixture of excitement and dread. But mostly dread. These days she didn't get him. She really had no idea what to expect. One minute he was a lover, the next a stranger. She felt like she was caught in a landslide, unable to find her footing. Which meant she should keep her distance as much as possible until this whole thing was over.

She parked in front of the store and watched Finn direct his motorcycle to the small alley that ran between the jewelry store and the adjacent building. She waited until he reached the front facade of the store before she got out of her car. He paused, his head bent as he looked at his cell phone. "If you get into trouble in there," he murmured barely loud enough for her to hear, "just call out my name."

"Right-o." Keira drew in a bracing breath and entered the store.

After the manager seated her at a small table, he went into the back to retrieve some of their raw diamonds. Keira took the time he was gone to palm a couple of the fake stones she'd brought with her. When the manager returned, he carried a tray covered with a square piece of black velvet and sat across from her. He uncovered the tray and pushed several of the stones across the surface, putting distance between each of the diamonds.

She leaned over to look at them. Glancing up at him, she said, "May I?" with one hand reaching toward a diamond.

"Oh, by all means." He smiled. "You really can't get a good sense of the stone unless you hold it."

"No, you can't," she agreed. Again, she would replace the real stone with a fake that was the same approximate size and weight. As she picked up one she thought might work, from behind her she heard Finn mutter a swear word.

Then in a louder voice he said, "This is all worthless crap. I thought you were reputable jewelers here."

"Sir," the saleswoman said, "I assure you these are the highest quality stones in these settings. Perhaps you'd rather see something in platinum instead of gold?"

Finn capitulated but within thirty seconds had become belligerent again.

Keira glanced over her shoulder to see him standing there, arms akimbo while the biggest scowl she'd ever seen hung on his face. "Oh, dear." She turned back toward the manager. "Perhaps I should come back at another time," she said and started to place the diamond back on the tray.

"Please, give me a moment." The manager sent her a harried look and stood, motioning to the saleswoman who was dealing with Finn.

Keira let the fake diamond slide between her fingers and put it on the tray, keeping the real diamond hidden in her palm. She dropped the real stone into the hand she rested in her lap. While the manager stood in front of her, talking to his employee, Keira went through the motions of looking through the other stones. She picked up a few and set them back down without making an attempt to swap them. When Finn started up his noise again, the saleswoman hurried back to try to appease him, the manager watching the scene. Keira made one last swap, holding the real diamonds in the palm of her left hand while she prodded at the ones remaining on the tray with her right index finger.

"Do you see one that will work for what you want?" the manager asked.

She pointed to one of the fake ones she'd just deposited on the tray. "This one, perhaps." She looked up at the manager and pushed at him with her empathic abilities. She filled him with a sense of goodwill and well-being, and anticipation of making a big sale. She stood, dropping the real diamonds into her clutch purse while she fastened the clasp. Between the glamour and her adroitness at sleight of hand, the man never saw it.

"I won't be shopping here again," Finn exclaimed and stomped out of the store.

"Thank God," the manager muttered. Then his face

turned pink and he apologized. "I shouldn't have said that."

"It's quite all right," Keira responded. "It does take all sorts to make the world go 'round, doesn't it?"

"It certainly does," he agreed.

Keira glanced at the tray again and then lifted her gaze to the manager's face. "Thank you for your time. I hope to be back soon."

"It was my pleasure, miss. Shall I set this aside for you?" he asked, the hopes for a fat commission swimming in his eyes.

She pretended to think it over. "Ah, no, I don't think so," she finally said. "I'd hate for someone else to lose out on a great stone while I try to make up my mind. If we're meant to be together, it will be available when I come back." What a load of claptrap, but he seemed to buy it.

"Well, now, you come back anytime."

"Thank you, I will." When Keira went outside to her car, she saw Finn leaning against the side of the building, a big smirk on his face.

"Was I shifty enough?" he asked.

She shook her head and then shot him a grin. "You were bloody perfect, actually."

His answering smile tightened her belly. "Good," he said. He sobered. "I guess you should get those to Stefan."

She gave a nod and got into her car. With the lift of a hand she waved farewell and drove away. She only hoped that Stefan would be satisfied and it would be the last time she had to do something like this.

Finn pulled out into traffic and marveled at how adept Keira was at grifting. Man, she must have been something to see back in the day when she was doing it for a living. Her sweet face looked so sincere, so innocent, so lovely that any man with a heartbeat would have a hard time believing she could be as devious as she was.

He still had a hard time with the fact that she was doing this. He knew it was irrational, but he felt personally betrayed by her actions. Like if he couldn't look up to her, use her as a role model for striving to be more than he was, then what was the point in any of it?

He knew she remained upset with him for being in the rogue group. Which, now that he thought about it, made him pause. He knew at one point she had wanted him to be more than an enforcer. But if they were both on the same side in this new fight, what did it matter? He would have thought she'd be happy to have him as an ally.

And yet, as much as he'd like to tell her what was going on he couldn't confide in Keira only to have her betray him. He knew he had to completely win over the delusional Liuz's trust in enough time to find the rift machine and destroy it. If he didn't, not only would it mean the mission would fail, but it would most likely cost him his life. And maybe even hers, because Liuz might not believe Finn had acted alone.

He knew not calling her after they'd made love had caused her to draw back, to put emotional distance between them. She'd seemed genuinely concerned about him, and he still couldn't tamp down the jealousy he felt every time he thought of her interactions with Liuz. She'd let him hold her hand, had even seemed to enjoy his touch. What the hell was she doing? Was it possible her role in the group wasn't what it seemed, like his? Though for the life of him he couldn't come up with one reason that she'd be playing Stefan, except that it was what grifters did. They played with people's emotions.

He exhaled. Whatever her motivation, he could only be responsible for his actions. He hoped, once his deception came to light, she forgave him and would give him another chance.

Chapter Fourteen

I want you to do another job for me." Stefan Liuz lounged on the small sofa in the private room at Devil's Domain. His dark gaze centered on Keira, he tapped two fingers against the arm of the sofa as he waited for her response.

"Another job?" She pressed back against the opposite end of the sofa, trying to keep distance between her and the vampire. She'd allowed herself to relax over the past week, convinced Liuz was done using her after that last job. She should have known better.

"Yes." His eyes took on an excited glitter. "Another grift, of course, to use your considerable skills. Only this time I'm going with you."

"You?" Keira pressed her lips together and tapped into her empathic abilities. She didn't like the thought of him going anywhere with her, let alone hanging out while she pulled off a job. "Um—"

"*I'll* pose as your fiancé while we shop for engagement rings. You must admit you and I make a much more believable pair than you and Evnissyen." He smiled, looking pleased with his plan. "What do you think?"

She made her smile widen. "I think it's great." With

the way he was looking at her, like a dirty old man offering candy to a kid, she knew where this was heading. Her dread grew. Maybe she could talk him out of it, or at least postpone it until two days from now when it wouldn't matter anymore. "But the rift is in two days," she said. "Can't this wait? People are jumpy enough as it is."

"Are you afraid?" He leaned forward and stretched his arm along the back of the small couch. His hand dangled inches from her shoulder.

She didn't see why she shouldn't admit to a certain amount of trepidation. "Are you saying that with tensions running as high as they are I shouldn't be?" she countered.

He gave a careless shrug. "Really, what can they do to us?"

"Remember villagers with pitchforks and fire?" she muttered. "They can do plenty, I'm thinking."

Stefan chortled and shook his head. "Humans are like toothless dogs, Keira. They're all bark and no bite."

"What about other preternaturals? The council?"

He made a scornful noise. "After tomorrow neither humans nor the council will be in charge. They'll have to follow our rules, not the other way around."

She bit back a sigh. He was so full of blarney she hardly knew where to begin. With a frown, she said, "I thought there weren't going to be any rules. That's what anarchy is all about, isn't it? Or have I misunderstood completely?"

His eyes narrowed. His suspiciousness smoldered between them like a steaming pile of crap.

She hastened to add, "I'm not trying to be a smartass, Stefan. I just don't understand how humans, let alone council members, are going to be required to follow rules in an anarchistic society."

"Later they'll have to follow our rules," he murmured, his narrowed gaze focused on her face. "Unfortunately anarchies rarely last long, but every democracy needs a good overthrowing from time to time." He paused, moved his hand to her shoulder. Through the silken material of her dress, he stroked his fingers along her collarbone. "Let's talk about something else for now."

She forced herself to plaster a soft smile on her face and not shrink from his touch. She found him to be repulsive and utterly without morals. In her life before the rift she would have had no issue with being in cahoots with someone like him. Now, though, she could barely stand to be in the same room.

Let alone allow him to touch her. And she was very much afraid he had a lot more touching he wanted to be doing. Knowing that as a vampire he'd be able to sniff out her emotional state, literally, she turned her empathic ability inward to mask her true feelings. She wasn't quite sure how or why it worked. At one point she'd thought maybe it was a coping mechanism she and others like her had in order to be able to deal with being bombarded with emotions all day long. Whenever she began to feel overwhelmed she could calm herself, much like throwing a warm, comforting blanket over her psyche.

Knowing she couldn't alienate him this close to her goal, Keira reached up and placed her hand over his where it rested against her collarbone. As a grifter she'd often had to fake interest in another person, but none of her marks had been as loathsome as this one.

She tipped her chin down and peeked up at him like

a coquette. "What would you be wanting to talk about, then?" she asked, making sure to pour on the Irish.

"You. And me." He turned his hand to grip her fingers and brought them down to rest on his knee.

She studied his hand. It was on the small side with slim fingers tipped by fingernails that badly needed a trim. She couldn't help but compare Stefan's hands to Finn's broad hands with their long, square-tipped fingers. Stefan definitely came out the loser in the match.

"You must know I'm attracted to you," he went on. "I'd like us to get better acquainted." His grin was one that no doubt had won women over before, but Keira could barely stomach it. By all the gods in all the universes, why was this little cockroach so interested in her?

She wrapped herself with a cloak of affability and interest. "Oh, I'd like that, too." She gave him a wide smile.

He slowly leaned toward her and lifted one hand to cup her chin. Keira forced herself to hold still, though her skin began to itch where he touched her. He brought his face close to her ear. "I need a strong woman like you by my side, Keira. A woman who understands me, who can assist me." His warm breath stirred the hair by her ear, tickling her. She remained still. "You have amazing skills, skills I can use." He drew back slightly and stared down into her eyes. He moved his hand, stroking his fingers down her cheek. "Soft," he whispered. "So soft."

His lips pressed against her temple before he drew back again. She closed her eyes so she wouldn't have to look at the man. She was fairly certain she was holding on to her cloak well enough to fool him. She wasn't so certain her distaste wouldn't show in her eyes.

When he took her hand in his, she opened her eyes. He brought it to his mouth and pressed a kiss to her open palm. She fought back a shudder of revulsion and instead pushed out with her abilities, sending forth a sense of contentment and sexual interest. He moved his mouth to her inner wrist, and she focused on keeping her heart rate as steady as possible. Though any change in tempo he most likely would interpret as due to sexual interest.

He'd be dead wrong. She dearly wanted to pull her hand out of his grip but didn't want to upset his contented mood. She'd seen how quickly a vampire could go from satisfied to furious before, and she didn't want to be on the receiving end of any nastiness. But when he kissed her wrist again and then nicked it with his fangs, she gasped and jerked her hand away.

He was unrepentant and seemingly not offended by her action. He ran his tongue across his teeth and gave a low groan of approval. "Yes, you taste as good as I knew you would." He stood and drew her to her feet. With heels on, she actually stood a couple of inches taller than him, meaning she had to bend her head to stare into his eyes. That he clearly didn't like. "From now on," he ordered, "wear shorter heels."

"More rules?" She couldn't resist the jab even as she told herself she should make nice with Stefan. By getting closer to him she could gather more intel. Finn must be rubbing off on her, and she couldn't afford to take a page out of his book. Time was running out.

"I don't like my women to be taller than I am," he said. "We could always have your feet cut off, I suppose. That would solve the problem, wouldn't it?" When she stared at him, unable to hide her horror at his words, he gave an airy laugh. "Oh, for God's sake, Keira. Lighten up. I'm only joking."

"Right." She walked over to the door and picked up her purse from where she'd set it on the floor. She knew enough about him, about the lengths he would go to, that she didn't doubt he'd cut off her feet if it suited him. She looked at him and forced another smile. "Where should I meet you tomorrow, and what time?"

"I'll be in touch."

She nodded and let herself out of the room. Making sure she kept her emotions masked, she headed out of the club. Not knowing who might be watching, she resisted the urge to scrub her hands across her mouth. She wanted to get the taste and feel of him off her lips. It wasn't until she was halfway home that she relaxed. Not only was Stefan crazy for thinking he could succeed at his rift madness, he was also crazy if he thought he was going to get anywhere near her without clothes on. He would not be dipping his wick with her, no sir.

The last man she'd been with was Finn, and he was like a Lay's potato chip. You couldn't have him just once and be satisfied. But while the physical attraction had been what had initially drawn her to him, the more she got to know him, the more she liked. The more she loved. He didn't take himself too seriously, for one thing. He actually seemed to get a kick out of it when she teased him. He had a real sense of right and wrong, and when it was warranted didn't have much trouble crossing that line. She admired someone who could make hard choices and live with the consequences.

However, what she'd been seeing since he joined the rogue group made her worry that he would cross the line and stay there. Hunting down loose cannons in the demon community was one thing. Killing a member of the council was something else entirely. He'd changed since meeting up with Stefan. Or maybe it was that she'd never really known the real him. He seemed harder. More ruthless.

She didn't think she could be with someone as ruthless as Stefan, or as self-centered as she used to be. She couldn't begin to guess how he was going to react when he found out she was instrumental in bringing Stefan down and putting the kibosh on his plans. It all depended on how far into the dark side Finn had gone. And whether she could bring him back so they might have a future together.

She'd once upon a time thought Finn was a good guy trapped in the bad-boy image of a demon. Evidenced by the callous way he'd dispatched Tobias Caine, she wasn't so sure now. He didn't seem to like the fact that she was getting closer to Stefan, reacting almost like a jealous boyfriend. But he hadn't been too concerned when he had sex with her and then didn't communicate for two days.

She sighed. Damn it to hell. Men were more trouble than they were worth sometimes.

The next morning she met Stefan at a small coffee shop doors down from the jewelry store they were planning to hit. As she sat there sipping her coffee, in walked Finn, looking dark and dangerous in his black leather jacket and matching scowl. He didn't bother going to the counter to order anything. Instead he came over to the table where she and Stefan sat and pulled out a chair. "So, what did you want to powwow about?" he asked as he plopped into the seat.

The wood creaked under his weight. Keira half expected it to crumple beneath him, but somehow it held fast. The look he shot her spoke volumes. She hadn't *wanted* the chair to collapse, not really. But it would've been funny just the same.

Finn leaned forward. In a low voice he said, "You don't need all three of us to scam a jewelry store." He glanced around and added, "And it'd be nice, next time, if we could do something different."

"It's funny you should suggest that." Stefan wrapped his hands around his mug. Lifting it to his lips, he blew on the liquid a few seconds before taking a sip. As he lowered the cup to the table, he said, "Actually, I've changed my mind about doing a grift with you. Instead, I want the two of you to go over there and bring me a hundred grand."

Following his gaze Keira looked out the window while Finn twisted in his seat. They both looked back at him. In disbelief she said, "You want us to rob a bank?"

"I don't expect you to go in there with guns drawn," Stefan drawled. "You can use that finesse you're so famous for and con the manager out of the money." He stared at Finn. "You're there as backup. Like before, you'll distract or deflect if needed."

"We need time to plan," Keira protested. She leaned forward and placed her hand over his. She gently pushed some of her glamour onto him, imparting a sense of attraction and a desire to please while burying the truth of how she really felt. She gave him a soft smile. "Stefan, you can't expect me to go in there and ask the manager to hand over a hundred thousand dollars. It's not that simple."

"Make it that simple." His eyes went Manson scary for a second before a smile softened the madness. "You can do this, Keira. You have the skills." He turned his hand over and clasped her fingers. "I know you won't disappoint me. More of our brothers and sisters will arrive tomorrow, all over the world. They'll see newspaper and TV ads advising them of what steps they should take. We have to make sure we have adequate funds to take care of their initial needs."

"Shouldn't we do an electronic transfer then, rather than cart out physical money?" Finn traced a random pattern on the tabletop, his gaze fixed on Stefan.

Keira sensed anger radiating from him, and more jealousy. At least she knew he had feelings for her other than lust.

Stefan's mouth tightened. "We have our local needs as well, situations where cash is the preferred method of payment."

In other words bribes, Keira thought. Either that or Stefan wanted more money for himself. She wouldn't put it past him to use the grand revolution to fatten his own coffers. Rarely had leaders of revolution thrown over a government solely for the good of the people. Their overriding motivation was usually something a lot closer to home.

He stood and looked down at her. "I'll leave you two now so you can formulate a plan of action. You only have until the bank closes today to get this done." He glanced at Finn. "I'll be in the first room on the right in the private area at Devil's Domain. Bring the money to me there." His gaze went back to Keira. He bent and placed a lingering kiss on her cheek.

She watched him walk out of the coffee shop, trying with little success to ignore the furious vibe coming off Finn and the equal desire to wipe her face clean of Stefan's touch, the latter without success. "I'm going to the ladies' room," she said and stood up. "I'll be right back."

Finn sat back in his chair and fixed his gaze on the hallway Keira had just walked down before going into the women's restroom. What the hell was she doing, touching Liuz? Letting him touch her? Did she actually like the slimy little bastard?

Finn wanted to punch someone. Since he couldn't punch Liuz, he might have to go find a demon who was breaking the rules and pound his head. But first he'd find out from Keira if she was serious about Liuz. Because if she was, he'd subtract himself from the equation. Or, better yet, wait until after the rift machine was disabled and subtract Liuz from the equation. Permanently.

He'd never been one who enjoyed math, but this was one problem he could solve. Three minus one equaled two. If Finn calculated correctly, he and Keira would be the two left standing.

Deciding he'd get something to drink while he waited for Keira and wondering why it took women so damn long to pee, he went up to the counter and stared at the menu board. There were dozens of tea-based drinks and even more coffees. Finally he looked at the young barista and said, "Give me a Coke."

"Regular or diet?" she asked.

He grimaced. He didn't drink that diet crap. "Regular."

"What size?"

Oh, for God's sake. When had ordering a drink gotten

to be such a pain in the ass? He had a feeling he wouldn't be here very long, because Keira wasn't going to like the conversation he planned to have with her and would probably walk out. Since he couldn't carry a drink with him on his bike, he said, "Give me a small."

He paid for the soda and as he turned away from the counter, Keira approached the table. She took her seat and wrapped her hands around her probably lukewarm coffee. He set his soda on the table. "You want me to get you a fresher one?" he asked.

She shook her head. "No, this is fine." She took a sip. "I like it cold."

"Okay." Finn sat down and stretched his legs out beneath the table. "So, you're fine with all of this?"

She frowned. "Why wouldn't I be?"

He shifted in his seat, looping his arm over the back of his chair. "I thought you had gotten out of this kind of life. I *thought* you'd changed."

A muscle twitched in her jaw. He'd scored a hit. She took a sip of coffee and didn't meet his eyes. "Sometimes we can't have what we want."

"Really?" He leaned forward and braced his elbows on the table. "All you have to do is say no, Keira. Say no and walk away."

"Didn't they give you the same warning I got? There's no saying no, there's no walking away." She lifted her eyes to his. "I'm in this now. My choice."

"But why?" Dissatisfied with her explanation, and remembering that she had never really answered this question when he'd asked it before, he asked again, "Why in the hell did you get involved with this group?"

"Finn, look," Keira said with a shake of her head,

"we've been over this before. I have my reasons, and I'm sorry but they're none of your business."

"Is it Liuz?" he asked.

"What do you mean?" Another frown furled her brows.

"Do you have feelings for him?" Finn asked. When she didn't respond right away, he decided to be more direct. "Do you want him, Keira? Is that it? You want to be with him, have sex with him."

Something flared in her eyes, but had gone too fast for him to decipher. Annoyance wafted off her with a slight aroma of burned toast. "If I do, again, it's none of your business. It's not like we agreed to be exclusive."

"Didn't we?" Finn narrowed his eyes. "I seem to recall some talk of caring about each other. But, hey, maybe it's that you want Stefan more than me. Is that it? You want him?" Before she could respond, he said, "You know what? It doesn't matter. It doesn't. Because he can't have you." For all his intensity, he kept his voice low so that the people around them couldn't overhear their conversation, but he had to get this out. "You belong with me, even if you don't want to admit it."

"Finn—"

"You have no idea how dangerous he is, Keira." He had to be careful how he phrased this. She couldn't know how it was he knew exactly how dangerous Stefan Liuz was. "I know you know how crazy it makes me when he touches you. And not only because I'm jealous." There. He'd admitted it. "But also because the closer you get to him, the deeper into his world you'll get. I only want to protect you."

"Finn." She paused and stared out the window. Her

tongue swept out to moisten her bottom lip, and she met his eyes. "I do care about you, and I'm glad you feel the same way about me. I want to explain, but I can't. As there are times when you can't tell me everything, this is one of those times for me. I hope you understand." She reached out and placed her hand over his where it rested on the table. "Please be careful. It's obvious Stefan is interested in me, and if he thinks you're in his way, he might try to eliminate the obstacle." Her eyes went dark with worry. "I don't want anything to happen to you because of me. I couldn't live with myself."

He turned his hand over and lightly clasped hers, feeling the coolness of her skin against his. "Nothing's gonna happen to me."

"I hope not." She stared at their hands a moment and then drew away. "We need to do what Stefan wants. Let's just go to the bank and get this done." Without waiting for his response, she walked toward the door.

Finn heaved a sigh and hauled himself to his feet. Damn it. She was so intent on following Liuz she might get them both killed. He caught up to her a few steps outside the coffee shop and took her arm. "What's the plan?"

"I don't suppose you have an account at this bank?" she asked with a hopeful look.

"Nope." Finn stood with her at the crosswalk, waiting for the signal to change. "How do we do this?"

"Stefan is right," she said, either not seeing or ignoring his grimace. "You need to be prepared to act as a distraction, but I think I'll be able to, ah, sweet talk the manager into giving me the money."

The pedestrian sign flicked to WALK, and they crossed

the street. As they headed down the sidewalk toward the bank, Finn said, "I can't hang out inside the bank. Somebody's bound to notice."

She shot him a dry look. "No kidding." They reached the front of the bank and stopped. Keira put her hand on Finn's arm. "Let me go in first. In a few minutes, you come in and get a good look around—quickly and unobtrusively—and then tell someone you want to open an account. If I come out with a bagful of money, you can always abort the account opening and tell them you changed your mind."

"Like that's not suspicious."

"People do it all the time," she said with a wave of her hand.

"And if you don't come out with a bagful of money?"

She met his gaze. "Then get the hell out of there, boyo." She took a deep breath. "Are you ready?"

"No, but I suppose that doesn't matter. What Stefan wants, Stefan gets," he singsonged.

"Men," she muttered. "Even ones thousands of years old can still act like whiney little babes." She sighed and entered the bank.

Finn waited several minutes, as instructed, then went through the door. Once inside, he stopped at the center counter and reached for a deposit slip. He took a pen from a plastic container and started to fill out the slip while glancing around the bank. There were no security guards on duty that he could see. However, cameras were in several locations, and as far as he could see there weren't any blind spots.

After a few moments, he approached the desk of a loan officer. "Excuse me," he said.

A pretty young woman looked up from her computer screen and smiled. "Yes, sir?"

He returned the smile. "I'd like to open an account."

She stood and came around the desk. "I think Ida in new accounts can help you out there. Here, I'll take you over to her." Her last few words came out breathy, and her face grew pink as she kept glancing at him from the corner of her eye.

It wasn't that big a bank, he figured he could have found the new accounts desk all by himself, but he obligingly followed along behind her. She stopped by another desk. The woman behind this desk, gaze fixed on her computer monitor while she tapped away at the keyboard, wasn't as young or as pretty.

"This gentleman would like to open a new account," the loan officer said.

"Have a seat," Ida responded in a deep, harsh voice. She didn't look up or smile.

Finn knew he'd have his work cut out for him trying to charm this one.

She coughed and typed a few more words onto the keyboard.

He could smell the cigarette smoke oozing from her skin and clothes even without using his preternatural olfactory abilities.

"I'll pull up the application." She finally looked up at him from over the frames of her glasses. "Please, have a seat."

He sat. From here he could see Keira inside the bank manager's office. She was seated across the desk from him, her hand outstretched, covering his. The guy had a besotted look on his face and Finn had the fleeting thought that they were lucky the manager was a man. Though with her empathic abilities, Keira would be able to affect a female the same way.

As he watched, she stood and moved around to the manager's side of the desk. She moved her palm to his cheek and held it there, talking to him the whole while. Finn couldn't make out what she was saying, not even by employing the use of shapeshifter hearing, but whatever it was, it produced results. The manager gave a nod and stood. He walked over to a credenza and opened a drawer. When he turned around, he held a canvas money pouch in his hand. He smiled at Keira and murmured something to her. She smiled back and sat down in the guest chair. When she saw Finn, she tilted her head ever so slightly, giving him the signal that all was well. So far.

Ida started asking him questions for the application, things like his name and address. He looked at her and answered, giving her truthful information because he figured it would be easy enough for authorities to figure out who he was by pulling surveillance video.

"Opening this account does require that I see some form of picture ID," Ida said.

About that time Keira walked out of the manager's office, a wide smile on her face and the canvas pouch in her hand. The pouch was ridiculously small to be able to hold so much cash. He knew each bundle of hundred-dollar bills equaled five thousand dollars and was only about half an inch thick. The bag was only about five or six inches wide. Still, one would expect a hundred thousand dollars to be bigger.

She shook hands with the manager and walked out of the bank.

Finn looked at Ida and adopted a chagrined expression while he patted his pockets. "I don't believe this." He gave a low chuckle and shrugged his shoulders. "I must have left my wallet at home." He flipped his wrist to check his watch and said, "I won't be able to return before you close, so would you just delete that? I'll come back another time."

Her sigh came out on a gust of aggravation. "Of course, Mr. Evnissyen. Come back any time."

Finn smiled and left the bank. Keira was waiting for him by her car.

"I'd almost forgotten how much fun this is," she said. Her eyes danced with blue sparks of excitement. "I mean, the sleight of hand at jewelry stores is one thing, but this, really laying it on and grifting money out of people, it's something else entirely." She laughed and looped her arm through his, hugging it to her side.

Her enthusiasm had totally chased away the curmudgeon mode she'd been in before. While he liked to see her happy, her reaction was just what he'd been afraid of. Grifting, for her, was like a drug—one job was too many, and a dozen wasn't enough. He needed to see what kind of space her head was in, see if maybe he could talk some sense into her. Though she'd been right earlier when she'd said there was no walking away. If he was successful in encouraging her to leave the group, he'd damned well make sure it was safe for her to do so.

"Hey!" She leaned against her car and stroked a finger down his chest. "Why don't we go to my place and celebrate?"

This was the Keira he was used to, a woman confident in her appeal and not afraid to show her passion. "Sure," he said. If he was at her place, he'd have her alone and they could have a private chat. Among other things. He nodded toward the money bag she held. "Aren't we supposed to get that to Stefan?"

"And we will." She went up on tiptoes and pressed her lips to the corner of his mouth. "Just not right away."

He put his arms around her waist and tugged her closer. "What kind of celebration did you have in mind?"

She winked at him. "You'll find out when you get there, boyo." She planted her mouth on his, giving him a kiss that stole his breath and started a fire burning low in his belly. When she drew away, both of them breathed heavily. She smiled and whispered, "Don't take too long." She hopped into her car and drove away, still with that huge smile on her face.

Finn strode to his bike and pulled out into traffic. He'd thought perhaps she'd been distancing herself from him, but maybe he'd been wrong.

Of course, he didn't know exactly how she planned to celebrate her achievement. It was hard to tell with her. She might want to break out cake and ice cream. Maybe some champagne.

In which case his hopes would be dashed and he'd be wrong again.

Chapter Fifteen

Keira went into her house and waited, hand on door-knob, until Finn sauntered past her. Then she closed and locked the door. Taking his hand, she led him back to her bedroom. She set the money bag on the dresser by the door and stared at him.

By all that was holy, she felt like she was on fire. Her blood sang, her skin tingled, her thoughts scattered except for one.

She wanted this man like she'd wanted no other.

With a small smile, she turned on a lamp on the table in the corner of the room. Soft light brightened the room. It was enough to be able to see clearly, yet it was still romantic in tone. Her queen-size bed with its green patchwork quilt looked lonely. She planned to remedy that quite soon.

Keira walked back over to Finn, kicking off her shoes as she went. Stopping in front of him, she let her gaze wander over his body and appreciated, not for the first time, what a strong, virile male he was.

As she slid her hands down his back and then up and across his broad shoulders, she felt the warmth of his skin beneath his clothing. Clothing that was in the way. She wanted the feel of him beneath her fingertips. Skin on skin.

She'd never before been so utterly consumed by a man. Oh, she'd had sex before and it was one of her favorite things to do, but this all-encompassing need was something new. Different. So different that it frightened her a little. What was it about this man, this demon, that moved her so?

She lifted her eyes to his, seeing how passion darkened his blue eyes, and knew what was different. She loved this man. With his arrogance and his hardness, she'd experienced such gentleness from him that she knew he had it in him to be kind, softer than he let on. She was certain what she felt was love.

Yet she saw no reciprocity in his gaze. Lust was there, to be sure. Plenty of lust. But no love. She knew it was a bad idea to feel this way. Stupid, even. But there it was.

While it might be a bad idea, love itself was never bad. She loved Finn, and she would do what she could to keep him from harm.

Right now, though, she wanted him naked and in her bed. And she would take the lead on their coming together. She wanted to entice him. Not through any glamour, but through emotion. Through her love, perhaps he could find it in himself to do more than "care" for her. She wanted him to love her back.

Keira pushed his leather jacket off his shoulders and let it fall to the floor. Then she set her fingers to the buttons of his shirt. She slid that off his shoulders, too, and it joined the jacket. Unable to resist the allure of his musculature, she traced her fingers up his biceps, over his collarbone and across his pectorals. She thumbed his tight little nipples, eliciting a sharply drawn breath from him.

Leaning forward, she pressed a kiss into the hollow of his throat, then on his Adam's apple, pausing only to draw back to study the tattoo that spread from the right side of his neck down onto his shoulder. "Why do you have this?" she asked.

"It's a holdover from my rebellious youth," he murmured.

"Really?"

"No." He chuckled. "I got this in a ritual my people performed. When a boy reaches manhood, he is given a marking." He brought his hand over and briefly touched the side of his neck. "It identifies our demon and our place in demon society." He dropped his hand back to his side.

She traced part of the tattoo, smiling when he tilted his head, his eyes closing at her touch. "This line?" she asked.

"That one marks the place where I was born. Everything above it is a replica of my grandfather's tattoo. My mother's father," he clarified before she could ask.

She gave a short nod and ran her fingers over more of the black lines. "I'm sorry," she whispered. "It just looks like a bunch of squiggly lines to me."

He grinned and looked down at her. "That's all they are, but they have meaning. Or rather they had meaning a couple thousand years ago. Today, not so much."

"Whether or not they have meaning, it's still sexy." She placed her lips against his neck. His pulse beat against her mouth, and soon hers matched its rhythm.

Keira brought her hands to Finn's head, cradling it in

her palms, and gently urged him toward her. Their lips met, breaths mingled. This was what she'd been craving. The feel of him under her hands, beneath her mouth.

She skimmed her tongue across the seam of his mouth and he opened for her. She slipped inside, softly caressing his tongue with hers, enticing him to follow her when she retreated. He gathered her closer, his big palms flat against her back. She moved her hands to his shoulders, curling her fingers into his firm muscles, testing his strength. When his mouth moved down her neck, she sighed and tilted her head to give him better access. His hot breath against her skin, the feel of his erection pressing against her belly...it was all going too fast. *She* was going too fast. She wanted this to be about him.

With a soft sigh she pushed him back and moved her hands to his belt buckle. "I want to touch you." Holding his gaze with her own, she whispered, "I want to taste you." She unbuckled his belt, feeling his stomach muscles jump as the backs of her fingers brushed against his skin.

She went to her knees in front of him. Unzipping his jeans with care, she pushed them down his legs. Beneath his gray boxer briefs, his cock lay as a thick wedge along his thigh. She tugged his underwear gently down his legs, freeing his erection. He stepped out of his clothes and kicked them to the side.

Keira wrapped one hand around his shaft and touched the fat tip with a light flick of her tongue. He jerked and let out a harsh moan. She liked his reaction, so she repeated her motion. Another groan made her smile with feminine delight.

With her left hand she palmed his balls, rolling them over her fingers, lightly massaging them. The muscles in his thighs grew taut, a fine trembling setting up in his legs as he fought for control.

She aimed to make him see that all the control here was hers. Standing, she urged him backward until his knees hit the edge of the mattress. With a light shove, she pushed him onto the bed and stood between his spread legs.

"God, Keira, you're killing me." When Finn's heated gaze, full of yellow demon fire, fell on her, it was like the entire world held its breath.

"Oh, now, I don't want you dead, not by a long shot." She reached up and began to unbutton her blouse. His eyes tracked her movement, heating even more when the upper slopes of her breasts were revealed. "I very much prefer you alive. And moaning. In my bed." She slipped out of her blouse and did a slow shimmy out of her slacks. That left her in a barely there red satin bra and matching lacy panties.

The way his eyes lit up made her decide to leave her underwear on a bit longer. She slid her hands up his thighs, enjoying the feel of his hair-roughened skin against her sensitive palms. When she bent to take him in her mouth, her long tresses cascaded over his body, brushing against his flat abdomen and eliciting another moan from Finn. As soon as her lips closed over the head of his cock, his hips jerked, driving more of him into her mouth.

He muttered an apology that she waved away with one hand. She twirled her tongue over him, tapped on the sensitive underside, and stroked over the weeping tip. All the while she caressed his inner thighs, coming close but never quite touching his sac.

Without warning he surged up, grasping her waist to toss her onto the bed. He came down over her, wedging his knee between her thighs. As he stroked her hair away from her face, she grinned up at him. "You men never like foreplay," she mock complained.

"Yeah, well, we're simple creatures. It doesn't take much to get our motors revving at full speed. You don't want me putting that engine in gear without you along for the ride, do you?"

She gave him a pout. "I was in the driver's seat, Finn. How much more 'along for the ride' could I have been?"

"I don't mind you driving," he said. With economical movements he removed the rest of her clothing and came back down between her thighs. She could feel his hard length against the folds of her sex. He gave her that slow smile of his, the one that started in his eyes and landed on his lips. "But I prefer you to be fully engaged, if you know what I mean." He tested her readiness with one hand.

It was her turn to gasp and moan as he stroked two fingers into her sheath. In, then out. In. Out. He set a rhythm that had her hips rising and falling to his touch.

He brought his mouth back to hers, his kiss slow and deep. Carnal excitement raced through her, making her toes curl, legs sliding restlessly across the coolness of the quilt beneath her. His chest lifted with a deep, sharp intake of breath and the kiss turned hungry. Urgent with a need that was almost desperate, the pressure of his mouth just this side of painful.

His hands urged her thighs farther apart, then he was pressing inside her, one slow, tormenting inch at a time. She shoved her hips up, trying to make him go faster, but he only laughed and kept up his maddeningly slow pace. Finally his pelvis rested against hers. As he began to move he braced himself on one arm. His other hand came between her thighs to circle and stroke her clit.

Her arousal ratcheted up another notch. Soon the room filled with the sounds of their breathing, rasping and heavy, joined by the slap of flesh against flesh, sharp cries and harsh groans.

Keira felt her sensual tension rise to a fever pitch, stretching taut like a rubber band, before it snapped, throwing her into a maelstrom of ecstasy. Her entire body clenched and shuddered, and she cried out and clutched onto Finn.

He held her while she thrashed beneath him, his jaw tight with the control he exerted over his own pleasure. As soon as she quieted, he gripped her hips, fitted himself to her more solidly and began pistoning into her. Hard. Fast. His eyes gleamed with yellow demon intensity, and she felt a renewed quickening of her body.

She thrust her hips up to meet his downward plunge and reached around him to grip his tight buttocks. His movements came even faster, then he let out a shout as his completion emptied him.

He collapsed on top of her, his breathing harsh and heavy, his cock giving a final few twitches inside her. When he started to move away she stopped him, wrapping her arms and legs around him. "Don't move yet." She gave a soft sigh. "I want to stay like this for a while."

"Like this?" he asked in a deep voice and canted his hips forward, driving his still semierect cock deeper into her sheath.

Her breath hitched. "Yes," she breathed. "Just like this."

They were silent several moments until the laws of physiology took over and his softened shaft slipped out of her body. "All good things must come to an end," he murmured and turned onto his back. Despite admitting to herself that she was in love with this man, she couldn't tell him. Not yet. Not while she was so uncertain about so many things—his role in the rogue group, the old way of life he'd seemed to embrace all too eagerly. Would he give it up for her? Would he ever be free of Lucifer even after the group was finished? If he didn't, if he stayed on as Lucifer's enforcer, could she accept that?

Once the job was done, would they have something strong enough to keep them together?

He lay there a few minutes and then sat up and put his feet on the floor. With his back to her, he said, "As much as I'd like to stay, we have to get that money to Liuz."

She wanted to say, *To hell with the money. To hell with Stefan.* But he was right. She'd forgotten herself in Finn's arms and had blanked out on the bag of cash sitting on her dresser. The sooner they got this to Liuz, the better. And she would try to get him to show her where the rift machine was so she could go and destroy it. They were running out of time.

She'd hold on to the confession of love she dearly wanted to make and hope once she was able to tell Finn exactly how she felt, it wouldn't be for naught.

Of all the prets in the world, how had it fallen to her to save the whole damned world?

Chapter Sixteen

Keira and Finn cleaned up after their lovemaking, taking separate showers because bathing together would have served to delay them even further. She knew his self-control where she was concerned was tenuous, and when it came to her self-control, well, it was nonexistent. If she were to be in a hot, steamy shower with him, his big, naked body pressed against her, they'd never leave. Nearly an hour later she walked into the Devil's Domain with the money bag in her hand and Finn on her heels.

She made her way straight back to the private rooms, where the vamp standing guard let her in. The first door on the right was the room where Stefan had said he'd be. She'd give him his money and be on her way. Adrenaline still sang in her veins and the high of the job and memory of making love to Finn amped up her awareness of those around her, especially Finn.

She got the sense that he wasn't happy she'd had such a good time on the job, and on one level she wasn't, either. However, she did recognize the joy she felt in doing what she was good at. Being successful always brought about a sense of well-being. She paused outside the door and looked at him. "Are you ready?" she asked.

"Let's do this and get out of here," he responded. "I'm thinking maybe we need another celebration. What do you think?" His voice came out low and languid and so full of desire and affection it softened everything feminine inside of her. She fought it back, knowing their time for intimacy was past until the next Influx had passed. After that, well, she really had no idea how things would end up.

For right now she couldn't let Stefan see how Finn affected her. The vampire thought he had a chance to get in her pants, which was where she needed him. In her experience with men, they were more malleable when they had sex on the brain, and she aimed to use that to her advantage. A Stefan she could manipulate was a Stefan she could defeat.

She knocked on the door and heard him call "Enter." She went inside. Finn came in behind her and closed the door. Without any fanfare she went over to a seated Stefan and handed him the money bag. "Here."

A slow smile curved his lips and he hefted the bag a moment before sliding open the zipper. He took out one of the bundles and fanned it. He laughed and looked up at her. "Job well done, my dear." He glanced at Finn standing at her back. "You did your part, too, I'm told."

Keira glanced over her shoulder and saw Finn's eyebrows shoot up. "You were told?" he asked. "You had someone watching us?"

"Of course," Stefan said, his tone evincing his puzzlement that Finn would be surprised to find this out. "I always have someone keeping an eye out on our new members."

Keira shared another glance with Finn.

"That's why I'm surprised it's taken you so long to bring this to me." His stare was pointed. "You completed your assignment over an hour ago."

What excuse could she give? She didn't want to let on that she and Finn had been intimate with each other. She was pretty sure Stefan wouldn't like that, and if he got jealous it might jeopardize her mission. "I needed to freshen up afterward," she said. "Not to mention refresh my energy," she added. Hopefully he'd form a picture of her frolicking naked on the grass.

From the light in his eyes, she was fairly certain that was what he was thinking. He looked at Finn. "And what were you up to while she was doing all this freshening and refreshing?"

Finn gave one of his half shrugs. "I took a nap."

"Is that right?" That one Stefan didn't seem to buy, but he also didn't seem too interested in pursuing it further.

Keira decided to steer the conversation back to the matter at hand. "Why do you keep new members under surveillance?"

His upper lip lifted in a sneer. "Because they aren't always what they seem, that's why."

"You mean you've had people join who didn't believe in the cause?" Keira asked. *Imagine that.*

"Several months ago, as a matter of fact. A vampire joined our ranks, we think at the behest of the council. He managed to be with us for a few weeks before we caught on." Stefan's eyes hardened. "He was dealt with."

By "dealt with" she knew he meant the vamp had been killed. The same thing that would happen to her if they ever found out she had joined in order to bring them down.

"I'm satisfied that you two are genuine in your aspirations," he said. He stood and walked over to the phone on the wall. Holding the receiver to his ear, he dialed a number and waited. When someone came on the line, he said, "Come see me." He hung up and walked over to Keira. Ignoring Finn, who stood only a foot away, he cupped her chin and stared into her eyes. "I knew you wouldn't let me down." He leaned forward as if to kiss her, and she drew back before he could make contact. He straightened with a frown.

With a flick of her eyes, Keira indicated Finn. She couldn't fake an attraction to Stefan and really sell it to him, with a protective and disapproving Finn standing behind her. Finn, the man she loved. Even pretending to like Stefan was an affront to what she felt for Finn. It left a sour taste in her mouth.

Thank God the comet was due tomorrow. Then, one way or another, this would all be over. She'd either be victorious and Stefan would be behind bars awaiting execution, or he'd be successful and she'd be halfway around the world in her attempt to evade him.

Or she'd be dead. That possibility was never far from her thoughts.

A knock sounded on the door. "Enter," Stefan called out.

Keira altered her position so she stood sideways to the door. That way she could keep an eye on Stefan, Finn, and the vampire Javier who had walked in.

He directed a cool glance toward Finn, a much more heated one to Keira, and a subservient, almost docile look at Stefan. "You need me?"

Stefan handed him the money bag. "Secure this. And meet me later at the machine."

Javier took the money with a nod and left the room.

Stefan stared at Finn. "You may go as well. Thank you for looking out for this lovely lady today."

"Sure." Finn hesitated, his gaze going from Keira to Stefan and back again. "You'll be all right?" he finally asked.

"Your need to protect her is over," Stefan snapped. "She's quite safe with me."

Still Finn didn't budge. Keira sensed anger roiling up in Stefan, like a cauldron of slippery crude oil about to bubble over. "I'm fine," she assured Finn. "I'll call you later."

He gave a nod and reluctantly left the room.

"As a reward for a job well done," Stefan said, taking her by the arm, "I'm going to show you the machine that will bring all our schemes to fruition."

She raised her eyebrows. "Really? How exciting." This had been one of her goals, and it was finally going to happen! "When?"

"Now." He escorted her out of the room and headed toward the back entrance.

"Now?" She glanced over her shoulder but there was no one to come to her rescue, even if Stefan would have let them. If he really had bought her act she was in no danger. But she couldn't stop a shiver that worked its way up her spine.

"Is there a problem?" he asked as they reached the parking lot. The sun had set while she'd been inside, and the lot was illuminated with multiple lamps. She didn't have a jacket with her, and she shivered again as the cool night air caressed her skin. "Oh, no. No problem. I'm just surprised we're going now."

He smiled and helped her into the passenger seat of a large luxury sedan. She watched him as he walked around the front of the car, his wiry frame almost effeminate looking when she mentally compared him to Finn. Looking at him now, if she didn't know what she knew, she'd never guess how incredibly devious and dangerous he was. He had a fairly nondescript appearance. It was only when his eyes took on that mad light that one began to see his true nature.

She wasn't sure what had twisted him, but if he'd been working on this plan ever since he'd come through the rift, it had obviously begun in the other dimension. And she thought it must have been something pretty spectacular to cause such a reaction.

He climbed behind the steering wheel and started the car. "Ordinarily I have a driver, but I don't want to share this moment with anyone else tonight." He sent her a smoldering look. "No one but you."

Oh, no. What else did he have planned other than showing her the machine?

She noticed as he drove he kept checking the rearview and driver's-side mirrors, and the more he did it the more she realized he was checking to make sure they weren't being followed. She stifled a sigh. If she was in trouble here, she could rely only on herself to get out of it.

An hour later he stopped the car at a trailhead northeast of town. "We'll have to hike in from here," he said as he opened his door and illuminated the inside of the car.

Keira glanced down at her feet. She wore her favorite pair of shoes—a bright pink peep toe with a two-inch platform and five inch spike clear acrylic heels. "Ah, Stefan. I can't hike in these." She looked over at him.

"Of course you can't." He got out of the car and came around to her side. After he swung open the door, he held out his hand, palm up in invitation. "Come with me."

She accepted his help to get out of the car and followed him back to the trunk, which he opened using his remote. Inside the trunk was a shoe box. He bent and flipped off the lid, then straightened with the box in his hands. Inside was a pair of brown hiking boots with a pair of white socks lying on top of them. "These should fit."

Keira raised her eyebrows but took the shoes out of the box without comment. She went back to the passenger side of the car and sat sideways on the seat. Taking off her heels, she dropped them onto the floorboard. She rolled the socks onto her feet then pushed her right foot into the hiking boot. So far, so good. She laced it up and then put on the other one. She stood and stomped her feet, walked around in circles a bit, then stopped and looked at Stefan. "They fit."

His smile was pleased. "I thought they would." He reached into the car and took a flashlight from the glove compartment. He shut the door and flicked on the light. "I'm an excellent judge of size."

She'd known many men who could look at a woman and guess her dress size. But shoe size? That was something new.

Setting an easy pace, Stefan took the lead, telling her to stay close. "It's cold enough at night now that snakes aren't out," he said. "But there are always mountain lions to be concerned about."

She blew out a breath and hurried to close the distance between them. After an hour, she was beginning to puff a little. "How much farther?"

"We have at least another hour's walk." He stopped and looked at her. "Do you need a rest?"

She stopped and put her hands on her hips, dragging in deep lungs full of air. "No, but I wish we'd brought some water. My mouth is so dry."

"There's plenty of water at the mine," he said. "Let's go."

"We're going to a mine?" She started walking again, this time at his side.

He gave a nod. The beam of the flashlight threw shadows onto his face, giving him a devilish appearance. "It's a copper mine that played out over a hundred years ago. It's deserted, and the main shaft has a spot that's large enough for the machine."

"And whatever it is that this machine does, it can do it even though it's essentially encased in rocks?" She wasn't an engineer by any stretch of the imagination, but she knew her cell phone cut out whenever she went through a tunnel.

"We have an amplifier that points the radio waves toward the opening of the cave. There is a certain degradation of the signal, but it's still strong enough to get the job done. Once we have the numbers we need, we can dismantle the machine and reassemble it out in the open."

"Why would you need to do that?" She frowned and accepted his help over a rough patch.

He took on that creepy serial killer expression. "I mean for every human being on the planet to become preternatural. With this machine I can open the rift any time I want to."

Her heart rate increased, and not merely from exertion. The climb got steeper and they fell silent. Keira struggled to make sense of what he'd said. He really planned to have prets take over the world.

He was insane.

Finally they stood in front of what appeared to be an abandoned mine, complete with crisscrossed boards blocking the entrance and a sign that read DANGER! DO NOT ENTER attached to them.

Stefan tugged on one side and the boards swung open like a gate. He grinned at her start of surprise. "This way," he murmured. He pulled the gate closed after them and led the way down the mine shaft. They reached a dead end, and with a frown she looked around. Her heart started beating faster, even though she willed it to be normal. She knew Stefan's vampire hearing would pick up on her increased pulse, but she couldn't completely suppress her rising panic. He'd brought her into a mine with only one exit. He knew she was a fraud and was going to kill her, and leave her body up here for the coyotes to scavenge.

"Don't be alarmed," he said. "We're not trapped."

Thank the gods he'd misinterpreted her agitation.

He pressed a protrusion of rock and the wall in front of her slid open.

"It's just like in the movies," she said, wonder in her voice.

"Isn't it, though?" He grinned, his glee like that of a nerdy schoolboy. If he wasn't such a complete whack job, she thought they could have been friends. She wondered what could have happened in the past to have turned a seemingly ordinary guy into a madman. "Come on."

The rock face closed behind them, and lights flickered on, showing a tunnel that headed into the mountain hundreds of yards deep. "This way," Stefan said.

* * *

Finn padded on four paws around a mesquite tree. He'd followed Liuz and Keira, at first on his motorcycle and then, after they'd started up the trail, he'd drawn on his chameleon abilities and shapeshifted into a mountain lion. He'd made sure to stay downwind of them so Liuz with his superior vampire sense of smell wouldn't detect him. Finn didn't know how Liuz would react if he thought he was being stalked by a mountain lion or, rather, a shapeshifter in the form of a mountain lion.

At first Finn had followed the two because he'd been jealous. He was certain Liuz had been about to take Keira home with him. He wasn't sure what he would have done if that had been the case. He really hadn't thought it through. But when the vampire had turned the car off the freeway and headed up into the mountains, curiosity had overtaken jealousy. When Keira changed her shoes it became apparent to him there was going to be walking involved. He knew he'd have an easier time of it going four-footed, so he'd shifted. That had been two hours ago, and he was having a hard time maintaining this form.

He'd slipped down to the mouth of the cave in time to see the rock face slide away to reveal the rest of the tunnel. He knew he couldn't move fast enough to get there before it closed, so he'd decided to reconnoiter the area. Liuz was a lot of things, but he wasn't stupid. There would be guards posted. Finn needed to see how many, and where.

It felt odd, seeing the world through the eyes of a large cat. While colors didn't seem as bright, things were much more defined, and he could see farther and over a wider field of view than he could even with the sharp vision of a demon.

Things smelled differently, too. To take advantage of the superior smell of the cat, he dropped his jaw and wrinkled his muzzle, opening the passage to the sensitive Jacobson's organ at the roof of his mouth. He smelled mesquite, a jackrabbit not that far away, a few deer closer to the foot of the mountain, and there, finally, a waft of preternatural. There seemed to be three distinct types— a werewolf, a vampire, and something else, some sort of shapeshifter he'd never smelled before.

He sidled around a few barrel cacti, made his way past a small group of scrub trees and stopped, straining to see in the darkness to find what his nose told him was just up ahead.

After a few minutes he saw him. The guard, cradling a high-powered rifle complete with scope, was high above the mine, at least two hundred feet up on a rocky ledge. Finn stared at him, trying to figure out how in the hell the guy had gotten up there. He must have rappelled down, he finally decided, because even in his cat form Finn would have a hard time with that terrain. That guard wouldn't be easy to take out, and he had a bird's-eye view of everyone who approached the mine.

Which meant Finn had been spotted, but he didn't sense any alarm on the parts of the guards, so mountain lion sightings around here must be common. He circled around and found the other two prets he'd smelled earlier, one on either side of the cave. Both of them held the same type of weapon as the first man. Their preternatural abilities wouldn't help them take out threats from a distance, but these rifles surely could.

With Keira inside, he didn't want to kill the guards and alert Liuz there was trouble. The vampire would most likely assume Keira had something to do with it and immediately strike out at her. Finn would have to wait and remove the threat when he came back to destroy the machine.

The next time he was here, he'd have reinforcements, and they'd make sure Liuz never completed his plans.

"My comrades in arms in the other dimension have been using the Detention Center to hide criminals who are sympathetic to our cause." Stefan stooped to avoid a low-hanging protrusion. "I set things up with a couple of friends before I used the rift to escape the law all those years ago. I didn't know technology in this dimension would be so primitive. Our people are long lived in the other dimension, but not immortal. So I am now working with the next generation. The sons and daughters of my original friends. Children who were raised to believe in the cause."

Keira didn't respond, willing to let him continue his delusional ranting so she could gather the information she needed.

He seemed happy she was hanging on to his every word. The more he talked, the more full of himself he grew. On her part, she became more and more alarmed at how insane he was.

As they reached a widening of the tunnel, Stefan swept out his arms and said, "Here it is."

Keira stepped around him and stopped to stare at the machine in front of her. It was larger than she'd expected, nearly van size, gunmetal in color with something that looked like an antenna array on one end. Lots of knobs and dials took up the side she could see. Lights blinked, yellow and green, and one button gleamed red.

"Isn't it beautiful?" Admiration colored Stefan's tones in broad strokes.

"I've never really thought of machines as being beautiful," Keira replied. "Though I do think my car is pretty," she allowed.

He laughed. "See? You *do* think they can be beautiful." He crossed his arms and stared at the rift machine like a proud papa. "This thing is the key to my plan. It will keep the rift open for as long as it's running. My comrades on the other side have assured me that there is quadruple the number of prets ready to come through the rift." He glanced at her. "Right now preternaturals are only about three percent of the population in the U.S. According to my comrades' records, every seventy-three years approximately twenty thousand people are stripped of their bodies and sent through the rift."

Those were not exactly staggering numbers. "Three percent of the population is something like…" She did a rough calculation in her head. "A little over nine million?"

"Right." He looked impressed with her mathematical skills. "Imagine with this Influx that we can multiply that number by four. That puts us up to ten percent." He stepped closer to the machine and ran his hand over the metal. "As soon as my friends have more preternaturals ready, we can activate this machine and open the rift on our own, any time we need to. Any time we *want* to."

Keira walked a little closer, too. "Does the rift work both ways?"

Puzzlement dropped his brows low over his eyes.

"I mean, can you fix it so entities can be sent from this dimension to the other one?" Maybe one way to help save humanity would be to send the entities from the other dimension right back to where they'd come from. Perhaps the souls could be salvaged without lasting damage, letting humans continue to live out their lives as they were meant to.

He cocked his head. "I suppose it could be done to make the rift available to either side. But we don't have the technology available for the body-stripping process," he said. "And, besides, why would any of us want to go back? There we would grow old and die. Here, once our essence combines with our human hosts, we can live forever." He stroked his hand across the machine again. "It won't be long before we outnumber humans, or at least aren't as much of a minority. Then we'll see who has the power."

Keira turned around and made a pretense out of studying the rest of the roomlike structure they were in. As soon as she was able to get out of here, she had to contact Caladh and let him know the location of this mine. She also had to make it clear to him that, whatever happened, Finn was not to be hurt. As long as she stuck close to him she might be able to keep him out of harm's way. With everything they'd been through, it had to count for something.

One thing was certain. Stefan must not be allowed to succeed.

Chapter Seventeen

Just after sunrise the next morning, Finn put in a call to Nix's cell phone. He figured if anyone from the rogue group was still watching, he was safe to call the daughter of his father's girlfriend. Thus far, no one had suspected him in Tobias's murder. When she answered and realized it was him, she put him on speakerphone. Finn let her and Tobias know what had been happening, and gave them directions to the mine, "I'll meet you there around noon," he said. "I have a little business to take care of first."

"Business such as?" Tobias asked.

"Liuz has sentries posted. I have to take them out before we can even hope to get into the mine."

"We can help you with that, you know."

Finn snorted. "They'd smell the two of you coming a mile away. It's better for me to do this on my own."

"All right." Tobias shushed Nix when she started to object. "Trust me, honey, Finn will be all right. They won't know what hit them."

Finn felt burgeoning pleasure at the unexpected praise. "You know, for a vampire, Caine, you aren't half bad." He laughed at Caine's pithy response and rang off.

While mentally preparing himself, he physically

geared up for battle. He attached his holstered Glock to his belt, shrugged into the scabbard sheath that held a short sword between his shoulder blades, then finished dressing. Before heading out the door he grabbed a plastic bag—he'd need that for his clothes later on. He hadn't thought about it last night, and had to shake a lot of dirt out of his clothing before he could redress.

Two hours later he paused about half a mile away from the mine. Stooping behind a large boulder, he got undressed, putting both his clothing and his weapons into the bag and stashing it between a big boulder and a smaller one.

With a slight grunt he focused his energy inward and reached for his chameleon ability. In a few seconds he was a mountain lion again, panting through the pain of the metamorphosis. His eagerness to take care of business helped mitigate the discomfort, though, and he was soon on his way.

The sentry who'd been on the ledge above the mine was higher up, in a spot that would be easier for Finn to reach. He ran his wide tongue over his whiskers and padded forward. He stalked toward the guard, sometimes moving only a millimeter at a time. The sun was nearly overhead when he was finally able to pounce on the man from behind. Finn quickly chomped down on the sentry's throat, ripping away his ability to scream and ending his life.

As he padded off, he knew it had taken him longer than he'd anticipated to reach the sentry. He had to take out the other two quickly, before Tobias and Nix started up the trail, or this fight would be over before it got started. Liuz would realize that Tobias wasn't dead, which would lead him to the realization that Finn had not carried out his orders. That would make him realize Finn wasn't on his side after all, and things would go seriously downhill from there.

The other two guards were easier to take out than the first one had been. It was over before either of them could get off a shot. Finn clamped his powerful jaws in the vampire guard's shoulder and dragged him into the brush to hide him, then did the same to the other pret. Once finished, he loped back to where he'd left his clothing and weapons.

He pushed his chameleon demon back and shifted to his humanoid form. He closed his eyes and leaned against the side of a large boulder, panting through the last of the transformation, and tried to ignore the fatigue tugging at his muscles. He got dressed and rearmed, then made his way back to the mine, this time on two feet. As he approached the entrance, he smelled the sweet grass scent of heather and stopped moving. He looked around but didn't see anyone. Yet, as soon as he took a step toward the mine Keira stepped out into the direct sunlight.

She wore black pants that hugged her shapely legs, a knit top, and thick-soled boots. When she shot a quick glance around, he saw that her gorgeous hair was in a tight braid wound around the back of her head. She turned toward him and stared. "That's far enough, Finn," she said. "Did you do something to the guards?"

What the hell was she doing here? She was going to ruin everything. "Yes, I did. Now, Keira, get out of my way."

"No." She shook her head. "You need to go. I can't let you ruin everything I've worked for."

"Don't you mean we?" he muttered.

She scowled. "What nonsense are you spouting now?"

"We as in you and your toothy lover boy."

"Stefan?" Her scowl darkened and a look of distaste flickered in her eyes. "I've told you. He's not my lover."

Finn shoved back the elation that tried to surface at her disavowal of the rogue leader. He walked a few feet forward and scowled when she moved to block him. "Keira, get out of the way."

"You shouldn't be here," she said.

"Me?" He glared at her. "What about you?"

"I—" Her fists clenched at her sides. "What does it matter to you?"

"It matters because I care about you. I want you to be safe." He took a deep breath and held it a moment before exhaling. He had to get through to her. "Look, I know you want Stefan's plan to succeed, but I can't let that happen."

She gasped. "Finn, I don't want him to succeed." Guilt passed through her eyes. "I'm here to take care of that bloody machine once and for all."

Finn felt like he'd come into a conversation midway and didn't have a clue what was going on. "What exactly do you mean by, 'take care of the machine'?"

"I mean to destroy it," she said.

Now it was his turn to be stunned. And disbelieving.

Her gaze turned pleading. "Finn, don't you see? What he wants to do is wrong, on so many levels. Not least of which is the fact that bringing such a high number of new prets through the rift will only further enflame relations between preternaturals and humans. He's putting all of us in danger."

Finn moved closer to Keira and studied her, trying to

gauge her sincerity. "You've been acting as a spy all this time?"

She nodded. "For Caladh. He came to me months ago and asked for my help." She paused and her lips tightened. "No, that's not quite accurate. He basically blackmailed me into helping him."

Finn's gut tightened. He knew Keira had history. Hell, she was three thousand years old, so of course she'd done things she might not be proud of, above and beyond grifting. But something she could be blackmailed over?

"It's true," she whispered. "Many years ago I fell in love with a man who I thought loved me, who I thought I was helping by agreeing to run a job on a wealthy mark. Even though I'd stopped grifting several centuries before, I came out of retirement. And just like now, on the jobs I pulled with you, there was no getting back into the groove, no trying to remember how to do something. It was as easy and natural to me as breathing." Her blue eyes took on a slight sheen of tears. "He was only using me, but that's not the worst of it. Due to our actions, the mark died. Not by our hands, but because of the circumstances we manipulated." A tear slid from the corner of her eye and she quickly wiped it away. "It's something I'm deeply ashamed of and an action which I've been trying to atone for ever since. I thought if I could do this, if I could stop Stefan from ruining countless lives, it might make up in some small way for my lack of judgment before."

Finn had to accept Keira was telling the truth. His initial instinct about her had been right—she was trying to be better. She studied him as closely as he had her. "You believe me then?"

He gave a nod. "I believe you. That's why I'm here, too. To stop Liuz."

"You..." Her eyes widened. "You killed Tobias!"

"No, I didn't." When she looked doubtful, he said, "You'll see soon enough. Let's go."

The thought crossed Keira's mind that Finn might be lying, trying to fake her out. However, if that was the case, why hadn't he killed her while he'd had the chance?

Either way she'd get close to the machine. She wasn't quite sure what she was going to do once she did, she was making this up as she went. She'd been a warrior queen once upon a time, but that had been fighting other tribes with spears and arrows, not trying to take out a great metal beast.

Finn checked his watch. "The next rift is due to open in two hours. We're cutting it close." He frowned. "I've already contacted Tobias and Nix. They should be here pretty soon."

She gave a nod, then what he'd said really filtered in. "Wait." She watched a slow grin curl his sensual lips. "You really didn't kill him?"

"I told you I didn't."

Keira allowed herself to feel hope for the first time in a long time. Something else fought its way up from the depths of her soul, too: a sense that, working with Finn at her side, there wasn't anything they couldn't do.

She was relieved that Finn wasn't the bad boy she'd thought he was. There was good in him, even though he did his best to downplay it. She'd known that; it was one of the reasons she'd fallen in love with him. She should have had more faith in her own judgment.

Finn cast another glance at his wristwatch then looked at the trail. "Damn it. Where are they?" His gaze snagged hers. "I don't think we can wait. Liuz is probably in there right now firing up that machine."

"What's your plan?" she asked.

"We go in there, fight the bad guys, and disable the machine."

She blinked. "That's it?" She couldn't keep the shrill incredulity from her voice.

"I never said it was a good plan," he defended.

"How about we go in, you take care of the bad guys, and I'll sweet talk Stefan until I can get close enough to the machine?"

"I'm not sure that plan's any better than mine," he muttered. "But I like it. Let's go."

She shook her head at his grin and followed him into the mine. They reached the juncture right before the shaft seemed to dead end. Two burly vampires stood on either side of the shaft, leaning broad shoulders against the wall of the mine. Upon seeing the intruders, they straightened from their relaxed posture.

"You're not authorized to be here," the one on the left said.

Keira took a step forward and pushed out with her empathy. "Oh, Stefan asked us to come," she said. She tried to wrap both vamps in a comfy cloak of camaraderie, but they weren't having any part of it.

"Oh, the hell with it," Finn muttered and launched himself at both vamps. "Get out of here," he told Keira as he dodged their fists. "I've got these two."

One of the vampires struck him in the jaw, sending him staggering back several feet.

"Oh, you do, do you?" Keira drew her dagger and stepped into the fray. She was smaller and lighter than her opponent, who looked like he'd been a boxer back in the day. She couldn't tell how old he was, though she sensed he had been turned rather than coming through the rift. He was probably one of Stefan's converts after he'd arrived on Earth.

She figured as long as she stayed out of reach she'd do okay. So she took a page out of Muhammad Ali's playbook and danced around, jabbing out with her dagger every time she saw an opening.

Soon the vamp was bleeding from several cuts, some of them deep, and he was getting madder by the minute. Which suited her just fine, because the more he let his emotions control him, the bigger her advantage.

"I am gonna gut you with your own knife," he promised her, his pupils so dilated she couldn't see any hint of iris. Crimson filled the whites of his eyes, unspoken testament to how she'd riled him. Vamps were fast, but she was pretty quick, too. He charged her, a move she easily sidestepped. She hadn't counted on how quickly he'd recover his momentum, though, and he grabbed her arm as he turned around. "You're mine now, you little fey bitch."

"I don't think so," she muttered. Reaching forward and down, she grabbed his balls and squeezed as hard as she could. His free hand came up and wrapped around her throat. Okay, maybe not the smartest move she could have made, but it would be interesting to see who passed out first: Her or Mr. Numbnuts. If she could only get her bare skin on the Earth beneath her feet, she might be able to get a boost of energy.

She sagged in his grasp, pulling him off balance. They went down in a tangle of limbs. She still had her hand wrapped around his testicles, and he continued to choke her. As soon as her head hit the dirt, she focused on drawing more energy from the Earth. There wasn't much to draw on, and she realized it was because nothing was alive here. It was all soil and rock. There was some energy because of the surrounding area that had plant life, but directly beneath her...she might as well be in a barren desert.

She was able to draw enough to give herself a tiny boost of strength. He must have realized what she was doing, but it was too late. His eyes widened just as she broke his hold on her arm and brought her dagger to his throat. A couple of quick slashes ended him, and she pushed his corpse off her. She grimaced at the warm blood she could feel sliding down her face. She swiped at it with her sleeve, wiping it off as best as she could, then turned to see how Finn was faring.

He slammed his vamp up against the wall of the mine with enough force to split his skull. He let the vampire fall to the ground and looked around, his gaze a little wild. When he saw her, his eyes widened and he hurried over to her. "Keira," he said, his hands coming up to cup her face. "You're bleeding."

"It's not mine," she whispered. He didn't seem to hear her, and now his gaze was fixed on her throat where she imagined the imprint of the vamp's hand still showed. She rested her palm on his lean cheek and said, "Finn, I'm all right."

He looked into her eyes and some of the worry left him at her words. "Good," he muttered. "That's good."

She dropped her hand and took a step back. She cleared her throat. "What do you say we go take care of that machine?"

Finn ran his tongue over his lips. "Why don't you hang back and let me take care of that? You've done enough."

She sighed. On one level she understood his need to protect those he saw as weaker than himself; he wasn't one to exploit weakness unless it was in the enemy. On the other hand, it rankled that he wanted her to stay behind like a good woman should. "You know what? You have more machismo in your little finger than any other man I know." She propped her hands on her hips and scowled at him.

"You sure it's not this finger?" he asked, flicking up his middle finger.

That made her laugh. "Come on," she said with a shake of her head. "We still have work to do." His face, as he realized she wasn't going to stay behind like a good little woman should, would have been comical if the circumstances were different.

As they approached the sliding wall, she sobered. With her hand on the rock mechanism that operated the wall, she looked at Finn. "You ready?"

"Wait a sec." He searched around until he found a sizable rock. He hefted it in one hand and nodded. "Let's do this."

She opened the wall. As it began to close behind them, Finn set the rock on the ground in the opening, making sure it blocked the doorway from completely closing. Then they made their way into the large chamber of the mine where the machine was housed.

Liuz stood beside the machine, twisting dials and fiddling with the array. Several other prets were there as well, each engrossed in their duties. One was bent over a laptop, another stood next to the antenna array, and two others prowled on the other side of the machine, no doubt guarding it from intruders who might find another way into the mine.

She caught the thumbs up that Finn gave her. He stayed to the shadows and moved soundlessly around the wide shaft, heading toward the man on the laptop.

Keira drew in a deep breath and started walking in Stefan's direction. He wasn't yet aware of her presence. Pulling a cell phone–size device out of the front pocket of his slacks, he twisted a dial and started talking in the standard language of the other dimension. She heard the tinny response from the person on the other end, assuring Stefan that all was ready on that side of the rift.

Good God, this really was happening. Her heart stuttered and her palms began to perspire. They had to stop this madman!

Stefan lifted his head, nostrils flaring, and looked at her. Confusion, irritation, and then growing anger flitted over his face. "What are you doing here? You weren't invited." Concern flicked through his eyes. "You're bleeding."

"I'm fine, Stefan. It's not my blood." Having replenished her energy from her time on the ground beneath the now dead vamp, Keira projected a feeling of lust and pride toward him. "I couldn't miss this, Stefan," she said, putting just a bit of whine in her voice. "I want to be with you during your time of triumph." She continued moving forward, keeping one eye on the gal who, when Stefan hadn't sounded the alarm, turned back to the array.

In her peripheral vision Keira saw Finn put his hands on the laptop guy. She started talking to cover up the sound of the man's neck breaking as Finn twisted his head. She pushed a little harder, focusing her empathy directly on Stefan.

He relaxed, his face going a little slack, and let her get closer. But as soon as she reached him he seemed to overcome her empathetic push. He let out a little growl and said, "Why are you covered in blood? If it's not yours, as you say, then whose is it?" He looked over her shoulder. His eyes widened and she had no doubt he had seen the stone doorway was ajar. He reached out for her, his face dark with rage, but Finn jumped forward and punched him in the face.

Stefan staggered back, but quickly recovered and launched himself at Finn with a roar of fury. Keira drew her dagger and headed toward the young woman who stood at the antenna array, the woman's face holding an expression of indecision. "Make your choice," Keira told her. She hefted the dagger. "I've already taken out a vamp with this. Don't underestimate my skills or my determination."

"I...I'm only here because of my boyfriend," she stammered.

The young woman didn't smell more than fifty or so years old. She'd probably been born here on Earth, of two fey parents who had most likely kept her very sheltered.

"Go," Keira said. "And don't come back."

"Thank you," she whispered. She took off running.

Keira turned to face the other two prets coming toward her. One was a demon—a big, tall man with gleaming yellow eyes and nasty written all over his flat face. The other one, a werewolf by the smell of him, was smaller than the demon but still bigger than she was.

"Don't think you're going to scare us with that little dagger," the demon said. "As soon as we get through with you, we're going to take care of your friend there." He looked entirely too enthusiastic about the prospect for her comfort.

She couldn't let them get to Finn, not while he was grappling with Stefan. She had no doubt he could hold his own against two, but three was pushing it, even for him. The demon and werewolf came at her together, and she ducked and struck out with her dagger, catching the werewolf along his ribcage as she rolled out of the way.

"You're gonna pay for that," he snarled.

"Yeah, yeah," she muttered.

The rest of the fight went by in silence punctuated only by the grunts and growls of the combatants. She took a punch to the face. The flash of pain across her cheekbone made her eyes water. She swiped them away and lashed out with one foot, catching the werewolf in the midsection and knocking the breath from him.

The demon reached for her, and she heard Finn say, "Don't let him touch you, Keira. He's Surtur."

Her eyes widened. She bobbed and weaved, eluding the Surtur's reach. She'd never met one before, but she'd heard of them. They were the fire giants of legend and were the worst of the worst.

She tried to keep the machine at her back, and keep her eyes on both assailants, without success. The werewolf grabbed her from behind, his arms trapping hers at her sides. She struggled, bucking and twisting, but couldn't break his hold.

The Surtur started forward with an unholy glee glittering in his eyes. "You picked the wrong side, sweetheart. Now it's time for you to die."

Keira's heart pounded against her ribs. She wet her dry lips and waited for him to get close enough. Then with a soft grunt she pushed her feet off the ground and slammed them into his chest. The action knocked him back several feet, and it also rocked the werewolf off balance. His arms loosened. Not by much, but it was enough.

She broke free and slashed out with her dagger, catching the werewolf behind one knee. He went down with a yelp, holding his leg. She knew if he'd fed recently he wouldn't be down for long because his metabolism would enable him to heal rapidly. No, she had to do more damage. Permanent, not-able-to-recover-from damage.

With another couple of quick slashes, she cut a deep gash across his belly and one across his throat. "I'm sorry," she whispered. It had been millennia since she'd been in battle, but the sadness of taking another's life, even if he was the enemy, was the same now as then.

She twisted to face the Surtur and froze as she saw him closing in on Finn. "Finn!" she cried out in warning. "Behind you."

Finn whirled to face the new danger. He avoided his assailant's grasp and threw a sneer his way. "You've backed the losing team, Phoebus," he said. He lifted his arm and drew his short sword from the scabbard between his shoulder blades.

"Funny, I was just about to tell you the same thing," the Surtur demon responded. "Guess we'll see who's right."

"Guess we will." Finn dodged Phoebus's lunge and slashed downward with his blade.

Phoebus drew back in time and only the tip of the sword raked across his biceps. Still it was enough to cause pain, and yellow flared in his eyes. The next time he lunged, Finn closed the distance and thrust his sword forward deep into his enemy's gut.

Phoebus's eyes widened and he gasped. As Finn withdrew the sword and retreated a few feet away, Phoebus pressed his hands to his wound and staggered back. He lifted bewildered eyes.

"You always did rely too much on your ability," Finn muttered. He hefted his sword. "You should've learned how to fight." With that his blade sliced through the air and Phoebus's neck. Finn stared at the head at his feet. "Well, it's not on a platter, but it'll do."

He turned to see that Keira had squared off with Liuz. As Finn started forward, the vampire got past Keira's defensive moves and wrapped an arm around her throat. She'd lost her dagger at some point, and dug her fingers into his arm to try to loosen his hold. Her gaze, filled with anger, fear, and exhaustion, met Finn's. He realized whatever energy she had was depleted, and she wasn't strong enough to break free from Liuz.

"Back off," the vampire snarled, "or I'll kill her."

Finn forced all emotion aside. He couldn't allow himself to be distracted by fear for Keira or rage that Liuz had dared to threaten her. Coldness filled him, an iciness that drove out everything but the certainty that Liuz was a dead man. "Go ahead," Finn finally responded to the vamp's threat. "I'm here to do a job. Regardless of any peripheral damage, that's what I aim to do." He met

Keira's gaze and kept his free of emotion. "I don't care about her." He put his attention back on Liuz. "As an enforcer I've been trained to focus on what matters. I care only about the successful completion of my mission." He lifted one shoulder in a shrug. "Kill her and you lose your advantage. You'll make my job that much easier."

Chapter Eighteen

Keira felt her pulse jump in her throat. Finn had to be bluffing. He couldn't really mean it. He couldn't care more about his mission than he did about her life. She reached out with her empathic ability and drew a sharp breath. There was no insincerity from him, no doubt, no fear. Just the certainty that what he was doing was right.

She searched his eyes, looking for a hint of the gentleness she'd sensed in him before, the softness she'd experienced firsthand. There was only hardness. He might as well be wearing armor.

He was a warrior first and foremost. Always. Only.

This was the real Finn, then. This man toughened by his experiences, jaded by the life he'd lived. And she was to become the latest casualty of war, not even a blip on his radar.

The Finn she'd seen before, the one who'd told her he wanted something different, had all been an act so he could get past her defenses. So he could use her body to assuage his lust.

He must have lied to her when he told her that Tobias was still alive. If it furthered his mission, whatever that mission was, she believed he would kill Tobias.

And lie about his feelings for her.

She stiffened in Stefan's grasp, listening with disbelief and sorrow as Finn told him how he'd gotten into this to gain his freedom from his father, who for his own reasons didn't want more preternaturals coming through the rift.

"Personally," Finn said, "I don't care what kind of havoc you plan to create." He took a few steps forward. "And if a few prets have to die in order to preserve the old order, so be it." He moved a little closer. "Sorry, doll," he said to Keira.

"I'd tell you to go to hell," she replied, blinking back tears. "But you'd probably enjoy it there."

His lips twitched. "I might." He walked forward several steps, stopping only when Stefan told him to. "There's no way out, Liuz," Finn murmured. "Let her go and let's settle this between us."

Stefan tightened his arm, closing off her air supply even further. Keira clawed at him and fought to breathe.

Over Finn's shoulder she saw movement, and as she was about to call out a warning—she couldn't help it, she still loved the bastard—she recognized the man and woman walking into view. Tobias Caine and the woman that Finn had gone to see at her house.

Hope unfurled within Keira. If Tobias was here, obviously alive and unharmed, that meant Finn hadn't killed him. He'd been lying all along. She met his gaze. He obviously knew she'd thought the worst of him, because his eyes chided her yet held such affection for her. She was ashamed she'd ever doubted him.

Stefan, on the other hand, wasn't feeling so generous. Rage emanated from him. "You!" he snarled. "I thought you were dead."

"Obviously not. Once again the master manipulator missed," Tobias rejoined. A world of satisfaction and triumph rode the curve of his lips.

Stefan's arm tightened again. Keira choked, gasping for air. She wished everyone would stop yacking and get on with it. She'd like to start breathing again, soon.

"Everything you've told me, everything you've done," Stefan said, "has been a lie?"

Finn raised his eyebrows. "I'm surprised you didn't have more people joining your group so they could stop your insanity."

"I suppose you were in on it too, weren't you?"

She felt Stefan's face move against hers and guessed he was talking to her. She couldn't respond—she didn't have enough voice to speak, and the way he had his arm wrapped around her throat limited the movement of her head.

"Let Keira go," Finn said. "If you don't hurt her, you might come out of this with your head intact."

"We have over an hour until the rift," Stefan said. "I can hold on to her that long, and then I win."

Keira slumped a little in his grip. Part of it was playacting; a larger part was because her vision was beginning to go dark from lack of oxygen.

"There's no way you come out of this as anything but the loser you really are," Tobias said. Satisfaction rode every lean line of his body. And something more, a savage fury that radiated from him in waves.

The woman with him—another vampire—felt just as strongly, though Keira sensed she was restraining herself a little more than Tobias was. The female vamp took a step forward. "You and I have some unfinished business,

Natchook. There's a little matter of you putting out a hit on my husband. And, oh, yeah." Her eyes narrowed. "You nearly killing me a year ago."

"Nix, my dear. How good to see you again. You're looking well." Keira couldn't see his face, but she heard the smirk in his voice. Stefan asked, "Has it been a year already?" By Dagda's balls, the man did not know when to quit.

"Nearly." Nix took another step forward. "And I see nothing has changed, you're still hiding behind a woman." Disgust colored her tones. "Can't fight your own battles, eh?"

Keira felt rage and anxiety rolling off Stefan and, for a brief second or two, doubt. She took advantage, letting herself go completely slack as if she'd fainted. Her action pulled him off balance, and he loosened his hold. She jabbed back with her elbow and ducked beneath his arm.

Finn jumped in, pushing the vampire away from her, and he and Stefan went at it with their fists. Very quickly blood smeared both their faces as lips split and knuckles crunched into bone.

"He's mine," Tobias bellowed. Keira looked to see him heading toward the combatants, his eyes black surrounded by crimson.

Stefan bit down into the fleshy part of Finn's shoulder. Finn yelled, his face contorted in pain. "Then come and get the bastard," he snarled and slammed his fist into the vampire's temple. It loosened Stefan's hold on him and Finn shoved him away.

Tobias jumped into the fray, landing several blows before Stefan turned and ran deeper into the mine. Tobias, Finn, and Nix all started after him, Keira on their heels.

Tobias caught up with him after several yards, but Stefan shrugged out of his jacket, leaving it hanging in Tobias's grip, and kept running. They took up pursuit again.

The further into the mountain they went, the colder it got. The shaft sloped downward, then hooked up with other shafts so that they zigzagged their way after Stefan. Keira hoped to God someone remembered the way back, because she was now completely turned around.

She was chagrined to realize they were all so much faster than her. Not because she was a slacker, but because Tobias and Nix were vampires who naturally were capable of moving at much greater rates of speed than other preternaturals, and Finn... Well, this was what Finn did for a living. He was used to chasing after fleeing subjects.

She redoubled her efforts and turned the corner into another shaft. The others were several yards ahead of her and it looked like Tobias was once again closing the gap. Stefan glanced over his shoulder, his expression a mixture of anger and disillusion, and maybe even a little fear. As he turned his head forward again Caladh stepped out from a cross-shaft, a wooden stake in his hand.

Stefan's own momentum drove him into the stake. He let out a gasp and looked down, then dropped to the ground.

Keira ran up to the group and stopped beside Finn. She wrapped her arm around his inner elbow, gratified when his bigger hand came up and curled over hers. The warmth of it took away some of the coldness of her skin. And, more than that, it gave her comfort.

Tobias knelt beside the fallen vampire. His face grim, he muttered, "Damn it."

"Isn't he dead?" Finn asked.

"Yes. Damn it."

Finn shared a glance with Keira. "I, uh, thought that was what you wanted. Him dead."

"He wanted to be the one to do it," Nix said. She walked up to her husband and urged him to his feet. Bringing one hand to his face, she cradled his jaw. "It's done, Tobias. He's finally paid for his crimes."

He reached up and clasped her hand in his, and turned his head to press a kiss into her palm. The love between them was obvious, and Keira felt a pang of envy. Why did that type of love always seem to elude her?

Tobias let out a long sigh and turned away from the body, keeping his wife's hand in his.

All of them stood in silence for a few seconds. Keira knew everyone else felt as much relief that the crisis was over as she did. All that remained was the dismantling of the machine. She was about to suggest as much when Tobias spoke again.

"You have perfect timing, my friend." He held out his hand to shake Caladh's. "I only wish we'd known we were on the same side."

"Hey!" Finn shot the vamp a frown. "Just because Liuz was running didn't mean he was going to get away. We would've caught him."

"Of course," Caladh said, a jovial smile on his face. As usual he was dressed smartly, his white long-sleeved shirt crisp and bright, his charcoal-gray slacks tailored to a perfect fit. "I am happy I could be of assistance to such brave and fearless people."

"I don't know about the fearless part," Keira muttered. "I was plenty scared." Finn slid his arm around her shoul-

ders and gave her a quick squeeze. She slipped her arm
around his waist and stared at Caladh. "How did you
know to show up when you did?" When the others looked
at her, she said, "I was working for him, that's the whole
reason I infiltrated the group. To stop them. At his behest."

She heard Finn's sharply drawn breath and glanced up
at him. "I couldn't tell you," she whispered. "I wanted to,
many times."

"Same here." His dark blue eyes began to shimmer
with hope and something she was afraid to even dream
that looked like love.

Dragging her gaze away from his, she looked at Caladh again. As she realized what his being here meant,
her heart started a reggae beat behind her rib cage. "You
didn't return any of my calls. I never had a chance to
tell you the location of the machine." She took a few
steps away from Finn and closer to the selkie councilor.
"How did you even know where we were? Where the machine was? And how did you get in here without coming
through the main entrance?"

Finn went cold, then hot as the impact of Keira's words
hit him. "The council was behind this?"

"No." Tobias stared at Caladh. "They weren't." He
glanced at Keira. "Were you working for the council at
large? Did Deoul have Caladh ask you to do this?"

She shook her head. "It was just Caladh. He said he
wasn't sure who on the council he could trust, so we were
to keep this between us." She bit her lip and then whispered, "I trusted you."

"I told you not to trust anyone." He seemed pleased

with himself, an odd attitude to take considering he was so outnumbered. Tobias still had a look of bloodlust about him, and Finn looked ready to strangle Caladh with his bare hands.

"You put Keira in danger for nothing?" Finn took a step forward. "Why the pretense? Why hide behind Liuz?"

Caladh didn't respond.

Finn thought he understood. "It kept everyone's focus on Liuz, and off you." He narrowed his eyes. "That's it, isn't it? You let him manipulate people, use them, but all the while he was only a marionette dancing to your tug of the strings. Did he even realize you were using him?"

Caladh chuckled. "He was such a stupid little shit. Of course he never realized he was merely another cog in the wheel. He thought he was the wheel, turning and shaping events to bring in a new world order."

Finn took a deep breath and held it a moment while he sorted through his racing thoughts.

"What are you up to, Caladh?" This from Tobias, whose face had darkened as he came to realize the extent of his coworker and friend's perfidy. "What exactly didn't you want anyone to see?"

"His bid to take over the council," Keira answered. "*You* killed Deoul so you could be moved into the position of president. Start with the regional council, then work your way out to what? Setting up a national council? Or a worldwide one?"

"That would presume my ambitions are limited to the preternatural community," Caladh said.

Finn noticed he didn't deny killing Deoul.

"And they're not, that's what you're saying?" Nix's

lovely face creased in a frown. "Oh, for God's sake. Don't tell me this is a ploy to take over the world." She rolled her eyes. Finn was happy to see she was still as snarky as ever, and not only with him. She hadn't let a little thing like being turned into a vampire change her for the worse. She propped her hands on her hips. "Couldn't you come up with something more original than that?"

"You watch your tone, Ms. de la Fuente." Caladh's face blackened with a scowl.

"Or what? You'll fire me? Oh, you can't do that, 'cause I don't work for the council anymore." Her scowl matched his in ferocity. "And it's Mrs. Caine now, thank you very much."

"Enough!" Finn took a step forward. As much as he enjoyed watching Nix cut the selkie down to size, they had to get moving. "We need to disable that machine and take him"—he jerked his chin toward Caladh—"to council headquarters. Let them sort out what to do with him."

"Are you sure none of them are involved in this?" Keira asked.

Finn looked to Tobias, who shrugged. "I have no idea," the vampire said. "But we have to start somewhere."

Finn started toward Caladh. The councilor drew a pistol from behind his back. "This is loaded with silver bullets, for the werewolves. And I have enough iron mixed in to cause any fey extreme discomfort. Of course, they won't do lasting damage to a vampire, but one of these will put a vamp down for the count for a while. And if it stays in the body long enough, werewolf or fey, you will die."

"Neither silver nor iron is poisonous to demons." Finn stopped and stared at the selkie. "You'd better have good aim, brother, 'cause you've only got one chance before I rip your heart out."

"And here I thought you were going to take me in." Sarcasm dripped from his words like poisoned honey.

"That was before you pulled a gun. So make it count." Finn watched as the gun started to swing toward Keira. Without thinking, he drew on his chameleon abilities and shifted into a vampire, vaulting through the air to crash into Caladh, deflecting his aim.

Being the slippery seal he was, the councilor rolled to his feet and ran down the mine shaft.

Finn took off in pursuit, the others charging behind him.

"We don't have time for this," Caine called out.

"You go take care of the machine," Finn yelled. "I've got this."

Caladh pointed the gun over his shoulder and pulled the trigger, firing blindly as he continued to run.

A bullet ricocheted off the rock wall near Finn, sending sharp shards of stone hurling toward his face. As a couple of them struck him, he grunted at the pain but didn't slow his pace.

Another couple of shots. He heard Keira scream. As he slowed and looked over his shoulder, he saw her fall to the ground. He stopped short and headed back toward her. Caladh wouldn't get away. Not from him. But right now all Finn could focus on was saving his woman.

Chapter Nineteen

Keira saw the indecision in the gazes of those gathered around, but there was nothing they could do for her. "Go," she told them, trying not to cry at the agony. Keira pressed her hands against her wound and fought for breath. By Dagda's balls, it hurt. As the iron from the bullet seeped into her blood, tendrils of fire licked outward from the wound. Keeping one hand on her injury, she placed the other one palm down on the packed dirt floor of the main shaft and tried to draw energy from the Earth.

It was like trying to strain peanut butter through cheesecloth. The iron in her bloodstream blocked almost all the absorption of any of nature's vitality. Maybe if she could get outside, where there were plant roots to also draw from, it might be better. Right now she knew that moving would be a very bad idea. Without letting on how badly she was hurt, she said, "I'll be all right."

"Go," Finn echoed as he knelt beside her. "I'll stay with Keira."

Tobias hesitated for one more second, then muttered "Come on" to his wife. The two vampires took off at a full-out run.

"Boy, I do not envy Caladh when those two catch up to him," Finn said. "Ultimately it's his fault that Nix was turned, since Caladh, as you so eloquently put it, was the one pulling Liuz's strings." He stared down at her and brushed her hair from her sweaty brow. "I'm so sorry, Keira. I should have done something, stopped him."

She shook her head. "There wasn't anything you could have done. You should go, help them," she whispered. She struggled to sit up and bit back a cry. Her left arm was numb, but the wound pulsed with flashes of pain that she'd aggravated by moving.

Finn braced her with his bent leg behind her back. "A couple of vamps can handle one lone selkie." His face was grim, his eyes churned with worry mixed with anger. "I'm not going to leave you while you're hurt and unprotected."

"Well, if it weren't for this," she said, dipping her chin toward her chest, "I could take care of myself."

Finn's grin lightened his beautiful eyes. "I have no doubt about that at all. I always figured you had some Boadicea in you. Tonight proved me right." The smile left him and he stroked his fingers down her cheek. "God, you were gorgeous. A little scary, to be honest."

She laughed and then grimaced as her chest hurt in protest. "You've never been scared of me."

"You don't think so?" He shook his head. "You'd be surprised." He gave her a short, sweet smile and then stared down at her with eyes gone dark and tortured.

"Don't, Finn," she said. "This isn't your fault."

He didn't say anything, but she could see by the look on his face that he didn't agree with her.

From deeper in the mine came the sound of a struggle.

When she thought she heard the snarls of wolves, Keira frowned. Within a few minutes, Caladh stumbled into view. His appearance was no longer crisp and neat. Blood streamed from his nose and mouth and stained the shoulder of his torn, dirty shirt. He was followed by Tobias and Nix. Behind them came a woman clad in a long shirt and a man wearing only pants. Both were barefooted.

She recognized the woman. It was Tori Joseph, one of the werewolf liaisons to the council. The man was familiar as well, but Keira couldn't recall his name.

"Sorry we were late to the party," Tori said. Her gaze strayed to the body of her cousin lying on the floor of the mine shaft. Her full lips tightened.

"Better late than never," Finn responded. "Though you're both a little underdressed."

Tori looked at him, a slight blush staining her cheeks. "You know if we want to preserve our clothes we have to take them off before we shift. Mine fell down a hole. A really deep hole. So I'm wearing Dante's shirt."

That was who he was, Keira thought. Dante MacMillan, a police detective with the city. Well, probably not anymore, since she could sense he was a werewolf.

"And she knocked our shoes down the hole, too," Dante offered. His lips curved into a grin but even through the filter of pain Keira saw his sharp gaze didn't miss a thing.

Finn gave a slight roll of his eyes and muttered something about werewolves and idiots. "And why are you here?" he asked.

"I thought we might need their help," Tobias said. He had one hand wrapped around Caladh's upper arm.

Nix stood nearby, her eyes stormy yellow. If Caladh

made a move, Keira knew the female vampire-demon hybrid would be on him in a flash.

Tori moved away from Dante and went down on one knee beside Stefan. She reached out and lightly touched his cheek. "Damn you, Natchook," she whispered. A tear slipped from her eye to trail down her face. "Damn you."

Dante helped her up and slid his arm around her waist, hugging her to his side.

Tobias said, "Dante and Tori studied the smaller rift device and the schematics that go along with it. They might be able to figure out how to disable the larger machine."

"Can't we just turn it off?" Keira asked. She bit the inside of her cheek to help take the focus off the pain radiating from her shoulder. She couldn't let them take her anywhere until that infernal rift contraption was destroyed. "It is a machine, after all. They have power switches."

Tobias shot her a look.

Finn chuckled. "She has a point." He paused and sobered. "We can't stay here, though." He looked down at Keira. "I'm going to pick you up now, sweetheart. And it's going to hurt. Ready?"

She bit her lip then shook her head even as she whispered, "Yes."

He sent her a tight smile. "All right, then. Here we go." Finn carefully slid his arms beneath her.

She knew he was doing his best not to jostle her, but, gods above, it hurt. She trapped cries of pain in her throat, but as he stood and got her settled in his arms she couldn't contain a low moan.

"God, baby, I'm so sorry." She saw him look at Tobias.

"It's a damned two-mile hike to get from the entrance of the mine back to the trailhead. She'll never make it."

"We'll figure it out, Finn. I promise you," the vampire said. He glanced at the others. "We'll take care of the machine on the way out." His gaze hardened on Caladh. "Move it."

As they walked, the selkie yammered on about his plans for the rift. "You don't know what you're doing," he said. "Think about it. No more subverting our darkest desires, no more kowtowing to humans and their laws."

"Watch it," Dante muttered. "Some of us were human not all that long ago."

"And some of us like humans," Tori added.

"Then you're stupid."

Keira followed the conversation with numb fascination, appreciating the distraction from the flames burning her insides.

"Boy, you are a piece of work, you know that?" Nix shot Caladh a scowl. "You acted all benevolent and kind on the council, while all the while you were plotting behind their backs. Behind Deoul's back."

"Oh, don't talk to me about Deoul," Caladh snapped. "You couldn't stand him."

"No, I couldn't. And I don't feel bad that he's dead," Nix admitted. They turned into the main shaft. "But I wouldn't have killed him, despite how much I might have wanted to sometimes."

"Hear, hear," Tori muttered.

They entered the larger portion of the shaft where the machine was. Keira knew Finn did his best to keep her as steady as possible, but each step he took was pure torture for her. When they were a few feet from the machine, he stopped and went down on one knee. "We'll rest here for awhile," he murmured. His voice was hoarse and his eyes held self-recrimination.

"This isn't your fault," she managed to tell him again through a throat tight with pain. She was vaguely aware of the others gathered nearby, talking in low voices. Nix, however, stood a short distance away with a gun in her hand, standing guard over the defeated and now silent Caladh.

Keira wondered for a moment where the female vampire had gotten a gun, but then remembered that Caladh had brought one. It must be his.

"I didn't protect you," Finn said, drawing her attention back to him. His face was taut, a muscle in his jaw twitching furiously.

The last thing she wanted him to feel was guilt. "I don't need your protection. I was wounded because of my choices, Finn, not yours." She'd known going into this that it would be dangerous, perhaps even deadly. She'd expected that danger to be from Stefan.

Not even once had she suspected Caladh wasn't everything he'd appeared to be: concerned, determined to protect the status quo. However he'd done it, he'd flown so low under her radar she hadn't had an inkling of his true emotions. She wanted to say more to Finn, but she suddenly felt so tired. Her eyes fluttered closed and she exhaled.

"Keira?" His voice went raspy. "Keira!"

"What? I'm okay," she managed, her words slurring together. Everything took so much effort. Talking. Breathing. Even trying to open her eyes, which was why she didn't. "I'm just so sleepy."

"Try to stay awake, sweetheart." She felt his fingers against her cheek, then stroking through the hair at her temples, brushing it back from her face. "Maybe if we get your skin against the ground, you can heal yourself."

It was time to 'fess up. "I already tried. It didn't work." She rubbed her face tiredly against his shoulder.

"What do you mean?" Finn drew a sharp breath. "How could it not work?"

"It's the iron from the bullet." She forced her eyes open and looked up into his face. "While the bullet is in me, it blocks Earth's energy. I can't absorb it. It might be different outside of the mine, where there are trees and plants with life-giving root systems." She sighed. "I don't know."

"We should go try that." He started to gather her up.

"No, wait I want to see this through. Please," she added when he seemed about to argue. "There isn't much time before the rift, and I want to know for sure that the machine has been destroyed. Or at least turned off." She turned her head and watched the others.

Dante gestured to the large button that glowed red. "I'm telling you, this is the power switch."

"So turn it off," Tobias said.

Dante pushed the button. Nothing happened. He pressed the button again, and again nothing happened. He swore. "That should have worked," he said.

"Maybe Natchook hooked up a failsafe," Tori said. "Rigged the machine somehow so that it couldn't be shut down."

Tobias frowned. "That would mean the thing would keep running indefinitely and would keep the rift open twenty-four seven." He shook his head. "That doesn't sound feasible to me."

"Remember we are talking about a madman here," Dante said.

Tori winced and looked away.

Keira wondered about her response, but before she could say anything, Finn bent closer and murmured, "Liuz was Tori's cousin."

"Oh. Wow."

"I think I may have a solution." Tobias walked over to a workbench and picked up a sledgehammer.

"This is how you're going to disable it?" his wife asked.

"You know how men are," Tori chimed in. "If they can't get something to work they smack it."

Tobias shot her a look and swung the hammer into the side of the machine where the various dials were. Sparks flew but the machine kept humming away. He swung again and again. The last wham of the hammer punched a five-inch hole in the side of the machine, exposing a variety of wires. With an oath, Tobias reached in and yanked out the wires.

The lights on the machine flickered and then went out. The hum stopped.

"Is that it?" Finn asked. "Is it off?"

"I believe so." Tobias glanced around. "I think we should also destroy this whole area so it and this machine can never be used again."

"I can take care of that," Dante volunteered. He thumbed over his shoulder. "I saw a box of dynamite back there; they must've been using it to blast out new sections of tunnel."

"No way I'm letting you loose with a bunch of dynamite," Tobias responded.

"Listen, I was in the Rangers, remember? I have explosives training, and anyway it's probably like riding a bike. You never really forget."

"It's probably like riding a bike?" Tori put one hand on his arm. "Dante, I'd really like you to be a little more sure than that."

He grinned. "I know what I'm doing. Don't worry."

"Okay, if you say so." She looked at Tobias. "To be on the safe side, though, I think I'll stay with him to supervise."

"That'll make me feel better, at least," Tobias murmured. He glanced over at Keira. "How's she doing?" he asked.

"I'm all right," she said. But she misspoke. Numbness set in, traveling from her upper chest down her side. Her hip spasmed, making her leg kick out, then it, too, went numb. She stared up into Finn's face. "Or maybe not. I can't feel my left side." She thought that might be a very bad thing, but she couldn't get her brain to work out why.

"God." He looked up at the others. A muscle ticked furiously in his jaw. "I've got to get her off this mountain."

"Let's go." Tobias led the way, then Caladh with Nix right behind him, and Finn carrying Keira.

When they exited the mine, Keira squinted in the bright sunlight and took a deep breath of clean mountain air. The sun had passed its zenith, and she guessed it was somewhere around one in the afternoon. Birds sang their cheery songs as if nothing had changed, and she found herself envying them. "Put me on the ground," she whispered.

Finn immediately went down on one knee.

"Let me try again." She put her palms flat on the

ground and sent out a call to the earth beneath her. Energy began to trickle into her, but it wasn't enough. "I need more of my skin on the ground," she muttered. She looked up at Finn. "Help me take my clothes off."

His brows raised but he complied without hesitation. A button went flying with his haste. "Sorry," he muttered. "You know, I always love it when you let me take off your clothes, but I never thought I'd be doing it under this kind of circumstance."

"Me, either." She glanced up to see Tobias and Nix had turned Caladh away and all three had their backs to her. "I don't think I can completely heal myself," she told Finn. "But I might be able to do enough so I can get off the mountain."

He supported her as she lay back down. Now she was skin to ground from her shoulder blades to her heels. She felt an immediate difference. The numbness left her, which as the pain flowed again made her think maybe this hadn't been such a great idea. After several minutes had passed, she said, "I think that's as good as it's going to get."

"You sound stronger." Finn drew her to her feet and helped her get dressed. "You can turn around now," he said to the others.

"Thank you," Keira said. It wasn't as if people other than Finn had ever seen her nude, and she wasn't shy about her body, but she wasn't an exhibitionist, either. She appreciated their care for her modesty.

"Can you walk?" Finn looked down at her, concern darkening his eyes.

"For a while, I think." She glanced down at her feet with a wry smile. "Good thing Stefan bought hiking boots for me."

"Hmm." Finn didn't seem ready to be thankful for anything Stefan had done, and Keira couldn't blame him. Stefan Liuz had been a delusional maniac. This world was better off without him.

Heading back down the trail was slow going. Even if she'd been in peak physical condition she'd have had difficulty climbing down the rocky path. Every time her footing slipped, it jostled her shoulder. After about the twelfth time she could no longer hold back the grunts of pain.

"Let's stop and rest a few minutes," Finn said.

She nodded, grateful for the suggestion. "I don't suppose anyone has water."

All but Nix shook their heads. "I have some in my bag," she said. "It's, ah, in the car."

"It sounds like your plan was ill conceived from the start." Caladh's voice conveyed the same smugness that was written across his features. "You all went up the mountain with nary a drop to drink."

"Oh, shut up." Nix shot him a glare.

"You used to be so respectful," the councilor murmured. "Is this what turning into a vampire has done to you?"

"No, this is what you being a douchebag has done to me."

Keira licked her lips. She wasn't going to get any better until doctors could remove the bullet. "Let's go."

"Are you sure?" Finn asked. He looked so worried, it warmed her heart. "You know what? I can carry you the rest of the way."

"You need your hands to be able to maintain balance," Keira countered. "If you're carrying me and lose your footing, we'll both go down." She sent him a dry look. She was giving short little pants, both from pain and exertion, and realized she wasn't scoring any points with her argument. "The way my luck's going today, you'll land on top of me."

"She's right," Nix said, glancing over her shoulder. "The terrain's too rugged through here. You can be all macho when you get to the trailhead."

"We're almost there," Keira whispered. "Just help me, Finn."

"All right." He put his arm around her.

She leaned on him as they made it the rest of the way down the trail. The five of them stopped and stared at the three vehicles parked at the trailhead. Keira pointed to the luxury sedan. "That one's Stefan's."

"The truck is Dante's. This one's mine," Tobias said, indicating a dark SUV. "We'll drop you two at the hospital and then take Caladh to council headquarters." He gave the councilor a dismissive glance. "His injuries aren't that severe." He glanced at Keira. "It might be best for Keira to ride up front. Finn, you and Nix can sit on either side of Caladh. Keep him out of trouble.

"Fine. Let's just get out of here." Finn helped Keira into the front seat and carefully fastened her seatbelt.

She felt herself beginning to fade again because everything took so much effort. Finally she gave up the fight and closed her eyes, letting her head loll against the back of the seat. The drone of the voices of her companions faded, then she knew no more.

Chapter Twenty

Finn sat by Keira's bedside, holding her cool hand in his. He stared at the beeping machine monitoring her vitals. By the time they'd gotten her to the hospital, the iron from the bullet had been in her system for several hours. The doctors had successfully removed it and were getting fluids into her as quickly as possible, but ultimately it was up to Keira and her body's ability to heal itself. The medical staff wasn't sure what kind of lasting damage, if any, there might be. The fey weren't like shapeshifters, who could heal from almost any wound, or vampires, who only needed to feed.

Iron was deadly to the fey, and Keira had sat around with a chunk of it near her heart. If something happened to her, if she didn't survive this...he was going to kick some doctors' asses from here to forever and back again.

If he lost her, he would never know how bright his life could have been. He knew as surely as he knew his own name that he'd never find another woman who touched his soul in the same way.

Over the past weeks, months even, while he was fo-

cused on his mission, this woman had barreled past his
defenses. She'd carved out a spot in his heart, a spot that
now took up most of the space. If she wasn't there to fill
it, he'd have a great, gaping emptiness within him for the
rest of his life.

Finn tightened his grip on Keira's hand, willing her to
get better. And finally admitted to himself that he did love
her. He could no longer deny it. This slender, stubborn,
beautiful redhead was the love of his life. Whenever he
was with her he had the time of his life, even outside of
her bed. That, for him, was a rare thing. She was the closest thing to a best friend he'd ever had.

He figured when one could find a lover and a best
friend rolled up into one person, it was magic and it
should be guarded as the piece of heaven it was. He'd
never thought he'd get so lucky. But here was his slice of
paradise, lying before him.

He wasn't going to let her go without a fight. When
she woke up—and it would be when, not if—he'd tell her
how he felt. There'd be no more secrets. If she let him,
he'd spend the rest of his life making it up to her.

He'd successfully completed his mission, even if it had
taken five other people to help him. He'd checked in with
Lucifer and had given him a brief update. The important thing was the machine was destroyed, and his father
would have to uphold his end of the bargain. For the first
time in a long time Finn would be free of Lucifer's influence. Free to be his own man. And the first thing he
wanted to do was shackle himself to Keira.

Finn stared down at her. At some point the medical
staff had bathed her. They'd even washed her long hair
then fashioned it in a loose braid that draped over one

shoulder. He brought her hand to his mouth and pressed a kiss to her palm. Bending his head, he held her hand against his mouth. He clenched his teeth and fought back the heaviest fear he'd ever experienced. He'd never been so helpless in his life. If he could fight this battle he gladly would, but it was something taking place on a battlefield he couldn't reach. There was nothing he could do now but pray, to whatever deities might be out there listening. "Please," he whispered. "Please."

Minutes ticked by. An hour. He stood and stretched. Loath to leave her, he paced the small room, desperation riding him. On his hundredth trip from the window back to the bed, he noticed his father standing in the doorway. "How long have you been there?" Finn asked.

"Not long." Lucifer shoved his hands in his pockets and walked into the room. His voice quiet, he lifted his chin toward the bed. "She's not doing well, I take it?"

"No, she's not." Finn sighed and stood at the foot of the bed. "They were able to get the bullet but it's taking a long time for the iron to work its way out of her system. The best thing for her is to be outside where she could absorb energy from the Earth, but it's too dangerous to move her just yet."

"So bring the Earth to her."

Finn gave a nod. "I thought of that, too, but according to one of the fey doctors on staff, it's not that simple. The energy she draws upon is from the interconnectivity all living things have to each other. It's not just from the dirt, it's from the tree that's in the dirt. It's from the bugs and animals in the tree and in the ground." He scrubbed the back of his neck. "It's . . . complicated."

"I see." Lucifer stared at Keira for several seconds,

then put his hand on Finn's shoulder. "I'm proud of you," he said, his voice deep. He met Finn's eyes. "I knew you could do this, and you proved me right."

"Thank you." Finn searched his father's gaze and was met only with veracity. It was the first time in recent memory that the old devil had praised him for anything. Maybe it was because Finn had given up on trying to please Lucifer, but he'd given up because he'd never gotten any recognition. At least now, when it really mattered, his father had said the words a son needed to hear.

"I know I'm not the kind of father that engenders the warm fuzzies," Lucifer went on. "It's not because I don't care."

"I know that." Finn realized his father was uncomfortable with sharing his feelings and, in fact, preferred not to acknowledge them at all. He supposed that kind of attitude was in large part what made him so successful as the leader of demons.

"Even though you won't be working for me anymore," his father went on, "I hope you'll let me throw work your way from time to time. Once your security business is up and running, that is."

Finn frowned. He was pretty sure he'd never spoken his dream aloud in his father's presence. "How did you..."

Lucifer shrugged. "People tell me things."

"I guess they do." Lesson learned there. If Finn didn't want his father to know something, he had to keep it to himself. Although there were prets out there who could pluck the thoughts right out of your head. They were rare, and he'd never met any, but he'd bet his last dollar his father knew at least one. And that one probably owed him a favor or two. "Guess I need to learn to keep my mouth shut."

His father grinned. He looked at Keira and the smile left his face. "You let me know if there's anything I can do for her, all right?"

Finn gave a nod.

"And call if there's anything I can do for you, son."

"I will."

Lucifer patted his shoulder and walked out of the room, pausing in the doorway. He turned back and looked at Keira. His face tightened. "Caladh MacLoch has much to answer for." He shook his head and left.

Finn took up his vigil beside the bed. He took Keira's hand, gently sandwiching it between his much larger ones. He wasn't sure how long he'd sat there when her fingers moved within his grasp. At first he thought it was his imagination, but then they twitched again. He jerked up his head and stared into her face. "Keira? Sweetheart? Can you hear me?"

Her eyelids fluttered and after a couple of tries they swept up to reveal her blue eyes, seemingly alert but for the lingering grogginess of sleep.

"Hey, there." He smoothed her hair off her forehead. "How're you feeling?"

"Better." Her voice was raspy.

Without letting go of her hand, he reached for the cup of ice chips a nurse had left on the bedside table. He dipped the spoon and pulled it out with a piece of ice. "Here," he said. When she opened her mouth he placed the ice on her tongue. He replaced the spoon in the cup. "The doctors say you should be fine," he said, not wanting to give her the full truth until he thought she'd be up for hearing it. That truth was they were hopeful, optimistic even, but really didn't know. "Do you have any feeling in your left side?"

She thought about it, her face scrunching up. "My leg tingles a bit. And it hurts on that side when I breathe, so I suppose some of the numbness must be fading." She shifted against the sheets, a wince tightening the corners of her mouth.

"Well, that's a good sign," he said. "At least you're feeling something now. Can you move your legs?"

Her right leg slid under the covers, then her left, and she let out a cranky, "Ow."

"Let's not do that again for a while," Finn offered.

"Yes, let's not." She stared at their joined hands and began to play with his fingers. Finally she whispered, "I should have trusted you."

"When?" he asked. Deciding to be fair about it, he added, "When I was lying to you, maybe? Or telling Liuz it didn't matter if he killed you? Is that when you should have trusted me?"

"That bit did worry me a smidge," she admitted with a small smile. She raised her eyes to his. "I believed you when you said all those months ago that you wanted to do more with your life. I should have come right out and asked you what was going on instead of letting my own insecurities allow me to make assumptions. I should have been there for you, like a friend would be."

Finn brought her hand to his mouth and pressed a kiss in her soft palm, folding her fingers over as if he could keep it stored there. God knew she had his heart in her hands. "The same could be said of me, you know. You'd cleaned up your act. And there I was, ready to believe you'd so easily slide back into old habits."

"It wasn't easy, yet it was." She wet her lips and it made him want to lean over and kiss her. But she was in no condition for him to get frisky, so he reined in his libido. Keira went on. "I was amazed myself at how simple it was to walk right back into that old life. It's very addicting."

"That rush when you're on a job?" he asked. She nodded and he huffed a sigh. "Well, regardless, I should have trusted you more, too. So I guess both of us were a little too quick to believe ill of the other. We have a lot to learn about trust. About each other."

"Yes, we do." She paused. Just as he said, "Keira, I have something to tell you," she said, "Finn, look, about us."

They both stopped, stared at each other while an awkward silence grew. Finally he said, "I know the gentlemanly thing to do would be to tell you to go first, but I need to tell you something."

"All right." She sat quietly, holding his hand, her calm gaze on his.

He couldn't meet her eyes and tell her what he needed to. Give him a big, badass demon or vampire to kill and he was Mr. Mighty. Confess his love for one woman? Mr. Wimpy. He cleared his throat. "I should have told you this weeks ago, Keira. When I first realized it. But I denied it even to myself. Especially to myself. Because I didn't think I was ready. I had too many other plans."

When he didn't go on, she said, "Finn? What exactly is it you're trying to tell me?"

"I shouldn't have hidden behind a mediocre word like 'care.'" He swore he could hear her in his head, saying

You need to look a woman in the eyes when you tell her you love her, you great big lummox. He knew she didn't have that capability, but if he mumbled it while staring at her hand, he'd be depriving them both of something special. Something worthwhile. He cleared his throat again and met her gaze. "Keira O'Brien, I love you. When I thought you were going to die…" He pressed his lips together and blinked to clear sudden moisture from his eyes. "I knew if you weren't in my life I'd be empty the rest of eternity."

Her mouth opened and she stared at him with wonder swirling in her gaze. "I need to sit up," she said. She craned her neck, wincing, her hands patting along the bed. "Where's the control thingy?"

"Take it easy. It's right here." Finn picked it up where it lay slightly beyond her fingertips. He gave it to her and she pressed the up button. When she got it where she wanted, he stood and adjusted her pillows.

"Thanks." She searched his eyes. "You must know I love you, too."

His heart expanded until he thought it might blow a hole through his chest. "You seemed fond of me, but not really interested in anything deeper than that. Every once in a while I wondered if there was something more between us." He shook his head.

"I couldn't let you see how I felt. I didn't want to jeopardize the mission. And you seemed so sincere, even if you were a tad uncooperative, with the rogue group. I chalked that stubbornness up to you being you." She swallowed, the movement drawing his gaze to the soft column of her throat. "I do love you," she whispered, bringing his gaze back to her face. Tears flooded her eyes and suspended on her lashes. "With all my heart. But sometimes I feel like my heart's only this big." She held up one hand, her forefinger and thumb about an inch apart. "I try, Finn. I do. Caring and compassion aren't natural for me. They never have been. Maybe it's because I got drawn into grifting early in my life and was surrounded by people who used me, who betrayed my trust. And it seems like when I let my guard down, someone like Caladh comes along. I have to work at it. Trust and caring, I mean."

"Sweetheart, we all have to work at it. And don't you dare let Caladh's deception make you doubt yourself. He fooled us all." He leaned forward and placed his lips on hers, a gentle meeting of hearts and souls, for the first time their emotions truly laid bare. He drew back and swiped at her tears. "For those to whom love comes with difficulty, when they give it it's that much more precious. I wouldn't change a thing about you, Keira. Not one thing. You're my match in every way."

He slanted his mouth over hers again. Her lips parted and he drank down her sigh.

"Well, I guess this is a sign she's feeling better," came a feminine voice from the doorway. It was pain-in-his-ass Nix.

Finn released Keira and gave her a grin, then twisted so he could look at his almost sister. "Hello there, little cousin."

She scowled. "Don't call me that." By now she gave him that directive without much heat. She looked at Keira. "The docs say you're gonna be fine," she said. "Anyway, I thought you both would like to know what's been going on."

Finn took Keira's hand in his again. Keira nodded, her eyes wide and dark. "What's happened with Caladh? Was he the one who killed Deoul?"

"Tobias is certain he did, but they're still running tests and questioning the bastard." She frowned. "He's not talking. They're holding him in the cells in the basement of the council building, awaiting trial for treason and, most likely, murder in the first degree." She folded her arms over her chest. "There's no way he'll be able to argue a lesser plea, since it's clear he premeditated Deoul's murder. Allegedly." Her scowl deepened.

"I can't believe it," Keira murmured. "I never picked up on anything like that from him. Of course, I was barely around him when he was with Deoul. Plus, I think he was quite adept at masking his emotions."

"Probably. He's obviously much better at being sneaky than any of us gave him credit for." Nix glanced at Finn. "Tori and Dante called right after we dropped you off here and told us they set off several charges, both on the machine and in various places throughout the mine, including the entrance. No one's going to be able to use that machine ever again."

"You mentioned schematics? And what about the smaller device Liuz was using as a radio transceiver?" Finn stroked his thumb idly back and forth on Keira's wrist.

"As soon as we figure out where he was living, we'll search for the schematics." Nix shrugged. "As far as the device, we can only hope the one he had was it. And it got buried with him in the mine."

"I met him once at a house," Finn offered. "I don't know if it was his place or not—it was decorated in early thrift-store style, and I always figured him to be someone who would surround himself with nice things. Expensive things. Maybe he was waiting until he was ruler of the world."

"Do you remember where you met him?"

Finn gave a nod. "I'll text you the address."

"Great. Thanks." She looked at Keira. "I hope you feel better soon. We should do lunch once you're out of here." With that she gave a small wave and left.

"I'd love to do lunch," Keira murmured. She laughed. "I like her."

"You should have known her when she was part human. Boy, was she cranky."

Keira's smile widened. "I'm sure that had nothing to do with you."

"Of course not." He shot her a grin.

She shoved the covers off her legs and swung them to the side, then pulled the pulse oximeter from her finger.

"Whoa, whoa, whoa!" Finn stood up. "Where do you think you're going?"

"Home." She rubbed her forehead with her fingers. "I'm ready to get out of here. I need to feel the Earth against my skin."

"Is the numbness completely gone?" he asked.

"It sure is."

"Uh-huh." Finn shook his head. Her tone had been falsely light. "Don't kid a kidder, sweetheart." He gently swung her legs onto the mattress. "Back in bed you go." She started to protest and he said, "Until the docs clear you, this is where you need to be. And you know it." He put the pulse oximeter back on her finger, knowing he did it only because she let him. "I'll bring in some dirt or something for you."

"Very funny."

He could see by the paleness of her skin and the bruised look around her eyes that she was still tired and weak. The fact that she went back into bed so easily only confirmed what his eyes told him. He had no doubt that if she could get to her little grassy patch of ground in the backyard that she'd be able to heal herself. But it was the getting her there that could cost her her life. For now she had to stay put and let the medical staff do what they could to shore up her strength.

She dug her head into the pillow, trying to get comfortable, and winced. "See?" he asked in a gentle voice. "You're not ready to go home, warrior princess."

Her lips twitched. She looked into his eyes and whispered, "Stay with me."

"Always. And for us, that's a long time." He sat on the edge of the bed and brought her hand to his mouth and pressed his lips to her knuckles. He rested their hands on his knee. "We have a life to build together. Just think: with my background as an enforcer and your grifting skills, we can run a top-notch security company, a solid foundation to build our future on."

"Sounds lovely." Her eyes drooped.

He dropped his mouth lightly on hers. "Sleep well, sweetheart. I'll be here when you wake up."

If fate were willing, he would always be there for her, and she for him. And if fate had other ideas, they'd fight it together.

Epilogue

Bartholomew Maxwell "Ash" Asher stared at the TV screen in the employee lounge at council HQ. The news had been going nonstop for almost twenty-four hours, following the occurrence of the rift and newest influx of preternaturals. Several amateur videos had already run that showed an actual habitation of a human by a being from another dimension.

No one could see the incorporeal entity, but the shock to the human's system and the disorientation and confusion were plain to see. The fallout from this latest rift was just as easy to determine—with dozens of local people affected, the human government would move forward with their plan to forcibly implant microchips into preternaturals, their way of "protecting" themselves.

Ash gave a snort. *Yeah, right.* It was the humans' way of keeping tabs on wild animals and nothing more. Well, he'd be damned before he let someone stick a hunk of metal in his arm or anywhere else for that matter. He was his own master, and he didn't need to be GPSed like some damn pet. Or car.

The council was in disarray after the last two presidents were removed from office in quick succession. The first, Deoul Arias, who was murdered by the second, Caladh MacLoch, who now awaited trial in the cells in the basement of the building. Ash had been tempted to go down and talk to the councilor, to try and figure out why he'd done what he'd done. Or, at least, what he was accused of doing. Ash trusted Tobias Caine and Victoria Joseph, and both of them seemed confident of Caladh's guilt.

But right now he had bigger issues to deal with. All liaisons did. They had to get out on the street and round up newly turned preternaturals before they could hurt anyone, or themselves. They had brand-new lives to get used to, abilities and predilections they'd never before experienced.

Ash shoved his hands in his pockets and stalked from the room. It was time to get to work.

...page ... an excerpt from

Kiss of the Vampire.

Chapter One

Arizona Daily News, February 13, 2012

From the Editor

By Simon Tripp

In just under two years this planet will see another Influx of incorporeal beings. Most of them will be criminals, but some will be political dissidents or religious prisoners. The dimensional rift itself is caused by the return of the Moore-Creasy-Devon comet making its 73-year journey through the solar system. Beings from the other dimension have been using Earth as their own Botany Bay for millennia, and as of yet our scientists have been unable to find a way to stop it. These interdimensional marauders will stream through the rift like Vikings of old riding the rough waves of the sea to take possession of human bodies without any regard for those they displace. Or, more accurately, suppress.

We know little more about them now than we did when we first became aware that vampires and werewolves and all those other creatures of myth were, in fact, real. According to Dr. Nandi Wesley of NASA, an Extra-Dimensional (ED) takes possession of a human and the combination of their otherworldly essence with that of their host determines just what creature they become. How that happens still remains a mystery. No one in this world can explain on a genetic level what makes one a vampire, another a werewolf, still another a pixie, not even the renowned Dr. Wesley. As well, governments around the globe are as unprepared now as they were three years ago when word of this rift became public knowledge. Following the hysteria that caused families to turn on each other because they suspected their loved ones had become EDs, the United States passed a law that protects EDs from discrimination in housing, employment, and other aspects of life. The Preternatural Protection Act (PPA) also includes strict penalties for hate crimes directed toward EDs.

I've always pretty much been a live and let live sort of guy, but I'll admit I'm troubled by this laissez-faire attitude we have toward the monsters in our midst. Just because they say they'll police themselves doesn't mean they will. It's up to the everyday citizen to protect him- or herself, since our government won't, because in less than twenty-four months we'll have even more EDs to contend with, vampires being the worst of them.

Everyone knows these beings have been preying on humans for centuries. Just last month a woman was brutally attacked and died while her two small children looked on in terror. The vampire who was responsible has yet to be brought up on charges. More accurately, he or she has not been found. I don't know about you, but it seems to me that more often than not preternaturals literally get away with murder. Maybe some of these anti-preternatural groups that have sprung up over the last few years aren't all wrong. Maybe, just maybe, the people who killed that vamp in Scottsdale yesterday had the right idea.

I'm not satisfied to leave things as they are. Are you?

* * *

Nix de la Fuente scowled at the editorial as she made her way from her car to the latest crime scene. She folded the newspaper and stuffed it into her oversized bag. It was garbage like this in the media that kept people stirred up. At least the guy hadn't mentioned demons at all. She supposed she should be grateful for that. Thousands of years of propaganda foisted on humans by various religious establishments had definitely made demons out to be the bad guys. Some of that negative press wasn't wrong. Okay, most of it was pretty accurate.

Since she was only half demon, though, she considered herself one of the good guys. Most of the time, anyway. And it was her somewhat unique heritage that had landed her the job as one of the liaisons between the region's Council of Preternaturals and the local authorities. That hadn't earned her many friends on her mother's side of the family, because most demons wanted nothing to do with the council. They figured it was their right to live and kill others as they pleased. Her mother had been downright pissy about Nix taking a job with the council, but Nix didn't see any reason to placate a mother who'd been mostly absent from her life, letting Nix's paternal grandmother raise a child she'd resented and sometimes had even seemed to hate.

As Nix neared the crime scene, she paused outside the taped-off area and grabbed a pair of shoe covers to put over her boots. In between two tall saguaro cacti, she braced herself against the wall of the building and slipped on the covers. Flashing her ID at the uniformed Scottsdale police officer, she ducked under the yellow crime scene tape he held up for her. Taking care where she placed her feet, she walked several yards to where a corpse was covered with a black tarp. She pulled a pair of latex gloves out of her purse and with a sigh squatted down, slipped them on, then folded back the plastic sheeting.

Under the setting sun the blood appeared dark and dull on the victim's face and streaked the once beautiful but now grimy blond hair. Vacant blue eyes, clouded over, still held a look of surprise in their depths. In death her fangs hadn't retracted, the tips resting against her lower lip.

Nix's heart gave a thump. She knew this victim. Amarinda Novellus. Nix would never have thought she would see her like *this*. She blew out a breath and lifted the tarp higher to see more of the body. What was once designer clothing hung in bloody tatters. The rib cage gaped open, some of the bones broken. Most of the victim's internal organs were gone. One leg lay bent beneath her at an unnatural angle. Her right arm was at her side, palm down, while the left one was bent above her head. All of her fingers were gone; no doubt her attackers had removed them to hide the bits of flesh and blood Amarinda had gouged out of them with her nails. Deep slashes scored her forearms, her thighs. She hadn't gone down easily.

There were any number of preternaturals with the capacity and the desire to do this sort of thing, but the suspects greatly decreased when victimology was taken into account. Vamps were strong. Really strong. And fast. Even alone, this one should have been able to defend herself against almost anything.

Except there'd obviously been no defense against whatever had done this to her. At this point it was difficult to tell whether she'd been gutted by claws or knives.

A pair of men's scuffed brown shoes moved into Nix's field of vision. She glanced up past a potbelly to the ruddy face of one of the assistant medical examiners. "George. How're you doing?"

The porcine shifter scratched the side of his nose with a stubby finger. "Can't complain. Wouldn't do any good if I did."

"Family all right?" she asked. "Your youngest just went off to college, right? How does she like it so far?"

A broad grin creased his face. "Family's fine, and my baby's lovin' the college life. Worries me a little," he muttered, his smile losing some of its brightness. Knees cracked as he squatted next to her. "Helluva thing," he said with a slight gesture toward the body.

"Yeah." Nix sighed. "What d'ya got?"

"Murder by person or persons unknown. Just like the one yesterday." At her exasperated look he shrugged. "What do you want from me?" He gestured the length of the body. "She's been cut open and disemboweled. The how of it I'll know once I get her on the table. The why of it's your job. I can tell you she fed within the last twenty-four hours. That's determined by how soft and pink her skin is." He reached out and lifted her upper lip. "See how red her gums are? That shows she's fed recently, too." He let her lip fall back into place. "'Course, it could be that she took a long draw from the bastards that did this to her. I can't say for certain." He paused, shaking his head, then blew out a sigh. "It's a damned shame." He stood with a groan and stretched his back. "The boys should be here shortly to collect her. I'll let you know what I find out from the autopsy."

Nix watched him amble off and then looked back

down at Amarinda. As with the earlier victim, there weren't any visual clues that she could see on the body, but maybe there was some scent left. Nix leaned forward slightly. Just as she started to draw a breath to focus on the various odors from the body, a spicy, woodsy scent tickled her nostrils. A man moved into her peripheral vision and hitched up his black slacks to hunker down beside her.

"Nice of you to come," Detective Dante MacMillan murmured, shooting her a sidelong glance. Dante had been assigned to the Special Case Squad only a month ago. Even though it usually took her a while to warm up to people enough to call them friends, she and Dante had been on several cases together already and she knew he was a man of deep integrity and an abiding sense of justice. Plus he made her laugh. Nix wouldn't hesitate to name him as a friend, even after such a short amount of time.

She grimaced. "I came as soon as I got the call." Damned werebear dispatcher had a thing about demons, and he always waited until the very last minute to call her about a new case, making sure she strolled on to the scene later than everyone else. She'd probably hear about it from her bosses afterward.

"I've been here ten minutes. First officer on scene secured the site and started jotting down makes, models, and license plate numbers of cars on the street." He clasped his hands between his knees. "I have uniforms doing a canvas of the area. So far no witnesses. At least none that want to tell us what they know."

She looked down at the body. "I know her. Her name is Amarinda Novellus."

"How do you know her?" Dante's voice was hushed, his tone compassionate. Finding out that you knew a victim was never easy. It brought the violence of the murder all that closer to home.

"She was a friend." Nix clenched her jaw against the pain of her loss. She and Amarinda had drifted apart over the last five years because being around the female vampire had dredged up too many memories Nix hadn't wanted to deal with. Now she'd never have the chance to renew their friendship. Her emotions rose, her gut churning with demon fire as if the beast inside was trying to burn its way out.

Nix stared at what was left of her friend and pushed the guilt and grief aside. She had a job to do. Had to focus and get it done. She could grieve and wallow in regrets later. After she found Amarinda's killer.

Dante glanced at the victim, his face drawn and taut. A heavy sigh left him. "The second dead ED in as many days. God, I thought humans could be vicious to one another, but what EDs can do to each other..." He gave a slight shake of his head and gestured toward the gaping rib cage. "I mean, an ED had to have done this kind of damage, right?"

"Could have been a pret." Nix refused to call them EDs. It wasn't that there was anything technically wrong with the term, "extra-dimensional" really was quite accurate. But most humans said it with such disdain in their voices that it had become an insult and wasn't used by most preternaturals. She replaced the tarp and rose to her feet, removing her latex gloves and tugging the back of her short leather jacket down over the knife scabbard at the small of her back. She might possess more strength than an average human female, but it never hurt to have actual weapons at your disposal. Like a blade made of silver at her back and the Glock 9 mm at her waist.

Dante stood as well, towering over her. Of course, most men did, since her human DNA contributed to the fact that she was only five four in her stocking feet. Good thing she had on her three-inch-heel boots tonight. That way, at least, her eyes were level with his chin instead of his Adam's apple. She met his gaze. "There don't seem to be any bite marks that could make it a vampire kill, and I don't see any bites or scratches or tufts of fur on Rinda that would suggest a shape-shifter. Until the coroner can take a closer look, we won't know if the damage was done by humans with knives or prets with claws and teeth."

He cocked an eyebrow. "You really think humans could've done this?" He gestured toward the covered body.

"Maybe." The editorial she'd read just before she'd entered the taped-off scene came to mind. "Some of the anti-pret groups might have moved from rhetoric to rampage." She shrugged. "I've met some pretty violent humans, especially on this job."

"Yeah, me, too." He paused. She could tell by the look on his face he was really hoping humans hadn't been involved. Of course, if they weren't, that would mean that both of them would no longer be involved on this case. If this incident were pret against pret, human authorities would back off and allow the preternatural council to resolve the issue. Dante added, "This didn't happen here. Not enough blood." He gestured around the site. Criminalists were busy doing their jobs, from those taking photographs and placing evidence in paper bags to the one at the edge of the scene making a video recording. "There should be spatter everywhere, but there's only what's on and under her body."

Nix agreed. "This is definitely a dump site. She was killed somewhere else." The killing hadn't taken place that long ago, either. What blood was there was still fresh. One of the human techs walked by, the air disturbed by his movements wafting the rich smell of blood toward her. She could almost taste the coppery tang on the back of her tongue, making her stomach knot even more.

Demons didn't ingest blood like vampires did, but the smell of the stuff still brought out a primal response. A dull throb set up in her forehead and she brought one hand up to rub under her bangs, willing her horn buds to stay hidden. The last thing she needed was to start showing her demon at a crime scene. None of her human colleagues except Dante knew she was anything but 100 percent bona fide human being. She planned to keep it that way. While most people had settled down fairly well after finding out that vampires, werewolves, and the various fairy folk were real, they were downright hostile about demons. She didn't need the prejudices of the cops and the crowd gathered on the other side of the yellow tape hindering her work.

"George says based on rigor mortis she's been dead about an hour. No more than two." Dante rubbed his jaw. "He went into some mumbo jumbo about how it's different with a vampire 'cause they're technically already dead. My eyes glazed over after about the fifth time he said 'Adenosine Triphosphate.'"

Nix shot him a look of commiseration. The assistant

ME was a verbose little shape-shifter who loved the sound of his own voice. Especially when he was able to trot out long, complicated words. She was amazed he hadn't gone into more detail with her, but maybe he figured he'd already given the information to Dante, so why bother? "So once we have a suspect list we'll want to check alibis between the hours of two thirty and five thirty, just to be sure."

Dante nodded. "Hey, can you…" He looked around and lowered his voice. "Can you smell anything?"

Dante was always discreet, and Nix was forever grateful. She took a deep breath and held it, pushing past the scent of blood for other odors. The sounds around her faded as she focused on her olfactory sense. There was a light smell of vamp, some lingering aroma of shape-shifter, but nothing recent enough to support or discount their involvement. There was something else there, though, a smoky odor lingering just beneath everything else, something… like demon.

Nix stilled. Why in the hell would demons have attacked a lone vampire? As far as she knew there had been no blood feuds called. And most demons wouldn't dare strike out on their own without sanction from their leader. Of course, there was always a possibility that a few had gone rogue and were having fun like in the old days, ganging up on a vampire who'd been foolish enough to venture out on his or her own—but she didn't think that was what was going on. The scent of demon would be a lot stronger if that were the case.

She drew another breath. While her sense of smell was better than a full-blooded human's, it wasn't as good as a full-blooded demon's. And nowhere near as good as a vamp's or any of the shape-shifters. But even she could tell there was something wrong here. The demon scent was too faint. If actual demons had been here, the odor would be much stronger. Maybe it was residual from earlier in the day. But still, it troubled her. It wasn't enough to definitely say demons were involved, but it was too much to rule them out.

"The strongest smell is of humans," she murmured. "I'm no bloodhound, though, and I can't tell older scents from the current ones," she added with a glance at the technicians working the scene. She kept her voice low. "All of the pret scents are so faint, my first assumption is that the attackers were human. It's just too difficult to sort out all the other smells." Plus if vamps fed on humans just prior to the attack, they'd have an overriding odor of human on them. She said as much to Dante.

His low sigh drew her attention back to him. His eyes looked tired and soul weary, like most of the other human cops she knew. Poor guy. He looked a little pale, the lines around his mouth testament to the strain he was under and the confusion he was trying to sort through.

"What is it?" she asked.

He scrubbed the back of his neck with a big hand. "It's just... all this." He drew a deep breath. "Here we were, going along for thousands of years thinking we were at the top of the food chain. We gave names to things we didn't understand, like vampires or werewolves or goblins. And then to find out we weren't kings of all we surveyed, that these things were real, just not in the way we'd imagined them."

"What do you mean?" Nix crossed her arms and stared at him.

"Vampires aren't vampires, shape-shifters aren't shape-shifters. They're all just a bunch of interdimensional squatters."

She grinned. His metaphor was accurate. "Technically they *are* vampires. They have fangs. They don't eat, they drink blood."

"But they're not reanimated corpses like in the legends. That's what I mean." When she started to correct him, Dante waved her off. "Okay, okay, I realize that the entities that turn into what we call vampires can only take over dying or newly dead bodies, so I suppose that makes them reanimated corpses. But... you know what I mean." Frustration colored his deep voice. He gestured toward Amarinda. "She's not human. Not really. She's an alien possessing a human body. And in just under two years even more entities will come through the rift and nobody knows how to stop them."

"It's not like it's going to be the end of the world," Nix said slowly. She wasn't sure how she felt about the next Influx. She was part demon, so the fact that more prets were going to come through the rift didn't frighten her. If anything, she felt a little sad for all the humans who were going to be possessed by strangers, completely unable to do anything to prevent or avoid it. Thousands of families would become dysfunctional overnight. "We'll adapt." She hoped that was true.

"Yeah, I suppose." He took a few steps away from the body and began moving around the crime scene, following in the footsteps the criminalists had already taken.

Nix pulled a small but powerful flashlight out of her purse and followed him, looking closely at the ground, at the adobe walls of the nearby building. Except for the body, there didn't seem to be any other evidence of a crime, which supported their conclusion that Amarinda had been dumped here.

"Something this brutal tells me it was personal." Dante circled back toward the body. "You just don't do this kind of damage to someone you don't know."

"You don't think so? Remember, if it was prets that killed her..." Nix gave a quick shrug. At his questioning glance, she reminded him, "Werewolves eat people. And the internal organs are the yummiest."

"Oh, hell." He grimaced. "I really didn't need to be reminded of that. I don't think I'll ever get used to seeing stuff like this." He hooked his thumbs in his belt, fingers framing the large silver buckle. "I wonder what's keeping Knox?"

"I don't know." Nix looked around the crime scene for any sight of the quadrant vampire liaison. It was unusual that he wasn't here yet. She stared down at the tarp, her heart beating like bongo drums in her chest. Amarinda was the second vamp to be killed, and Knox was late. What if... She drew in a breath and held it, trying to calm her fears. She hoped he was all right.

Dante gazed toward the edge of the scene where the techs were beginning to pack up their cases. "Hey, Marks!" When the man looked up from the computer tablet he was jotting notes on, Dante asked, "Did you get word to the council dispatch that the vic is a vamp?"

The man nodded.

Dante glanced at Nix. "Then they should've called him by now." He brought up his wrist to look at his watch. "Wonder what's keeping him." He dropped his hand, hooking his thumb over his belt again. "So, what can you tell me about your friend here?" He gave a quick nod toward Amarinda's tarp-covered body.

Nix wet her lips. She realized she was thirsty and reached into her bag for a bottle of water. She usually carried at least one bottle with her because in the low humidity of the desert it was easy to become dehydrated. "She came through the rift somewhere around 330 BC, give or take. There are vamps older than her, but not many." Being immortal, like a vampire, didn't mean you couldn't be killed. It just meant it took a lot to do it, especially the older a vampire was. "She works..." Nix broke off and swallowed, surprised at how much this hurt. She twisted off the cap of the bottle and took a swig of water, using the few seconds to recap and replace the bottle to get her emotions under control. "*Worked* with Maldonado."

"The quadrant's vamp leader?" Dante gave a low whistle. "Someone must have a death wish, to take out one of Byron Maldonado's people."

"They may not have known. Or cared," Nix said.

"Who didn't know or care about what?" The raspy bass voice with a flavor of South Carolina came from behind her.

That deep voice stopped her heart. She turned, and when she saw Tobias Caine duck under the crime scene tape her stomach lurched. He was pulling on latex gloves as he walked. His thick black hair was in its usual rakish mess with a few strands falling over his forehead. He straightened and loped toward them with an easy long-legged stride that belied his underlying intensity.

Five years. It had been five years since he'd walked out on her. Five years since he'd thrown away her love.

It was like a dagger to the heart, seeing him again. He

looked the same as ever, tall, lean, handsome as sin. His gray shirt matched his eyes and his leather coat fell to midthigh, drawing attention to those long legs encased in dark blue denim. He looked damned fine. His presence revved up her pulse and that made her mad. There should have been some sort of sign that he'd suffered as much as she had, the bastard.

Nix stiffened her legs, telling herself it wasn't seeing him again that made her weak in the knees. There was no denying that lust surged through her body in tune to her quickened heartbeat. It didn't seem to matter he wasn't hers anymore.

Some people used meth. Others drank themselves into a stupor. Her drug of choice was Tobias Caine. And it seemed that even after five years of sobriety, she was still as addicted as ever. Her eyes began to burn, signaling the rise of her demon. Tobias had always had that effect on her, as if his darkness called to her own. When they'd been in the middle of making love it hadn't been a problem, it had even enhanced the experience. But now, while she was on the job...She gritted her teeth and forced the demon back.

Dante shifted, his right hand sliding over to unsnap the safety strap on his gun holster. He let his hand rest on the butt of his weapon. She could see how tense he was, his shoulders taut, hand ready to draw his pistol.

Nix didn't blame him. She was tempted to draw her gun, too, but for an entirely different reason. Battling back the urge to tear into Tobias, she asked him, "What're you doing here?"

His hard, stormy gaze locked on hers. "Nix. It's good to see you."

She ignored the throb between her thighs as her body reacted to his voice and those damned pheromones that spilled from him. Vampires had the ability to influence the behavior of others through these pheromones, excreted colorless chemicals that human senses were too dull to detect but pret senses could identify just fine. Some vamps were better at using them than others. Tobias was one of the best she'd seen. Or, more accurately, felt. "I asked you a question," she stated with a glare.

Tobias reached into the inner pocket of his leather jacket and pulled out a wallet. He flipped it open and showed ID that looked suspiciously like hers—that of a council liaison. "I'm your vampire liaison."

"You're not my anything." She folded her arms over her breasts. "What happened to Knox?"

Tobias shrugged. "He's been temporarily reassigned."

"Mr. Caine." Nix heard Dante's hard swallow but his voice held steady as he said, "I'm Detective MacMillan."

"No need for formality. Call me Tobias." Tobias reached out and the two men shook hands in greeting. Tobias tucked his ID away. "It's Dante, right?" Upon receiving a nod of affirmation from Dante, Tobias looked at Nix again.

As he took a step forward, she raised a hand to ward him off before he thought to come any closer. The pheromones still rolled off him in a steady stream, making it hard to breathe through the sensual fog they created. She ground her teeth to keep from leaping into his arms. Or baring her throat. Or both. "You need to ramp it down, Caine," she muttered.

"Don't know what you're talking about," he returned blandly.

She glanced at Dante. His hand rested once again on the butt of his gun but he didn't seem to be overly affected by the pheromones. While it was true he wouldn't sense them, he would still be influenced by them if that was what Tobias wanted. Since he wasn't, that meant Tobias was deliberately directing them her way. Her human DNA made her more susceptible to the effects than a full-blooded demon would be, and he knew it.

"Caine!" she bit out, taking a step backward, putting more distance between them and ignoring the confused look Dante sent her way. "Just what the hell are you doing here? Since when are you a council liaison? And why was Knox reassigned?"

Tobias gave her a cocky grin, making her heart flutter in unwanted longing, though his stare remained as penetrating as ever. "I arrived in town early this morning. As soon as word of this came to the council, they asked me to be a special liaison because of my background and the spate of murders that's happened recently."

She scowled and ignored, for the moment, the fact that they'd be working together. "Since when are two deaths a 'spate'?"

"Since today." His gaze snagged on the body. "Let me take a look at the victim."

Oh, crap. Amarinda and Tobias went way back. She was the one who had introduced Tobias and Nix. When he had left town, Nix had gone out of her way to avoid Amarinda after that, effectively ending their relationship. Something she would never be able to fix.

As he started forward, she put her hand on his arm. "Tobias..." There was no easy way to say it. "It's Rinda."

Tobias's face became drawn and the spill of vamp

pheromones increased, though now they vibrated with building rage and sorrow. "Damn it." He breathed out a sigh and crouched beside the body. He folded back the tarp to reveal her face.

Nix noticed a slight tremble in those long fingers and couldn't deny the sympathy she felt for him. Despite his meeting Amarinda more than a hundred years ago, the two had managed to maintain a close friendship. Before he'd left Scottsdale, they'd both worked for Maldonado— Tobias as one of Maldonado's enforcers and Rinda as a kind of jill-of-all-trades. Nix had never really been sure exactly what the female vampire's job had been.

Nix moved to the other side of the body so she could see Tobias's face better. His expression was controlled, placid even, but she could detect the stirrings of rage in the way his pupils dilated until there was only the smallest circle of gray rimming them.

She pushed aside the feelings Tobias's reappearance in her life engendered and focused on the job. She could get through anything if she just kept things on an impersonal level. *Just forget you know what he tastes like, how his skin feels against yours, how full you feel when he's deep inside you.* She tried to ignore the eager thump her clit gave and drew in a steadying breath. "Can you smell anything?"

He closed his eyes and inhaled. After a few seconds he grimaced and opened his eyes. "There's a little bit of shape-shifter and some vamp other than Rinda's scent. That could be odors here at the scene and not necessarily on her body. And then, there's you." The look he gave her suggested he could sense her physical reaction to his presence, probably even smell the involuntary stirring of arousal within her. "But there's something more, something beyond this overpowering odor of all these humans." He glanced at Dante with a mumbled, "No offense."

Dante scowled. "Offense taken."

Nix pressed her lips together while the two men sized each other up. Even as alpha as he could be, Dante was one of the most easygoing guys she knew, yet she wouldn't be surprised if Tobias managed to rub him the wrong way. When he wanted to be, Tobias could be a real charmer. Most of the time he didn't bother to put forth the effort.

Tobias cocked an eyebrow but didn't respond. With slow deliberateness, almost as if he were taking the time to say good-bye, he drew the tarp back over Amarinda's face and stood. He shoved his hands into the front pockets of his jeans, drawing Nix's gaze there. The material pulled taut across his groin, showing the outline of his cock. She jerked her gaze away and glanced at his face. Thankfully he hadn't seemed to notice where she'd just been looking.

"There is something...It's familiar, yet not. I don't know what it is." Frustration colored his voice, made the low tones tight and even raspier. "Who the hell did this?" His gaze caught Nix's. "Humans? Or someone trying to make it look like humans?"

She didn't have an answer. Not yet. "Since she wasn't killed here, it's hard to say. But the strongest scent is human, not pret."

"That might be technically accurate," Tobias murmured. He pressed his lips together and drew in another slow, deep breath. "That other smell. It smells like...demon." All demons had an underlying scent of burned wood or paper that was undetectable to humans. From the scent you couldn't tell one demon from another, but you could separate demons from other prets. Vamps and shape-shifters had no trouble picking it up. He looked at her, a hint of accusation in his eyes that immediately made her mad.

Not back in her life five minutes and already he was pointing fingers. She couldn't help being part demon, damn it. "Not every unexplained murder has a demon behind it, you know." She darted a glance around, making sure the police officers and assorted crime scene specialists weren't within earshot, then looked back at Tobias in silent warning. He should know better than to bait her about her lineage in front of the cops.

Of course, he probably figured there wasn't a whole hell of a lot she could, or would, do about it. And he'd be right. If he really did want to "out" her, he could. But she didn't think that was what he was after.

"It's not demons," Nix muttered, glaring at him. So, yeah, she'd caught a whiff of the same scent, but it was too faint to mean anything. She was about to say more when activity from beyond the yellow crime scene tape caught her attention. Two tall, slender men in dark blue one-piece uniforms stood on either side of a gurney upon which lay a folded crimson body bag. Council-appointed corpse retrievers, though they generally called themselves body snatchers, were there to collect Amarinda's body.

Tobias waved his hand at the cop at the perimeter. "Let them in." Since the victim was a vampire, authority in this case fell to Tobias. He took a few steps back from the body, making room for the two men.

Nix stepped back, too, and watched in silence as they unfolded the body bag and stretched it on the ground next to Amarinda. They picked her up and placed her with great care in the open bag, then pulled the top portion over her, zipping it until she was completely covered.

It wasn't until the men had wheeled the laden gurney to the other side of the yellow tape that Tobias, his gaze on the departing body of his friend, said, "There's really not much else you can do, Nix. The crime scene techs will gather enough evidence so that equal measure can be tested by human forensics as well as turned over to the council for testing by our lab. You don't need to stay."

In this ebook short story, Sirina lan Maro, a fearless warrior from beyond the Rift, fights to save her world. But when her own cousin plots against her, Sirina is forced through the Rift and finds herself in nineteeth-century London. Alone and trapped in the body of a human host, she struggles to survive in this strange new world—until she meets a man who offers everything she needs...

Please turn this page for an excerpt from

Into the Rift.

Chapter One

Sirina Ian Maro set a small plate in front of her cousin and smiled to see him start in on the slice of chawberry pie. He ate with the same gusto as when he was a youngster. She took a seat in the dining alcove and cut into her own piece of pie.

Her living quad consisted of sleeping quarters, a central living area that could double as a guest room, a small scullery, and a dining alcove. She'd been allotted this quad once her conscription with the Talisian global security forces had been fulfilled. Ten years she'd been out, ten years of making a living by doing some of the same kind of work she'd done in the service. Only now she did it as a private citizen, providing security consultation to local enforcement officers.

Sirina looked at her cousin. His normally verdant skin seemed pale, a sure sign he was agitated about something. His eyes kept straying to the row of still images she had on her small workstation in the main living area.

She leaned over and put her hand on his, halting the motion of him scraping the last swirls of pie filling onto his utensil. "Natchook, what is it? What's wrong?"

He pushed away from the table and walked to where

the pictures were. He gazed at an image of their squad in their tan desert uniforms. The four members of the elite team stood straight, arms around each other, wide smiles curving their mouths. With his index finger he traced the features of the other woman in the group of four, and sadness pierced Sirina like the bite of a giant pincer. Yura Ian Xarchai, her best friend and Natchook's wife.

She and Yura had grown up together here on Avasa, a colony of the much larger planet Talis. As such, they had been second-class citizens, conscripted into service in defense of their ruling planet. Natchook, who was part Talisian, had already served for five years by the time she and Yura joined.

Shortly after their arrival in the service, Yura and Natchook had fallen in love. They'd been allowed to marry and serve in the same unit. Three years later, when Sirina's brother, Kester, was drafted, he, too, became part of their squad.

Kester at first balked at the idea of serving as a combatant. The last place a pacifist like her brother wanted to be was in the armed services. But the longer he served, the more he came to appreciate the discipline he learned. It helped him control his compulsive behaviors. That there had been peace between the planets also helped, so his anxiety-induced disorder was easier to handle. His constant access to a behavior modification expert hadn't hurt, either.

After Sirina and Yura had satisfied their requisite eight years, they'd been released from service. Natchook had taken his retirement soon after. Kester, enjoying the regimentation the security force provided, had decided to make a career of it.

They should have all lived out their lives happy and healthy. Only it hadn't gone that way for Yura. Three years ago, after a lingering illness, she had died. Sirina still missed her, though time had softened the pain, and she knew Natchook missed her, too.

"Kai Vardan is responsible for Yura's death, you know." Natchook picked up the still image and stared down at it. Sirina knew he had eyes only for his deceased wife. "Someone should make him pay. Someone..." He trailed off, his jaw flexing as he tried to control his emotions. "Someone needs to kill the bastard."

"Are you crazy? No, someone does *not* need to assassinate Kai Vardan." Sirina stared in shocked horror at her cousin. She knew he blamed the Talisian leader for what happened to Yura, but this...this was insane. "What would make you say that? Have you heard something?"

His gaze darted to her before he again looked down at the image. "I haven't heard anything. I just think it would do everybody a big favor if someone did."

Even talking about the assassination of a world leader was treasonous. "Look, I realize you're upset, but this isn't the way to resolve your grief. Visit with the priests at—"

"Don't you think I've gone through all the grief rituals and sought counseling? I have. Several times." Natchook surged to his feet. "Vardan killed Yura. Someone needs to make him pay."

"He did not kill her. She died because of a regulation that's been in place for centuries." Sirina put one hand on his shoulder. "Yura was Avasan. Talisians get service at hospitals before Avasans, you know that."

"I'm a citizen of Talis. She was my wife, and she was

sick. She should have gotten tests. A diagnosis. Treatment!" He shrugged off her hand. "Our Most Benevolent Leader," he said with a sneer, "could have taken action when this regulation went to referendum fifteen years ago during his tenure as a member of parliament. Once he became world leader, he could have pushed to change the legislation. He *should* have..." He turned away, one hand going to his face.

She knew he fought back tears. He'd loved Yura with a fierceness Sirina had never known. And he still did, all these years later.

Natchook turned again to face her. His eyes were wet, his face hard. "It's not just the health-care edicts. There are many laws that disadvantage Avasans. Laws that are equally unjust. They've been unjust for centuries. Yet no one seems bothered by it. They just accept it. *You* just accept it." His lips curled with disdain. "She was your best friend, Sirina. Surely that meant something to you once."

"Of course it meant...*means* something." She scowled. "And don't you try to make me out to be the villain in this. I'm Avasan. I have no vote. No voice. What could I have done to change anything?"

"Maybe you couldn't have done something then. But now..."

"No." She slashed one hand through the air. "Killing the Talisian leader isn't going to solve anything. It will just make things worse."

"Wait, just listen to me." His voice lowered and took on a pleading tone, but she heard the dark intensity that rode beneath the surface. He went back to the dining alcove and sat down, waiting until she retook her seat before going on. "This one thought has been rolling around in my mind for years now: Righteous men live in peace and think they're free; only the enlightened can know true peace through anarchy and chaos." His eyes glittered with fanatic fervor. He tapped one finger on the table. "That's the key, Sirina. Overthrow the government by ushering in anarchy and chaos."

"Natchook, no!" She grabbed his hand. Ice crawled from her belly up her throat. This idea of his was deranged, and he scared her with his sincerity. "You listen to *me*. Kai Vardan didn't pass the laws that keep Avasa under Talis's rule. He wasn't the one who kept moving Yura's name to the bottom of the list for medical treatment—"

"She never got the chance for *treatment*!" He jerked his hand away and sat back in his chair. "Because of these archaic, discriminatory edicts, a Talisian with a hangnail gets to see a physician before any Avasan, no matter how sick they are."

"It's not that bad."

"Right. The next time you get sick and can't get in to see a doctor and just keep getting sicker and sicker, you tell me you still think that way." He leaned forward, his expression set. "If there is no rule of law, everyone's on the same footing. Chaos makes us all equal." He spread his hands. "Avasans will finally be the same as Talisians, free to do what they want, *be* what they want. Tell me that's not tempting."

Oh, it was tempting all right. Not that she would admit it to him. But she'd lived her entire life being told what to do, when to do it, how to do it. She had enjoyed her time in the service, but she hadn't had a choice about serving. Now that she was her own person again, she'd managed to eke out a living as a consultant for the local security forces. But she'd often wondered what her life would have been like if she'd been born on Talis, if she'd been able to actively make choices instead of having them foisted on her.

No matter her upbringing, what Natchook thought needed to happen was ill-advised. Insane. "What you propose isn't the way to bring about change. There has to be another tactic, something we haven't thought of yet."

"Since my wife's death all I've done is think, trying to find other ways. But I keep coming to the same conclusion. They don't care about what happened to her. She isn't even a footnote on any legislator's agenda." He stood and began to pace the small room. His voice low, he said, "I made sure to become friends with Jarrad T'heone, the captain of Vardan's personal security cadre. Through him I've met Vardan. He's not as good a man as you think he is. He's Talisian, with Talisian interests first. Always."

While a member of their squad, Natchook had a knack for infiltrating enemy ranks. He still exuded charm and confidence, qualities of a natural-born leader. But Sirina couldn't let him get involved in something like this. "And if someone does assassinate Vardan? Then what?" She stood and grabbed his arm. "If you get mixed up in this, they will *execute* you. You won't live to see what, if any, changes are made."

He gave a bark of laughter. "They can't execute me if they can't catch me." His grin and quick wink were sly with self-confidence. "Hypothetically speaking, of course."

"Right." She stared into his eyes. "And are you sure your hypothetical escape plan is good enough to evade every security force in the system?" Trying to get through to him, she tightened her fingers. "Natchook, the assassination of a world leader is a huge thing. They'll put a price on your head. Anyone who is remotely involved will be hunted down like rabid beasts. You won't find a hole to hide in on any planet."

He shook his head. "I've thought about that, too. If someone wanted a handy escape route, all they'd have to do is lay some credits on a couple of technicians at Rift Central," he said, giving the detention center the nickname most Avasans used.

It was the place where society's undesirables—political dissidents, religious heretics, and criminals—were taken after trial and sentencing. Once there, their souls were stripped from their bodies, and the incorporeal energies that made up the essence of what was left were placed in specially designed holding tanks.

A rift between their dimension and another occurred every seventy-three rotations of Talis around their sun star. Because the rift opened from the other dimension, all the authorities could do was wait for it. But when it happened, the holding cells were opened, and the gravitational forces of the rift sucked the entities into it. No one knew what happened on the other side after that point.

Not very many people cared to know, either. This solution had been practiced for millennia, and most system inhabitants were just glad to be rid of the troublemakers.

Her cousin looked confident in his plan. "The timing is perfect. The rift is due in just over a week. Once someone is placed in a holding cell and the rift opens, they'll make their way through. The authorities could never touch them."

She was through talking about all this hypothetical nonsense. "You think bribing a technician or two at the detention center will get your soul removed from your body so it can be sent through the rift when it opens?" Sirina couldn't believe she was having this conversation with her cousin. He'd always been so levelheaded. So strong-minded. Yura's death had affected him much more deeply than she'd thought. She had to convince him not to go through with this. "Let's say you go through the rift. What then? Nobody knows what happens once you're in the other dimension. You could simply cease to exist."

"So I die either way." He shrugged. "I'll be with Yura again." His voice dropped to a soft pitch as if his last words were murmured in prayer.

She gave his arm a little shake. "I can't believe you. There's no evidence at all that anyone survives being sucked into the other dimension. You're going to die. How does your death honor Yura's memory? The only thing you'll accomplish is to remove a moderate leader from power. The vice chancellor is much more hard-line in his beliefs about Avasa. You could make things worse for us."

He stared down at her. "I hadn't thought about that."

"Right." Sirina let go of him and moved away. "Please let this go. Don't get involved. This won't fix anything."

"Maybe you're right." Her cousin didn't seem as sure of himself as he had moments ago.

She pressed her advantage. "You know I am. And this isn't something Yura would have wanted. You know that, too."

Some of the hardness left his expression, to be replaced with the softness of sorrow. "I do know that." He heaved a sigh and sat back down. "I guess you're right. Maybe…" His head bowed. "Yura's love made me whole. With her gone, I lost what was best about me." He looked up at Sirina, his eyes dark with grief. "I miss her so much."

She went down on her haunches beside him and placed one hand on his knee. "I miss her, too." She held his gaze. "Promise me you won't do anything stupid."

He dipped his head. "I promise"

She wasn't sure he was serious. "I mean it. I don't want to lose you, too."

He looked at her again. "I won't do anything stupid. You have my word."

She searched his eyes. Satisfied she'd dissuaded him from his vengeful, ill-advised plan, she got to her feet. "Great. That's great. Thank you."

He stood as well. "I need to get going."

"Listen, why don't you come over for dinner tomorrow night? I'll fix a salad and broiled marbox," she promised, tempting him with his favorite meal.

He gave a groan. "Oh, gods. You know I can't resist."

She grinned. "Yes, I know. And I'll top it off with more chawberry pie."

"It's a deal." He leaned down and pressed a kiss to her forehead. "See you tomorrow."

Werewolf Tori Joseph, council liaison, knows more about a recent spatc of attacks on humans than she can ever let on.

But as she gets closcr to her human colleague, Detective Dante MacMillan, her attraction to him becomes the secret she must hide...

Please turn this page for an excerpt from

Secret of the Wolf.

Chapter One

Hard muscles rippled beneath skin and fur. Sharp teeth reformed themselves. Bones crunched, shifted, and re-aligned. Glossy brown fur receded, leaving behind only silken, tanned skin as wolf became human.

Became woman.

Hugging her knees to her chest, Victoria Joseph took several shuddering breaths and fought her way back from the mind of the wolf. Perspiration dotted her skin. Her body ached, muscles flexed and quivered, recovering from the shock and pain of transformation. As the last of the wolf retreated inside, giving her one final slash of pain through her midsection, a soft moan escaped her. She took another deep breath, the humidity of the August morning traveling deep into her lungs. The rain overnight had cleared out, but not before it had tamped down the pollen and dust that ordinarily floated in the air. It was monsoon season in the Sonoran Desert. Even with the rise in humidity, unbearable with the hundred-degree temperatures, she loved this time of year. Monsoon storms were wild, swift, and deadly, yet they spoke to her soul.

She skirted a large saguaro and, with arms that still trembled, shoved aside a large rock to retrieve the plastic bag she'd stashed there earlier. She pulled out a bottle of water and took a long drink, then another and another until she'd downed it all. She'd learned a long time ago to rehydrate as soon as possible after a shift. Otherwise she'd be in real danger of passing out from the strain of the metamorphosis.

Dropping the bottle back into the bag, Tori drew out clean clothing and shoes. Once dressed, she tucked her cell phone into the front pocket of her jeans and plaited her long hair in a French braid. She hiked the mile back through the desert to the trailhead where she'd left her car. Whenever she went wolf, she wanted to get out where she'd have some degree of solitude, and the McDowell Sonoran Preserve afforded that, especially at night.

As she steered the Mini Cooper into her driveway, the sun began to rise over the eastern mountains, sending alternating shafts of light and shadow across the valley floor. She shut off the engine and sat there a moment, enjoying the stillness of the dawn, and wondered if her brother was awake yet. Randall had shown up four days prior without warning. The last time she'd seen him had been just before they were stripped of their bodies and put in a holding cell for decades. Their souls had then been sent through a rift between dimensions as punishment for a horrific crime committed by their cousin. As incorporeal entities they'd been drawn to Earth, to the bounty of human bodies available for the taking, for instinctively they'd known if they didn't take a host they'd die. She'd ended up in London in the body of a woman making her living on the streets of the East End. Through the years, she'd managed to get away from that kind of lifestyle, and the new Victoria Joseph had made her way to the United States at the turn of the twentieth century.

Rand, she'd found out just recently, had gone into a man in a small village outside of Manchester. It might as well have been the other side of the world. In 1866, it had been impossible to even begin to try to find him. She'd been alone, a stranger in a borrowed body, overcoming the guilt at displacing the rightful owner while trying to find her way in a primitive world. Staying alive was about all she could do for a long time.

She and her brother hadn't seen each other in nearly a hundred and fifty years until he'd shown up on her doorstep, a familiar spirit in a stranger's body. She'd known him instantly. He was the same sweet brother she remembered, yet he was different in some ways. More withdrawn and evasive with a chaser of surly. But even with the newfound secrecy, she would take what she could get. He was family. She was willing to overlook a few eccentricities and irritating behaviors to have him with her again.

Tori just wished she knew what to do to make him more at ease. He'd had some predisposition toward obsessive-compulsive behavior before the Influx of 1866, but those tendencies seemed to be exacerbated here. Perhaps the human he'd ended up inhabiting, Randall Langston, had also had such predilections.

With a sigh she got out of the car and let herself into her small two-bedroom rental. Smells of lavender and vanilla assailed her from the various bowls of potpourri she had scattered around the house. Her job as werewolf liaison to the Council of Preternaturals was more often than not dark and full of violence, and as a werewolf she was predisposed to be more aggressive in nature than an ordinary human woman. So when she came home she wanted calm and tranquility. She needed it in order to slough off the stress of the day.

Tori drew in a breath and held it a moment, letting the tranquil setting of her home seep into her spirit. Neutral beige and cream furniture was piled with blue and green pillows, and the same color scheme played out on the walls. The wooden wind chimes on the back patio clinked, the sound coming to her as clearly as if she were standing beside them.

She didn't need to use her keen werewolf hearing to pick up the snores coming from Rand's bedroom. He rarely arose much before noon, preferring to stay up until the wee hours of morning and run as a wolf as much as possible.

She tried to get over his choosing to run alone instead of with her. After all, he'd been on his own just like she had, and he was much more of a loner than she'd ever been. But it bothered her. Why had he gone to the trouble of locating her if he didn't want to spend any time with her? It was as natural for werewolves to run as a pack, even a small pack of two, as it was to breathe.

Tori moved quietly through the house, not wanting to wake him. She undressed in her bedroom, putting her cell phone on the nightstand. After she took a quick shower, she slipped into a robe and padded barefoot into the kitchen. She was starving, which wasn't unusual after a shift. She pulled some raw hamburger meat out of the fridge and gulped down a couple of handfuls—just enough to satisfy her inner wolf. She'd long ago gotten over the gross factor of eating raw meat.

That first time, she'd been half asleep and had come wide awake when she realized she was chowing down on raw liver. She'd soon discovered that the longer she denied the wolf its meal, the more violent it became when it finally got out. As long as she fed it regularly, she could shift without worrying that she'd kill someone.

She dumped some granola into a bowl and added a few diced strawberries. She poured herself a cup of coffee and went into her bedroom, closing the door with a soft *snick* behind her. She placed the cup and bowl on the end table and went over to her bookshelf. Reaching for a well-worn paperback, she pulled it off the shelf and went back to her queen-sized bed. She perched on the edge and opened the book in the middle, staring down at the pages before her.

She spooned cereal into her mouth and slipped a finger into the book to retrieve the small black device nestled into the area she'd cut out. The size of a cell phone, it was about half an inch thick with a couple of small knobs and two retractable antennae at one end. Tobias Caine, former vampire liaison to the preternatural council and now a member of the same, had given it to her two weeks ago. Apparently, he and his wife, Nix, had acquired it months ago but held onto it in secret, waiting for a safe moment to hand it off to her.

As Tobias had put it, he'd chosen Tori because she had two things he needed: a background in radio communications and the ability to keep her mouth shut. Discretion was most important until they figured out the gadget's purpose. She'd been honored that he trusted her with such a task.

He'd also given her the schematics, though they weren't very useful in getting the thing to work. Oh, she'd managed to turn it on, but within minutes a voice had spoken in the standard language of the other dimension, asking for a password. She'd quickly turned the device off. Now, as she studied the thing, turning it over and over in her hands, she tried to figure out how to activate it without having someone on the other side know. The schematics didn't seem to indicate that, at least not that she could tell. Perhaps it wasn't possible.

She wouldn't know until she tried. As far as she knew, only three other people knew she was in possession of this little doohickey—Tobias, his wife, Nix, and Dante MacMillan, a human detective who'd been right in the middle of the action when the device had come to light. Her resources were limited.

Tori finished her cereal and set the bowl back down on the nightstand. Grabbing her coffee, she took a sip and carried the cup as she went to her dresser. She opened her lingerie drawer and lifted her panties out of the way so she could pick up the folded schematics. She shoved the drawer closed with her hip. Going back to the bed, she spread out the plans and stared down at them while she sipped her coffee.

There were drawings of gears and lines and sections for a first amplifier and a second amplifier, R-F output, a resonator, and at least two doublers. Mostly though, it was a lot of letters and numbers that must have meant something to the person who'd drawn them up, but she couldn't decipher it. Not yet, anyway.

She placed her empty cup on the table and folded the paper up again. Sitting on the edge of the bed, she slid the schematics under her pillow for the time being and stared down at the device. The idea that this little thing could open up a mini rift amazed and frightened her. What was the purpose? Oh, she knew enough to figure that right now it was used to communicate from one dimension to the other. But there had to be more to it than that. What nefarious plans were being hatched, and by whom? Tobias hadn't told her from whom he'd gotten the device, just that the person had been mad with ambition.

Tori picked up the black apparatus and brought it closer to peer at the small knobs. She couldn't discern any labels or hash marks on the casing, nothing to indicate what function each knob had. She needed to get a magnifying glass to tell for sure.

The more she studied this thing, the more intrigued she became. It really was an ingenious contraption created by an imaginative and clever inventor. What had been his intention behind building it? Had he meant to make mischief? Or had his plans been more altruistic than that?

A quick rap on her bedroom door was followed by the door swinging open. Rand poked his head around the edge. "Good morning. You went out early. Or is it that you came in late?" His head tipped to one side as if he were considering a complicated brain teaser. "Oh well, no matter. What's that?" he asked, his gaze on the device in her hand. He came into the room wearing jeans, his chest and feet bare.

"Rand!" Tori closed her fist around the object in question and fought the urge to hide it behind her back. She wanted to deflect him from the device, not call attention to it, and putting her hand behind her back would make him all the more curious.

Lifting a hand, he lazily scratched his chest. His mouth opened wide in a huge yawn.

"You can't just barge in here. You need to wait for me to tell you to come in." She scowled at him. "What if I'd been getting dressed?"

"Then I'd have seen bits of you I don't necessarily want to see," he said. Tori had lost her East End accent long ago, but even after all these decades, Rand's tones still held the flavor of his British human host. He stuck his fingers into the front pockets of his jeans and hunched his shoulders. "I daresay I'd have recovered from the shock eventually." He glanced at her hand. "So, what *is* that?"

Though she was certain she could trust her brother, she was duty-bound not to divulge the secret. She liked Tobias. More than that, she admired him. She wouldn't betray his trust in her. As nonchalantly as she could, she replied, "It's just an MP3 player a friend asked me to try to fix for him."

Rand raised his brows, skepticism shadowing his eyes. "And why would he think you could fix it?"

"I was a radio communications technician back in the day. I've kept up with all the new gadgets as a hobby," was all she offered. She didn't want to talk to him about serving as a communications officer in the American Army during World War II. If he was as pacifistic as he'd been before their Influx, he wouldn't approve. She was sure he'd felt right at home during the sixties. Hell, he probably started the whole "Make Love Not War" movement. He would overlook the nobility of the cause, and right now she didn't want to get into an argument with him. Not when they'd just found each other again.

It was time for a change of subject. "So, what do you think of Arizona?" She kept her eyes on him and her hand wrapped around the device. It wouldn't do for him to get too close a look or he'd see it wasn't an MP3 player. She kept her voice cheery, hoping to distract him. "I mean, I know you've been here only a few days, but how do you like it so far?"

Her brother looked like he wanted to pursue the other topic, but for now he let it drop, for which she was grateful. While ordinarily she had no problems discussing her job or, in this case, a special assignment, this situation was different. He was her brother, and she didn't like being deceitful with him. She wanted him to feel like he could trust her because maybe, just maybe, he'd be more inclined to stay. But if he thought she was being disingenuous with him, it could be all the encouragement he needed to leave.

"I don't know," Rand said. His shoulders hunched further. "I like it well enough, I suppose. I don't believe I'll be staying here for the long term, though." He grimaced. "It's hotter than hell, for one thing. I mean, who the hell lives where it's a hundred and ten degrees, for crying out loud?"

"Right now it's hot, yeah. But it's perfect in the winter months." Tori bit back her disappointment. Rand didn't have to stay in Scottsdale with her, but she'd like him to be close. "And of course I want you to stay here, but wherever you end up, we have to stay in touch."

"Absolutely." He walked over to her dresser, making her stiffen for a moment. Not that there was anything he could get into—the schematics to the device were under her pillow. When all he did was stick a finger into the glass bowl of potpourri, she relaxed. He stirred the fragrant mixture around, making the scent of lavender and vanilla permeate the room. "It's been great to finally find you," he said without glancing her way, his tone one of a stranger making small talk. They might as well go back to discussing the weather.

He sounded less enthused about being with her than she'd like. It befuddled her. What was going on beneath that brush cut? She'd thought they had been on their way toward rebuilding the relationship that had been put on hold by their trip through the rift all those years ago, yet he seemed remarkably disinterested.

Before she could delve into it further, her cell phone rang. With a murmured apology, she slipped the rift device under her pillow and then grabbed her phone from the nightstand. She noticed her brother's sharp eyes hadn't missed the fact that she'd hidden the alleged MP3 player. She'd have to make sure to find a better hiding place than a book and her underwear drawer. She answered the phone on the second ring. "Hello?"

"Got a brouhaha over on Chaparral, just east of Hayden," the council dispatcher said without any formal greeting. He was an irascible werebear who didn't put up with a lot of crap, though he sure could dish it out. "Local LEOs have things in hand at the moment, but you need to get your furry self over there."

"What happened?" All business, she rose from the bed and headed toward her closet. For now, at least, the Scottsdale police had things under control. She paused as she reached for a blouse and wondered if Dante MacMillan was already at the scene. A sensual shiver worked its way through her. There was something about that man, something that, even though he was human, called to everything feminine and primal within her.

"Some kind of skirmish between a werewolf and a vamp," the dispatcher answered, drawing her back to the conversation, "with a human bystander caught between 'em. Think the human's okay, though. Well, mostly okay." The werebear gave a little growl. "As okay as one of 'em can be in the middle of a fight between two prets, I suppose. But you need to get over there pronto."

"Ten-four." She grinned at the dispatcher's disgruntled snarl. He really hated it when she used police codes. Tori rang off and looked at her brother. She shoved the phone into the pocket of her robe. As she pulled the blouse from its hanger, she started, "Rand, I—"

"Let me guess," her brother said. His voice held a hint of sarcasm that dismayed her. "You have to go."

She nodded and went to her dresser to pull out a clean pair of jeans. "Rand, we really—"

He slashed a hand through the air. His face darkened, glittering gaze meeting hers. "Just forget it, Tori. It's always been this way with you. Job first, family second." He sounded like a sulky child.

She tamped down a surge of irritation even as she felt the need to defend herself and her choices. "That's not true!" She dropped her clothing on the bed and went over to him. She put her hand on his shoulder and gave it a squeeze. "I love you, you know that. And I love having you here. It's just like old times. With you around, it makes this place, this planet, feel like home." For the first time since she'd arrived in this strange, new world it felt... comfortable. Family made all the difference.

She was surprised to see a film of tears make his blue eyes shine. "It's not that I don't like being here with you," he said, his voice low, a little hoarse. "It's just..." He shook his head with a sigh. "I've always felt like I existed in your shadow. 'Why can't you be more like your sister?'" he mimicked in an excellent approximation of their father's bellicose tones. "'Your sister never disappoints us.'" He went back to his normal voice. "I knew he was disappointed in me. Always disappointed. And I'm just not sure that, if I stay, things will be any different. I'll be known as Tori's little brother, the inept one. The loser."

"Rand, no you won't." Tori felt much more compelled to build up Rand's self-esteem than to defend her father. He had been strict, demanding perfection from a son who was too emotionally fragile to withstand the pressure. She gave her brother's shoulder another squeeze. "You're not inept. And Father loved you. You know he did."

"Did he?" Rand shrugged. His fingers started tapping against his thigh. "Whatever." He wore the same churlish expression he had when he'd been a teen. She felt momentary dismay that he could still be so immature. Hadn't he learned anything from his trip through the rift? Had he not grown at all in the century and a half they'd been on Earth? He seemed to shake his mood, because a slight smile tilted his lips. He lifted his hands, spreading them in a sheepish gesture. "Listen, I'm just being..." He shook his head. "Don't pay any attention to me. Go. Get to work. Save the day," he said in an approximation of a superhero's voice.

She returned his smile, though she couldn't get rid of the worry niggling at the back of her mind. He was lost and alone and resisting her attempts to make him part of her life again. If she pushed too hard she might lose him again. On impulse, she hugged him and quickly released his thin but firm body. Anyone who made the mistake of thinking he'd be physically weak might make the last mistake of their lives. She pressed a kiss to his cheek and tried to ignore the sour-milk scent of his sullen discontent. "I'll see you later, all right? We'll have dinner together. Think about what you'd like, and I'll stop by the grocery store on my way home." She searched his eyes, looking for a sign, any sign, of what he might be thinking, what he was feeling. "We'll talk. Catch up some more."

"Yeah. Sure." He gave another smile, though this one was definitely forced. With a nod he left the room, pulling the door closed behind him.

Tori grabbed the device and schematics from beneath her pillow. She slipped the folded paper into the pocket of a fleece jacket she hardly ever wore and tucked the device into the toe of one of her boots. The jeans she shimmied into were formfitting, and the blouse was frothy in various shades of turquoise. Her women's athletic shoes were serviceable with bright purple along the edge of the sole. Being a werewolf was so much a part of what she was, she needed to find ways to feel like a woman. To be feminine. To be more than the beast. Purple shoes and filmy blouses helped.

She brushed her still-damp hair and braided it, then slipped her brush into the fanny pack she usually wore instead of carrying a purse. After shrugging into her shoulder holster, she retrieved her Magnum from the gun safe. It was a requirement of the council that all liaisons, in essence law enforcement officers for preternaturals, had to carry guns. Tori didn't usually mind, but sometimes the gun was the least favorite part of her job. While it often made her feel sexy, it rarely made her feel feminine.

Besides, when it came to defending herself or running down a suspect, all she really needed were her claws and fangs.

Acknowledgments

Many thanks to my readers. I appreciate your support!

As always, huge thank you to the team at Grand Central Publishing who did such great work getting this book out, with a special shout-out to Latoya Smith for all her help.

Thanks also to Susan Ginsburg, who rocks the house!

THE DISH

Where authors give you the inside scoop!

♥ ♥ ♥ ♥ ♥ ♥ ♥ ♥ ♥ ♥ ♥ ♥ ♥ ♥ ♥

From the desk of Kristen Callihan

Dear Reader,

I write books set in the Victorian era. Usually we don't see women with careers in historical romance, but one of the best things about exploring this "other" London in my Darkest London series is that my heroines can lead atypical lives.

In WINTERBLAZE, Poppy Ellis Lane is not only a quiet bookseller and loving wife, she's also part of an organization dedicated to keeping the populace of London in the dark about supernatural beasts that roam the streets—a discovery that comes as quite a shock to her husband, Police Inspector Winston Lane.

Now pregnant, Poppy Lane develops a craving for all things baked, but most especially fresh breads. Being hard-working, however, Poppy has little time or patience for complicated baking—an inclination I share! Popovers are a great compromise, as they are ridiculously easy to make and ridiculously good.

Poppy's Popovers (yields about 6 popovers)

You'll need:

- 1 cup all-purpose flour
- 2 eggs

- 1 cup milk
- 1/2 teaspoon salt

Topping (optional)

- 1/2 cup sugar
- 1 teaspoon ground cinnamon
- a dash of cayenne pepper (to taste)
- 4 tablespoons melted butter

Directions

1. Preheat oven to 450 degrees F. Spray muffin tin with nonstick spray or butter and sprinkle with flour. (I like the spray for the easy factor.)
2. In a bowl, begin to whisk eggs; add in flour, milk, and salt, and beat until it just turns smooth. Do not over-beat; your popovers will be resentful and tough if you do! Fill up each muffin cup until halfway full–the popovers are going to rise. (Like, a *lot*.)
3. Bake for 20 minutes at 450 degrees F, then lower oven temperature to 350 degrees F and bake 20 minutes more, until golden brown and puffy.
4. Meanwhile, for topping, mix the sugar, cinnamon, and dash of cayenne pepper—this is hot stuff and you only want a hint of it—in a shallow bowl and stir until combined. Melt butter in another bowl and set aside.
5. Remove popovers from the muffin pan, being careful not to puncture them. Then brush with melted butter and roll them in the sugar mix, shaking off the excess. Serve immediately.

Inspector Lane likes to add a dollop of raspberry jam and feed them to his wife in the comfort of their bed.

He claims they make Poppy quite agreeable...*Ahem*. You, however, might like to enjoy them with a cup of tea and a good book!

R. Call

♥ ♥ ♥ ♥ ♥ ♥ ♥ ♥ ♥ ♥ ♥ ♥ ♥ ♥ ♥

From the desk of R.C. Ryan

Dear Reader,

To me there's nothing sexier than a strong, handsome hunk with a soft spot for kids and animals. That's why, in Book 3 of my Wyoming Sky series, I decided that my hero, Jake Conway, would be a veterinarian, as well as the town heartthrob. Now, who could I choose to play the love interest of a charming cowboy who has all the females from sixteen to sixty sighing? Why not a smart, cool, sophisticated, Washington, D.C., lawyer who looks, as Jake describes her, "as out of place as a prom dress at a rodeo"? Better yet, just to throw Meg Stanford even more off her stride, why not add a surprise half-brother with whom she has absolutely nothing in common?

I had such fun watching these two try every possible way to deny the attraction.

But there's so much more to their story than a hot romance. There's also the fact that someone wants to harm Meg and her little half-brother. And what about the mystery that has haunted the Conway family for twenty-five years? The disappearance of Seraphine, mother of Quinn, Josh, and Jake, chronicled in Books 1 and 2, will finally be resolved in Book 3.

In writing the stories of Quinn, Josh, and Jake, I completely lost my heart to this strong, loving family, and I confess I had mixed emotions as I wrote the final chapter.

I hope all of my readers will enjoy the journey. I guarantee you a bumpy but exhilarating ride.

Happy Reading!

R. C. Ryan

RyanLangan.com
Twitter, @RuthRyanLangan
Facebook.com

♥ ♥ ♥ ♥ ♥ ♥ ♥ ♥ ♥ ♥ ♥ ♥ ♥ ♥ ♥ ♥ ♥ ♥

From the desk of Margaret Mallory

Dear Reader,

Ilysa is in love with her older brother's best friend. Sad to say, the lass doesn't have a chance with him.

As her clan chieftain, Connor MacDonald is the sixteenth-century Highland equivalent of a pro quarterback, movie star, Special Forces hero, and CEO all rolled into one. And the handsome, black-haired warrior never even noticed Ilysa *before* his unexpected rise to the chieftainship.

Other women, who are always attempting to lure Connor into bed —and failing, by the way—are drawn to him by his status, handsome face, and warrior's body. While no lass with a pulse could claim to be unaffected by Connor's devastating looks, Ilysa loves him for his noble heart. Connor MacDonald would give his life for the lowliest member of their clan, and Ilysa would give hers for him.

Connor MacDonald is the hope of his clan, a burden that weighs upon every decision he makes. Since becoming chieftain, he has devoted himself to raising his people from the ashes. With the help of his cousins (in *The Guardian* and *The Sinner*) and his best friend (in *The Warrior*), he has survived murder attempts by his own kin, threats from royals and rebels, and attacks by other clans. Now all that remains to secure his clan's future is to take back the lands that were stolen by the powerful MacLeods.

Through the first three books in The Return of the Highlander series, Ilysa has worked quietly and efficiently behind the scenes to support Connor and the clan. None of her efforts has made him look at her twice. Clearly, it's time for me to step in and give Connor a shake.

The poor lass does need help. Her mother thought she was protecting Ilysa in a violent world by covering her in severe kerchiefs and oversized gowns and admonishing her to never draw attention to herself. Ilysa's brief marriage left her feeling even less appealing.

But Ilysa underestimates her worth. After all, who helped our returning heroes in The Guardian sneak into the castle the night they took it from Connor's murderous uncle? And who healed Connor's wounds and brought him back from death's door? Even now, while Connor fights to protect the clan, Ilysa is willing to employ a bit of magic to protect him, whether from the threat of an assassin or a deceitful woman with silver-blue eyes.

Unfortunately, Ilysa's chances grow more dismal still when Connor decides he must marry to gain an ally for the clan's coming fight with the MacLeods. As I watched him consider one chieftain's daughter after another, I knew not one of them was the right wife for him or the clan. What our chieftain needs is a woman who can heal the wounds of his heart—and watch his back.

But Connor is no fool. With a little prodding, he finally opened his eyes and saw that Ilysa is the woman he wants. Passion burns! Yay! However, my relief is short-lived because the stubborn man is determined to put the needs of the clan before his own desires. Admirable as that may be, I can't let him marry the wrong woman, can I?

Despite all my efforts, I fear Connor will lose everything before he realizes that love is the strongest ally.

With Ilysa's life and his clan's future hanging by a thread, will he be too late to save them?

I hope you enjoy the adventurous love story of Connor and Ilysa. I've found it hard to say goodbye to them and this series.

You can find me on Facebook, Twitter, and my website, www.MargaretMallory.com. I love to hear from readers!

Margaret Mallory

♥ ♥ ♥ ♥ ♥ ♥ ♥ ♥ ♥ ♥ ♥ ♥ ♥ ♥ ♥

From the desk of Cynthia Garner

Dear Reader,

My latest novel, HEART OF THE DEMON, takes two of my favorite preternaturals—demon and fey—and puts them together. Tough guy Finn Evnissyen has met his match in Keira O'Brien!

I come by my fascination with the fey honestly. My family came to America from Donegal, Ireland, in 1795 and settled in the verdant hills of West Virginia. One item on my bucket list is to get to Donegal and see how many relatives still live there.

My fascination with demons, I guess, has its roots in my religious upbringing. Just as I have with vampires and werewolves, I've turned something considered wicked into someone wickedly hawt! I hope after reading HEART OF THE DEMON you'll agree.

To help me along, my Pandora account certainly got its workout with this book. From my Filmscore station that played scores from *Iron Man*, *Sherlock Holmes*, and *Halo 3*; to my metal station that rocked out with Metallica, Ozzy Osbourne, and Rob Zombie; to my Celtic punk station that rolled with the Dropkick Murphys, Mumford & Sons, and Flatfoot 56, I had plenty of inspiration to help me write.

I have a more complete playlist on my website extras page, plus a detailed organizational chart of the Council and their liaisons.

Happy Reading!

Cynthia Garner

cynthiagarnerbooks@gmail.com
http://cynthiagarnerbooks.com

VISIT US ONLINE AT

WWW.HACHETTEBOOKGROUP.COM

FEATURES:

**OPENBOOK BROWSE AND
SEARCH EXCERPTS**
•
AUDIOBOOK EXCERPTS AND PODCASTS
•
AUTHOR ARTICLES AND INTERVIEWS
•
**BESTSELLER AND PUBLISHING
GROUP NEWS**
•
SIGN UP FOR E-NEWSLETTERS
•
**AUTHOR APPEARANCES AND TOUR
INFORMATION**
•
SOCIAL MEDIA FEEDS AND WIDGETS
•
DOWNLOAD FREE APPS

BOOKMARK HACHETTE BOOK GROUP
@ WWW.HACHETTEBOOKGROUP.COM